SHOOTER IN THE SHADOWS

DAVID HEWSON

ACKNOWLEDGMENTS

I'm grateful to my good friend Steve Feldberg for his help and inspiration in steering this project from an off-the-wall idea into reality. And to all his many colleagues at Audible who brought it to life in its previous incarnation as an audiobook with Audible.

Cover design based on original concept by Brobel Design, LLC.

1

VENICE, TUESDAY

The moment the water taxi sped away from the jetty at Venice Marco Polo Airport, Thomas Honeyman's phone rang.

'Lauren? Is that you? How are things? Look, I... Where are we supposed to meet? I mean... I want to...'

A man's voice, good English with a gentle veneer of Italian, came on.

'Thomas! This is Giorgio Morosini. Welcome to Venice, my friend. Who's this Lauren? You have a friend joining you? Good. It's best not to be alone.'

'Sorry. It... it doesn't matter.'

'I trust your journey was comfortable. Is it at all possible you brought some rain?'

The flight from Kennedy had landed hours late. He'd spent most of the delay on the runway not moving an inch. Then halfway through the long wait, the text came in.

Dad. Thanks for the money and everything. It was sweet. God, this has gone on so long. Time heals and all that stuff. See you soon. Can't wait.

Ciao. All my love.

He'd tried to call back but just got a robotic voicemail. The text was a mystery. He hadn't sent Lauren money or anything else, hadn't heard from her in years. Honeyman had no idea where she was or how to contact her. Even her Facebook page hadn't been touched in years.

'No, Giorgio, no rain.'

'Oh well. Perhaps come winter. This is such strange weather. So arid. There are fires in the countryside. People are worried. We've never known a summer like this. Still, it's none of your concern. Tell me. Are you writing something now?'

How many times had someone asked that same question?

'Writing's what I do. That's like me saying "Are you selling anything now?"'

There was a pained sigh down the phone.

'I'm selling lots of things. It's just getting harder and harder finding buyers. I wish you well with your latest masterpiece. This is your habit, I think. To arrive a few days before the Feast of the Redeemer. Then go home when you are happy.'

'You're an observant man.'

'Not really. You told me this was your habit. When you took me on. What was that... four years ago?'

Honeyman didn't recall. Maybe it was at the end of the long and liquid lunch they'd enjoyed when he hired Morosini as agent for his remote island hidden away near the northern marshes, a distant reach of the Venetian Lagoon where the most intrepid of tourists never ventured. In truth, his annual visit was much more than a habit. It was a ritual. A superstitious sacrament to a year's labor on whatever was the work in progress.

The process was always the same. Wrap up the manuscript as much as possible back home in Manhattan. Then fly to Italy, bury himself in the villa, cut off from everything—people, communications, the world. Start work on the final revision the moment he arrived on the Tuesday, barely sleeping between edits, stopping just for food and drink in the hope the story was so alive there was nothing else in his head. Then finally, the Saturday night the *festa* began, with fireworks searing the sky across the water, he'd hit "save" for the last time and make himself a celebratory Negroni.

Job done.

Another book ready to dispatch into a marketplace that seemed more unwelcoming with each passing year.

He'd been working as a full-time author ever since the dollar tsunami hit with his true-crime debut eleven years before. The success of that first book proved so rapid, so breathtaking and lucrative, he barely had time to believe it was happening. Then the rot set in, slowly, relentlessly. Book after failed book as his sales dwindled with each passing year. All the while he clung to the belief that one day writing, the thing that had put him on this pedestal, would surely return him there too. If only he could find the right words, another great story. An old pulp author—someone he'd admired for years though the guy had never sold that much—told him at a festival in Melbourne that a real writer couldn't give up. Do that and you were dead in the water. A blank page never sold. Besides, a real writer had no choice. You had to keep trying, however futile it seemed.

Trying was all he'd done of late. His last manuscript, a techno-thriller, had been deemed unsellable by his New York agent after the thing had spent a year in limbo only to be turned down everywhere. The book was, they all said, imitative and lacking originality. Which was exactly what he felt they'd been asking for in the first place. A year spent chasing the market he was told to pitch for, only to see every minute, every last sweated word, go to waste.

'So tell me, Giorgio. Are we ever going to make any money out of that place?'

To begin with, Honeyman had hoped to use the island in Venice for rentals when he wasn't there writing. But no one would touch it. Too remote, too primitive. He couldn't even get insurance. Then, as his finances worsened and he didn't have time or money to visit Italy much, he begged Morosini to find an outright buyer. Not that they'd had any luck there.

'I wish I had better news. Business is terrible at the moment. Even for properties you'd think would be easy to move. It's not for want of trying, I assure you.'

Every recent conversation they'd had was marked by that particular undertone: Honeyman had bought a ridiculous liability in the first place. The only way to get rid of it was to find someone foolish enough to relieve him of the burden. One mug looking to exchange his place for another. Morosini, to his credit, seemed to appreciate Honeyman wasn't too happy with that idea.

'We've cut the price forty percent already, Thomas. You want me to go lower?'

It was still hot, though Honeyman could begin to detect the cool and welcome breath of evening in the sweep of wind from the speeding boat. The lagoon sky was as gorgeous as ever, like a watercolor painting where the tints washed into one another as they fell to the darkening shadows in the east. Tonight, not even the lack of sleep and the jet lag would stop him from beginning work in earnest. Four days of hard labor would follow until the Night of the Redeemer, sleep a luxury, seized briefly between frantic periods of writing. This time it wasn't a book he was trying to finish but an idea, an outline he meant to get down in sufficient detail for it to sell outright. A last, desperate throw of the dice in the hope of salvaging his career, of trying to convince the publishing world at large he was more than a one-hit wonder sinking into obscurity.

'Will it make a difference?'

'To be honest, Thomas, I really don't know. You paid all that money, and how much time do you get to spend there? No. Don't answer. I know. Not enough. People don't want to live like a hermit. Especially surrounded by the dead. They want life, they want the city. Music. Museums. Restaurants. Bars. Vaporetti a minute's walk away. Power. Water. Communications. Comfort. Dorsoduro or San Marco. Not somewhere they can't find on a map. You must have understood.

The place was on the market for ages before you came along. You told me.'

'I didn't think I'd ever have to sell, Giorgio. I thought it was my paradise. Somewhere to write. In peace.'

Morosini's gentle laugh was kindly meant, he felt sure.

'You know one thing I've learned in the real estate business? It's the places you think are heaven that one day turn out to be hell. You're aware what the locals call your little paradise?'

Of course Honeyman knew.

Maledetto. "The Cursed."

Shopkeeper, fisherman, waiter; all the locals he met on the nearby inhabited islands of the lagoon—Burano and Mazzorbo were the closest—scratched their heads in bafflement when he told them where he lived. Then they nodded in vague recognition and looked at him as if he were crazy.

The contract used the island's official name, Santa Maria dell'U-milità, originally a remote leper colony with its own small, derelict chapel. When the city needed it, a necropolis too, a burial ground for victims of the plague. So numerous were the corpses buried beneath the island's dark, hard soil that on occasion the rain would wash away enough earth to expose their remains. It was a haunting wilderness abandoned for two centuries until a German industrialist acquired the island in the 1950s and began to convert what was left of the old hospice into a private villa.

Honeyman still remembered the first time he saw it from a boat. At a distance the house looked enchanting. Two floors, ochre stone, large pointed Venetian gothic arch windows and a magnificent carved stone front door. Almost a baronial home, set apart from everything on its low rock platform in the wilderness of the lagoon marshes. At the time, he was breathless from his instant success, locked inside a dream, swimming in money from the movie of his story that had just launched at the film festival on the Lido. He'd made the decision to buy the place before he'd even set foot on its rocky shore. Ernest Hemingway had stayed there a while, or so the German's pretty, talkative daughter told him. Writing, drinking, a one-time reporter turned literary novelist. Flush with money and confidence, head turned by the starry company he was keeping, Honeyman hoped he might achieve the same.

In private he was unsure of his talents. Were they real, or did he just get lucky with the chance to document a brutal double murder in his hometown, and invent a good few facts along the way? To drown out those doubts, he'd conned himself into thinking that what counted more than anything were the material things a writer surrounded himself with. That location, the ambience, the computer you used, the process of structuring a narrative, the way you placed your pens around the desk, the right music in the background, the view from the window—these magical elements could provide inspiration when, in the plain light of day, it seemed lacking. That a magical place to work might furnish the right words when all you could find were the wrong ones. All that was needed was the key to unlock the creativity that kept evading him. A private villa on a tranquil lump of rock with nothing but a tumbledown graveyard and an abandoned chapel for neighbors surely had to provide that.

Soon after he'd paid close to three quarters of a million dollars for the island, he discovered the story about Hemingway was a myth. There was hardly a corner of Venice that didn't claim the old man had been there, boozing and bedding in between turns standing up in his loafers as he tapped away at his portable typewriter. Honeyman had tried that too. All it gave him in return was backache.

The German who originally bought the place eventually rammed a shotgun in his mouth and pulled the trigger, ruined by the cost, crazy from drink and dope. The building Honeyman had taken on was still in much the same state the man had left it, and for much the same reasons. Every last brick and piece of furniture had to be shipped there by boat, at huge cost and inconvenience. Even if you could find someone to do the job, and that was never easy.

Maledetto.

∾

HE NEVER NOTICED the damage to his family until his wife, Diane, strode naked into Mohawk Lake and kept on walking as the gray-green water took her. That was July 12, 2012, four years to the day from the deadly blaze that kick-started Honeyman's career.

There was nothing to mark the spot of that tragedy, not even a bunch of flowers for the teacher and the sixteen-year-old boy burned to cinders inside the hut hidden away in the woods close to the water's edge. Still, everyone knew where it was. Always one to make a point, Diane had stripped right by it, folded her clothes neatly on the bare ground, placed her wedding ring on top, then stepped in and kept on going through the shallows. A ranger found her body three days later when she washed up close to the parking lot a mile away. There was a note next to the ring that said: *There's a shooter in the shadows and I can't bear this anymore.*

Lauren, their only daughter, had just turned twenty and was away at college. Honeyman was sequestered on his island retreat, his head inside a month-long struggle to fix a mystery novel, one more piece of fiction that never did quite work even though it sold to a tiny publisher for a pittance. He had no idea anything was wrong until he took the boat to Burano, tried to call home and found the cops answering the call.

By the time he got back to their home in Prosper, New York, Lauren had identified her mother in the morgue. Not a pretty sight, the medical examiner said. The fish had done their work.

Diane's blood alcohol level showed she must have consumed half a bottle of vodka or so before she died. Lauren blamed him for her mother's death. Then she quit college, adopted her mother's maiden name, Taylor, and was gone from his life—bumming around the world, last he heard, singing and dancing on cruise ships. When a private detective he hired tracked her down in Aruba one time and got her on the phone, she refused to speak to him no matter how much he begged and tried to apologize. Twenty-eight now, wherever she was. Maybe still a wannabe star, offspring of a wannabe novelist. Or married with a kid, and discovering family was a lot harder than you thought.

With any luck he'd soon find out.

'I ADVISE PATIENCE,' Morosini went on. 'We can cut the price again if need be. There is interest. Well.... kind of.'

'Kind of?'

The long, sleek speedboat bucked and bobbed as it hit the wake of one of the lagoon ferries working its way from Burano to the city. Spray splashed Honeyman's face. The briny fragrance of the lagoon, salt and mud from the low water and the nearby marshes, the faintest whiff of gasoline behind, filled his head. In a sudden flash he could see himself in the study, getting down to work. That brightened his exhausted spirit. A page unwritten always had to offer hope. So many dreams had started there. It was surely time for one to deliver, even if he had no clear idea how.

They'd left the main navigation channel to Venice and were breaking for the secluded wetlands of the north. He'd heard about the drought affecting Europe. Its effects were dramatic. There didn't seem to be a green patch anywhere in the lagoon, even on the island of Sant'Erasmo where Venice grew her vegetables, which sat as a low outline, the color of high summer savanna, toward the Adriatic. Soon the phone signal would vanish. By the time he was in his dilapidated home he'd be without main power, running water, internet, a phone. There was no way Lauren could contact him on the island. He could take the dinghy over to Burano in a couple of days and check his phone there. It was either that or abandon work altogether. Which he'd happily do if he knew where she was, how he might get in touch. But she'd offered none of those details. Maybe it was all a ruse, a game. She hadn't been above those when she was a kid. He hadn't sent her any money either. That part of the message was simply wrong.

Lauren had cut herself out of his life for years. Until she came out into the open, it was important to remember why he came here.

To work.

To think.

To be trapped in that solitary spot with nothing to fight but himself, his imagination and its shortcomings in the hope of salvaging what little was left of his career. Until the Night of the Redeemer and that final tap of the keyboard: job done. Or in this case, job started, with a desperate plea for work he'd dispatch as soon as he found a signal on the way home.

~

'Last week I was contacted by a curious young man through the website. American,' Morosini said. 'At least he sounded like it.'

'You don't know?'

The sigh again.

'To be honest, if someone asks to see around a place like yours, I would never ask too many questions. On Thursday I took the fellow out there on my boat. He said he wanted to be left alone for a few hours. He said... he needed to feel the atmosphere, to understand if it would suit his particular taste. I came back for him at the end of the afternoon.' He hesitated. 'There seemed no harm. I feel I owe you every chance I can find.'

Morosini liked to cruise the city canals in a small, smart leisure craft, the kind residents used to dodge and weave through the warren of Venetian waterways, large and small. Space enough for six people at the most. He was in his forties, divorced. Once, a year ago, he'd stopped by Maledetto unannounced, with an elegant Englishwoman in the stern alongside a shaggy black Labrador. They were out for a picnic and wondered if Honeyman wanted to join them. The woman looked so happy and taken with her new Venetian friend, he couldn't bring himself to break the spell.

'This gentleman seemed to know it was owned by a writer.'

'Really?'

'Yes. He wondered if you were coming back. Whether he could meet you. I said you were due this week. I do hope that wasn't a mistake...'

'I really don't want to start giving people tours, Giorgio. That's not why I came. If he's seen it already...'

'Of course. I understand. But I said I'd ask.'

'Will he make an offer?'

'It was strange.'

No straight answer. Which was as good as one.

'What was?'

'Did you ask for something to be delivered there?'

'Just the usual. Food and drink. There's a local guy in Burano, a fisherman, Paolo. He handles the gardening and maintenance for me.'

'Must have been him, I guess. I wondered if our visitor had invited someone else along while he was there. There was another boat headed in that direction as I was leaving. So few people go that way. Never mind. It was your Paolo, I imagine. Bringing the hermit's essentials.'

'An offer. Do we have an offer?'

The line was getting weak and crackly. Any moment Morosini would be gone.

'He told me he was going to be around for a couple of weeks before returning to Switzerland. I tried to call him this morning.'

'Switzerland?'

'Quite. Where there's money. You understand my enthusiasm?'

'And?'

'The number turned out to be wrong. I emailed him and the message got bounced back. Either my writing is getting worse or he just isn't interested. Or maybe he was some kind of... time waster. A voyeur who wanted to look around the place for free. We get them occasionally. They like to tick off our odd little islands. Especially those with a macabre history. I'll keep trying. All the same, I think it best you check nothing's missing when you get there. Which is why I called. He didn't look like a thief. Not that there seemed much worth stealing, to be honest. Still, these days you never know.'

Again the speedboat bucked as it crossed the wake of a ferry, this time one headed north. It would be the last conventional traffic they'd meet. From this point on they were in the wilder reaches of the lagoon, where the water was so shallow in places you could step straight out of the boat into the thick brown mud. No one came here except a few fishermen seeking mantis shrimp or clams and, in winter, the occasional duck hunter toting a shotgun. The water taxi men hated the area since navigation along the few working channels was slow and difficult, a winding path through the shallows indicated by lines of ancient double pylons emerging from the muddy surface.

Maledetto appeared on the horizon, an uneven mound of desiccated brown grass and palms rising above the sluggish gray water and scrappy marshes. The low orange-tiled roof stood out from a thicket of tall vegetation that ran like a dead forest around most of the perimeter. By the landing jetty the boathouse looked more rickety than ever and close to collapse. At the eastern end of the island stood what was left of the chapel: a square ruin of low stone walls, the stump of a campanile—most of which had long since tumbled to the ground—and the leaning outlines of gravestones, close to following the same course. Everything seemed overrun with wild plants and bushes anxious to swamp what brick and mortar was left.

'If I don't sell this soon, the bank will be doing it for me. Neither of us makes a penny.'

A pause. He wondered if the signal had gone already.

Then Morosini, his voice resigned but firm, said, 'I feared that was the case. You've always been straightforward and honest with me. I appreciate that. Let me do the same in return. This fellow I showed around... if he was interested, I feel he would have got back to me by now. I'm not sure I can find a buyer soon. Perhaps not at all. You took on a strange fantasy for yourself. From what I've gathered it's been accompanied only by sadness and pain. I wish I could help. Truly.'

Honeyman gritted his teeth. From time to time he got reporters on his back wanting to write stories about one-time celebs on the rocks, especially if there was a tragedy to be revisited. Not just Diane's suicide and the estrangement of his daughter but the two strange, grim deaths that made him briefly rich in the first place. They didn't put it that way, of course, always feigning sympathy and a little jealousy for a former hack who supposedly made good. He avoided them, but they went ahead with their stories all the same. It was hard to get mad. When he'd been doing the same job, he wasn't past inventing a few facts himself when the need arose.

Giorgio Morosini probably knew every last sorry detail of his life, from sudden fame to shattered family and waning fortune. All it took was a few easy searches online or a glance at his Wikipedia page.

'You said "from what I gathered." What have you gathered?'

The line crackled more loudly.

'Maybe that place truly is cursed.'

'I don't believe in curses, Giorgio.'

'Perhaps that doesn't matter. They only need to believe in you. I appreciate that you want some time on your own. That there's an element to your life that is, of necessity, solitary. But let me break it for an hour or two. I can come out in my little boat any day you like. We can ride over to a little restaurant I know on Sant'Erasmo. Everything on the plate will come from the lagoon. The wine they make from their own vines. We can get stinking drunk together and curse the cruelty of the world. Like Hemingway must have done.'

'I'm not Hemingway.'

'I know.'

'Giorgio. I have to work. I *have* to work.'

'Ah.' He enjoyed talking to Morosini, not least because the man was perceptive. He didn't need desperation spelled out, letter by letter. 'Perhaps another time then. A happier one. It will come.'

'Can't wait,' Honeyman muttered, but there was nothing on the line except static, broken by the beating of waves against the polished wooden hull of the speedboat and the persistent rhythm of its engine.

THEY WERE EDGING CAREFULLY into the rotting timber jetty. There was much to avoid: broken planks, iron railings hanging off the edge, stinking seaweed and algae clinging everywhere. The local behind the wheel looked pretty much like every taxi skipper he'd met—

tanned, slick black hair, shades and a white polo shirt. He was frowning as they approached, as if it was beneath his sleek and polished vessel to stoop to such a lowly destination. When the prow nudged the pier he leapt out and threw a rope round the firmest-looking pole he could find.

'You're a writer,' the man said as Honeyman stumbled along the deck to the steps.

'You were listening.'

'Couldn't help. You talk loud. Most Americans do. You think I've ever read something you done?'

Another perennial author question to go along with Morosini's 'Are you writing anything now?' How many times had he heard this one? How long since he'd been able to say... yes?

Honeyman passed over his bags then took the man's hand and hauled himself up onto the landing.

'I wouldn't know. What kind of books do you like?'

'All kinds.'

'I wrote something called *The Fire: An American Tragedy*. True crime. About... about two murders in upstate New York. About the town too.'

Maybe more about the town than he'd intended. Which had consequences, good and bad.

The fire happened in 2008. The publisher got Honeyman's book through the lawyers and into print in October the following year. It caught the mood of the time somehow. The world seemed to be filled with doubt at that moment. Wall Street and the banks were in trouble, people losing their homes, their savings. There was a sense that beneath the calm, outward, respectable face of society lurked something dark and rotten. A shadow that had always been there but either people had forgotten or, in their craving for an easy life, pretended it never existed in the first place.

That was the secret fear Honeyman latched onto. A story of small-town America's dark secrets exposed after a brief and darkly violent episode of insanity. Drama—sex, hate and two bizarre and terrible murders that remained, for all the evidence available, quite unexplained—all in the kind of white-picket-fence community everyone thought a perfect haven from the horrors of the city.

In the space of twelve frantic months he'd gone from obscure, poorly paid local reporter to riches and a fleeting moment of international fame. The tiny island retreat outside Venice—a city he'd dreamed of for years after reading about it back home—was a well-deserved present to himself.

Diane had hated the place from the moment she stepped off the boat. The seclusion, the primitive conditions, the creepy ruined chapel with its graveyard, all of which she found more distasteful than macabre. And the fact it was impossible to get anywhere without climbing into his shabby little motorboat for a journey that would take twenty minutes to the nearest inhabited island, and an hour or more to the city jetty at Fondamente Nove. Even there she loathed the food he loved, hated that most locals spoke no English.

Lauren, for her part, was simply bemused. One day she came into the kitchen with a skull she'd found near the ruins of the chapel, astonished something so 'cool' was just lying around beneath the surface of Maledetto's dusty ground. But mostly she just missed being able to waste away the day online, chatting, listening to music, dancing when she felt like it, lost in her own little world.

After two visits, Diane said she and Lauren would never set foot in Italy again.

THE LAUREN AND DIANE SHOW. He wished he'd never come up with that sour little joke. They loathed it. Though some of his wife's silent anger stemmed, he knew, from jealousy. She'd been a journalist too until Lauren came along. A more persistent chaser of facts than he'd ever been. But one of them had to give up work to look after the kid. Logic or convention or something they never talked about seemed to dictate it would be her.

A local reporter was all Diane was, all she ever wanted to be. Her ambitions never extended beyond being a daily chronicler of life and the occasional death in the small town of Prosper where she grew up, where Honeyman, a city man, product of a peripatetic childhood in Ohio, found himself in the end. For him, the job on the *News-Ledger* was always meant to be a stepping-stone to something bigger. He had ambition. He could write quickly, glibly, attractively, in pretty much any style people wanted. Those were skills Diane had never possessed. Her prose was workmanlike and serviceable, never stylish, and she knew it. Nor was there ever a time when she felt the need to adjust how she spoke or wrote or acted to the tune of others. She was her own woman and always would be.

'The murderer locked a teacher and a boy from her school inside a hut in the woods, poured gas all around and set fire to it,' Honeyman said to the water taxi driver. 'Cops couldn't find who did it. I could.'

The man took off the shades, stared at him and shook his head. His eyes were small and dark, squinting at the sun, his skin the color of tan leather.

'Why the hell would someone do that?'

A question everyone asked. Including his editor when he wrote the book. Naturally, Honeyman speculated. Jealousy of some kind was the obvious answer. But of what? Had Jorge Rodriguez, the troubled firefighter who set the blaze, been a secret lover of the dead woman? Or simply furious that she'd maybe taken more than a casual interest in his own son?

Honeyman never did find out. That was a hole in the book, one the critics pounced upon. Not that it stopped the thing from selling.

'*The Fire: An American Tragedy,*' Honeyman repeated. 'I don't remember what they called it in Italian. '

The man shrugged and said, 'Doesn't ring a bell. That's a hundred and fifty.'

'It's usually a hundred.'

'Not for me. No one's crazy enough to live out here. I got no chance of a customer until I get back to the airport.' He glanced at the skeletal contours of the chapel at the eastern end of Maledetto, and the spiky headstones rising out of the wilderness, then held out his hand. 'Only you and dead people, and you don't look like you're going anywhere. A hundred and fifty.'

Across the terrace the grass was desert pale. Beyond, on either side of the villa, tall masses of weeds and thistles and shrubs rose dry and a desiccated shade of gold, like rampant wild corn waiting for the harvest.

'I'll need a ride back to the airport in a week. How much for the return?'

'A hundred and fifty times two. Which makes three hundred where I come from. You want to make a reservation?'

'Maybe later,' he said and threw the guy his money.

NO BREEZE DISTURBED the dying palms and scrub that rose from Maledetto's caked brown earth. The grass and weeds had a peculiar smell of their own—dusty, marshy, saline. The heat meant their debris formed a hazy swirling cloud like pollen dancing in the still, dry air. Sometimes Paolo would collect a fleshy-leaved weed from the margins of the rocky shore. The furnaces on Murano used it to make their glassware. He'd taken Honeyman to see them at work once—sweating, burly Venetians blowing ornate goblets and sculptures out of nothing but silica and flame. Honeyman had stared into the searing white-hot oven then grunted an excuse and headed for the door. Paolo couldn't understand why the sight of Murano's fierce, blazing furnaces affected his guest so badly. Any more than he could comprehend why a foreigner would wish to lock himself away in the creepy, deserted prison of Maledetto, unvisited, lacking in all modernities.

Inside the decrepit open boathouse—little more than a garage shell over the shallow water—was the ancient blue-and-white dinghy Honeyman had bought when he moved in, rocking gently on its frayed rope moorings. There'd be a spare can of gas somewhere. On Sunday morning he'd steer over to Mazzorbo, eat one ceremonial meal—seafood followed by duck—in his favorite restaurant, Ai Cacciatori, then order a water taxi for the following day.

A direct flight left just after one. With the time change he'd be in Kennedy before five in the afternoon. Hoping for a meeting the following day with his agent, and the prospect, finally, of a new publishing contract with one of the big houses.

Focus. That was what writing entailed. He had to keep his mind on the job in front of him, setting up a new book to sell, something different. At least an idea for one. A long and detailed outline he'd write over the next four days. One that would get him back in the bestselling game.

He'd hit on the idea a few weeks back, alone in Manhattan, more than a little drunk. The answer seemed so obvious that perhaps it was only what was left of his pride that had prevented him seeing it for so long. There was a bleak, unshakable truth to his brief career, such as it was. Only one book he'd ever produced had caught the imagination of the public. The first.

Much as he'd prefer to be known as a novelist, it was the town of Prosper and the terrible events of the summer of 2008 that made his name, not the attempts at fiction that followed, all handed to smaller and smaller publishers as the years went by until finally even those sales ran out. The only sensible road to follow was to return to the territory that made him. To work out some kind of sequel that exhumed afresh the story of a vengeful firefighter named Jorge Rodriguez and how he'd locked Mia Buckingham, a teacher at Lafayette High, in a cabin in the woods three miles outside Prosper. With Scott Sorrell, a sixteen-year-old student in her art class. Trapped them in there, both naked, soaked gas around the perimeter, then threw a match and vanished, covering his tracks with the knowledge he'd gained from his job. Even Suzanne Barclay, Honeyman's literary agent, had expressed an interest in resurrecting that story. It was the first idea he'd suggested in ages that had produced any kind of positive reaction from her.

He didn't let on that he didn't have a clue how he might tell the same narrative again. Not that Suzanne didn't notice. She could see right through him just as easily as Diane once did.

Honeyman watched the speedboat turn and head back across the lagoon, throttle on full, mud and water churning in its noisy wake. The stifling summer air was thick with mosquitoes and buzzing, biting gnats. He'd need the net around the bed at night, and even then some would get through.

The only electricity came from a set of solar panels on the roof feeding a battery system. Enough to keep a laptop going, a tiny refrigerator and a few lights, not much more. That was all he needed. His research for the first book was on the laptop already: recordings of original interviews, newspaper clippings, crime scene photos, court documents, everything.

Gold was lurking somewhere.

It had to be.

Paolo, the old man from Burano, was usually there in a flash, asking polite questions, shyly presenting his bill. What he'd paid for the food—packets of pasta and jars of sauces, some bread, crackers, cheese, ham, milk and cereal—and the drink—gin, Campari and Cocchi Vermouth di Torino, the only red vermouth Honeyman would touch. Then an accounting for the hours spent on the garden and maintaining the villa during the bitter winter.

He was a hefty man of the lagoon, ruddy-faced, seventy or so, cheeks whiskery and creased from all those long years working the sparse marshes for fish and wildfowl. A character out of Hemingway. Four years before, Honeyman had used Paolo in an opportunistic stab at a techno-thriller about an environmental spill that paralyzed Venice during Carnival. Not that he ever knew. The work never appeared outside the U.S., and there in ebook only. Reading was surely not one of the old man's pastimes.

Still, he was good to talk to for a little while. And it felt odd he wasn't there already, offering a warm welcome before asking for his money.

Honeyman dragged his two bags up the broken concrete path. The house was built from the remains of the old leper hospice and the neighboring chapel, hulking stones five hundred years old sitting alongside cement and tiles from the 1950s. Upstairs there were, in theory, six bedrooms, but only one of them was habitable anymore, and that barely. On the ground floor were two large living rooms; what was meant to be a bathroom but never got finished; a study at the back; and a huge kitchen looking out to the rear, a battery radio on the counter the only concession to the outside world. There, surrounded by a wilderness of weeds and trees, was a pool that had been empty and broken since he bought the place, a crack like the legacy of an earthquake running through the dirty blue tiles, straggly weeds poking through the length of it.

'Paolo...!'

There was a flash of something swift and threatening, so close Honeyman felt the hot summer air swirl around him. Stunned, he stepped back and saw a black, curved blade sweep by his cheek. It took a moment to realize he'd just missed a flashing scythe by inches.

'Shit.' He was struggling for breath, for words. 'What the hell are you doing?'

It wasn't Paolo at all.

The man was tall, strong, short of breath as he hacked away at the tall, rampant weeds of the garden. Mid-twenties maybe, curly black hair shiny with sweat, burly in the stained blue overalls, though his bare arms weren't as tanned as Honeyman might expect from someone who worked the fields in the blazing Veneto summer. His face was almost entirely obscured by a dark beard so bushy and wild it looked wrong, artificial.

The guy stared at him, puzzled, mouth open as if stupid, holding onto the scythe as if he couldn't quite work out what he'd done.

'And you are?' Honeyman demanded.

The stranger grunted something, and it wasn't even a word. Honeyman asked again. Then, after a long moment, the gardener reached into his pants, pulled out a wadded-up piece of lined paper, and passed it over.

The writing was hard to read. Paolo's usually was. The first page was a scribbled list of the drink and groceries he'd ferried to the house and the transport costs. Three hundred and eighty euros due. The second sheet was a note.

SIGNOR HONEYMAN—

My brother and his family are in Jesolo for a couple of days so I cannot be there to meet you on your arrival. I send my nephew, Gianni. He a good kid. Good worker. Deaf and dumb but not stupid if you get me. He take care of the garden today. Gianni got a boat of his own, a good one, so he can get all the way back home to Sant'Erasmo when he's done. He lives there with his grandma. I send him back to work for you in the morning. Cheap too. Ten euros an hour to you and him not being able to talk back he don't argue.
—Paolo

HONEYMAN PACKED the note into his pocket, pointed at the scythe and said very slowly, 'You be careful with that.'

As if the guy could hear. As if he'd understand English.

All he got back was another wordless grunt and a wave of the hand that might have passed for an apology.

A drink, he thought. If Paolo had done his job right there'd be ice in the small fridge he kept hooked up to the solar panel batteries. A drink would be good.

THE HALL WAS EMPTY, the living room too, the whole place dark and fusty, with the cloying smell of a home that hadn't been aired or lived in for a while. The faint but distinct aroma of a recent cigarette was hanging round. Maybe the gardener had been inside smoking... Though why?

He dropped his bags and yelled, 'Hello? Lauren?'

No answer. Not that he should have expected one. This was a refuge for a hermit. The place didn't get visitors. So who the hell was the guy Giorgio Morosini had been talking about?

He went into the kitchen. The old wooden table at the center was spotless, not a speck of dust upon it. A pristine tumbler and dinner plate sat upturned in the big ceramic sink as if someone had just used them and couldn't be bothered to put the things away. Inside the refrigerator was a hunk of fresh parmesan and two lemons, more water, two bottles of Soave and, in the freezer compartment, a couple of bags of supermarket ice cubes. And a chunk of English cheddar, unwrapped, with what looked like a bite mark.

Maybe the gardener had wanted to try a new kind of cheese.

Bewildered by the strange and unfamiliar state of the place, Honeyman made himself a strong Negroni with that quick, unthinking, practiced manner he'd managed to master over the years.

THE BLINDS WERE HALF-DOWN in the study, the room in semi-darkness. Must have been more of Paolo's doing, because Honeyman never worked that way. A rambling fig tree draped its pendulous branches and fleshy leaves over the windows. That was normally enough against the bright lagoon light, and free fruit if he was lucky.

Honeyman drew back the shades. Rays of evening sun streamed in, yellow and green like the fading drought-stricken foliage through which it fell. There was an aroma from somewhere. A perfume. Maybe a flower he didn't know existed outside the window. Though it reminded him of home life too, of family and a house shared with women.

Then he popped the computer on the desk and listened to the familiar boot-up chime as the laptop came to life. Within seconds, a sudden and quite unexpected sound startled him. The brisk sting that introduced the TV news in upstate New York had started automatically, and with it the station's logo, both unwanted memories of a life he'd long left behind. A video began running across the whole of the screen. It was a clip he knew well, one that was probably somewhere among his reference material on the drive. Though why it should come alive like that...

When he saw the anxious newscaster, her hair, her dress, everything took him straight back to 2008.

'This just breaking. We understand there's a significant development in the case of the Mohawk Lake fire tragedy. Law enforcement officers have surrounded a trailer one mile from where the murders occurred. Our crime reporter Jim Preston, who's been on the case since the start, is in the Seven News helicopter overhead now. Jim?'

There was the chop of helicopter blades and a powerful engine. Then a face Honeyman knew so well, Preston, the local TV guy who handled crime stories when they cropped up.

'That's right, Sue,' the reporter announced over the racket. 'After weeks of seeming mystery over the perpetrator of the terrible murders of a young teacher and her pupil, a horror that shocked the nation, it appears police may be chasing a significant breakthrough this morning. This follows the publication online of a story in the *Prosper News-Ledger*, claiming that Jorge Rodriguez, a local firefighter, is likely the prime suspect in the killings of Mia Buckingham and Scott Sorrell, the two who were burned to death in a school cabin outside the town a month ago. According to the report, Rodriguez may have been involved in some kind of relationship with the dead woman, and there's photographic material in his possession to tie him to the crime.'

The picture switched to Sue in the studio making a face that said: *You got to be kidding me.*

'And you're telling us this is the first the cops have heard of the guy?'

'So it seems. Right now we're flying over Rodriguez's trailer close to Mohawk Lake. Like I said, one mile from where the teacher and Scott Sorrell were burned to death. You've got our live feed on the screen. As you can see eight, no, nine squad cars are taking up position and—'

'Wait, Jim. You're saying this case got broken by a small-town newspaper? Not by the local police department?'

'The police have been sidelined on this case pretty much since it turned big, Sue. Word is that the town's police chief, Fred Miller, could face disciplinary proceedings before long.'

'I've got to ask this again, Jim. The paper cracked this case open?'

'The reporter, Tom Honeyman, named the guy—'

'That doesn't seem right.'

'To be honest with you, Sue... nothing much has seemed right about this story right from the get-go.'

'You think Chief Miller could lose his job over this?'

'Not really uppermost in anyone's thoughts at the moment. But in due time... Christ—!' A panicky Preston yelped into the mike as the helicopter engine rose into a roar.

'You're over the scene. Talk to us, Jim.'

'We're having to move fast from here. OK, OK. The guy's coming out of the trailer. Oh my god. There's shooting... We're getting... There's... there's gunfire. I don't think—'

Honeyman killed the clip with a shaking finger, still unable to figure out why it had popped up like that when he turned on the computer.

Sweating now—and it wasn't just the close and humid heat—he glanced at the status bar. The laptop's Wi-Fi was on. He was connected to some kind of network, not that there should have been such a thing out here. When he pulled up a browser it came back with nothing. This was all local, as if there was a router somewhere on the island and he was hooked up to it.

The webcam was staring straight at his face, and the light above it was blinking. Maybe whoever it was could see him, hear him... Maybe they'd been watching him all along.

Fingers shaking, he clicked on the dropdown to turn off the connection. All he got was a warning: *You have insufficient access privileges.*

When he tried again, a deafening electronic laugh almost sent him screaming out of the room. For a moment he couldn't begin to think what it was. Then it came again, and he zeroed in on the source. Second drawer down in the desk. There was a walkie-talkie there, the voice bellowing out from it.

Welcome to Maledetto, Tommy boy. You and me need to talk. And don't even think of turning the computer off. How the hell are you gonna work then? How are you gonna fix this shit you're in?

The TV clip started playing again, and Honeyman hadn't even touched the laptop. He slammed his fingers on the keyboard, trying to stop it.

Hey, Tommy. That's an expensive machine you've got there. Don't hurt it.

Hands shaking, he picked up the handset, lurched to the window, pushed the blinds back all the way, peered outside. All he could see was wild green shrubs and lanky weeds. All he could hear was the buzz of insects and the distant squawks of lagoon birds. And the smell... stagnant water and fresh-cut vegetation.

There was no sign of the gardener.

'How did you get into my computer?'

You're a lazy man. You take shortcuts all the time. You did back then when you were writing that first book. Didn't you?

'This is my home. I don't know how the hell you got here—'

We walk on water, Tommy. All dead people do. Maybe Saturday night we get to walk together 'cross all that shit and mud and flat lagoon, go meet your redeemer. You like that idea? I hope so. Your clock's ticking, man. Running out by the minute.

Tom Honeyman was barely listening. He didn't have much of a temper, but when it came the sudden, unwanted heat was hard to control.

'I don't know who the hell you are. This is my home. I want you off the island. Now!'

Come on! Is that any way to talk to a friend? I'm the only one you've got right now. Watching over you from this dump of a church on this dump of an island. Come all this way to help you find your mojo. You really think you could turn yourself into Hemingway by squandering your stupid money on this piece of rock? Christ. Cash don't

make class. One book don't make a writer. Look out the window
again...

Beyond the leafy green branches of the figs he could see the
ragged stone wall of the ruined church at the very tip of Maledetto.
As he watched, an arm waved briefly from what must once have been
a parapet. It appeared then vanished so quickly he barely had time to
register what he was seeing at all.

It was an invitation, though. One he wasn't going to refuse.
Honeyman went in the kitchen, found the sharpest knife he could
and stomped outside.

HONEYMAN WALKED down the rough pebble path that led to the
boathouse, keeping his head down, trying to work out what to do. A
sudden sweep of movement caught his attention to his left, close to
the sprawling fig tree that drooped down on the villa, half-hiding the
study's windows. The scythe going back and forth.

'Gianni,' he whispered, getting closer. The gardener didn't look
up. Eyes on his work, he just kept swinging his long blade, now
stained green with stalks and severed leaves.

Deaf and dumb.

Wonderful.

Gingerly, Honeyman threw a few pebbles his way and waved his
arms high in the air.

'Gianni.'

That made him look up. But how the hell do you communicate?
Honeyman tried to signal there was someone else on the island by
mouthing the words 'Un'altra persona. Un ladro'. *Someone else. A thief.*
But he wasn't sure at all the message got through.

'You...' Honeyman pointed at him, then the boathouse. 'I need
you take...' His hand gestured at the flat gray lagoon. 'Take the guy
out of here. OK?'

All he got back from behind the heavy black beard was a wordless
grunt that could have meant anything.

'The boat.' Honeyman pretended to pull the motor cord then steer with the tiller. 'You. *Il ladro*. The thief...'

The gardener shrugged. That seemed as much as he was going to get.

Honeyman nodded too then set off up the path.

Think...

The mystery man had set himself up in the church. But clearly he'd been inside the house, might have been hanging around a day or two. And somehow he'd hacked the MacBook.

Can't have done that here, Honeyman thought. Not in the short time he'd been on Maledetto.

Maybe the guy knew he'd been in Prosper asking questions. Maybe that was where he got into the computer. How else? At Kennedy? On the plane?

He walked through the leaning headstones of the graveyard then crossed the rickety wooden bridge that led to the tiny islet where what was left of the church remained. The outer walls were a good ten feet high in places, more solid than he remembered. What must have been windows were now little more than holes in the stonework, a few like medieval weapon slits. As he got closer he realized there was something much more recent behind them. A tent—khaki, military—and he could just make out some modern equipment scattered around: antennae and cables. Exactly the kind of thing he wanted to avoid here. Maledetto was his escape from all that crap, from the world, distractions, complications. People.

This was an intrusion. An outrage.

Honeyman yelled a few obscenities then took out the knife and waved it in the air.

'OK, *man*... You're going to leave. The gardener can take you. I want you gone. I want you...'

He stopped. There was music, loud music, coming from behind the pale walls not more than five yards away now. *Familiar* music. The knife felt loose and slippery in his sweating hands.

The racket got louder. Deafening, and just the sound of it, the relentless ratchet of a hip-hop beat and a rapper chanting rapid lyrics over rolling synths, took him straight back to the summer of 2008, the time everything turned on a few weeks and that bloody climax by Mohawk Lake.

Lauren adored that song. Maybe because she knew how much her father loathed it. The work of some rapper whose name he couldn't recall even though the damned thing got played everywhere that summer and she wouldn't stop watching the stupid video on her laptop in her bedroom. Dancing like she was in a nightclub, not just sixteen, shameless when he caught her messing around in front of the laptop instead of doing her homework.

Low.

The name of the song came back and the picture in his head got brighter, the sound louder. The memories even more cruel.

'Low.'

'Turn that off!' Honeyman screamed. 'I don't know what the hell you're doing here, but this needs to end. Now!'

A couple of seconds more and the music ended bang in the middle of a repetitive riff.

Fine, he thought, standing there sweating, breathless.

The corner of the khaki tent was visible as he got closer, along with a couple of backpacks and a pile of military-style gas containers.

You stop right there, Tommy!

The voice was loud and distorted, not quite human. Played through the sound system, he guessed.

Honeyman stood up, waved the knife in the air, yelled, 'Screw this. I want you out of here. There's a boat. You're going to get on it. You're going—'

The words just died then. Something had appeared in one of the slits next to the door, and it was like the music, a memory taking him back years to a time he'd been a reporter covering a military exercise in Ohio. They had these weapons there, the kind the army used in Iraq and Afghanistan. It was a sniper rifle, black and shiny, and a pair of swift hands were positioning it on a bipod. Behind, he could just make out the head and shoulders of someone in army fatigues, a black ski mask over the face, shoulder falling to the stock. He didn't need to look where the barrel was aimed.

There was a crack of gunfire and a puff of smoke.

Hey, Tommy. You've gone all quiet. Cat got your tongue?

Another shot, a brief burst of flame and smoke. Over his shoulder. Somewhere the shell hit stone, on the house, he guessed. This close the guy could have killed him easily for sure.

Honeyman turned and ran.

Ran like he was a kid again, arms pumping, legs aching. Dashed and stumbled through the crushed grass and weeds, back toward the villa.

He tripped, fell to the ground, felt his fingers sting as they hit nettles and brambles. The knife slipped from his fingers and vanished into the rotting trunk of a dead palm.

No match for a Bushmaster XM-15.

There. It all came back from his reporter years. The thirst for detail. The hunger for facts and names and certainties, and the burning need to concoct them if maybe they weren't there.

Run.

He stumbled for the villa.

The gardener was still out front, hacking away at the weeds by the path to the boathouse. Deaf to it all.

'Gianni!' Honeyman yelled. 'Gianni. Get inside...'

He was going to have to drag him into the villa, think this through. Work out... what?'

'Come on...'

Five paces away, the gardener seemed to see something. His head went up. His eyes narrowed. He threw the scythe to one side, squinting back toward the chapel.

There was another gunshot, and then Gianni fell, screaming, hands high in the air, the scythe flying off to nowhere, vanishing into the tall weeds he'd been trying to cut. Honeyman called his name, started to dash toward him.

Then the rifle sounded again, and angry clouds of dust began to make a bead from the point where Gianni had disappeared into the thick undergrowth by the trees, each one a yard or so closer to Honeyman.

He stopped. He stood his ground. Another shot whistled past, then another that took out the bark of the carob tree by his side.

Through the open door of the study he could just hear the walkie-talkie.

Get inside, Tommy boy. Last chance, genius. Get in the house. Stay there. We got work to do.

There wasn't a movement, not a sound from the gardener.

He walked inside.

HONEYMAN WENT STRAIGHT to the desk and grabbed the walkie-talkie. His fingers didn't stop shaking. There was no way he could get the memory of the gardener—deaf, stupid eyes, big, bushy beard—out of his head.

'You just shot a man. Let me go and see if I can help him.'

Why'd you want to do that? You don't know the guy from Adam.

Crazy. No other word for it.

'Because maybe I can do something.'

No helping there, Tom. Sad to say. Your Italian friend's gone for good. Some guys just walk in the wrong place at the wrong time, and there's nothing any of us can do.

'You shot him.'

Now you're repeating yourself. A good reporter doesn't do that, does he? A good reporter gets the facts. Or makes them up.

Honeyman went to the front door, stood in the shadow of the porch and looked out toward the jetty. There was no movement out there. No sound.

'What the hell do you want?'

Same as everyone. Even you, if you know it. The truth about Mohawk Lake. A little justice.

'I... I did my best with that story.'

Best wasn't good enough, was it? You know you been living a lie all

*these years. Still, we're gonna fix that. Third drawer down. Time you
learned this is about more than your own miserable skin.*

Honeyman went back into the study and scrabbled through the
mess of papers and pens and old cables in the desk. He uncovered an
airline luggage tag in the name of Lauren Taylor. By its side he found
a Polaroid of his daughter in torn jean shorts and a t-shirt, brown hair
short, sweaty, unkempt, standing stiff and scared and awkward
beneath a bright and searing sun. A blue-and-white-checked blind-
fold was tied over her eyes. Her mouth was open, in shock or terror.
She looked a lot thinner than he recalled, tanned, older, though she
still stood with that awkward teenage stance.

Diane always said she'd look fifteen even when she was fifty.

The photo was taken outside by the ruined chapel, on the
scorched and rock-hard earth that must once have been the nave.
To the side was a relic from the old days: the statue of an angel,
right hand outstretched, blind eyes turned to the sky, left arm
leaning on a crutch. A nod to the true purpose of Santa Maria
dell'Umiltà.

He punched the talk button.

'What the hell have you done to her? Where is she?'

One thing at a time.

'Who are you?'

Mister Honeyman's bestest friend. Not that you know it yet.

'What... whatever you're after you can have it. I don't care. I want
Lauren safe. *Where is she?*'

*Oh. All the loving father now. You're reading this all wrong, man. Just
like you did back then.*

The news clip started playing again. Honeyman slammed the
keyboard to stop it.

'Lauren's got nothing to do with this...'

*Shut up and listen. You don't even know what this is. I'm not saying it
again. Don't try and turn the laptop off. I'd know. I wouldn't like that.
Neither would your kid.*

The line went quiet. Honeyman thought he heard words but he
couldn't make them out.

Then there she was, the same sharp, young, awkward voice audible over the crackly line.

Dad, please, this time you got to do what someone asks. Just this once. I didn't mean... Don't fucking touch me! Don't—'

'Has he... has he hurt you?'

I'm sorry. I'm really sorry I got you into this.

'You didn't. Just ask the guy what he wants. He can have it.'

There was a tussle on the other end. He could see Lauren in his mind's eye, recall how she'd always give in to defeat in a way that never quite said *you won.*

What I want? Here's the deal, Tommy—

'The deal is you let her go—'

You're going to need me to write this book of yours. The one you've been trying to talk to everyone 'bout, back in Prosper, and getting nowhere. Well, now you got your writing partner. I know stuff you couldn't even dream of. Real things from back then. I got clues to help you put things right this time. Sometimes I'll use these walkie-talkies to jog your memory. Sometimes I'll send you a little gift across the wires. When you write— and you will write — I'm gonna read every single word you say, right when you set it down. Lucky boy. You got your own personal editor, twenty-four hours a day. I trust you're grateful.

'I'll do whatever you want. If you let her go.'

That I cannot do. Lauren Honeyman... What's that, sugar? Correction... Lauren Taylor's a part of this story. Just like her old man. She's mine now.

'And your part?'

Jesus, Tommy, don't you know? I'm that thing you've been missing all these years. Your inspiration. Your muse. Your... spark.

A video came up on the laptop screen, live, shot from a phone, it looked like. Someone was holding it, walking around, camera at waist height, parched earth and grass and paving stones rushing past, a tent, a camping stove, sleeping bags.

Then, neatly laid out over sheets as if on display, weapons. Handguns, seen so briefly he couldn't count them, a sniper rifle with a bipod stand, two long-blade field knives with horn handles.

Finally the shot found a pair of sneakers, skinny tanned legs, cut-off jeans rising, a t-shirt tight above the navel and a logo on it above the image of a gigantic cruise ship: *See the World on Board Apollo.*

The camera rose. Lauren's shoulders, bare neckline, then her face, blindfolded, shaking her head in terror, whimpering as the lens came and stalked all around her.

The guy was breathing hard, enjoying this as he came so close there was nothing in the frame but her quivering mouth, bright, white teeth, a bloodied lip, purple and stained with dried blood in the left corner.

Then the image froze. Right on her wounded mouth.

Your kid does not make good conversation.

'I want to talk to her again. I want you to take that thing off her face.'

You've seen enough.

'Don't hurt her. She's done nothing. Let her go. Take me.'

Maybe I should. You murdered Jorge Rodriguez with your lies. Killed your own wife—

'Don't say that—'

Stupid bitch walked straight into Mohawk Lake—

'Don't say that!'

Be funny if your daughter went the same way. Out here, middle of nowhere. Italian nowhere. Christ. Your parenting skills are as great as your talent for husbanding. You know that?

Honeyman stormed away from the laptop, into the hall, away from the peeking, peering webcam. Now that the day was fading he could see tiny red lights throughout the house, above the study door, visible in the hall. He walked through the ground floor, then the upper rooms. There were small cameras, the kind people used for security and as baby monitors, set in corners and crevices everywhere. Plastic boxes with bulbous lenses. He had a couple like this back home. They could run on batteries for weeks.

In the last bedroom was a massive backpack so crammed that the seams bulged like veins on muscles. A tag on the strap said: *Lauren*

Taylor, Apollo. He must have grabbed her at the airport somehow, dumped her bag here, taken her off to the old chapel.

He and his daughter were trapped just as much as Mia Buckingham and Scott Sorrell out by Mohawk Lake, twelve years before.

OUT TO THE WEST, over the ragged outline of the Dolomites, the sun was dying, a blazing golden ball. There seemed to be no colors in the world except fire and the growing dark.

Honeyman went back to the study.

That's right, Tommy. I've got you nailed. Had time to prepare. Got my eyes all over the place. You can't take a crap I don't get to see. Step out of that door without me saying and I will know, and I will burn this little bitch of yours. Then you. Annoy me just a little again and I cut off a finger of hers and let you hear her screaming.

Stay calm. Keep cool.

'OK. Again. What do you want?'

You're really asking? Same as everyone. The truth. Justice. Jorge Rodriguez never killed those people.

Honeyman's heart sank. He'd had to write the book. The contract was there. They needed the money. He craved the chance to escape Prosper. But it wasn't perfect. In a way he was lucky no one fact-checked everything and tore apart his version of events.

'You're wrong. I saw the evidence. I *found* the evidence. He came out of that trailer like he knew it. It was him—'

Don't ever tell me that again, Tom! Just say it one more time and we are done. I will burn the pair of you and leave your miserable corpses black as coal on these rocks.

'No, listen to me—'

The moron came out of that trailer stinking drunk! The way he was most of the time since that crappy town started beating on him. Jorge Rodriguez was a scapegoat for all you tight-ass hypocrites in Prosper. You know you've been living a lie all these years. Time to fix that, Tom.

The cursor started moving on the screen, hunting for something.

The word processor fired up, opened a new document showing the title—*The Fire Revisited: A True Story* by Thomas Honeyman—and saved the file as 'Fire2'.

How are we going to open this? Don't want anything literary. Got to grab 'em by the balls from the start. That's where you went wrong writing your stupid novels. You thought you had talent. We both know that's bullshit.

'This is insane...'

Don't ever say that to me again. You're going to work, Tom Honeyman. I want to feel you hurting right inside this story you're going to tell. I want to see your pain like you're just some dumb character in one of those dumb novels you wrote. Except this time we make it real.

The cursor blinked.

This is no fairy tale, Tommy boy. This is real flesh and blood. Dead flesh and blood. I even got you your tagline. You know what a tagline is, don't you?

The words began to appear, letter by letter across the screen:

Here's the truth. Jorge Rodriguez didn't kill the teacher and her student. It's time America knew who did.

Honeyman clutched the walkie-talkie.

'How do you know?'

How do I know what?

'How do you know it wasn't Jorge Rodriguez?'

Is that a serious question?

'What do you think? *How do you know?*'

I know, dumbass. How is irrelevant. You got him killed. You sucked on Mia Buckingham's guts the way she sucked on Scott Sorrell's dick. Then made yourself a pretty fortune. Thomas Honeyman. The guy who was into fake news before fake news got invented. You never did have the whole story right. What you didn't guess, you invented. Here's the deal. You always give yourself a deadline, don't you? That real estate guy told me. When the fireworks go up over the water, you sign off on some new piece of shit. Eleven thirty Saturday night. Well, let's stick to that. You've been asking questions back in Prosper. You've got a bunch of material on that laptop of yours. Like I said, I got a few pointers of my own. So, Ace, we go back and look at everything again. You're going to put a name to whoever poured gas around that shack and killed two people. And this time you're going to get it right.

Honeyman knew there were gaps in the story he told. Some facts he'd never disclosed, a few he'd distorted for the sake of the narrative. Some he'd hidden from himself. There'd been no time to stand on principle. The publishers were begging for a finished manuscript and offering a small fortune for him to deliver. Hesitate, and the money might have gone elsewhere. All manner of vultures were hovering around the ashes and charred timbers by Mohawk Lake, scrabbling for dollars in the ruins.

Oh, right. You're thinking: Where the hell do I start? Christ, the favors you're getting here.

A heading appeared on the laptop: *By Mohawk Lake.*

Then a stream of pasted text, which ran down the screen so quickly he couldn't read it.

My gift to you. Enjoy. Absorb. Between the two of us we're gonna write the biggest story you'll ever put your name to. Third person, Tommy. You're a player in all this, not the star. Wrap it up right come the Night of the Redeemer, when the fireworks start lighting up the sky—

'Sounds like you have the answer already.'

Or maybe I just know it wasn't that loser Rodriguez. Safe bet that whoever killed that woman did so for personal reasons. She used that study hut a lot on her own. Well, not so much on her own. More for extracurricular activities, if you get my drift, and not just with that little idiot Scott Sorrell. You do get my drift, don't you, Tom?

'It doesn't matter what she did with her private life. She didn't deserve to die. Any more than that kid.'

Christ, man. You're gonna have to do better than that. You come up with the name of whoever did light that fire by Saturday, then you and your girl get to walk out of here free and never hear from me again. That I promise. You keep telling me it's Rodriguez and I make a fireworks show all of my own. Your kid first, then you right after. Burn the pair of you, and that's a promise too. Oh... And if you're thinking of running...

There was a sound Honeyman couldn't nail at first. Then he saw a point of purple flame shooting out from the darkness close to the shore. After that came a roar. Finally an explosion.

He ran to the front of the villa, threw open the front door.

It was a flare, he guessed. Aimed at the boathouse and his dinghy. Soaked in gas, they had to be, just like Mia Buckingham's shack by Mohawk Lake. Both the shed and the boat were alight, orange and yellow flames fanning sooty smoke up to the starry sky. He could smell the fuel and the fire, see flakes of black debris rising on the wind.

There was no one near that he could see. The man must have retreated back the way he came. Back to where he was keeping Lauren with his guns. And nothing in the house but knives.

Honeyman sat down at the computer and folded his arms.

Who needs a boat, Tom? Not you.

'Then how do we get out of here?'

Like I said. Maybe we walk on water. Like your dead wife was trying all those years ago. Walk all the way to the city, underneath a sky of beautiful fire.

Don't answer him, Honeyman thought. *Stay silent. Don't make things worse.*

'That Buckingham lady surely liked to spread her favors around, didn't she? But I guess you know that. Being an investigative reporter and all. Must run. Got business, and you got work. We'll talk in the morning. Ciao.*

'I need to speak to my daughter.'

Oh. And one more gift for you.

A clock came up in the laptop's menu bar. Counting down to the moment the fireworks were due to start across the lagoon.

Deadline: 3 days. 23 hours. 46 minutes.

The time ticked away in front of him.

It was dark beyond the window, insects buzzing everywhere. Honeyman swept a few away, bent over the laptop and began to read.

2

BY MOHAWK LAKE

Prosper, New York
Saturday, July 12, 2008

F red Miller was six-foot-four, lean, a little bent with age but hard muscle and bone all the same. A widower who liked to live in his uniform even when he was at home watching TV, beer in hand. The pants, the shirt, the jacket, they all felt comfortable, and besides, after Sue died and their kid Vern went to college in Seattle and never came back, who was going to moan? Sometimes, when booze and exhaustion took hold, he'd found himself sleeping in his blues, waking on the couch in the morning wondering if it was fine to go to work the way he was even if Molly the station secretary would wrinkle her nose and tell him he was a pig.

Vern was a good son, but Seattle might have been in another country, and the tech job he got after college, moving all over the place, didn't seem to give him much in the way of free time. It wasn't a surprise or an affront that his boy found it hard to come back to Prosper more than once a year. The place was boring for the young. Hell, it was boring for the old, not that many would admit it.

With his gray hair slicked back and a craggy face dominated by a hook nose, some of the braver kids called Miller 'Beaky'. But only behind his back. He was one day into his fifty-ninth year, alone in the station, when the fire department called and said didn't he know something had been burning bad out by Mohawk Lake.

The last piece of Molly's birthday cake was in front of him along with a card from Vern, a cup of coffee and a copy of the *Prosper News-Dispatch*. A paper he read out of duty, not pleasure. He didn't like reporters, especially not Tom Honeyman, the pushy hack who covered what few crime stories the town produced. Nor Jeff McAllister, the paper's owner and publisher who'd inherited the rag from his late mother, a decent woman who knew what to print and what to keep quiet. Jennifer McAllister would have put Honeyman in his place, told him nothing hereabouts was Watergate and Prosper had no call for a wannabe Woodward or Bernstein. But her son just shrugged and said they needed something to fill the pages and keep the dwindling handful of advertisers happy. Not that it was working. What with the banks and big companies and Wall Street falling over, lots of little mom-and-pop outfits were in trouble too. The paper was getting thinner and thinner by the week, and McAllister had taken to writing editorials along the 'use it or lose it' lines that failing businesses spin before they go belly up.

Prosper was a quiet, contained little town where shady things happened behind closed doors and drawn curtains, rarely even gossiped about because gossiping was admitting they existed in the first place. Fred Miller didn't mind. It made his job easier. It meant the statistics—the idiot numbers he got judged by—looked fine and within what the town council termed 'acceptable limits'.

If he'd wanted he could have torn the place apart, rooting out the weed-smokers and the coke-heads, the drunk drivers and, just for fun, busting some sneaky adulterous couple when they were pulling on their pants in the back seat of an SUV in Prudeaux Wood. Prosper knew all about that too. Just to remind them and keep the stats in line, he'd throw a DUI case in court from time to time, and anyone he found beating on a woman. A peace existed between the town and its sheriff. An uneasy one, more so than Miller appreciated, but to him, at least, it felt fine.

That Saturday he'd spend as the lone officer on duty, nothing to do until the evening, when he might have to kick a couple of drunks out of the bars and tell them if they were stupid enough to try to drive home they'd wake up in a cell covered in bruises.

'I'm Police,' he barked at the nervous-sounding youngster on the line. 'You're Fire. Deal with it.'

The kid grunted something Miller couldn't quite hear. There was the sound of motors running in the background, pumps maybe.

'You need to be out here, Chief. We thought it was just youngsters messing with that hut the high school uses out in the woods.'

'They do that all the time. The little bastards like setting fires and causing trouble. If you can point me toward the moron who did it I'll spank them hard if their old man won't but—'

'There's bodies inside.'

Miller grabbed his hat, his gun, his car keys.

Hell of a way to hear.

ONE HOUR later he was standing next to the high school study cabin, wondering if he'd ever get that smell—charred wood, burned flesh, and the cloying stink of gasoline—out of his head.

He remembered the cabin from times he'd had to deal with kids messing around close by. Smoking dope. Drinking. Screwing. Doing all the kid things they thought they could get away with out in the woods. The place had been there a good thirty or forty years. Vern had gone a couple of times at school—study visits only, not that he was into nature much. The building was fashioned after someone's idea of an old-style wooden lodge. Heavy timber planking, big entrance door, just one window and that had bars all over it to stop intruders stealing some of the art supplies and science equipment the teachers left inside.

Now it was hard to imagine what it had been like at all. There was just a low, crooked skeleton of blackened timber stumps, smoking away. The fire crew said they'd found the window grate on the ground, still padlocked. There was a chain and another lock through what was left of the door. From what it looked like, someone had trapped whoever was inside, spread gas all around the parched grass and tinder-dry timber, then set the place ablaze.

The hut was tucked away in a seldom-visited part of the wood beside the lake. No one but the school used the place, and it being a Saturday it was odd anyone was here at all. No tire tracks on the shingle. Just a couple of mountain bikes thrown on the ground next to some trees, one newish and it looked like a woman's, the other older and probably a kid's.

The fire department had taken down what was left of the burned timber walls. Men in heavy work gear were tiptoeing among the foam and debris, not looking too hard at what they were stamping through. Sweating like pigs in all that clothing, Miller guessed. And maybe over more than the heat. In the center of the devastated cabin he could make out two charred corpses crouched in contorted agony, both so badly burned you couldn't tell if they were young or old, male or female. Human either, really. Miller took it all in, silent, thinking, and knew in his gut this was going to be the worst thing he'd ever had to deal with in all his years as a Prosper cop.

'What the hell do I do?' he said to no one in particular.

'Won't be your job for long,' someone said. 'They can't let small-town cops handle a thing like this. Wouldn't be surprised if the State don't wash their hands and pick up the phone to the Feds.'

'You're a detective now?'

The fireman glared at him. He was mid-thirties, foreign-looking face covered in smoke, eyes wet with tears from the fire.

'No. Just seen this kind of thing before. Have you?'

'Everyone's a smartass around here, aren't they?' Miller snapped straight back.

It was only later, after the crazy case came to a strange end, that he realized who'd made that remark. Jorge Rodriguez. Two years living in town, which made him a rank outsider, kicked out by the fire department the following week after a fight with his wife wound up at work. Supposedly, Rodriguez had locked his victims in the shack that morning, set the deadly fire around them, then reported for his shift like nothing had happened. Seemed odd that the perp should have been asking for the Feds to turn up with all their science and clever college investigators. Odd, too, that he'd gone back to stare at his handiwork, tears in his eyes, which maybe weren't all down to smoke.

But then 'odd' was a word that was never far away when it came to events that July Saturday down Mohawk Lake.

If this thing was as bad as it looked—two people murdered in a blaze that was going to leave little in the way of evidence—Rodriguez was probably right. Miller was no fool. He appreciated right away that he was out of his depth, and that how he responded to this catastrophe might well affect his future. The Council and a few of the men who thought of themselves as town elders had been asking when he was retiring. He was getting old, getting crabby. Or crabbier, to be precise.

There was also the problem of how to proceed in the brief time he had before the outside teams started to show. With a road accident, and there'd been a good few of those, it wasn't hard to find the relatives or parents. He could call in his three deputies, though all were off duty and two were probably close to drunk in Reggie's Sports Bar by then. The four of them would work the phones, scrape the place for IDs, start the slow process of putting a name to those charred bones and burned flesh. Maybe they belonged to someone he knew already, Prosper being that kind of place.

But Miller had stared hard at those two incinerated shapes and realized there wasn't a chance he was going to get a shred of anything there. That meant he had no way he could break the news to the bereaved, to wait for the shrieks, the tears, the denials, then offer to make a cup of coffee or find some booze. Which was his job and always had been. The first thing a cop like him did when faced with sudden death. To be denied that opportunity left him thinking there weren't just relatives out there facing a loss that day. His position, his standing in the small upstate town, was on the line as well.

Standing by the burned-out shack, smoke and worse in his nostrils, Fred Miller wondered if he was going to throw up. Before the year was through he'd be out of a job, trying to get by on his pension with some night-time security work for a grocery store chain twenty miles away in Burnsville. The lack of money wouldn't trouble Miller too much. He was a bachelor, tending to find women more trouble than the enjoyment they handed back in return. The loss of status in the only job and the only town he'd ever known... that was different.

Something—the shack, the ground, the world—began to shift beneath him. It was as if an earthquake was rising up from beneath the hard, burned earth to shake Mohawk Lake and everything around. Before he knew it Miller found himself on the ground, arms flapping, head spinning, warm vile puke coming out of his mouth, spitting it straight and desperate at the dark and sooty soil because he sure as hell didn't want it on his uniform.

'Chief.'

He was rolling in the black and smoky filth, couldn't get upright, couldn't stop thinking all these fire guys had given up looking at the cabin and its corpses and were staring straight at him instead.

Strong arms came and pulled him to his feet. Another one of the firemen. Steve. That was his name. He couldn't remember the rest. Names were getting hard. Someone, somewhere was laughing, and a voice in Miller's head whispered: *They'll be talking about this in town before the night's out.*

Along with all the rest of the gossip.

Chief Miller fainted and threw up.

What kind of cop does that?

Jesus... No wonder they want him out.

Steve looked him up and down and said, 'You OK?'

'Yeah.'

'We all done it. No need to be ashamed.'

'Like that helped,' Miller growled.

'You know we had to call Albany. When it's a crime like this—'

'I do crime.'

'Yeah, but. I mean... it's way beyond us. You understand that, don't you?'

'I do crime. When they give me the chance.'

'Sure. When they show, can you give them this?'

Steve had something in his gloved hand, was holding it out to shine in the bright summer sun. A woman's necklace, silver heart-shaped pendant on a chain, everything stained by smoke and fire. Someone had rubbed off the soot so you could see what was engraved in a crude script that almost looked homemade: *To Mia. Always and forever.*

'Forever don't last long,' Miller said, then pulled himself together as best he could, took a tissue from his pocket and a plastic evidence bag, placed the necklace carefully in there. The firefighter was wearing gloves. That was something anyway. 'Where'd you get it?'

The guy nodded to a stand of trees close to a small clearing. There was a picnic table and some wooden seating next to it. Hunched over on a bench was someone Fred Miller had known since he was a kid at school alongside Vern. Jackson Wynn, wearing a park ranger uniform, kneading his felt hat in nervous hands, glancing in their direction.

'Jackson called us.'

'And?'

Steve shrugged and wiped some grime and sweat from his face with the back of a gloved hand.

'He was holding that thing. Started wailing like a baby the moment I opened my mouth and asked him about it.'

Miller had had words with Jackson Wynn a good many times over the years. When he was a student at Lafayette High and people said he was trying to peek into the girls' changing rooms. Later, when a couple of families thought he was stealing underwear from clothes-lines out among the new houses on the edge of town. Not so long ago, after someone complained he was trying to take pictures with his shiny new phone, sticking it under women's skirts.

Some of the older brats used to yell 'Got your rocks off yet, Jackson?' when they saw him around town. He lived on his own now his mom was dead, in a rundown shack off Madison that had all kinds of junk—sinks and old bicycles and a rusting Ford that was going nowhere—on what passed as a front lawn. The town had set him up with a park service job, which was ten percent sympathy and the rest a desire to get him off the street. No one wanted to see him hanging around with his long miserable face gawking at anything in a dress.

Miller pulled out his pocket tape recorder. Mia. There was only one woman he could think of with that name. A pretty one too, recently turned up at Lafayette High. So she'd know about the cabin for sure.

'I'll talk to him.'

Molly could type out the transcript later. Once she stopped sobbing. Because a thing like this...

He gagged. The sick came up again. He spat up what bile was left onto the black burned ground.

A thing like this wouldn't go away easy at all.

TWENTY MINUTES later Miller was sitting at the picnic tables watching Jackson Wynn sweat like a trapped pig across from him. He had his voice recorder on and was thinking up some questions. Miller needed something to do, someone to harass. The weedy park ranger fit the bill.

'You called the fire department, Jackson? Why not me?'

'Park rules. Didn't know anyone was in there, did I?'

'Where were you when you saw it was on fire?'

'Didn't say I saw it on fire. Was smoke I saw.'

Never a straight answer, Miller thought. 'Where were you when you saw the smoke?'

'The other side of the lake. Over by Pine Point.'

Miller laughed and made sure Wynn knew why. 'Now there's a surprise. You hanging around the girls' summer camp.'

'Wanted to see they were OK. That's all.'

Miller leaned forward until he was as close to the ranger's face as he could get. 'Don't give me that shit, son. It's the middle of summer. They got good people working there. Why wouldn't those girls be OK?'

'Got my job to do.'

'You're a creep, Jackson. Always were. I know you.'

'No need to keep going on about things from when I was a kid.'

'More recent than that. You watching those pretty things go swimming again? Taking pictures? I said I'd lock you up if I caught you—'

'N-no... I went there in my boat, doing nothing wrong. Saw there was smoke coming from the other side of the lake. So I went and looked.'

He was lying. Miller knew what that looked like.

'And...?'

'S-school shack was on fire. Used to go there when I was at Lafayette. Collecting bugs. Doing science. Not art like they use it for now.'

Miller nodded at the smoldering log ruin beyond the parking lot.

'Don't think anyone's going to be using it for a long while.'

'Looked like someone had splashed gas everywhere and put a light to it.'

'You could smell gas?'

'Oh yeah. Flames were twice as high as the place when I set off across the lake. Went up like tinder. Damned lucky we got no wind and it's bare earth 'round there or we'd have an incident on our hands here.'

If there hadn't been people nearby he'd have grabbed Jackson Wynn by the collar of his ranger shirt just then.

'Jesus Christ, boy. Two people dead. That *is* an incident. Did you see something? Hear anyone? A vehicle? Voices?'

'All I heard was them flames dying down. Climbed out my boat and the timbers were cracking like bones got left in a fire pit. I thought maybe some of those bad kids from town had torched the place.'

Miller got out his cuffs and placed them on the table.

'I ought to arrest you.'

Jackson Wynn looked ready to weep.

'What for?'

'You look the way you always do when you're lying.'

'About what? I'm not—'

'I don't know, Jackson. But I'll find out. You're not smart enough to hide things, not from me. Won't go down well with the park service if I take you in. Maybe you'll lose your job, and since that was a favor you won't be getting another too quick. Maybe—'

'Chief. Believe me. I didn't do nothing wrong. People are always picking on me. I was on the other side of the lake. Watching the girls.'

'Anyone going to back you up there? Did those pretty little things in bathing suits see you?'

Wynn looked shifty, glanced at the gray lake.

'Some counselor came up and told me to scoot out of there or they'd complain. *I wasn't doing anything but watch.* Then I saw smoke rising over here. Right through the trees.'

'And when it burned to the ground you stepped inside?'

'I didn't do anything wrong.'

Miller reached over and flicked some ash from his ranger shirt.

'You're covered in this stuff, Jackson. Smoke and dirt all over your boots and pants. You went inside that place.'

'Got curious. Place smelled funny. Like… like it was a barbecue or something. Meat… Burned meat.'

Miller took out the pendant he'd gotten from the fireman.

'How'd you get this?'

'Found it. Outside.'

'Got a name on this locket. Mia Buckingham. From your old school. Did you know her?'

'Didn't *know* her.'

'Did you see her now and again?'

'Park's my job. Got to keep tabs on people. She was always coming down here. School days. Other days. Weekends. She had a key. Told me Principal Rabbitt gave it to her and said she could use the place as much as she wanted. For her painting and stuff.'

'What kind of stuff?'

'I didn't watch. I stopped watching. Like you said.'

Fred Miller laughed. Now he was getting close.

'Ah, right. That kind of stuff. *Your* kind of stuff. You ever see her here with anyone you could put a name to?'

Jackson started to gulp, then blubber. Tears and snot running down his long, miserable face.

'I didn't know the lady was in there. I thought it was just bits of wood or them things she used to make out of branches and timber and crap. Just saw this pretty piece of jewelry glittering and thought maybe I'd take it. Keep it. Who else was gonna want it?'

'Quit crying like a baby, Jackson. Quit retching. You watched her here, didn't you? You watched her before. You knew what she was up to in that shack. You knew who with. Who—'

The ranger was bent over the table, shoulders heaving, looking ready to throw up.

Miller barked into the recorder, 'Hear all that, Molly? You type this out for me. Interview with Jackson Wynn concludes. For now.'

MIA BUCKINGHAM HAD TURNED up in Prosper the previous September with the new school term. Art teacher, came from San Francisco, one of the old families on Nob Hill, though time and money and a bad marriage—or so she said—meant she was on her own, pretty much broke, desperate to be anywhere but California.

Thirty-one, short, skinny, always smiling, elfin face, glittering brown eyes, hair in a ragged kid's cut with pink and blue stripes all through the natural glossy brunette. Everyone—man and woman, boy and girl—looked up when she walked in the room, torn jeans, tie-dye t-shirt, fingers often covered in paint or sculpting clay. Mia Buckingham had something about her. A glitter, an aura, a kind of spark that meant she always got noticed. The kids went quiet when she bounced all giggling into class and announced school sucked, education didn't matter, and what the hell... they were all going out into the yard to make installations and stuff out of any old junk they could find.

Or, for the lucky few, a trip out to the study shack in the woods by Mohawk Lake. There to paint, to sculpt, to talk, to sing with her as she played her guitar like a hippie from another time, another world, one they'd only seen on TV. A place that seemed so wild, so border-less, so very unlike the cold, dry town where they were growing up bored stupid, looking for anything to break the tedium.

Most women liked her, too, which was rare because pretty teach-ers, seemingly unattached ones, didn't usually meet with the approval of the mothers of Lafayette High. They envied her looks, her freedom, the way she'd swear, quite foully, in a whisper if someone, a man in particular, pissed her off. For that, for the quick laughter and brightness she brought to their own dull lives, they ignored—almost —the fact she'd never had kids of her own to ruin her figure and swamp her days with all the chores that family entailed. Single, bohemian, maybe secretly a little indiscriminate in her private life, Mia was empathetic to their complaints all the same. She'd listen to them moan about idle husbands, feckless offspring, money, or rather the lack of it, the monotony of being stuck in Prosper when really they wanted to be in a big city leading the life she must have led one time. And if she slept around from time to time, well, that was what they'd all do if only they had the courage to risk being catcalled as a slut if it ever came out.

The school had an unwritten rule: it was fine to bang your fellow teachers—and maybe expected once in a while. Just don't ever touch a pupil. Mia let it be known she understood this and agreed with it. She was smart. She was a listener too, and when that inevitable note of envy came into their tone, when they wondered what it was like being free and single and a woman in San Francisco, able to do what you wanted, she'd sigh just for a second, drop her eyes to the floor and say, with a sudden sadness, 'The grass is always greener. I came here for a reason...'

Though beyond a failed marriage they never knew what that reason was. Which helped greatly with the aura. Mia Buckingham, the mothers of Prosper soon realized, was a woman with a past, an unknown one, perhaps tinged with misfortune. Why else would you leave Nob Hill with all its glamor for the dreariness of their little town out in nowhere with nothing much to do?

With fathers she was different. There was a kind of flirtatious seriousness to her, a look that said *Keep your kid in line and make sure they get good grades, especially from me... and maybe?* Whether she ever did turn grateful, the mothers of Lafayette High never knew, though so long as it was someone else's husband, the truth was they probably wouldn't mind.

As the embers by Mohawk Lake were dying down, Chief Miller understood only a little of this, though in the weeks to come he'd learn much more. Right then—with the firefighters getting on with their work; Jackson Wynn, silent and terrified, hunched on the wooden bench by the picnic table; state police on their way—Miller realized he faced two choices: acquiesce to outsiders stealing this strange incident from him or get involved and quick, in a way they couldn't stymie.

Watching the smoke and steam rise from the blackened skeleton of Lafayette's study cabin, Miller knew his career could well die alongside the charred remains of Mia Buckingham and whoever burned to death with her, another black shape just a yard away, frozen in the same kind of charcoal agony—man, woman, boy, girl, hard to tell.

It wasn't much of a choice at all.

MILLER CALLED GARY RABBITT.

'Hey, Bunny. Chief Miller here. Where does that pretty little thing of yours, Mia Buckingham, lay her head at night?'

'You can call me Principal Rabbitt or Gary. That's it.'

'Apologies, *Gary*. Mia Buckingham. Where does she live?'

'Why do you want to know?'

'She's dead. I want to look at her place.'

Rabbitt gulped down the line. 'Dead?'

'Yeah. Very. Where does she live? I mean... where *did* she live, obviously?'

'Oh my god. Really?'

'Not the kind of thing I make up.'

'I can't believe it.'

Rabbitt never asked how. Which was what most people did in those circumstances.

'Why not? People die all the time.'

'I mean... Mia.'

'Don't you want to know what happened?'

'Well, um. Yeah. This is such a shock.'

'Oh, sure it's a shock. Looks like murder. Not had one of those here in twenty years. Now I got two. Not that I know who the other victim is right now. Just that they got burned to a crisp with her. Like a drunk's barbecue out here, I tell you.'

'Burned? Jesus. I can't believe it.'

'You're repeating yourself. It would save me a lot of time if you told me where she lived and whether she has any relatives hereabouts.'

Rabbitt finally managed to say Mia was renting an apartment on Maiden Lane, on the new side of town.

Chief Miller's principal source of gossip in the town was Molly, and she was as good a conduit for scuttlebutt as there could be. His secretary had started whispering rumors about Lafayette's new teacher not long after Mia Buckingham turned up. A hussy, Molly said. A word she liked, being a widow who'd never expressed an interest in men after her trucker husband Frank died in a crash out on I-90 ten years before and no one in the world could ever match him. Miller had soon learned that Frank was good and drunk at the time and expired with a Syracuse hooker in his cab. Molly knew that too but they never mentioned it. In Prosper being judgmental didn't mean being judgmental about yourself, only others. At that Molly Dunn truly excelled.

No relatives he knew of nearby, Rabbitt said. Only a husband—

maybe ex-husband by now—back in California. He didn't have a name for the guy let alone a phone number, email or address.

'Why would I?'

'Was Buckingham her own name or her husband's?'

'Her own. I remember she said she reverted. She's very much her own woman.'

'*Was*. Was her own woman. And by the way, the school's going to need a new shack down Mohawk Lake.'

A pause, then Rabbitt asked, 'What?'

'It's gone. Burned to the ground, your teacher with it. Locked inside. Someone else too, didn't I say? Any idea who this other party might be?'

'Christ...'

'Wasn't him. Pretty sure you can only kill that guy with nails.'

'Tact's not your thing, is it?'

'I like to travel light in this line of work. Never found tact much use, to be honest. It's Saturday. Not a school day. The woman was in there with someone. I need to know who.'

'She had a key. I said she could use it when she liked. She used to paint there. Make things. She was an employee. I delegated responsibility for the cabin to her.'

'You ever go there with her?'

'I'm a married man.'

'I'm aware of that. You ever go there with her?'

'No.'

'Any idea who did?'

'How would I?'

'Nothing so annoying as people who answer a question by coming back with another.'

'I need to tell the school.'

'Come six o'clock this evening, Bunny, there won't be a soul in town who don't know what's gone down out there.'

'Is there any other way I can help?'

'She had a pendant round her neck. Little silver heart. Cheap junk. Inscribed with a love message. Any idea who might have given her that?'

'How in God's name would I?'

Miller wasn't a detective. He was a street cop. Used to dealing with people face-to-face. He didn't have the skills for this kind of encounter and knew it.

'We can talk more about this later,' he replied, which was all he could think of.

The line went dead. Ten minutes to Maiden Lane. He'd keep Gary Rabbitt to himself. The state guys or the Feds or whoever was going to steal this case from him—they could find him all on their own.

Traffic was light that Saturday afternoon. People thought it was too hot to be traveling. Mostly they stayed home, lighting their Weber grills, making their hamburgers, doing all the small-town things small-town people did on a hot summer weekend when they couldn't face anything else.

There was a vehicle outside 109 Maiden Lane when Chief Miller got there. A battered VW, the kind of car preferred by the men of Prosper who had more ambition than money. Foreign, because it was chic, shabby because they couldn't afford any better.

The door to her apartment was ajar. Inside was the reporter, Tom Honeyman, going through her things.

'What the hell are you doing here?' Chief Miller demanded, watching Honeyman's face flush as he struggled for an answer.

3

VENICE

Honeyman read the chapter as soon as it turned up on the laptop. Then he went and got another drink, some cheese and bread, came back and read it again. It felt strange. This was like reading something he'd written himself and forgotten about entirely. Whoever was behind this knew his style: the linear journalistic prose, plain language, the use of colloquialisms. The dialogue that was invented but sounded real. It could have come straight out of *The Fire*. Except it hadn't. These were matters he'd never written about. Never known about in detail. Some were simply new. Some questioned the narrative he'd created himself about what happened at Mohawk Lake. Where the hell had the guy found this stuff? And how? He couldn't begin to imagine.

Fred Miller was not among his own sources. Or anyone's. The chief disliked the media with a vengeance and Honeyman in particular. With good cause, the way things worked out. His reporting was the spark that sent Miller careering off the rails. But the chief was already gone from Prosper around the time Honeyman quit work to write the book. The publisher had sent Miller a copy of the proof, in part to see if the guy was going to sue. Not that he had any reason. The draft had been lawyered to death already, and Miller's role in the whole story was minor at best. Then one dark night, just days before *The Fire* appeared and hit the bestseller list at number one, Miller died in what looked like a violent argument outside a sleazy bar in Burnsville. Sorry end to a sorry story that seemed to have little do with Mohawk Lake.

It was the early hours of Wednesday by the time Honeyman finished the chapter a second time, two in the morning. His eyes could barely stay open but his head told him he'd never sleep. He went upstairs anyway, counting the blinking lights of the security cams that followed him through the hall, along the corridor, into the spare room where he found Lauren's backpack. He took that into the one functioning bedroom and climbed beneath the mosquito net.

Eight cameras he'd counted in all, scattered throughout the house. The place was covered but not perfectly; that was impossible. Besides, he knew from the ones he had back home that at night, the pictures were grainy, the motion detection too uncertain to catch everything. Knowledge worth thinking about. But first he wanted to see Lauren's things.

That was a miserable experience. Old cheap shirts and jeans and underwear, not many of them either. Perhaps working the cruise ships meant you didn't need a lot. Several of the t-shirts had the shipping line branding and place names: Grand Cayman, Key West, Bermuda. And one a picture of a cruise liner and a logo, *Apollo Venezia*. So Lauren must have been close to Maledetto sometime and never thought to try and see if he was around.

He held the shirts for a while, clutched a couple to his face. Kids always had a smell of their own. Maybe it was one that, in another person, you'd hate. But they were yours so it was personal, close, private and never really left you. They were just a young woman's casual clothes, but they belonged to Lauren. She was a part of him and always would be.

At the bottom of the rucksack was a clear plastic wallet. His heart nearly burst when, under the dim yellow light, he saw the single picture it contained. There they were, all three of them, a family back in Prosper when money was short and opportunities seemed even scarcer: mother, father, daughter. This must have been the spring before the fire and, to his dismay, the shot was taken at Mohawk Lake. The parking area and picnic spot maybe half a mile from the school study shack. There was a portable grill on the brick barbecue stand. Diane held a full glass of chardonnay while he stuck to soda because, as usual, he was driving. Lauren sat next to her on the bench, head down. He was holding a barbecue fork and trying to smile for the camera, the only one who was. A stranger had offered to take the picture when he saw them there. Why, Honeyman didn't know.

Did they look miserable? Did they look *marked?* Maybe. No one knew what the future held. Not Mia Buckingham, who might have been in the shack at that moment, or Scott Sorrell, living out his miserable existence with his strange, single mother on their failing farm a mile north of town.

Death didn't announce itself any more than poverty or riches or divorce. But looking at the three of them, he thought he could see the fault lines beginning to appear. In Diane's taut, unsmiling face, once so pretty, so active and alert when she was still a reporter on the *News-Ledger*, better at scooping up facts than he'd ever be but never so quick and glib and convincing with the words to tell them.

And in Lauren's hunched and miserable teenaged frame, all tension and tight, barely restrained anger. He'd told himself back then most kids were furious at the world, and the strange ones had to be those who weren't. Maybe that was true. Maybe for Lauren it was just a stage like it was for so many others, a time when all her hormones were jumping around, not knowing which way to go. Even if that were true, what followed—his sudden thrust into the spotlight, the money, the constant travel trying to sell more and more books, the place in Venice, the cracks within the family and, finally, Diane's suicide—these things would surely tip anyone over the edge. As he gripped his daughter's thin, worn t-shirts he wondered if he could feel his own fingerprints on the push that took her there.

There were no choices, no obvious ones anyway. This was who they were. What they were. To question any of it, to peer behind the shadows, the darkness and the wretchedness, and ask for answers, was to try to open a Pandora's box they all knew existed but feared to acknowledge.

There were more memories where he was too. After Diane died and Lauren vanished he'd thought of moving to Maledetto for good, burying himself in the work and the life of a hermit. He'd even sent ahead some things: personal stuff from Prosper he didn't want near him when he moved to Manhattan. They were still there, unpacked, pieces of his old life trapped in amber. It was a crazy idea, one that was never going to work.

He went to the last room at the end, where the boxes were stacked against the wall. There was a red light blinking in there. This guy didn't miss a trick.

Honeyman found what he wanted: the photo album Diane had kept so carefully, right up to the point Lauren left home for college. He sat cross-legged on the floor with a flashlight and went through the pages one by one. There couldn't have been more than thirty or so. Was that enough to encompass the lives of three people across a couple of decades?

The first two pages covered the time in the hospital—Diane, exhausted, elated, a tiny Lauren in her arms. She looked so beautiful and happy back then, amazed, shocked, unable to believe this had happened to them. As was he when a nurse took a shot of the three of them.

A good quarter of the album covered the first six or seven years of Lauren's life. A happy toddler, waddling around the cramped one-bedroom apartment they'd rented when they first got married. Then an older, lively kid pedaling a tiny plastic bike around the garden of the house they rented. It must have looked like they'd come up in the world, to her anyway.

Then the space between the pictures began to grow, along with the distance between the three of them. The photos were less spontaneous. Records of events—birthdays and the occasional vacation they could afford. Not the life they led day to day.

A few were from Lafayette High. Lauren, older, skinnier, not smiling so much anymore, looking as if she'd rather be anyplace else but there, facing up to a lens. The last in that section was an official school portrait taken just a week or so before the fire. She didn't seem unhappy in her plain white summer shirt. She looked as if she didn't feel anything at all.

There was hardly anything after that. Just photos of the woods, the lakes, the countryside around Prosper. Diane liked to go for long walks and filled the solitude taking pictures of nature: animals if she could get them, landscapes if not. He stared at the bowers, the paths, the trails she'd taken, and realized he didn't recognize a single one. Their lives had separated by then—not that, in his endless travels and desperate efforts to write another hit book, he'd taken the time to notice.

He went through the photos again page by page, staring at a few long and hard, wondering what had happened to them over the years, why he'd never noticed until everything was too late.

Now Lauren was back. He'd often wondered what that might be like. If they could heal the wounds, find some kind of normality between them. But first he somehow had to rescue her from the creature beyond the thorns and palms and rocks and ancient, crumbling graves. That, he thought as sleep stole upon him, was the one redemptive act the Honeyman family, what was left of it, deserved.

DEADLINE: 3 days. 11 hours. 12 minutes.

WHEN HONEYMAN WOKE, harsh summer sunlight was streaming through the mosquito net that stood over the bed, with it the faintly miasmic smell of the lagoon marshes and the distant screech of hungry gulls. From the itches on his neck and arms and ankles, the netting hadn't done its job.

Downstairs he gulped some milk and ate a pastry out of the packet then read again the chapter the man in the chapel had left him—a name, he so needed a name—and waited.

One hour.

Nothing.

Perhaps the guy had left.

Perhaps he had a boat of his own on the far side of the island and could come and go as he pleased, leaving Lauren bound and gagged in the ruins of the chapel. But there was that arsenal of weapons. No point in trying to free her until Honeyman knew where he stood.

Then there was the gardener, shot, just forty feet or so from Honeyman's front door. That blurred, swift episode still puzzled him. Why kill the guy? To make a point. There could be no other reason. To emphasize: *This is real, I am dangerous, I will kill you too if you give me reason.*

Gianni must have had a boat. He'd have left it somewhere by the jetty, surely, not that Honeyman recalled seeing it. In any case it was doubtless a wreck in the lagoon mud now, much like his own.

Not long after midday he went to the front door, aware that the cameras were following his every step.

It was unlocked. He pushed it open a crack and peered outside, squinting in the sunlight. What greeted him was the bright yellow of dead, dry vegetation by the path to the jetty, then the burned-out debris of the previous night's fire that removed his only way out.

The boathouse was gone for good, a blackened timber wreck, not quite as finished as the shack by Mohawk Lake but not far off. His own blue-and-white dinghy was a sorry mess a good three hundred yards offshore, upside down, half-sunk, blackened too, a huge hole gaping in its planking. The man must have come down during the night and kicked what was left of it off into the lagoon. Making sure there was no easy way of escaping the island even if he could find some way of freeing Lauren from her captor's grasp. There was no sign of the gardener's boat at all. No sign of a body. Maybe he dumped the corpse in the water too.

Despite the danger, Honeyman's curiosity got the better of him. He took a couple of steps out onto the patio.

There was no one around, so he walked out and started toward the jetty, checking either side. In the searing early afternoon sun the island looked bigger, the shrubs and palms and weeds more wild. As he approached the water the lines of gravestones running toward the ruined chapel emerged like broken teeth trapped in a rocky jaw. A cormorant—black, sleek, alert—sat on one of the few remaining timber supports for the boathouse, hunched, gazing at the torpid water, looking ready to fish. Overhead, a jet whined on its approach into Marco Polo. Civilization, life, help were all a few short miles away, but there was no way he could reach them. Not by phone, not by swimming, not by trying to flag down a passing vessel, since this backwater of the lagoon rarely attracted visitors.

Maledetto was his world, his prison. Just him, an unknown assailant, Lauren a captive somewhere.

He kept walking, kept looking, heart pounding, feeling he was being watched all the way, not that he knew how or where from.

Then he froze.

He saw what he thought was the shadow of a severed human head swinging on a rope from the gnarled old olive tree ahead along the path. Two steps more and he saw the thing more clearly as it pivoted into the sun. A green-striped watermelon dangling on a piece of string, eyes and a grin carved into the skin, a yard or two from the point where the gardener got shot.

The heat was stifling, the air thin and damp. He wondered for a moment if he might lose his balance.

Then, the crack of a rifle, the same sound as before. And another.

The melon exploded into pieces, scattering scarlet fruit and juice, green skin and seeds everywhere.

He froze.

One more round took out the last remaining chunk, the top, like a cap, attached to the branch by a piece of string. Only a marksman could do that. No ordinary shooter.

There was a point to be made here. Being malleable he might admit to. But that wasn't the same as being scared.

He deliberately walked two steps forward, past the tree, on toward the flattened grass. Now he could see the brown earth that was maybe the color of blood, the gardener's, he wasn't sure. Then the shots came again, firing up dust clouds ahead on the path down to the jetty.

'Got the message,' Honeyman murmured, then retreated a couple of steps, picked up the nearest piece of fruit, popped a chunk into his mouth and meandered slowly but certainly back into the house.

HE SLAMMED the front door behind him, leaned against it, wondering what to do next. Maybe try to put a sign in the window, to attract the attention of a passing boat. Not that many came out this far. And it would be hard, perhaps impossible, to position it so that the man in the church couldn't see. Or maybe—

When I say stay in the house I mean stay in the house.

The sudden crackle of the walkie-talkie startled him. The guy seemed to be everywhere, watching him constantly. Honeyman walked into the study and picked up the handset.

'I thought there was a dead man in my garden.'

Housekeeping came overnight and took out the trash. You've got guts, Tommy. I'll give you that.

Honeyman thought before answering. It was time to try to even up this relationship.

'The watermelon. Waste of good fruit. Do you have a name?'

Who doesn't?

'So what do I call you?'

Sir is good enough for now.

'I need to talk to my daughter. Sir.'

That's a pity.

'I have to.'

You got this relationship all wrong, my friend. I ask the questions. You answer them.

'I'm not answering fairy tales. I read what you wrote. You're making Chief Miller say things.'

Whoa. Did I hear that right? You mean like you did? I read every word you wrote, twice over. That piece of crap's full of people spouting stuff when you weren't even there. Didn't have a clue what was said. Just made it up. Maybe I was following your lead. Maybe I know more than you think. Doesn't really matter, Tommy. How'd you enjoy it? Did I get close? Style-wise, that is.

'Yeah. Well done.'

Putting words in people's mouths. Terrible thing to do. Still...

At the time he wrote *The Fire*, Honeyman had wondered about that gray area as well. This was true crime, not fiction. But his editor cited people like Truman Capote and insisted this was how books like the one he'd been paid to write had to work. They weren't meant to represent the literal truth, word for word, action by action. More a reflection of the truth that was as accurate as he could make it. And maybe, in its own way, a better representation of what really happened than the literal, bare and boring facts. Besides, people had conflicting recollections of the same event, even a few days after. He knew from his most-recent visit there were people in Prosper who'd recount a wholly different version of the killings at Mohawk Lake. And a bunch of newcomers for whom it was little more than a dark fairy tale told by old folk.

Reality was never set in stone. In any case, most of the invention went into the mouths of people who were dead and couldn't scream they'd been misquoted. No one sued from the grave. If it was going to sell, the book needed to read like real life portrayed in the guise of a novel.

'You got things wrong. Sir. Like the pendant. I talked to the cops. The real cops. Not that old bastard Miller. They never found a pendant.'

That old bastard Miller, as you call him, hated the state cops. The Feds too. He was running his own show. Perhaps he didn't want to do them any favors by showing them what he'd got.

Honeyman didn't want to say it, but he could imagine Fred Miller doing just that out of spite and his own, largely undeserved self-confidence. Prosper was his town. He'd hate having outsiders poring over it to try to crack the biggest crime he'd ever seen.

Hell, Tom... if we're talking gaps in the story, you didn't even tell your readers you were the first person at the teacher's apartment the day she died. Why was that?

Not a question he expected. Or wanted.

'Didn't seem any point. I never found anything. Miller's statement...'

What about the names in there? Principal Rabbitt. The husband. Robert was his name.

'You're trying to say I should be interested in them?'

You tell me. This is your story, Tommy. Not mine.

'I ruled out the husband. Ex-husband. Schoon. He's a pilot in California with one of the regional airlines. He was on duty that weekend. I've seen a copy of his logbook. Couldn't have been him.'

You talked to him?

'On the phone. He was in San Francisco. Seemed like a decent guy.'

Seemed...

'The logbook checked out with the FAA and with the airline. He wasn't in Prosper that week.'

What did he say about his dead wife?

It hadn't been an easy conversation. The guy didn't want to be interviewed but Honeyman called back three times, said he was going to keep on calling until he talked. It was easy to come on strong over the phone.

'He said he still loved her.'

Well, she certainly liked her loving.

'That's unkind. I don't think it was quite so simple.'

Hell, you're the one who painted her in that book as some kind of hippie small-town nympho. So what about Principal Rabbitt?

'What about him? Jorge Rodriguez was dead. They shot him when he came out waving the gun. Went through his trailer. Found everything there I said they'd find.'

Because our anonymous informant told you?

'The cops said it was him. Case closed.'

'Yeah. When they'd blown the guy to pieces. A month after you tore that town apart. Put all its dirt and secrets out there for the world to see. Can't believe you strolled back there a couple of weeks ago and thought people might hail you as some kind of returning local hero.'

Honeyman didn't rise to the bait. He wasn't expecting a ticker tape parade in Prosper. In any event, the people who remembered him mostly showed him the door. Besides, the town seemed mostly occupied by newcomers who thought Mohawk Lake was one more piece of local color.

Why did you go back, Tom?

'I wanted to see... to see if I could find something new.'

The dog returns to its puke. Thinking of digging Mohawk Lake out of the grave and making another fortune?

'This chapter you wrote. It does sound pretty much like me.'

Lots of people read your first book, Tommy. No great secret what you sound like. Is that so hard to understand?

'Knowing what I sound like's one thing. Being able to reproduce it—'

I'm not here for writing lessons.

'OK. If you want me to consider Rabbitt, give me some reasons.'

Reasons? You put them out there yourself. The day you put his name in the paper saying the Feds had found his jizz all over her sheets. If he wasn't a suspect—

'It was news. People read it, didn't they?'

Yeah. And probably wondered who you were gonna name next. It was a horny middle-aged guy getting boss sex with a pretty underling, thinking he'd never get found out.

'He was a public figure. She was dead. There was a murder investigation—'

Come on, Tom. The guy's wife gave him an alibi. He was out shopping or something that morning.

'It was still news.'

It was lurid gossip. You served it up again in your book. Know what happened to Rabbitt?

'He got fired, left town three months after Mia Buckingham died. On his own. His wife sued for divorce. But I didn't make him sleep with Mia.'

One more life you crapped on. So many people out there with a grudge against you. And you've got the nerve to go back to Prosper and see if anyone wants to help you.

Maybe that wasn't so smart. And, now that he thought about it, that must have been where this creep crawled into his laptop, found out about the planned trip to Venice, came here ahead of him, talked to Giorgio Morosini, checked out the island. And lured Lauren here somehow.

'What do you want from me? How do I get you to let Lauren go?'

Already told you. It's a piece of cake. You face up to what you did. You look at all the facts, the old ones, the ones you lied about, the new ones I'm going to give you. Then you write down who really killed Mia Buckingham and the Sorrell kid. And you do it before midnight Saturday. You need to understand, Tommy. We're owed. All of us you touched with that filthy myth of yours. It wasn't the fire that ripped Prosper to pieces. It was you. Prying and lying. Making stuff up. Then feeding off the scraps and getting richer than anyone in that miserable burg could dream of.

Honeyman struggled for a response. What he said was true, to an extent. He'd lived with the fallout of the book for years, the way it made the town hate them as a family. Not that he'd been around to take the heat. Maybe that was what killed Diane. She came from Prosper, born and bred, though her parents were gone, so all she had was him and Lauren. Neither of them stayed around much after the book came out. Lauren went to college. He got on the promotion circus for a while, trying to sell the books he wrote after *The Fire*, writing on Maledetto, never finding the same success again. When Diane killed herself he was racked with guilt. He'd left her to live alongside the lie he'd exposed, the picket-fence pretense that Prosper was one more quiet, semi-rural paradise where nothing bad ever went down. Until the fire at Mohawk Lake blew that fable right out the water.

'I'm not rich anymore. I want my daughter—'

Jorge Rodriguez. They never found a trace of him in Mia Buckingham's place.

'And? Maybe they made out at the shack. That place was burned so badly the cops couldn't pick up a thing. Or maybe he had other reasons. Maybe he thought she was screwing his boy.'

You really wanted to nail that Mexican, didn't you?

'I just followed the trail. I never knew the man. I'd no reason to... nail him. Maybe...'

He couldn't get the idea of the pendant out of his head. If Miller had hidden a key piece of evidence like that, what else might he have kept away from the state cops?

Maybe what?

'I said in the book. Some things you never find out. It's a mystery. You can speculate—'

And boy, did you do that. Not a single fact, was there? Just guesses.

True, Honeyman thought. Rodriguez's motive was a huge, gaping hole in the story and he knew it.

'I did my best—'

Here's a thought. Maybe they didn't even know each another—

'But Rodriguez was seen arguing with Mia near the school. There was talk—'

Who saw them, Tom? You never said.

'Someone... someone I couldn't name.'

Who told you?

'I can't—'

Christ almighty! Who the fuck do you think you are? Some big-deal investigative reporter? Reality check. You were a two-bit hack on a two-bit paper. Now you're a failed novelist at the end of the line. Time to put things straight. You never did say much about where you got all this... proof from.

Just that bullshit you kept using. 'A trusted source.' Like you had your own Deep Throat in Prosper. Right.

Honeyman kept quiet.

Don't fret, Tommy. The time to get that weight off your shoulders is coming.

'Where did *you* get this... material?'

My own trusted source.

'The interview with Jackson Wynn—?'

Mister Ace Reporter sure is slow today.

A moment later something popped up on the computer. An mp3 file named *MillerWynn1*.

Honeyman clicked on it and heard two voices from the past.

'You CALLED THE FIRE DEPARTMENT, *Jackson? Why not me?'*

'Park rules. Didn't know anyone was in there, did I?'

'Where were you when you saw it was on fire?'

'Didn't say I saw it on fire. Was smoke I saw.'

THE QUALITY WAS POOR, but the sound of Fred Miller's voice—gruff, cold, suspicious—and Jackson Wynn—dumb, whiny, resentful—took him right back to Prosper and the time he was working on the story.

Enough. Honeyman turned it off.

Sounds like they're alive, Tom, doesn't it? Sounds like they could be here right now.

'Sure.'

Lots more where that came from. I got a treasure trove here. Things you couldn't dream of. Real things. Not fantasies from your imagination.

Chief Miller lasted until the fall before getting fired, trying to fling blame and anger in every direction, much of it at the newspaper and Tom Honeyman. None of that stuck. Jorge Rodriguez was guilty. The proof was there in his trailer.

By the time Miller got shot in an argument outside a lowlife Burnsville bar the following year, pretty much everyone in Prosper had forgotten about him. There was a lot people wanted to put behind them. Those who did remember likely said to themselves: Everyone's got to die one day, and surely that was the way Fred Miller was fated to go. Full of booze, with a bullet or two in his guts.

'So what happened is the chief stole files from his own office. Took them with him when he got fired. He had a grudge. He could have wound up in jail for that and—'

Miller had every right. The files were his. Private. No one wanted to know what he thought, not anymore, thanks to you. He had this feeling in his gut Rodriguez wasn't the murderer. There was a bunch of people he thought might have done it. And yeah, maybe I know who they are. Know lots more besides. Miller was on the way out of police work, but it was three months before they forced him out. In all that time he stuck to his guns. Made everyone—the state officers, the Feds, the medical people—made damned sure they gave him every piece of paper he could lay his hands on. Snapped it all with his phone. Copied files. All kinds of records. How do you feel about that, Mister *Honeyman?*

'Let me talk to Lauren. *Sir.*'

You got to earn it.

'How?'

Write me the missing chapter. The one that tells me why you were inside Mia Buckingham's apartment when Fred Miller got there. You never said in your book you even went there. Funny thing. Don't leave anything out. Because I will know, and your girl will suffer. Third person. You can talk about yourself for real that way. Oh. And one more thing.

'What?'

I want to feel you hurt. Give me something fresh. Something bad you never revealed before because letting it out's going to ache. The Night of the Redeemer is coming. There's no redemption unless you offer something. Besides, confession's good for the soul. You need to rip the lies right out and let them bleach and die on that dead ground out there. Do that... and who knows?

'Who knows what?'

The handset went dead.

Honeyman bent over the laptop, trying to fix his mind to work the way it did when he was writing and things came together. That was never easy, never a process he understood any more now than in the beginning. Try too hard, plan and organize until you convinced yourself you were on top of everything, and soon enough, hubris or whatever people wanted to call it would descend. The ideas would dry up, and with them, the words.

Writing really only worked when he lost himself inside the world he was trying to create, could see and hear the people there. To do that, he had to be a part of it. No excuses. No distractions. That was what Maledetto was for, and it was time it served its purpose.

So many memories were stored on the laptop. Documents and interviews, recordings and photographs. A few things he'd never set down in print before as well.

But mostly the story of Prosper and Mohawk Lake was in his head, clear as a bell, kept that way by the hazy stain of guilt that had been dogging him over the years. The way the mind worked, it was the things he'd never written about, never admitted to over the years, which were the clearest memories of all. And the hardest to tell.

The question was: Would the truth save them? Or damn them? He just didn't know.

The blank page on the screen seemed to taunt him, seemed to ask if he dared to fill it.

There was only one way to start.

4

A THIEF IN MAIDEN LANE

Prosper, New York
Saturday, July 12, 2008

I t wasn't Honeyman's turn to be on duty at the *Prosper News-Ledger* that Saturday, which meant he could spend the morning the way he liked when he was alone in the house: hunched over his ancient Compaq laptop in the spare bedroom, at the tiny desk overlooking their tiny yard, trying to work on the book he so wanted to write. It was a novel. Or meant to be. A thriller about a mysterious sniper who takes down five people at a parking lot then vanishes.

He had the opening incident and a vague idea of the perpetrator. As yet no idea why the crime had happened or the sequence of events from opening to close. Years later, when he was struggling to resurrect the brief career he'd enjoyed with his one genuine success, he'd find the files again and try out the idea once more.

But it wasn't working back in 2008, and he couldn't breathe life into it any time later. He knew the problem: he was trying to create people, and the world that enclosed them, out of events—the violent, soulless pieces of action he'd dreamed up. The only true way to work was to come at the story the other way around. Characters and place came first and always would. The narrative needed to emerge from them. But random acts of violence, shocks and artificial twists—they were so much easier to devise than convincing flesh and blood, and the places. Smells and panoramic vistas of real life.

There was nothing in the idea, however much time and energy he wasted on it. One more dead end when it came to making up stories from scratch instead of taking something real and reassembling it, adapting the lives and deeds of others into words on the page. If he was honest with himself, he already knew it that Saturday morning as he tried revising the scene he'd rewritten a million times already. But part of fiction was sleight of hand, deception, trickery. If you couldn't fool yourself into believing a lie, how could you convince others?

Racked with self-doubt made worse by his hunger to finish the damned book, he'd never told his wife, Diane, what he was up to. Though maybe she'd guessed it wasn't one of his usual schemes: writing a business plan for a crazy e-commerce site, or coming up with some get-rich-quick scheme that would set them free from their drab near-poverty.

She'd only have sneered if he'd told her the escape route was now a book. A reporter turned novelist. What a cliché.

How many of the hacks who'd passed through the *News-Ledger* over the years had toyed with that dream? Plenty, and not one had finished a first draft let alone sold it. But Honeyman told himself he was different. He'd find a way. He had to. Life in their confined, oppressive little town, working a dead-end job on a dead-end paper, was becoming unbearable. He felt like an animal in a trap, every movement constrained, every effort failing, stuck in their mean little house, a place they could barely afford, struggling to pay the bills from month to month, something that seemed harder and harder with the economy going sour all around them.

Diane's bitter skepticism about his 'hallucinations,' as she called them, wasn't just about the work, and they both knew it. Most of the time they'd been married she'd stayed at home, raising Lauren, keeping the place kind of straight, mutely resentful of the career she'd abandoned because, well, that's what a woman did, what she was meant to sacrifice on the altar of the great god Family, a hungry deity who'd devour your existence whole if you let it. As they had.

Still, she resented the fact he had a job, being a reporter, the only work she'd ever known or wanted. On occasion it would show. She'd rip one of his stories in the paper to pieces or walk straight up to his laptop while he was working and throw a few acid words in his direction. So Honeyman now wrote in secret, the door closed, keeping a password on the laptop, calling up the file only when he was alone, dreaming of the day he could turn around, show her a letter from a publisher, an offer, one that would take them out of the stifling clutches of Prosper. Though a part of him wondered how Diane would react to that too. With relief? With support? Or just the familiar, envious grudge she seemed to bear about pretty much everything?

LIKE MOST SATURDAYS, Honeyman's daughter, Lauren, had said she was going to see one of her friends, anything but tackle schoolwork. He'd tried so hard to help there, but the more he did, the more she rejected it. She was a bright kid, quick too. She could write, clear, precise prose. They'd talked about her going to study journalism at college one day, though that was mostly his idea, not hers, and he didn't have a clue where the money might come from. It wasn't a frequent conversation. Mostly she wanted to laze around and listen to music. She was sixteen. Nothing he could say or do was going to change a thing.

Diane had taken the car, he didn't know where. Shopping, he hoped. Which at least would mean she wasn't with her group of similarly minded friends—tired mothers, sick of their husbands, eager to gossip and drink cheap chardonnay, anything to stave off their persistent domestic misery. He wouldn't be surprised if he'd be eating alone again. Which was fine. He didn't ask where Diane went or what she did, any more than he did of Lauren. No point in inviting trouble.

Best stay out of their way for as long as he could, Honeyman told himself. Best try and write the book that would take him— take *them* — away from Prosper.

He'd deleted five paragraphs of pointless crap when the phone rang.

'It's Jeff.'

McAllister. The boss. He called on weekends only if there was work.

'What can I do for you, Jeff?'

'Got a tip from a guy I know in the fire department. Looks like there's something bad out at Mohawk Lake—'

Honeyman groaned. He hated fires. They were smelly and dirty, went on for hours and left people crying in the street. Which was good copy but tedious to be around.

'You want me to go?'

'No. I'll deal with it.' Jeff McAllister covering a story himself. On the weekend. That was new. 'I want you to do something else.'

'What?'

McAllister hesitated, which wasn't like him.

'This might be big. If people have died we need photos. Material. We can sell it to the TV stations and other places. I'll cut you in fifty-fifty. We could both use the money, couldn't we?'

The death knock, or so one of the hacks he'd worked with in Chicago, an English guy, had called it. Standard media practice when there was an unexpected fatality, especially a violent one or a bad accident. Get in quick while the relatives were still in shock, grab what photos you could, then race out of there before they wised up and wanted to punch your lights out or, worse, asked for their pictures back.

Honeyman had done a few over the years. The days when you could snatch some exclusive photos by sweeping the room and taking them with you were coming to an end. Lots of people kept backups on their PCs or Flickr. If you got in quick now you'd be first with the news, that was all. Which mattered, even on a crappy paper like the *News-Ledger*. McAllister had taken to running any significant stories on the web before the print edition came out. Brought in advertising, he said, and god knows the *News-Ledger* craved that. But if you found some original photographic material and had the only copy... it could be worth something.

Honeyman didn't enjoy death knocks. All the same they were a part of the job. And he liked to think of himself as a professional.

'Who?'

Again the hesitation. Then McAllister cleared his throat and said, 'You know that new teacher at Lafayette? The one from California?'

Honeyman said nothing.

'Come on, Tom. You must know. Pretty thing with the neon hair. Everyone's seen the way she sashays around the place.'

'I think I know who you mean. Lauren's in her class. Diane deals with school stuff mostly.'

'From what I hear, she's dead.'

'Christ. Are you sure?'

'Seems so. And one other, no ID yet. Know where she lives?'

'Not sure... Maybe Diane went there once to talk about Lauren's schoolwork or something.'

'Your wife went to talk to a teacher at home?'

'Why, wouldn't you?'

'I dunno. Don't have kids. 109 Maiden Lane, apartment three. Talk to the janitor. I called the guy and said she's been hurt in an accident. In the hospital. Needs some things. We own most of that block. Her place included. He'll let you in. Poke around. Grab anything you think might sell. Then get out of there.'

'Isn't that stealing?'

McAllister never liked it if you argued.

'She's dead. She lived on her own. Who the hell's going to know?'

Honeyman stared at the screen in front of him. There were even fewer words there than he'd started with that morning.

'I don't know. It's Saturday. I got things to do—'

'I'm aware of the day. Are you aware you're a reporter? That I pay your salary? If it's nine-to-five, Monday-to-Friday work you want, maybe you should look for another job. Get out there. Take anything

that looks useful. Make us some money for once, will you? I got business enough here.'

He hung up before Honeyman could say another word.

THIRTY MINUTES later he was inside Mia Buckingham's place, with
just a few minutes on his own, when the door opened and Chief
Miller walked in and bellowed, 'What the hell are you doing here?'

The janitor had vanished not long after he let Honeyman through
the door. In all, he might have had six or seven minutes to rummage
through the messy apartment, no more.

'Jeff McAllister asked me to stop by. It's his property. He owns it.'

Miller was sniffing, and Honeyman knew what it was.

'You been smoking weed, Mister Reporter?'

'Is that what weed smells like?'

'As if you don't know.'

'I don't.'

'Someone around here has.'

'Not me.'

Miller moved a cushion on the floor to one side with a toe then
stabbed his foot against an acoustic guitar. The strings thrummed for
a moment in the close, hot air.

'It's a woman's home. You creeps think you can sneak in whenever
you like. Why are you here anyway?'

'I told you. The place belongs to Jeff McAllister. He heard there'd
been an accident or something.'

'An accident.' Miller sniffed again and wandered around the living
room. 'Your boss inherited everything his momma left him, didn't he?
This place included. Couldn't make a cent on his own.'

He picked up a book from the coffee table and wrinkled his nose.
Honeyman had seen it already. Madonna's collection of supposedly
erotic photos, from the Nineties. They seemed distinctly anachro-
nistic a decade and a half on, but so did a lot of the things in Mia
Buckingham's life: the nude paintings, the risqué pieces of artwork—

some she'd doubtless made herself—littered around the living room. Some posters that looked like they came from Cuba, with Che and Castro on them.

Miller retrieved a butt from a brimming ashtray and sniffed it.

'Doubt she's the only one in town who's got that, Chief.'

'How the hell a woman like this gets to be a teacher... You want a story?'

'Paper always wants a story.'

'How about this one? Stuck-up young college guy inherits a crappy little paper and a bunch of property from his momma. Can't make money from his lousy rag. Lives off the rest. Then, when the mugs who rent the places can't pay their way... what does he do?'

Honeyman blinked. The question had thrown him.

'I dunno.'

'Think. Person who can't pay the rent's a pretty young woman who don't mind sleeping around. Again: What does he do? What would *you* do?'

Miller had cold and piercing eyes, icy blue, and they never left Honeyman at that moment.

'Not a question I'm ever likely to face.'

'Yeah. Well, you remind your boss what I said the last time he tried pulling some lady's pants down in lieu of the money he thought he was owed. Don't happen while I'm here. Found anything?'

'I only just got here. Is she okay? The teacher?'

'She's dead. Someone with her too. Fire in the high school's cabin out by the lake.' The blue eyes never wavered. 'Someone set it. Someone killed them.'

'Oh my god. It was deliberate?'

Miller kept looking at him, then said, 'You sound like you knew already.'

'All I was told... there was an accident. Look, I need to report the story. That's my job.'

'Some job. How well did you know this Buckingham woman, Mister Honeyman?'

'I didn't know her, not really. My daughter's at Lafayette. In her art class. I think maybe we met at school once.'

'She met lots of people, that woman. I got a busy few weeks ahead of me, I guess. Tracking them all down.' He walked over and pushed open the door to the bedroom. There was a king-size bed, the sheets rumpled. 'Guess all those smart asses in from Albany are going to be spraying their sprays so we can see who's been jerking their stuff here.'

Honeyman came and stood behind him.

Fred Miller wrinkled his nose in disgust.

'Even if this little slut was busy doing that in the school cabin out by Mohawk, they got nothing useful to find there. Just ash and cinders. Shame. Means the only kind of guy who knows how to get to the truth is an old dinosaur like me asking questions. Not some kid with a case full of toys. So I'll ask you again. What did you find, Mister Reporter?'

'Nothing, Chief. Jeff said maybe I'd find a relative here we could talk to.'

'A relative?'

'Yeah.'

'She was on her own here. Everyone knew that.'

'I just... Can you tell me some more about what happened? Out by the lake?'

Miller laughed.

'Maybe come Monday I'll be talking to the press. If I feel like it. Right now, you can get the hell out of here. I want to snoop around, and I want to do that on my own. So... git.'

Honeyman didn't move. Miller took a step closer and leaned so close the smell of old, stale gum was obvious.

'Am I being unclear in some way?'

'No. I just... nothing.' Honeyman took one more look around. 'Nothing. I found nothing. Didn't have the time.'

Miller nodded.

'Then you can go. And don't come back. If I find you snooping around people's places again when no one's there, I'll be looking at you for burglary. Won't get away with waving your reporter's card then.'

'Got you,' Honeyman said and left.

HONEYMAN SAT in his battered old VW, shaking a little. Then he checked that Miller wasn't watching him from the windows and pulled out the two things he'd found in Mia Buckingham's bedroom. One was a photo of her at school in front of her class. She was wearing a tie-dye t-shirt she probably made herself, and the life in her—the colored hair, the bright, vivacious smile she had—all seemed to light up everything, even a few of the kids around her.

The second picture he'd found in the bedroom, tucked beneath a pillow. It looked like it came out of an instant camera, one way of making sure there were no copies.

She was in bed, topless, shoulders a little hunched, slight breasts showing, eyes closed, head back on a pillow, a satisfied smile on her face. Next to her, naked too, grinning straight into the camera, was a Lafayette kid Honeyman recognized. Scott Sorrell. All of sixteen. Maybe not even that. One of Lauren's classmates.

He looked like the cat who'd gotten the cream and couldn't believe it.

Honeyman had given him a lift home from school a couple of times when he picked up Lauren, so he knew where he lived. Alone with an eccentric mother the other kids called 'Crazy Maeve'. It was a farm on the northern edge of town, a rundown place that seemed on the edge of collapse.

He called Diane's cell and a woozy voice asked, 'Not that I'm deeply interested, but where are you? Thought you might be here locked in front of your laptop when I got home.'

'Went out on a job. Jeff insisted.'

'On a Saturday? He treats you like shit.'

'He's my boss. He thinks it's his prerogative. It's a big story. Fire. People have died.'

'What people?'

'Can't say now. You and Lauren just get on with things. I don't know when I'll be back. Could be the biggest story we ever had out here.'

When she laughed at that he could hear the booze.

'Jesus, Tom. Who are you kidding? You sound like you think you're a real reporter. It's the *News-Ledger*, remember? If it's that big a story the TV stations will be here right away, and little you won't matter a damned bit.'

'Yeah. I'm sure you're right. Are you OK?'

'Why wouldn't I be?'

'Is Lauren home?'

'We've both been home for hours. Why?'

'Nothing. I'll call when I can.'

MAEVE SORRELL ANSWERED the phone immediately and, when he told her who he was, said, in that acerbic country voice of hers, 'My son there with that girl of yours?'

'I haven't seen Scott in a while. He doesn't come over anymore. I was wondering—'

'Guess she must have blew him out. Where the hell is the lazy little skunk? I got chores need doing. Useless kid don't earn his keep. Thinks this place is a motel or something.'

Lauren's friends came and went like the wind. Someone she adored one week she hated to pieces the next. He'd given up trying to keep tabs on who was in and who was out. Scott Sorrell, a quiet, good-looking kid who was maybe a date once upon a time—he wasn't sure, and Lauren certainly never said—he hadn't seen around in weeks. Not that Lauren had put him on what she called very vocally over their few shared meals her 'shit list', a revolving register of enemies and former friends from Lafayette she seemed to update on a daily basis.

'I'm doing a feature piece about the high school, and some of the kids there getting good grades. I heard Scott's doing really well. I was wondering if you could give me some personal stories. Email me a photo of him. We could use it in this week's paper.'

The Sorrells were farming stock, had lived in the area for three or four generations, or so people said. Steadily getting poorer and poorer over the years. Scott's father slipped the leash years ago and fled north to vanish in Canada. Maeve Sorrell stayed and worked the small patch of dirt they had left. Scott always seemed clean, well-spoken and polite. The very opposite of his mother. Maeve was well-known for having some strange and primitive beliefs. He'd always felt sorry for the kid on the rare occasion Scott came over. He looked like he never wanted to leave.

'Who said he's doing well? No one told me.'

'I believe—'

'He was supposed to be back here and help me in the barn. You know what they get up to, don't you? Filthy little bastards. Screwing around anyplace they can get it. I can smell it on him when he comes home with that stupid grin on his face.'

'When does he do that? After school?'

'Whenever he feels like it. God knows where he goes when he's not here. Hellfire and damnation coming his way 'fore long.'

Honeyman had to bite his tongue. Maybe Scott Sorrell was only one of Mia Buckingham's conquests. But maybe—it began to dawn on him—Scott was the second victim in the Mohawk Lake fire. What-ever... some more photos of him and a quote from his mother had to be worth something, if only he could get it quick and keep it to himself.

'If you like, I can drive over and look at your pictures. Easier to talk face to face...'

'Do that. If the idle little bastard's back by then, you can talk to him yourself.'

Probably not, Tom Honeyman thought as he started the car.

THE SORRELL PLACE was twenty-five minutes across town, more in Saturday traffic. He was passing Prosper's modest mall, a farm-style bunch of wooden buildings much like larger versions of the shack in Mohawk Lake, when McAllister phoned, sounding breathless, scared. Honeyman pulled over by the side of the road to take the call.

'Find anything, Tom?'

'Not really. I was barely through the door when Miller turned up and kicked me out. Old bastard threatened to arrest me for burglary.'

He wasn't going to let McAllister in on anything. The guy could have got him in trouble with the cops. Even if he did own the apartment, it didn't mean a stranger had the right to prowl around it going through her things. That was why McAllister was down at the fire while Honeyman risked his neck in Maiden Lane.

'Miller was just trying to scare you.'

'He succeeded there. What have you got?'

'State cops are here, throwing up barriers all around the scene. They won't say a damned thing.'

'You're sure it's her, Jeff? The teacher? Mia Buckingham?'

'They assume so. If she's not at home... where the hell is she? All her folks are back on the West Coast. They're still trying to work out who the other victim is.'

How much to say? How much to warn him?

'You knew her?'

'She rented one of our apartments. I told you.'

McAllister sounded snippy.

'Yeah. But you *knew* her.'

'What the hell are you suggesting?'

Say it, Honeyman told himself. It was going to feel good to push back at the guy who'd been giving him shit week in and week out these past few years.

'I think you might get a visit from Miller. The chief said... he said he'd had complaints about you pestering women in the apartments. When they couldn't afford the rent. You asking for... payment in kind. He's out for trouble. He doesn't like you. Doesn't like the paper.'

McAllister went quiet for a moment then swore down the line.

'Just passing on what he was saying, Jeff. If Miller yapped all that at me, he's going to be yapping it to other people—'

'One time he had a girl come into his office bitching about me. We fooled around for a while, and then she stopped and still couldn't come up with the rent. It was nothing.'

'Sounds like a good story.'

'Very funny. She never said no. Mom saw to it all. Paid her off to go back to Albany. No big deal.'

Taunting McAllister like this felt good.

'Mom's not around anymore. Chief Miller's on your case. Best you have a good story about where you were this morning. You do. Don't you?'

'Well, well, Tom. You found yourself a spine at last. Who'd have thought it?'

'Miller will—'

'I can take care of Chief Miller. That old fool's finished here anyway. If he tries pulling a stunt with me...'

'I was trying to warn you.'

'Thanks. Come up with something we can use in the paper, will you? That's what I'm paying you for. I'm going home. Try to wash the stink of smoke off of me.'

Honeyman leaned back in the old VW and smiled. He had a damned good idea who the second body in the cabin was going to turn out to be. Sometimes reporting wasn't just about the established facts. It was about drawing lines between seemingly unconnected events and people and places. Seeing if they linked in some way, then reaching the right conclusions.

All of which he'd sit on. The TV reporters would be on their way to Prosper soon. Maybe even the *New York Post.* Not that they'd pay good money for a salacious shot of a pretty teacher in bed with her pupil, after what looked like some good and sweaty fun. Both of them dead, murdered in a cruel and callous fashion in a place that belonged to the school she'd betrayed. There were seamier places he could get money for the photo, though, and as far as he could work out he had the one original.

Maybe, it occurred to him then, there was even a book in Mohawk Lake, once things had played out.

To hell with novels. He knew he could write real life. He knew how to embroider it too.

A vivid depiction of Prosper's crime of the century, one that exposed the town for the pit of hypocrisy it was.

Now there was an idea.

Honeyman drove along Main Street, glancing at the sullen shoppers on the sidewalk, a few arguing with their stony-faced kids, some of them familiar. A couple of women Diane used to hang around with were gossiping outside the kitchen store. A few doors further was Jim Langholm, the guy who owned the logging plant by the river, a place that hovered permanently on bankruptcy and now, with the latest financial crisis hanging over everyone, would probably tip right over, taking a hundred or so jobs with it.

Someone out there knew what had gone on in that cabin. A good few doubtless had an idea what Mia Buckingham had been up to in her spare time and maybe were even part of the fun. And somewhere there was a man—it had to be a man, surely—who'd burned two human beings alive that morning. Honeyman wondered what such a creature would be like. What they'd be doing at that moment.

Watching sports on TV?

Cracking open a beer?

Sitting with his kids or wife or mistress?

Or maybe, just maybe, dashing all over town pretending you were a genuine reporter—something Jeff McAllister had never really been in his life, except when he wanted to try to impress some woman. Jeff was where he was through birth and money. The son of the proprietor, and now that she was gone he was burning through her money faster than he could replace it. Honeyman couldn't believe McAllister would really turn out to be in Miller's sights. All the same he didn't mind if the bastard got to squirm a little under the shadow of the chief's suspicion.

What with the call and the traffic, it took forty minutes to get to the Sorrell farm, and even then he couldn't get close. A pack of cars, some marked, some plain, had turned up and monopolized the dirt track down to the grubby cabin where Maeve and Scott Sorrell lived. A couple of state guys, all uniform, sour faces and understated aggression, watched him pull up behind their convoy and were headed for him before he even managed to open the door.

'Press,' Honeyman said, pulling out his ID.

'Beat it,' the nearest cop said. 'Nothing for you here.'

'I've got a job to do. Just like you, sir. Also, the Sorrell boy went to school with my daughter. We're local. They were friends. If I can offer any assistance. Or sympathy—'

'Sympathy,' the other cop snarled. 'That's why you're here?'

'The town's going to hurt badly if what I hear is right. If there's someone I can talk to—'

'There isn't.'

They were maybe twenty yards from Maeve Sorrell's shabby front door. It was open, and Honeyman could hear cries and screams coming through it.

'Go back to town,' the second cop told him. 'When we're ready we'll let you know.'

Before he could leave the other guy grabbed his arm, squinted at him and said, 'You know their names?'

'I think so. Mia Buckingham. Teacher at Lafayette High. And the boy who lives here. Scott. He was a pupil. Same class as my daughter.'

'Who told you that?'

Honeyman shook his head and frowned.

'They were all talking about it in the store. Small town. News travels fast. Not much else to do except gossip and pass it on.'

An awkward moment. But they let it go.

Honeyman didn't return to the office, but drove home. Diane was in the garden, shades on, glass of spritzer by her chair, half asleep. Lauren was upstairs in her room. He could tell from the racket coming out of the window. That same damned song she kept playing again and again that summer, thrashing away to it, he could hear that too. All she wanted to do most days was dance. It made her feel free, she said. Made her think that one day she'd get the hell out of Prosper. Get the hell away from them as well.

'How'd the story go?' Diane asked without even turning to look at him.

'Early days,' he replied. 'Looks big. Shame... shame you're not still on the paper. May be a tough one. Door to door. In people's faces. More your kind of thing than mine.'

She took off her shades and stared at him.

'I'm just a homemaker, Tom. I haven't the faintest clue what you're talking about.'

'It's just... don't you want to know?'

'I'll read it all in the *News-Ledger* on Wednesday, won't I?'

She prodded her shades back on then leaned back in her chair, yawned, reached for her glass. Upstairs the music got louder. Lauren's dancing was so energetic he could hear the house's flimsy floorboards creaking under the strain. The same kind of noise the floor made on those rare occasions he and Diane still made love.

You won't read anything but the bare facts in the News-Ledger, Honeyman thought. Those he'd leak out gradually, daily in little teasers online, then a touch more fully in the paper during the week. *But one day... then you'll know. Soon you'll be grateful too.* He'd make sure of that.

5

VENICE

Wednesday
Deadline: 3 days. 1 hour. 17 minutes.

Storytelling wasn't usually about honesty. It was about drive and narrative, building a make-believe universe that would captivate an audience. The real world was somewhere they wanted to escape, whether it was inside the pages of a novel, a movie, TV or video game, or even a long-form piece of journalism that took them to a place they'd never hope to visit in their lives.

Revisiting the strange and winding story that had changed his life entirely turned out to be one of the toughest challenges Tom Honeyman had ever had to face. Too many hidden thoughts, too many buried memories he had been certain would never surface again. But by the time he'd completed the chapter, he felt he was settling into the task. There was something cathartic in pushing to one side the creative act he struggled with constantly and replacing it with simple, frank reportage: the contents, welcome or otherwise, of his memory. And there was something cathartic about admitting to the dishonest acts he'd hidden when he wrote *The Fire*. The sly theft of Mia's private, intimate picture of her in bed with Scott. The fact he'd kept details from Jeff McAllister that he should have passed on to the paper, which was still, then, his employer. The way he'd been quietly thinking, even on that first grim day, that the tragedy at Mohawk Lake might be the break he needed to escape Prosper.

The photo he'd sold to one of the supermarket gossip rags for $12,000. McAllister suspected he was the source and asked him straight out. Honeyman had denied it, naturally. And in any case, the *News-Ledger* was a family paper. Not the sort of place to run that kind of smut.

Lying came easy, which was just as well. There was a lot more ahead.

Thinking back to the material his mystery tormentor had sent him, it occurred to Honeyman he wasn't the only liar around. Fred Miller had kept that fire-scorched pendant to himself. The state cops had never mentioned it. If they had, they'd surely have made it public, released a photo, asked if anyone recognized it.

That was strange. Honeyman was all too aware that he'd taken risks with the book when it came out—cutting corners, inventing dialogue, drawing connections that maybe weren't real. He'd had to indemnify the publisher against getting sued just in case someone living crawled out of the woodwork with a lawyer at his heels. But it never happened. People wanted Mohawk Lake buried after all the white-hot heat of publicity had scorched the town of Prosper.

Except for Fred Miller, who'd died in a way Honeyman didn't fully understand, shot dead a year later. He'd never given up the chase, or so it seemed.

It was almost ten by the time he was done.

The prying ghost in his laptop presumably had read every word.

One way to find out. He typed as the last line in the chapter: *If you're there, kindly make your presence known. My schoolwork requires marking.*

Then watched, hands off the keyboard, as the cursor took on a life of its own and backspaced over the line, deleting every word.

The walkie-talkie crackled to life.

Do not soil this manuscript with your inane chatter, Tommy boy. Your lives depend upon what's here.

Fine, Honeyman thought. At least he'd prompted the guy into responding.

'You're the boss. Any questions?'

You outed Gary Rabbitt and ruined his whole life. Why did you wait 'til the book was out before you did the same for Jeff McAllister?

'Some things I didn't find out until later.'

Shit, Tom. Don't lie to me. You gotta assume I know everything. Dangerous otherwise. When you outed Rabbitt you'd seen the FBI's documents. You said that in the paper. If you knew then...

The laptop beeped and a photo of a confidential FBI forensic report came through. The exact same document Honeyman had found waiting for him in an envelope in the *News-Ledger* office one morning two weeks after the fire. It was the forensic sweep of Mia Buckingham's place on Maiden Lane. Semen from Rabbitt. Semen from McAllister. Scott Sorrell too. A few female hairs that didn't appear to be Mia's, not that the Feds seemed much interested in that. Could just be a cleaner or a friend who'd come by.

'To be honest, I didn't think Jeff McAllister was important. The cops had ruled him out. He had an alibi. He was out of town until ten that morning. He'd been at some girlfriend's in the country.'

Oh, come on, man! Rabbitt's wife gave him an alibi too, but you nailed him as sure as he nailed that teacher. Who sent you that FBI report, Tom? Got any ideas?

Honeyman had wondered at the time. The file just turned up with his name on the envelope. No clue who'd left it. And nothing else got leaked that way.

'I honestly don't know. It was sent anonymously. So where did *you* get it?'

None of your business. Jeff McAllister. He was part of the story. He was screwing the teacher too, for god's sake. Did you tell him?

Fine, Honeyman thought. *Did it really need saying?*

'He owned the paper. You think he was going to use his own rag to ruin himself?'

Did you even try? Did you ask him?

That was something else he'd left out in the book.

'I showed him the report. I tried to persuade him it was going to come out one way or another.'

And?

Dammit. This had to be said.

'He offered me a thousand bucks if I kept quiet.'

Whoa! And you took it. Blackmail too...

'It was his offer. I never asked. The bastard was paying me peanuts. So, no. It wasn't blackmail.'

Just a payoff then. Big difference, huh? This needs to go in the book. Everything does. Every last shameful detail. Go back to that chapter and write it. You want people to buy it or not? And I'll be watching. If you lie again I will know, and there will be consequences.

Maybe six or seven paragraphs would do. Piece of cake. Setting down the whole story had been that way, if Honeyman was honest.

'Whatever you say, sir. If you want me to expose someone else, I've got to know what you have.'

All in good time.

HONEYMAN WENT BACK in the kitchen and poured himself some San Pellegrino.

Then he sat down and typed up the story about Jeff McAllister and how he'd wept and wept when Honeyman showed him a copy of the FBI file. The Feds had hauled him over the coals already. Tore his apartment to pieces looking for evidence that could link him to Mohawk Lake. A few hours later, just for fun, Chief Miller and a couple of his deputies came back and did the same. Found nothing because there was nothing there except a stash of hard porn and some weed, which got McAllister a quiet warning and nothing more.

He was as close as Prosper had to aristocracy. The family had been around forever, owning businesses, property and the paper. A few rentals and the *News-Ledger* were all that was left. Two years after the fire, Honeyman long gone, the paper ceased printing and got sold to an e-commerce company that used it as little more than a vehicle for local ads.

Last he heard, McAllister had moved to Miami, where he was stretching out the last of the family dollars, an impoverished playboy heading into middle age. The guy had nothing—no talent, no journalistic experience, no management skills. People were as glad to see him go as they were delighted Tom Honeyman was no longer in town.

All of this he put in as an addendum to the chapter he'd written earlier. It was even easier this time. The words flowed. By eleven he was through. It was a beautiful night, moon almost full, sky clear and alive with glittering stars. There was the chirrup of insects in the trees and the occasional bird call.

When he was done he sat on the sofa in the study, staring out of the window, wondering what he could do to get his daughter back. To escape Maledetto and the ghoul out there beyond the graveyard.

He could see his latest effort was getting read on the computer. The page was scrolling up and down. *How do you do that*, he wondered? *What kind of skill do you need to steal your way into someone's laptop and take over their life?*

Not a lot if you knew what you were doing. Or so he guessed. Maybe that would be a part of the new book too. The unveiling of the catalyst, the masked figure who'd coerced Lauren into coming here, shot a man he can't have known in cold blood, then threatened them both to get the story— the real one, or so the guy hoped— down on the page.

The walkie-talkie crackled again. When he got to the laptop he could see his mystery tormentor had reached the end of the section.

Well, Tom. Pleased with yourself?

'I just put myself out there as a fraud and a cheat. That's what you wanted, isn't it?'

Confession is good for the soul, isn't it?

In a way it was. A burden lifted, and over the years he'd forgotten how heavy it was.

'I don't know who you are, but we have one thing in common. Whatever I got wrong, I'd like to set things straight. If you can help me there, we're on the same side.'

We're never gonna be on the same side, my man. But hey... I'm kind of impressed. I thought maybe you'd be stubborn. You're getting the idea. Time for your reward.

Honeyman couldn't work out what game the guy was playing now.

'Meaning what? You don't get to shoot me like that poor bastard outside?'

'Oh yeah. Him. I told you. He's dealt with.'

The walkie-talkie clicked the way he recognized now. It meant he'd hung up.

The only sounds were the insects, the birds, the occasional low murmur of a distant plane.

Then, so loud the noise made him jump half out of his skin, there was a rap on the front door.

A weapon. The best knife he had was out in the wilds somewhere, lost in the tangled roots of a palm tree. The best he could find in the kitchen had a short, serrated edge, a blade for vegetables, not that he'd ever cooked much here.

He went to the door and said, 'Who is it?'

A pause and then—her voice shaking, tearful, broken—Lauren, an older Lauren but still the same, said, 'Who do you think, Dad? For god's sake let me in.'

The blade tumbled from his fingers and clattered on the stone tiles. His fingers scrabbled to open the door.

He held his arms out wide, wondering how often they'd held one another in Prosper. They weren't that sort of family. There was always something that stood in the way, some silent resentment, some excuse.

Dirty, sweaty, shaking her greasy hair, weeping—maybe out of anger, maybe out of fear or embarrassment or something he couldn't name. The fat lip had gone down and didn't look too bad.

'God, I've missed you,' he whispered, clutching her head to his chest. 'I'm so sorry.'

She just kept crying. He did too. It was a start.

He didn't know how long they stayed like that. In the end, she retreated gently from his arms, wiped the tears from her pale, drawn face. She barely looked any different from the last time they'd seen one another, not long after the funeral, when all she'd done was scream and yell obscenities at him, then vanished.

'Don't believe a word he tells you, Dad. That guy's crazy. He's going to kill us. Doesn't matter what you tell him. He's going to do it. Soon as he gets what he wants.'

'Which is what?'

'He said everything you put in that book's a pack of lies.' She held him tightly again, and he could feel her shaking against him. 'Is it? Did you make it all up?'

'Not... everything.'

'He's got all these cans of gas. Kept talking about setting fire to things. And I heard shots. He said he took out some guy. Is that right?'

'The gardener. I think so.'

'He killed him?'

'Seems like it.'

'Oh shit.'

'He told me I need to come up with some new story... the *real* story about Mohawk Lake by Saturday night. Or...'

'Or what?'

'What did he tell you, Lauren?'

She hugged herself the way she did when she was little.

'He said there's some kind of fireworks thing happening across the water. And maybe there's more things that'll get burned than people know.'

'That's all?'

'I've been tied up most of the time, on my own. Will you level with me? I'm not a kid. What's going on here?'

'He says that I got it wrong about Jorge Rodriguez. That he didn't kill Mia and Scott. Unless I write the true story that uncovers who did kill them—'

'Then he burns us too?'

She swore and leaned up against him. His hand went to her hair again.

'So...' Lauren leaned back and looked straight at him. 'You've got to keep making up stories. Doesn't matter whether they're true or not. You've got to keep him going until we find a way out of here. It's like that fairy tale. You know... the one where the woman's got to tell the guy a new story he likes every night or else he kills her?'

'When you were with him, Lauren, did he say who he was? What's making him do all this?'

There was a quick flash of anger in her teary eyes. Then she blinked, squeezed it away.

'No. I told you. He's crazy. Did you know?'

'Know what?'

'Know you got it wrong when you said it was Rodriguez in your book.'

'Of course not.'

He wasn't sure she believed that.

'Does this place have water? I need a shower.'

'It's going to be cold.'

'I'll live with it.'

She wound herself out of his arms.

'I never thought I'd see you again, Lauren. I failed you both. You and Mom.'

She shrugged.

'Long time ago, wasn't it? What happened back then. I don't imagine I was... an easy kid.'

He bent forward and kissed her damp and grubby forehead.

'You're the only daughter I've got. The only one I'll ever have or need. And you're here.'

She smiled. 'I guess we've got him to thank for that.'

'We'll get out of here, Lauren. I promise.'

'Like we got out of Prosper?'

The moment she said it she winced. There was the old Lauren, always a bitter aside at hand.

'Sorry,' she whispered. 'I didn't mean it to sound like that. I...' She put a hand to her face and scowled. 'My head's not working right. Let me clean up.' She kissed him quickly on the cheek. 'You look good, by the way.'

Then she was gone up the stairs.

6

VENICE

Deadline: 2 days. 21 hours. 7 minutes.

J ust after two in the morning Lauren came down, towel around her long, wet hair, rubbing at it hard. She glanced at Honeyman as he sat at the computer, said something he didn't hear.

'Listening to us as well?' she yelled at she passed the winking red light of the camera above the door.

'You noticed?'

'He told me he'd wired the house.' She nodded and threw the damp towel on the tiles. 'Did it before he picked me up. Jesus... I'm really hungry, Dad.'

He followed her into the kitchen, went to the refrigerator and threw it open and watched as she grabbed a glass of wine and some slices of *prosciutto crudo*.

She'd found her backpack, put on fresh clothes much like the old ones—worn, sloppy, the kind she wore back when she was a teenager. They didn't look quite right now. Lauren had barely changed over the years. Maybe she'd lost what little baby fat she'd had and the occasional glint of bright enthusiasm in her eyes. From what he knew, she'd been doing what she'd wanted—dancing in the shows on cruise liners. There was something of the athlete—thin, taut, always tense—about her.

They sat at the table, opposite one another, their eyes hardly meeting, no easy conversation to be had. An awkward embarrassment hung around the room.

'This was never going to be easy, was it?' she said eventually.

He took her hands.

'I wondered if I'd ever see you again. What I had to do to make it happen.'

'Well,' she said with a roll of her eyes, 'you know... get me kidnapped.'

She laughed. He did too and then he said, 'You always were a tough kid. Brushed things off. You look okay.'

'I am, Dad. Not going to let that creep win. Are we?'

'No.'

She toyed with some food then asked, 'You ever find someone else?'

'You mean dating?'

'Yes, Dad. Dating. Company. A partner. Someone... someone to love.'

He didn't quite have the words to explain. So he said the best he could think of.

'I don't mind my own company. Never did. I didn't look, really. There was always work.'

'Always some new mountain to climb.'

'How about you? There must be lots of guys on the cruise ships. Maybe you could find yourself some rich banker or something.'

He got a caustic glance for that and knew he deserved it.

'I don't need a rich guy, thank you. Gotten involved with people a few times. Nothing lasted. Maybe... maybe we're pretty much the same, really.'

He glanced at the window.

'Do you have *any* idea who he is?'

'Dad,' she mouthed, nodding at the hall. There was a gap in the cameras there, a blind spot where the wall of the study blocked the winking light on the other side. Lauren walked through and leaned against the worn bricks in the shadows, still picking at the ham, sipping her wine. He followed and joined her, the two of them talking in whispers.

'Good question. I don't know. Thirty maybe. Sounds like he could come from anywhere. American, I mean. Big. Wouldn't want to argue with him. Knows how to use those weapons, though I guess you appreciate that already.'

'The guy he shot. The gardener. Did you see?'

She shook her head quickly, scared.

'No. He tied me up in the tent. I heard, though. I thought he was shooting you. I thought that was it.'

'What... what did he do with him?'

She shrugged. 'I guess he threw the poor guy in the water or something.' She gulped at the wine. 'I really thought it was you. He's crazy. I mean, you say one wrong thing he can just explode. There's all these cans of gas. Big cans. Got a generator out there and this rubber dinghy on the beach. But there's a hell of a lot of them.' She got closer, said in a hushed tone so quiet he could scarcely hear, 'I think he's planning a fire or something. Keeps talking about it. Setting things alight. Kind of an obsession.'

'You have no idea who he is?'

'Didn't I just say? White guy, stubble. Nice face actually, smiles sometimes. Not a... welcoming smile. More kind of... *Hey, you're mine. Isn't this cool? Wonder what happens next? You won't like it.*'

He watched her eating and knew he had to ask.

'Did he hurt you?'

'Say what you really want to say.'

'I meant did he hurt you?'

'Not really.' She shrugged. 'He kind of hit me when I wouldn't do what he wanted. I've had worse. You believe he'll let us go? If you give him what he wants? A name?'

Honeyman didn't know what to believe anymore.

'I don't know. He let you come here, didn't he?'

'Well, yeah. Not much of a gift, is it? The two of us stuck in this place. Two of us together make an easier target, don't we? He seems to think I know things you don't.'

'Is he right?'

Lauren put the glass and the plate on the window ledge and folded her skinny arms.

'You tell me. Mia Buckingham and Scott Sorrell died. You wrote a book. Got rich. What family life we had turned weirder, and you just kind of... vanished.'

'I was trying to make things better. For all of us.'

'Didn't work, did it?' she said sharply. 'For Mom. For me. For you. And then...'

They both knew she didn't need to say it. They'd never really talked about Diane's suicide at all. Right outside the funeral parlor Lauren had broken down in a yelling fit and screamed she never wanted to see him again. That was that.

'He told me he's got information about what went on,' Honeyman said. 'Maybe real, maybe invented, I don't know.'

'I was just a kid then. It all seems a bit like a dream. What kind of information?'

'Evidence. Something new. Something he found. I don't know.'

'How'd he get it?'

'Maybe he made it up. He said Fred Miller found a pendant that belonged to Mia Buckingham. Something a lover gave her. That was never in the evidence the cops went through. If it's true, then Miller kept it to himself. Even after he got fired. But I don't understand why—'

'You're asking me?' she cut in. 'I told you, Dad. I was a kid back then. All I know is what I saw.'

'A piece of jewelry. They should have made it public—'

She was laughing.

'What's so funny?'

'I'm a Honeyman. You're asking me about jewelry. Don't you

remember how much Mom hated all that stuff? Said it was a waste of money. You brought her something back once, didn't you? Fancy gold bangle… I don't know.'

He'd forgotten about that. It was the first time he came to Venice for the film festival, the day after he put in an offer on Maledetto without even telling Diane. She refused to join him, so on the way back he bought her a two-thousand-euro necklace from a jeweler on the Rialto. Back home, she screwed up her face in horror when she opened it. It was a stupid present. He should have known she didn't like jewelry or perfume or pretty much anything he came back with from his travels except booze. The necklace got sold, he imagined. He never asked.

Lauren must have noticed he got distracted, depressed by some memory.

'Dad. If I can help, just tell me how. But if we stay hidden like this, he's going to get pissed. We've got to play his game. For a while anyway.'

She went back into the kitchen and looked around the place, squinting the way she'd done since she was little.

'You got anything sweet here?' Her voice was louder. This was for the benefit of the camera. 'I could use some sugar.'

There were some pastries. He unwrapped a couple and they both sat in silence at the table, picking at them. She'd talk again when she was ready. Out under the watchful red light of the camera, a stranger listening to every word.

AFTER THEY'D FINISHED the pastries she pulled a phone from her pocket and said, 'Damn. There's no signal or anything here, is there?'

'If there was, you wouldn't have your phone, would you?'

'Got enough power in this house to run a charger?'

He found the one he'd brought and kept plugged into the outlet for the solar panels.

'This is the email he sent me. What I thought was from you.'

She held it out for him to read.

Lauren. It's Dad. We need to talk. It's urgent. I know things have been bad between the two of us, but it's time I made things right. Because time's something I don't have. Please come and see me. I'll cover all the costs. Tell your boss it's personal days, to see someone who's really sick. It won't be a lie. I saw your cruise ship was in England, so I've booked you a flight to Venice. I'm in the house in the lagoon. Reply to this message when you confirm the flight, and I'll arrange for a boat out to the island for when you arrive. Also I'm sending a couple of thousand dollars to your Google Pay. Use it however you want. I need you here. It's important. Please.

Lauren frowned and said, 'I didn't know what to think. I thought we'd lost touch. Me on the ship. You in New York. Or here. I didn't understand how you could know where I was.'

'I didn't. I had no idea.'

'*He* sure as hell did.'

The sender's address was an email account in the name of mister-honeybee543.

'Mister Honey Bee. That's what I used to call you when I was little, remember?'

'Sure I remember. But how could he know that? Who else knew?'

She thought about it and said, 'Mom, I guess. Maybe kids at school. They used to call me Miss Honey Bee for a while.'

'I didn't have an email address for you. I didn't even know you could send money that way.'

'Search me.' She glanced at the camera on the wall. 'Ask him.'

'Maybe in the morning. It's late. We've got work to do tomorrow.'

Lauren raised her glass.

'Right. Here's to the mystery of Mohawk Lake revisited. Getting the right answers this time.'

A little too much for the camera, he thought.

'I've been wondering if we'd ever meet again, Lauren. For years. Never once thought...'

She was on the old stone steps already.

'Me neither, Dad. Let's get some rest.'

He followed her upstairs, along the dark and dusty corridor, hot and stuffy, stale with age and damp. The camera for the main bedroom was set high on the entry wall. A bad position. When the door was open it blocked the sightline.

The summer moon shone through the window, its light rippling through the leaves of the fig tree against the wall.

Honeyman pointed at the device. 'I taped the hole where I think the mike is.' All the same he spoke in a whisper. 'As long as we're here I don't think he can see us. Or hear us. At least I hope so. This isn't really my kind of thing.'

'Or mine.'

Just for a second she held him, then delivered another daughterly peck on the cheek.

'Lauren, I need to know what you've told him.'

'About what?'

'About Prosper.'

She frowned.

'Nothing. He didn't even ask. He says he wants to hear it from you. All the stuff you never put in the book.'

'I'm not sure there's anything else to tell.'

'Well...' She glanced at the window. 'He seems damn sure there is.'

She was right. They had to stall. Or even better, get out of there unseen.

'What happened exactly when you got to the airport?'

'He was waiting when I came out of the gate. Had a sign with my name on it. We went to where all the fancy water taxis leave. I thought I was getting in one of them. But...' She leaned against him again. 'God, I can be so stupid. He had this crappy little inflatable like you used to see out on the lake. Hardly big enough for the two of us. I should have known.'

'That's how you got here?'

'Yeah. It's on the beach near that tent of his. When we arrived the guy let me go into the house and dump my bag. Then he said he wanted to show me something, and we walked to the church. That's when I realized this wasn't going to be the happy family reunion I thought. We stopped and he said he needed to take a picture of me. When I asked why, he slugged me in the mouth. Took a photo then dragged me inside the tent. Tied me up. Next thing I know there's some shooting and I think it's you and—'

'Where is the dinghy now?'

'Around the back, along from where he pitched the tent. There's a line of shingle.'

He nodded at the long bedroom windows. 'OK. We go out through the balcony. Me first. You let yourself down. I'll help.'

'Wait—'

'No. We don't wait. If we can just get to that boat—even if I have to paddle the damn thing—he's stuck here. We can make our way to Burano or somewhere. Find the police. It's a clear night. Plenty of light. We can see—'

'Which means he can too. He's got guns. He's smart.'

'He wants us here. That's as good a reason as any to get the hell out.'

Honeyman pushed the door right back so the camera would be blocked all the way to the window.

'Mister Honey Bee,' she murmured. 'How the hell did he know that? He's got to be from Prosper. When I think about it, he sounds that way.'

'Who cares? Come on—'

She didn't move when he took her arm.

'He said he'd kill you if he catches you trying to run. Said the same to me.'

'Yeah. That's why we don't get caught.'

The window was so old he nearly had to break the glass to get out. But eventually he managed to free the clasp, throw it open, and then they were out on the narrow concrete balcony, breathing in the cool night air, swatting away insects, looking out at the rough terrain of Maledetto and the distant ruins along the shore to the east.

Honeyman clambered over the iron railings, letting himself down on the old, wrinkled vine until his feet found hard ground. Then he held out his hands for Lauren, coaxing her every inch of the way, catching her in his arms as she reached him.

There was a sudden, loud flapping of wings from a nearby tree and the screech of an owl as it flew up into the starry sky.

This close, still amazed she was there, he knew something needed to be said.

'Sorry I was such a shitty father. I didn't mean to be. I fooled myself I was trying to make things better.'

'We were a shitty family, Dad. It's not your fault. We all own that.'

She glanced back at the house. They'd left the dim lights on downstairs and in the bedroom, which maybe wasn't smart. The red blinks of the cameras seemed to wink at them from everywhere.

'Do you know the way?'

'To the beach? Yeah. I took you there once. Remember?'

She nodded. 'Was that the time I found some bones?'

Honeyman squinted through the thicket of palms and shrubs.

'Exactly. We follow the graves.'

THE MOONLIGHT, the stars and the absence of cloud cover meant it was easy to walk through the rough and spiny vegetation toward the shore, ignoring the thistles and the buzzing night insects as best they could. The outline of a rickety wooden bridge stood out against the silvery night horizon, a strip of open water shimmering either side. It was the only way to reach the chapel and the graveyard, which sat on their own tiny islet, surrounded by a deep and fetid ditch.

All of this would be easy for the man in the chapel to see. If he was following the security cameras in the house he'd surely notice there was no obvious movement there. Maybe he'd interpret that as the two of them sleeping. Maybe he'd try to snatch some rest himself. All the same they had to assume time was short and opportunity limited. Best hurry to the beach, push the dinghy into the lagoon, paddle it offshore and then, when out of range of his rifle, try to start the engine.

The bridge was so shaky they had to creep across, Honeyman first. It creaked with every step. On the other side they entered a dune of soft sand, dotted with hummocks of marsh grass that stood against the night sky like bristly creatures frozen to the spot. Then the beach gave way to rock again and they dropped down a ledge, feet scrunching on hard shingle.

'Can you see it?' Lauren pointed toward a low shape just visible in a thicket of reeds where the pebbles ran into land. 'There. Right where he left it.'

This seemed too easy. Still, they got to the dinghy undisturbed. It was the kind of cheap craft some of the locals used when out dredging for clams in the dense lagoon mud. A small inflatable made of heavy-grade plastic, with a single bench seat and, at the stern, an outboard that smelled of gas. In the center was a pair of wooden oars still in their metal rowlocks.

The two of them untied the rope then dragged the boat down to the water's edge and pushed it into the lazy ebb and flow.

'Sit at the back,' Honeyman said. 'I'll row us out. Then kick in the motor in when it's safe.'

Lauren did as she was told and took hold of the rudder. Honeyman clambered onto the center seat and grabbed the oars. The night was tranquil, not a breath of wind, the lagoon as flat and still as a mirror. A long pale streak of moonlight dappled the water that ran to the seaward littoral, like the beam of a celestial lighthouse.

The oars felt new. Everything did. Maybe bought for the occasion. This man had planned.

Honeyman hadn't rowed in years, not since he used to take Diane and an infant Lauren out onto Mohawk Lake in one of the boats you could rent from the campground. Still, when his fingers fell around the oars, it wasn't hard to remember how.

Ten feet out they began to pick up speed.

To the south he could just make out the familiar night silhouette of the distant city, campaniles and towers making a ragged outline against the sky. Come Saturday, the deadline their captor had set, it would be alive with fireworks from the vast incendiary show that kicked off the Feast of the Redeemer. Now, just a couple of boats were moving across the lagoon. The closest must have been a good two miles away, but he had nothing to signal with, no hope of getting their attention.

He couldn't see the shore directly. Lauren, at the stern, was in the way.

'We're doing fine,' he whispered, thinking about when it would be safe to climb over and try to start the outboard.

It didn't sound like a shot, not at first, just the same muffled explosion he'd heard when the guy took out the gardener and then, the following morning, when Honeyman was looking for a body—the watermelon that was hanging like a decapitated head on the olive tree outside the front door.

All the same, a shot was what it was.

Straight into the empty bow, then passing through into the water where, as he turned, jumping out of his skin, Honeyman saw a plume of jet-black lagoon rise up in protest.

Lauren screamed, ducked down, hands over her head as if that could make a difference.

Then he could see. A figure stood on the beach, upright, a rifle in his arms, aimed right in their direction.

A second shot.

Again in the bow, and Honeyman could hear the escape of air alongside the crash of water as the shell spat through.

A chill cold rose around his feet, up to his ankles.

It was dank lagoon seeping into his jeans, with a swiftness that seemed unreal.

'He's holed the damned boat or something. See if you can stop the leak...'

'I can't fix it, Dad!' Her voice was close to a screech as she cowered behind the dead outboard, icy lagoon beginning to flood all around them as the dinghy started to sink. 'Look.'

The footwell was so dark he couldn't see where the damage was in the bow, only the gushing flood racing in.

Then a third shot tore through the night, and a spout of angry surf rose just a couple of feet to his right. That wasn't for the holed boat. It was a signal.

The guy was waving the weapon from the shore, yelling.

'Hey! Honeyman! You're in the shallows. As usual. Climb out of that thing. Come ashore. Or I shoot you from here like rats in a field.'

The dinghy was beyond help, cold water rising up to the knee, all with that familiar stink of mud and brine and something worse. The man must have navigated the craft into the beach this way. He was probably right. The lagoon couldn't be more than a few feet deep here.

'Lauren. It's me he'll blame. Not you.'

He dropped the oars and stepped out over the edge.

The water came up like a freezing tide, all the way to his waist. Then his feet reached soft mud, sank in and stopped. He looked up and held out a hand for his daughter. She swore, half leapt, half fell into his arms. Honeyman did his best to hold her, carry her as he struggled to stay upright.

'Bring the dinghy with you,' the guy yelled. 'It's mine. You stole it.'

Honeyman dragged his free fingers through the brine until they closed on a floating rope.

Soon the mud pulling at his feet gave way to pebbles and shingles.

The figure on the shore stood a couple of inches taller than him. A heavy guy, face hidden as he stood in the shadow of the moon.

'Let go of the girl. You. Stand over there.'

The voice, he thought, had the tone and accent of Prosper. Honeyman let go of Lauren's hand and she collapsed on the hard pebbles, sobbing.

'It was my idea. Not hers. She didn't want to do it. She...'

'You idiot.' The gun came up. 'You've made me mad now...'

Before Honeyman could say another word the butt swiveled around, flew out, caught him on the side of the head, then came back and hit him again. It was all so fast in the gray-white light he barely saw it.

Lauren was screaming. That was the last he heard.

HONEYMAN DREAMED FITFULLY, in images, not stories. Mostly it was about fire.

A searing orange inferno consuming a wooden cabin by a lake.

The white-hot core of the furnace on Murano where Paolo had taken him one day, only to be puzzled when Honeyman fled the room.

Finally, flames licking around their old home in Prosper, a place that, as far as he knew, had never been ablaze at all.

Someone—Lauren, it sounded like, or maybe dead Diane—whined and sobbed out of sight.

All the while he crept through the burning world, walking free, untouched among the heat and smoke. An observer—a distanced, detached eyewitness—there to describe what he saw, and never participate. Even to help.

Then the flames were gone and he found himself in a dead place, a bleakly surreal landscape of ashes and bones and smoldering, charred timbers, smoke drifting over a gray and watery landscape that might have been the marshes by Mohawk Lake, the lagoon hinterland or just the gloomy product of his own imagination.

When the dream was coming to an end, announcing its departure with a throbbing burst of pain, faces began to emerge, fading in from the shadows.

Jorge Rodriguez, the damaged, drunk firefighter who'd died that day the cops came calling, stumbling out of his decrepit trailer with a BB gun in one hand, whisky in his veins, yelling all manner of madness. Dead now, face smeared with dirt, blood streaking his dark and greasy hair. Sitting amidst the charred ashes of his trailer, looking out with bleak, accusing eyes.

Mia Buckingham. So very pretty, all the fathers said after she turned up at Lafayette High, which improved the attendance at school nights greatly. Honeyman among them a couple of times, though there was something about her—a fevered energy, the thought she was trying just a little too hard—that meant he left those meetings to Diane whenever he could.

She was dead too, naturally, though in this turn of the nightmare she made the perfect corpse, naked, legs splayed, pink-and-blue hair in geometric stripes gushing out behind her like she was ready for bed. Smiling, too, though her teeth were black and dull as everything else that stretched around her pale, slim corpse right out to a lead-dull gray horizon.

He looked and then didn't look. Closed his dream eyes. When he opened them there was no one there but Diane, ten feet high, just a face, eyes wide with fury, mouth curled and hard and cruel the way it could be.

His dead wife was screaming something, not that he could hear. Just that it was aimed at him.

He shut his dream eyes again. The pain became real, mundane, simple hurt.

Awake finally, he found himself on the floor of the study back in the villa, alone, clothes filthy and still damp from the lagoon.

DEADLINE: *2 days. 7 hours. 3 minutes.*

THERE WAS a sound from the desk. Honeyman was so lost in the dream and the hurt, it took him a moment to work out what it was: the yap of the walkie-talkie.

He struggled to his feet. Fierce summer daylight was streaming through the fig tree into the room, so bright it made his aching head feel worse. When he checked the laptop he realized he'd been out for the best part of twelve hours. It was past four in the afternoon, Thursday. Time was running out.

I warned you, Tommy. I said don't run.

'Where is she? What have you done to her?'

He felt his skull then caught his reflection in the window. There was a rising bump and a livid purple bruise from his temple to his ear. What looked like scratches down his cheek, maybe from getting dragged back to the villa. He seemed half-covered in mud. From the pain in his chest when he moved, he wondered if maybe he'd cracked a rib.

I said there'd be a price to pay. Christ. I give you a chance. And what do you do? Spit in my face. You want your kid back... you need to earn it.

'It's not her fault—'

Don't say that! Don't you dare say that!

The way he could switch from quiet and seemingly rational to outright bellowing anger was a warning, surely. It was like dealing with a child. A very dangerous one.

'What do you want from me?'

Fuck's sake, man. How many times do I have to say this? The truth.

Honeyman kept quiet.

Oh, silence, great. Sounds to me like you're finally starting to accept you got this all wrong.

'Seems that way. Might have helped if Fred Miller had told people what he found out there.'

Yeah. Blame someone else. Not the fact you were a shit reporter. Not the fact you downright lied.

'I never... never lied deliberately about anything.'

Right...

'Help me out, will you? If you've got more, send it to me. Stuff I can think about.'

Nothing.

'For god's sake... I don't know who you are. I don't even have a name.'

You got enough, man.

'Tell me—'

OK. I'll give you a break. I want to hear what put you on to Jorge Rodriguez before the cops blew him to pieces. That was when you lit another fire. I want to hear what started it. Don't give me any of that anonymous-informant shit. I won't buy it. You've got photos you shouldn't have had. Things you shouldn't have known. Now's the time, Tom Honeyman. Now you can get it all off your chest.

That was the last thing he wanted to hear.

You've gone quiet, Mister Honey Bee. Maybe it's too late, anyway. You wasted more than half a day on this dumb escape act. You've screwed the only way any of us have to get off this island. We're all in this now. You, me and her. Clock's ticking away until the lights go up across the water. All that fire in the sky. If you don't get me a name, you and your girl burn too. Though maybe...

He stopped and Honeyman could feel the taunting in his words.

'Maybe what?'

Maybe I'm just wasting my time here and I should just light up your kid right now, then sprinkle some gas on you.

'Don't touch her. I'll write it. Whatever you want.'

Good. I want the truth. Every last embarrassing piece. Remember, I got your little girl to talk to. I can fact-check you like no one did when you were putting together that piece of shit you got rich on. Tell it right and maybe she can come right back to Daddy. Lie to me again and you get a pile of blackened bones right on your porch.

The walkie-talkie went dead.

Honeyman walked to the desk, fell into the old office chair, let his fingers hover over the keyboard the way they had for so many years. Only now they were trembling, hunting once again for the words that always seemed so elusive.

Words he needed more than ever. Words that just might get him and Lauren off Maledetto alive.

7

PROSPER, NEW YORK

Prosper, New York
August 8, 2008

T he Honeyman family sat around the kitchen table, eating together for once. Diane's idea. It had been a strange and difficult month in Prosper. A teacher dead, a pupil with her. Scandal racing through the town. A good part of it fed and fired by Tom Honeyman—teasing and squeezing juicy morsels into the papers and on the web, tales that punctured the shallow and fragile lie that life was all sweet and bright and cozy.

The week before, Principal Gary Rabbitt was suspended from Lafayette High after the *News-Ledger* ran a leak from the FBI saying Rabbitt had left his mark on the sheets in Maiden Lane. Honeyman never let on where that came from, and claimed he never knew. Another annoyance for Fred Miller, the town police chief for as long as anyone could remember, a guy heading for the exit soon. Miller was increasingly getting pushed aside, first by state cops then the Feds, in the hunt—a fruitless one to date—for whoever set the fire that took the lives of Mia Buckingham and her pupil Scott Sorrell as they lay naked in the cabin by Mohawk Lake.

Stories like this didn't happen every day. The media had descended on the tiny upstate community, national and international, buzzing around like flies smelling an enticing corpse. Ordinary men and women going about their daily business were getting sick of TV crews pushing mikes and cameras in their faces and asking how they felt. True, money was flowing through the place for the first time in a while, and people felt happy with that. At least the ones who got it. The two Prosper hotels were full for once, the handful of restaurants and bars kept busy by reporters and producers and cameramen desperate for a story.

But as the shock of that July Saturday sank in, it was met with a growing sense of anger and outrage. Prosper was defined in the imagination of the people who lived there by its ordinariness. It was a place for the quiet, the unambitious, the meek and the tame. No one argued; no one broke the law much. No one got divorced if they could help it. Now the world was looking at the town and all its residents as if every last one of them was rolling around naked. A hive of unholy sin where death and adultery lurked behind neatly painted timber houses, in homes where perfect families drove to church each Sunday and sang the same hymns their parents had a generation before.

It wasn't just a school study cabin that caught fire. The flames had reached out to touch everyone, and a few still flickered, long fiery tongues out, hunting flesh.

'I heard guys talking...' Lauren began, mouth full of pasta, hair wet from the shower. 'They said—'

'Not now.' Her mother glared across the table. 'Just one time. One meal. One day where we don't talk about it, please.'

'Mom. *It* is all we've got to talk about. Word is...' Lauren never listened. 'Mia got into a fight with Billy Rodriguez's dad a while before she got killed. Someone saw them out by the parking lot, and he was so mad it looked like he'd hit her.'

'Jesus...' Diane reached for her glass. 'Why do I bother? And why would this come out now?'

'Search me. I just heard. Everyone knows it wasn't just Bunny Rabbitt she was balling. Or Scott. I mean, just look at her. Mia was cute. But hell...' She laughed. 'No one wore stuff like that here. Maybe California...'

Tom tried to calm things. 'Your teacher's dead, Lauren. A boy you know from school too.'

Diane waved her glass. 'Yeah. And I wish you'd quit using that stupid nickname. Sounds like you're four years old. Gary Rabbitt's the principal.'

'*Was* the principal. Bunny. It's what everyone in town calls him except you two. I am aware they're dead, Dad. Me and Scott kind of dated once. He was OK. So was Billy Rodriguez.'

'Try and be respectful. You're upsetting your mom.'

Lauren put down her fork and stared at them, mouth open.

'Wait a minute. You've been *personally* pissing off the whole town for weeks, lifting up the sheets and looking at what's stuck to the mattress underneath. Now you're taking a pop at me for upsetting people? I'm supposed to be *respectful*?'

'It's my job—

'McAllister needs the clicks,' Diane cut in. 'The paper's going bust along with everything else. You should try reading the news.'

'The news is boring. All about people with money losing it. What's that got to do with us? We're broke to start with.'

Diane glared at her. 'You don't know what broke is—'

'I heard Jeff McAllister was banging Mia too. She lived in one of his apartments.'

'Not true,' Honeyman insisted. 'Anyone who tells you that's a liar.'

'Listen to your father.' It was rare for Diane to use those words. 'He could be out of a job before long. You spreading rumors about his boss won't help. Think about it. If he's got no work, then what do we do?'

That idea didn't seem to have occurred to Lauren.

'Then he'll find another job, won't you?'

Diane laughed out loud, and he could hear the drink as she reached across the table and tapped Lauren on the arm.

'Yeah. Right. What? Here? How many reporter's jobs do you think there are? Anywhere? There's banks going under. People getting kicked out of companies everywhere—'

'Mom. This is Prosper. Dullsville. Things like that don't happen here.'

'Teachers getting burned alive while screwing one of their students doesn't happen here either.'

Honeyman tried to calm things.

'We'll manage. It'll be fine. Maybe this story... maybe it's got legs.'

'Legs.' Diane thought that funny, and he wondered how long she'd been going at the bottle before he came home from the office. 'Tanned and skinny ones like the lovely Mia's. Still thinking you could get a book out of it, Tom?'

'I could try. There's people interested. Big story. Good story.'

'Isn't that just a touch... opportunistic? For someone with such high ideals?'

'Someone's going to do it.'

'Hard to write a story without an ending.'

That was the wine talking. He felt sure of it.

'Meaning what?'

'Meaning... no one's got a clue who killed them! A month later and you can see them all wandering around looking lost and stupid. Fred Miller's out of the equation, just barking nonsense at people. The state cops, the Feds... all they've got is their computers and their science teams, and they haven't found a damned thing. Face it. No ending means no story. If it carries on like this for another few weeks, everyone gets bored. People only like mysteries when they're fiction, Tom. In real life we want certainty. Names. Faces in court. The reporters are already starting to leave town. Pretty soon this whole show is going to turn to dust in your fingers. Then we're back where we are. The three of us. Only one with a job, and that won't be around for long.'

Lauren glared at the two of them. This was her story, and she wanted to tell it.

'If you could stop arguing, maybe I'll tell you something useful. Couple of days before Mia and Scott got burned, someone saw Mister Rodriguez arguing with her in the parking lot.'

'So you said,' her mother muttered.

'Yeah. What I was going to tell you is the week after Mia and Scott died, Billy and his mom bolted for Syracuse. Never coming back. She and Mister Rodriguez are getting divorced. He drinks. He's mean, too. They think maybe Mia was banging Billy too and Mister Rodriguez found out. Came around and had a fight with her.'

'School gossip.' Diane stabbed a fork in the cold and clammy pasta. 'Why do we have to listen to this?'

'Because, Mom, nothing ever happened here before. And now it has. Billy's gone, isn't he? Mrs. Rodriguez too. Guess they didn't like living in that shitty trailer out in the woods. With a weirdo for a dad. They all got hated on 'cuz they were Mexican—'

'They came from Arizona.'

Honeyman glanced at his wife when she said that. 'Really? You knew them?'

'Not exactly. I knew *of* them. The kid was at Lafayette, like Lauren said. If you went to school meetings maybe you'd learn things.'

'I went to plenty of school meetings.'

She laughed, and he could hear the wine again.

'Yeah. When Ms. Buckingham showed.'

Lauren rapped her knife on the table. 'Cut it out, you two.'

Diane pulled a face and said, 'I did hear there was bad blood between Rodriguez and that teacher. Mia Buckingham told me herself, couple of days before she died. When I was picking up Lauren. He'd been... rude.'

'And you never told the cops?'

Diane closed her eyes and let out a long, sarcastic groan. 'When did you last exchange a meaningful word with a teacher?'

'I don't—'

'They get shit from kids. They get shit from awkward parents. If you were more of a father you'd be in there with me giving some of those lazy SOBs at Lafayette shit too. Starting with Rabbitt. School's even worse than when I went there.'

Lauren tapped her finger on the table. 'Too late. Bunny's gone. Mia wasn't lazy. She was cool. Wasn't she, Mom? You liked her. Everyone liked her.'

Honeyman said, 'Except this Rodriguez.'

'Crazy man. Drunk. He doesn't like anybody, Dad. Nobody likes him. That's why Billy and his mom are in Syracuse.'

'Are we finished here?'

It wasn't really a question. Diane was on her feet already, taking away the dirty plates.

Lauren stared at her father.

'Mister Rodriguez. He had a fight. Mia was messing around all over town. It wasn't just Scott Sorrell. Everyone knows that. Maybe it was Billy too. Maybe it was Mister Rodriguez. Both of them. I don't know. But they had a fight. Anyway, I'm out of here.'

She got her dance shoes and some clothes and said she was going to a friend's to try some new moves, some new song.

They watched her leave in silence.

Diane got herself another drink.

'Do you have to?' Honeyman asked.

'Yeah. I do.'

She sat in the chair in front of the TV, crossed her legs and stared at him.

'Listen, Tom. You were always a great writer. Never a great reporter. Me, it was the other way around, and we both know it. But I'm telling you. If you don't kick some life into that story now, it's going to die right in front of you. Like the *News-Ledger* will soon. Then what do we do?'

He went upstairs and turned on the laptop. His connection was slow as a tortoise, all they could afford, to Lauren's fury. Still, he had access to the paper's online library, a few others too.

Plenty of places to look.

Twenty minutes of digging was all it took.

THERE WAS a profile of the newcomer to the Prosper Fire Department written for the council website two years before, when the Rodriguez family landed in town. Thirty-four, from Mexico City originally, in his teens Jorge Rodriguez had moved to Phoenix with his parents. Legal —the article emphasized that. Prosper wouldn't have taken him otherwise. His wife, Maria, was from Mexico too. Their son, William, was fourteen, a keen baseball player hoping to turn pro one day.

A photo of them by Prosper's shiny fire truck didn't tell him much at all. Rodriguez was an unsmiling guy, maybe six foot and muscular, his wife very short, grinning for the camera in an embroidered Mexican blouse and a flowing bright red skirt she had to hold down, presumably because of the wind. Billy, the story said, was at Lafayette High and good at sports.

They'd come north, it went on, because the wife had relatives in Syracuse and wanted to be near them. Billy, a Yankees fan, would get to see his team.

Honeyman drilled through the new files. There was no mention of the guy in any of the fire reports. This wasn't surprising. They only ever quoted Lou Barclay, the chief, a man who liked to get his picture and his words in the paper, taking so much credit people used to joke he ran the department all on his own.

Always a talkative guy when it came to publicity.

Barclay answered his phone straight away.

'Hey, Lou. Still at work?'

'Who wants to know?'

'Tom Honeyman.'

There was a deep, guttural chuckle down the line.

'Jesus, Mister Trouble. If you're gonna say I slept with that woman, I'm warning you. I'll sue. And before it gets to court, my Elaine will be over and rip your nuts off.'

'Wouldn't dream of it.'

'Well, it's good to know I'm off the list.'

'I don't have a list. I just report the news.'

That amused Barclay too.

'Yeah. Right. That school's going to need a principal. A good few fellers in this town wondering if they're gonna be next in line for the axe. So who've you got in your sights now? Do tell.'

'No one. Truly. I was kind of hoping we could broaden the story a little. It's my job to report the news, not make it. A paper's here to reflect... reflect the community.'

'Sure doing that right now. Most folk wish you'd do a bit less reflecting. What's this got to do with me?'

'I was wondering if maybe we could do a story on how something like this affects your men. I mean, we take it for granted you guys are tough. You must have seen all kinds of things...'

'Been in this job thirty years and witnessed plenty. Nothing like that. We ain't had arson in this town as long as I've been working here. Just kids messing around sometimes. Never had people dead that way either. Christ...'

'That's the kind of thing I thought might be interesting to write about. The human angle. Take one firefighter who was there and tell the story through his eyes.'

'Happy to do that for you.'

'You'd be great. But I really need to get someone new here too. A different perspective might help. I'll get you in, of course. I saw from the records you've got this guy from Arizona. Rodriguez.'

Nothing but silence. Then Barclay snapped, 'What the fuck is this?'

'Sorry?'

'Don't give me all this bullshit. Human angle my ass. What are you asking about him for?'

Fine, Honeyman thought. *Might as well say it.*

'OK. It's just... I heard him and the Buckingham woman had a falling-out. Some kids saw the two of them arguing at school.'

'What kids? Who told you this bullshit?'

'Doesn't matter.'

'You asked him yourself?'

'No. Thought I'd come to you first—'

'With some lying crap about doing something good?'

'We can still do that. No problem. From what you say, I gather... maybe there's something in these stories.'

'There's nothing in it! Never heard the guy even mention the school. Or her. Not even after she got killed. Shit. He didn't give a damn about that kid of his. Or the wife. He had someone on the side. Liked to drink too. Phoenix didn't come clean about that when they sent me his papers. I never hire drinkers. Don't work out in this job.'

'Someone on the side...'

'Yeah. Week after the fire down Mohawk, the wife came in here screaming at him. Suitcase was in the car. Their kid got tugged along, looking like he was terrified. Said she was leaving town and Jorge could go screw himself. Right in front of the guys. What kind of behavior's that? Should leave domestic stuff at home. No place at work.'

'The other woman. Could it be Mia Buckingham...?'

'Nah. From what I heard she was way out of his class. The idiot was screwing some waitress in the Hawkeye, that dump of a bar down the road from him. Hung out there all the time, telling his old lady he was at work. She wised up, came in here to make sure we heard what an asshole he was. Jesus. We had to listen to it all, her screaming at him, trying to reach up and punch the guy. Then I threw the pair of them out and told him not to come back. Guy didn't fit in anyways. Got nothing against Mexicans. He just wasn't right.'

'When did this happen?'

'Couple of weeks ago.'

'After Mohawk Lake?'

'As I said.'

'What's he done since?'

'Search me. Not my problem.'

'His son was at Lafayette. Same class as my Lauren.'

'She told you all this, did she?'

'I didn't say that.'

'Didn't need to. Some reporter if you're getting your stories from kids now.'

'He must have known Mia Buckingham.'

'I told you. I never heard him mention her name. Not once.'

'Not even after she died, Lou? Biggest story this town's ever seen. Everyone's talking about it.'

'No. Everyone's trying to stop. Except you won't let them. Rodriguez was a stranger here. Never made friends. I don't think he gave a shit about Prosper. Any more than you.'

'OK. But—'

'Listen to me good, Mister Reporter. What I told you was in private. Don't want to see any of that in the paper. Put my department or my name within a mile of that story and I'll see you out of town for good, and there'll be plenty of others around here cheering. In case you hadn't got the message.'

'If you give me a chance to—'

'You're just a fucking parasite, man. Stay away from me and mine.'

Then Lou Barclay hung up.

HONEYMAN MADE a few notes on the Compaq, then went downstairs and got the car keys. Lauren was still out, Diane in the front room, TV off, eyes closed, doing nothing at all.

'I thought I might go and try to talk to this Rodriguez guy.'

She didn't move an inch.

'Why?'

'Maybe he knows something. Maybe there's a story there.'

'You're going to ask him if he was going to bed with her? Or his kid was or something?'

'No. I thought I might ask him why they argued. What was she like?'

Diane squinted at him.

'You're asking me?'

'Yeah. Mia Buckingham. What was she like?'

She shuffled up in the chair and reached out for her drink.

'You're assuming I knew her well enough to make that judgement.

It was just a few conversations. About how Lauren was doing. Or not doing.'

'I'm sorry. I should be more involved.'

She waved the glass at him as if to say *don't bother.*

'Everyone liked her. You know that, Tom. You've written it enough. Not sure she fit in quite as well as she thought, if I'm honest, but that doesn't matter anymore, does it? Come on. Those couple of times you came along at school. I saw you looking.'

'What?'

'I... saw... you... looking. No need to apologize. All the guys used to stare.'

He wasn't admitting to that. Even if it was true.

'It seems Lou Barclay fired Rodriguez a couple of weeks ago. He was drinking. There were problems with the family. The wife turned up at work and started yelling at him for having an affair. Could be the argument with Mia Buckingham was something to do with that.'

'Not sure he was really her type.'

'Her... type?'

'Whatever that was. Do you know where he lives?'

'I thought I might ask around in the bar he goes to. The Hawkeye. Maybe he's there.'

She laughed.

'Jesus. Only if you want to wake up in a hospital. He's got a place on that park a mile or so down Consett Lane. An old trailer set out on its own. You turn left when you drive in. Maybe when we're broke we'll end up there. Unless you save us all with your book, of course.'

'How... how do you know where a guy like that lives?'

'Because...' She opened her eyes wide. 'I took Lauren there a while back. She had some schoolwork to do with the kid. They were in the same class. Didn't she say?'

'I don't recall.'

'No. Your mind was doubtless elsewhere, as usual.'

He jingled the car keys in his hand and didn't move.

'No idea know how long I'll be.'

'Promise me you won't stop by the Hawkeye. Or any of the bars in town right now. There's more than one guy out there who'd like to kick your ass, just for starters.'

'Thanks for that. Seen my work camera anywhere?'

A couple of months before, McAllister had acquired a stack of digital point-and-shoot models as part of a promotion. They were meant as contest prizes for readers, but a few he handed out to people on staff. They were supposed to shoot anything they thought might turn out useful for the paper: silly animals, kids, car crashes, chance shots that could generate a few clicks on the web or maybe sell elsewhere. Most didn't shoot a thing. Why should they? McAllister wasn't offering a dime in return.

'Your camera...?'

'If I'm going to do a book I probably ought to start taking some photos. For research. Just for me.'

'When did you last use it?'

'Don't recall.'

'Jesus. Like my mom used to say... you'd lose your head if it wasn't nailed on. I think maybe...'

She got up and went into the kitchen, came back clutching a small black-and-silver model that had seen better days.

'Here.'

He took it and turned it on. Plenty of charge. Not a single picture on the memory card. Maybe he'd erased it. Or Diane did. Or Lauren.

'You really think you're going to save us with this, don't you?'

'Going to try.'

It was a hot night, and a part of him felt like driving and driving. As far as the gas would take him. Prosper was starting to close in on him. One day, soon, they had to leave.

But, for now, he went to Consett Lane.

It was eight, the light fading, when Honeyman pulled up beside the trailer. A sorry-looking, rusting thing, it stood alone at the edge of the park, a good two hundred feet away from the nearest neighbor. There were a couple of trash cans in the long grass by the front, one of them knocked over, the contents spilled on the concrete. Maybe the neighbors didn't like Jorge Rodriguez any more than his boss had.

He'd thought through his approach. Be friendly. Sympathetic. Say he'd heard there'd been trouble at the fire department. Which wasn't that unusual, given Lou Barclay's temper. If Rodriguez wanted to tell his side of the story, the paper was willing to listen.

Then, once inside, move the conversation on to Lafayette High and Mia Buckingham and see where that went. He wasn't great at this kind of thing. Diane was much more suited for the awkward stuff, and being a woman could push it further and get less heat in return. All the same, Mohawk Lake was his story, one he was keeping to himself even when the big papers and the TV networks begged for help and offered checks—not big ones, not big enough anyway—if he came up with a little local insight.

He rapped on the door. It popped open a crack, and out came a stale cloud of spilled booze and the sweaty stink of a man who lived on his own.

'Mister Rodriguez...'

No answer.

Not a soul in sight. No car or truck outside. A mile down the road stood the Hawkeye Inn, a roadside bar with a penchant for country music, cheap whiskey, cheaper food, along with plenty of fights. And, if Lou Barclay was right, a warm, female shoulder that was the only one Jorge Rodriguez might have to cry on at that moment.

'Mister Rodriguez...?'

There was a smell hanging all around the trailer, one that gave him pause for thought.

Gas.

Around the back, three metal jerry cans were stacked against the remains of an old brick wall.

He took out the Casio and photographed them, then went to the front again and rapped once more on the door.

Still no answer, so he went back to the car, found the pair of plastic gloves he kept for when he went to the gas station—he never could stand the smell of it on him—then pulled them on and went back to take a good look around.

RODRIGUEZ'S HOME was a bachelor cave. Clothes everywhere, empty booze bottles, a half-empty pack of condoms by a disheveled bed in the makeshift room at the end. Maybe this was new. The chaos that came from losing his family. It seemed impossible the guy's wife and kid had stayed in such a dump at all.

The Hawkeye was open until midnight or later. Five-minute drive away even for a drunk. Time was short. He turned on the lights and went to work.

In the cramped space between the entrance and the kitchen there was a bookshelf and a small desk with a tiny laptop on it, one that looked older and even cheaper than Honeyman's.

A stack of books and a pile of photo albums—three of them, two recent, one older.

Honeyman nosed through the books, snapping away with the camera. Jorge Rodriguez seemed to have only one thing to read about: fire. Some of the titles were operation manuals, the kind any professional in the business might be expected to own. A couple of true-life personal stories of firefighters and their experiences. One about the terror that ensued at the World Trade Center during 9/11. Another a hefty technical tome covered in scrawled annotations that appeared to be prep for technical exams in department operations.

Alongside were some far stranger titles. There were three books about spontaneous human combustion—people suddenly catching fire, getting incinerated for no good reason. A crudely printed conspiracy paperback about mass-fatality blazes around the world and how most of them might have been deliberate, not the accidents they seemed. A volume about the use of napalm and other incendiary weapons in Southeast Asia. Then four books covering the effects of atomic bombs in Japan at the end of the Second World War, complete with pictures of ravaged victims, some reduced to little more than charcoal—like Mia Buckingham and Scott Sorrell—others crippled and screaming, skin burned from their bodies.

All in all there were lots of photos, some of them fires, but mostly victims, corpses and burned bodies ringed in felt-tip pen. Just looking at them gave Honeyman the creeps. But Rodriguez was a professional in the fire department. Maybe there was a good reason why he'd have an interest in the subject. Not that Prosper had suffered a fatal blaze in years until Mohawk Lake came along.

Then he looked at the first two photo albums and started taking more snaps of his own. These had to be the guy's personal pictures, records of fires he'd attended over the years, mostly in Phoenix, judging by the houses and the surrounding landscape. Again, there could have been a good reason why he'd want to keep track of jobs he'd worked on. All the same... it seemed excessive.

The third album didn't contain photos at all. It was full of newspaper clippings starting from five years before in Phoenix. House blazes, all fatal. Then, halfway through, it turned to Prosper. Here were Honeyman's own stories about Mohawk Lake, coupled with stories from the *New York Times* and *Washington Post*, all neatly clipped, dated and folded into the album. He must have been cutting them every single day, mostly from the real newspapers, though the weirder stories from some of the supermarket gossip rags—pieces that told tales of Prosper's supposed dark side more luridly even than Honeyman's own—were in there too.

Behind the last album was a printout of a few pages stapled together, and a bulky Panasonic mid-range camera.

He picked up the paper and his breath caught, his fingers shook as he tried to take photos of it all. The desk light didn't work, so he had to squint at the sheets by the window to see them well.

The first page was a color inkjet printout of a photo of the cabin at Mohawk Lake before it burned down.

The second was a copy of it with scribble marks around the side, puddles of ink that looked like plans for setting gas.

The third reproduced the previous page, but with marks in red and yellow crayon that looked like tiny flames. Maybe possible ignition points.

Something told him he had to get out of there quick. But not before he looked at Jorge Rodriguez's camera.

He turned it on and hit the play button. There were just seven images on the card, all dated twelve days before Mia Buckingham and Scott Sorrell died. They looked as if they'd been snapped through the window of the cabin. There was the glass, with the iron security bars just visible in a couple of images. Everything was blurred by a lack of light and by movement. It was hard to make out who was there exactly, apart for Mia, naked, arching over someone on the cabin floor, head back, lurid hair flying down her back, mouth open, eyes closed, a wide, ecstatic grin on her face.

Two people making wild love on the floor of the cabin in the woods, someone spying on them through the window.

The final couple of shots showed it wasn't going to last. There was a blurry photo of Mia turning, getting up, and she wasn't pretty then. She looked mad as hell at getting spied on. Her pale, taut body hid whoever was with her. That much was going to stay a secret.

He thought of taking out the memory card, then wondered what the Feds, the state cops and even Fred Miller would make of that. So Honeyman snapped the photos on the screen as best he could. In a way, maybe they were better. The poorer quality gave them a kind of allure, a mystery that could come from him fudging how he got them. And there was only one person to be identified here. She was dead, ashes and black bones in a morgue in Albany.

He could barely stop shaking as he hit the shutter button on the Casio.

After that he fled back to his VW.

No one around. No sign of Rodriguez. He thought of going into the Hawkeye himself just to see if he was there. But Diane's warning stopped him. His face was known, he wasn't popular. Not a time to stick his neck out.

He had a key to the *News-Ledger* office and editor rights on the website. He had a story too.

BEFORE MIA BUCKINGHAM and Scott Sorrell died, people only went
to the *News-Ledger* site to look up the real estate listings and see
how far the price of their homes had fallen in this, the year of the
crash. Honeyman had changed that for good. Jeff McAllister let
him loose on the system, even ponying up extra money when their
hits busted the limits on the crappy, cheap web-hosting service he
used.

Honeyman could run whatever he wanted. The bigger question
was how to handle it. How to publish the photos of Mia Buckingham
and her mysterious partner and the evidence trail, while making sure
he took the credit as the guy who maybe cracked the mystery of
Mohawk Lake.

Diane would know. This was her kind of thing. He called home to
say he was in the office on his own. She didn't sound as woozy as he
expected.

'Find anything?'

'Oh yeah.' It felt good being able to say that. 'Quite a lot.'

'Really?'

He wondered if she sounded impressed.

'Really. Rodriguez wasn't there. His door was open. The place was
a mess. Stank of booze. I think he must have been out at the
Hawkeye.'

'Sounds like burglary, Tom.'

'Sounds like me doing my job. He's got lots of books about fire. A
map of the cabin, a sketch of how you could set fire to it.'

Silence.

'He's got photos on his camera. Looks like he was snooping on
Mia Buckingham. Caught her there when she was having fun with
someone.'

'Who?'

'Maybe one of the kids. Scott Sorrell. Maybe his son. Could
explain why he went to the school and had a fight with her.'

'You're guessing.'

'True. Can't see who it is. Just her. She seems to have noticed she had a Peeping Tom on her hands and came at him. I guess he fled.'

'Wow. Big guy running from a little woman.'

That was all she said. She almost sounded amused.

'I've got the proof, Diane. He was spying on them. Would you hang around if they caught you doing that? The question is... what do I do with it?'

'You're asking me?'

He hesitated and said, 'I am. I was always the features guy. You did news.'

'Last time I was in a newspaper office it still had typewriters and little pieces of paper you wrote on.'

'You've got that talent. You don't lose it.'

A moment.

'You could be in big trouble for digging around in there. That's career-ending stuff if you admit to it. Prison maybe.'

'I wore gloves.'

'Smart. Anyone see you?'

'No. In the big picture—'

'In the big picture you've turned this town over and there's plenty of people who'd love to see you pay. You got to hide how you got hold of all this. I don't want to do jail visits. Lauren might find that cool the first couple of times, but I suspect it would pale for her too after that.'

Something clicked in his head, a thought that had been hanging there for a few weeks and mostly ignored.

'Whatever happens, I'm done here, aren't I? No going back to how it was before. The place has changed. So have we.'

'I guess.'

'So what do I do?'

'Christ. Do you really not know?'

'That's why I'm asking.'

'You've already got an anonymous leaker, haven't you? They sent you that DNA info that sunk Bunny Rabbitt's boat. Are you at the keyboard?'

'I can be.'

'Good. Let me dictate your lead.'

He wanted to laugh. She was enjoying this, sounding energized in a way he hadn't heard in years.

Diane thought for a moment then said very slowly, very deliberately, in the voice she'd used to phone in copy back when they first met, 'Detectives are expected to interview a suspect in the Mohawk Lake tragedy later today after incriminating material, including intimate photos of the deceased teacher Mia Buckingham, along with plans for setting fire to the Lafayette High cabin, were posted anonymously to this paper. Inquiries by the *News-Ledger* have established that the materials belong to Jorge Rodriguez, a Prosper firefighter recently dismissed from his job. Thomas Honeyman, the *News-Ledger* reporter who was sent the material, is turning over the evidence to the police. The *News-Ledger* will cooperate in any way police agencies see fit, as they seek to close the case that has haunted Prosper for a month since Ms. Buckingham and her pupil, Scott Sorrell, died in the inferno set by a mysterious assailant.'

It was obvious, and quite brilliant. Put the onus for action on the police. Take any incoming heat off the paper. Claim the credit for himself. Place the responsibility for the incriminating photos on an anonymous informant.

'Okay, Tom. I take it you can write the rest? I take it, too, you're going to be damned careful to make sure no one's going to punch a hole in these lies when they come out.'

'Yeah.'

'These photos... you can use them online? They're not too explicit?'

'I can blur a few things. I didn't take the originals anyway. They're shot off the screen of his camera. Doesn't need much.'

Diane hesitated.

'Good... If you're right and it *is* this guy, it doesn't matter, does it? All people will talk about is how they can breathe again. Thanks to Tom Honeyman. Or rather his nameless, faceless source. Maybe you'll be redeemed. Kind of doubt it, though.'

'I couldn't have done this without you.'

'True. What about McAllister? You going to tell him?'

'No.'

'He'll be mad.'

'I'm beyond caring. He can look at the web numbers tomorrow and be grateful.'

'Then fire you when the noise dies down.'

'I'll be gone soon anyway. Better things to do. It goes out there in the morning. Eight o'clock. Breakfast reading.'

He'd thought this through already. The story needed impact. No point in letting it drift out late at night when the audience was bound to be smaller. The web system let him set up stories to go live at a specific time. This one he'd program to release right at eight. Then the networks could follow it up and start the ball rolling during the day.

'Sounds good, Tom. Seven thirty we can hit the phones and tell the wires and the big papers there's something coming they need to tune into. Oh, and make sure the site can handle the traffic. You're going to get more than Jeff McAllister could ever dream of.'

'Right. It's just...'

There was a note of doubt in his voice, and naturally she spotted it.

'Just what? You sound as if you're having second thoughts.'

The last few weeks he'd been praying for a breakthrough like this. Desperate for something that would give him the kind of edge on the story that might get them out of Prosper.

'Not for a second. I was remembering what it was like when we used to work together.'

'Oh.' That was it.

'I'll make things better for you and Lauren. I promise. Whatever happens—'

'Of course. You're doing this all for us, aren't you? Nothing selfish in it, no hunger for glory at all? Get on with it then. I'll be in bed by the time you're home. Try not to wake Lauren.'

It took an hour to set up the story, and another hour to tweak it so that the blurred and grainy pictures looked right alongside the text.

He went to the publishing controls and set the release time: eight a.m. Then his finger hovered over the button marked 'Schedule.'

Maybe Rodriguez was back from the bar by then. Maybe he ought to go out to the trailer park and give him the chance to try to explain.

But if the guy really was a murderer... where was the sense in that? The cops could deal with him. It had been hard work, no small amount of risk, and a degree of subterfuge too. But he had his story. He had to run it. Too late to back out now.

Tom Honeyman hit the "schedule" button, leaned back in his old office chair and closed his eyes. The *News-Ledger* was going to be history soon. He could feel the joyous release of escape getting closer by the hour.

8

VENICE

Thursday
Deadline: 2 days. 0 hours. 23 minutes.

Honeyman finished typing, closed his eyes and almost tumbled off the chair at the desk, straight down to the floor. Too little sleep. Too confused after getting knocked out when he tried to escape with Lauren.

Too much to think about as well.

Tell the truth or else.

Before his story about Jorge Rodriguez broke, Diane manned the phones, calling the networks and the big papers, tipping them off. Every last one started asking the cops when Rodriguez was going to be pulled in for questioning. A team of state detectives showed up at the newspaper office by nine-thirty, checking out Honeyman's story. Ninety minutes later, watched by the news helicopter from the local station, a full-blown SWAT team began assembling at Rodriguez's home. The standoff was short and shocking. As soon as the man stumbled out of the door waving what turned out to be an old BB gun, the shooting started. When his blood was on the coarse gravel outside the rusty trailer, they ransacked it. A picture soon emerged of a man at the end of his tether. Family gone, job lost, dwindling money going to drink and little else.

Whenever anyone pressed Honeyman on his sources, his answer remained the same. *I got an anonymous tip. An envelope through the office door. An SD card with some fuzzy images on it, a scribble on it saying they came from Rodriguez. Nothing else. Just like when someone sent me the DNA report.*

Rodriguez was dead, seemingly guilty as hell. No one thought to ask how Honeyman knew the photos really came from him. They found the originals in the trailer. Case closed.

That was his story, and he stuck to it.

The walkie-talkie stayed silent. As did the laptop.

He went into the kitchen, got some bread and gulped down some water. There was no way off Maledetto now, not unless the dinghy could be fixed, and it was unlikely there'd be the opportunity to do that. It was night. The only idea he could think of was to put up some kind of signal that passing vessels might see.

Except the easiest beacon was a fire. Which could take hours to set up even if he could manage it. By which time the two of them would be dead.

The red camera light blinked at him from the kitchen wall. He saluted it and said, 'A little feedback wouldn't be unwelcome.'

Then he went back to the study and waited.

Almost midnight, when he was back close to dozing, the walkie-talkie squawked.

Wow, Tommy. So your reporting talents extended to burglary. Mister Ace Reporter's a common thief. Some confession. No Pulitzer coming your way. Just jail time if they see this. Did it feel good letting it all out?

In a way it had.

'If that's what you want to hear. What have you done with Lauren?'

Me and your kid enjoyed a little talk.

'Don't hurt her.'

That's up to you, pal. Here's your reward...

There was a beep and seven images appeared on the desktop.

Honeyman clicked on the first and recognized it immediately. It was one of the pictures from the memory card on Rodriguez's camera. An original or a copy—it was impossible to tell—but it was sharper than the shot he'd run in the paper. If this guy had gotten hold of the actual pictures, he couldn't begin to imagine how.

Honeyman shivered as he stared at the photos on the screen.

There was Mia Buckingham naked, ecstatic, grinning, back arched, bright neon hair waving around her bony spine, straddling someone out of shot. Then, in sequence, he went through the others. Mia noticing they had a visitor, getting up, getting furious.

'Where did you get these?'

What does that matter to you, Ace? Better than the crummy copies you stole, aren't they?

Suddenly, it all made sense. *Fred Miller.*

As chief of police, Miller would surely have access to the evidence as it was assembled, even if he was being kept at the periphery of the investigation. He seemed to be the kind of guy who took a copy of everything. Made sense he'd print duplicates of any photos that came in along the way. Must have taken them with him when he left the police.

Miller was a widower. From time to time he talked about his son a world away in Seattle. It was one of the few occasions a note of warmth came into his voice. And when he got shot that night in Burnsville, his things had to go to someone...

How many possible explanations were there?

Honeyman took a deep breath, wondered what there was to be lost, and said, 'Good evening, Vern Miller. Pleasure to meet you at last.'

Silence.

'I'm sorry about your father. I'm sorry it all turned out bad. I wish it hadn't. He didn't like me. Didn't like anyone much, I think. But he was a good cop. Deserved more respect.'

Silence.

'Maybe we both want the same thing, Vern. Maybe if we work together...'

It was a long wait. Finally a voice came out of the speaker and it sounded deeper, colder, angrier than anything he'd heard before.

Well, fuck me, Mister Honey Bee, aren't you the smart one? Finally you made a connection. Yes, it's Vernon Miller here. With a stack of material my father sent me for safekeeping just before he got killed. October twenty-ninth that was, two thousand and nine. Where were you that night, Tommy boy?

It seemed the strangest question.

'Hell, I don't know. It was around the time the book was coming out. I was all over the place for interviews and signings. New York. Washington. L.A. Why did he send you all this stuff?'

That's a story for another time. You weren't anywhere near Prosper?

Honeyman tapped at the laptop. He wasn't keeping his calendar online back then. He really had no idea.

'I'm sorry. I don't know. There was a tour. Two, three towns in one day sometimes. Is this relevant, Vern?'

Keep using the name. Establish a relationship. Bring him in.

You're lying.

'No, Vern. I'm not.'

Another beep. A pdf turned up on the desktop. A story from the *Burnsville Examiner* dated October 31, 2009. Four paragraphs, a photo of Honeyman smiling at a small independent bookstore, six or seven people around him.

'You were there October twenty-ninth. The day my dad died.'

Honeyman scanned through the story. It seemed genuine. The months around the appearance of the book had been so busy his feet barely touched the ground. One day he'd be in Virginia. The next the other side of the country. TV interviews, magazines, bookstores— everywhere people asking him the same question: Why?

Why did Jorge Rodriguez kill that teacher and her teenage lover? What drove him?

All the time he could only give the rehearsed answers he'd elabo-rated in the book, with more than a little help from his editor: *The world's more full of doubt than certainty. Any reasons died with Rodriguez on the dried-up turf outside his trailer, leaking away onto the hard soil with his blood.* It was the best he had, and no one was in a position to argue.

'I was on a schedule, Vern. People told me where to go. I didn't hear your dad was dead until a week or more after it happened. Never made any connection—'

You were there—

'I don't know what you want to hear, Vern. I never saw your father after he left Prosper. Certainly not in Burnsville. That's the truth.'

Another incoming document. Another story from that week's Burnsville paper. The lead. A former police chief shot to death outside a lowlife bar, after a quarrel in the street, the local cops assumed. He had a reputation for arguments. They were 'pursuing leads'.

Those useless bastards never found who shot my dad.

'It wasn't me. Why would I?'

Now there's a question. He never gave up on Mohawk Lake. He thought he was getting somewhere. And then he's dead. So I'm guessing whoever killed him is the same person who lit that fire, Tommy. First... first we got another problem.

Honeyman found himself sweating.

'What kind of problem?'

Stop being so slow. I asked you to make connections. Find names. Mine was never one of them. You complicated everything again, man. How am I supposed to let you out of here now?

Damn, he thought. *That was stupid.* The old reporter in him being too clever for his own good.

'I'm sorry. I didn't mean anything. I'm trying to help here. Let me see if I can work this out. Then we can come to some arrangement. I still got a little money. Take what you want. Truly.'

Still nothing.

Then the walkie-talkie chirped.

He could hear them, hear her, Lauren, whining, crying:

Cut it out! Jesus...!

'Lauren! For god's sake, Vern! Please...'

Leave me alone!

Lauren squealed and shrieked, and pretty soon there was just one word in all the noises.

No!

Honeyman slammed his finger on the button and made it stop.

DEEP in the night the front door banged open. He ran out to find his daughter shuffling through, head down, bare legs emerging from a men's outdoor jacket more suited for winter and the woods of upstate New York than a sweltering Italian night. One quick sideways glance halfway between shame and anger, then she threw the jacket on the floor and dashed upstairs in little more than a t-shirt. Soon he heard the sound of the shower.

When she came down she was wearing a fresh shirt and jeans, her hair tied up in a towel. She went straight into the kitchen and grabbed a glass of wine. Her eyes were still pink and bleary. She hardly ever cried even when she was little.

'Lauren—'

'Don't ask.'

'Christ...' He fell on the chair opposite and grabbed some booze for himself. 'I'm sorry. I was trying... trying... I don't know. Trying to reach him.'

'I said... don't ask. We're alive, aren't we? I've been working cruise ships, remember? You'd be amazed what I've been through over the years.'

She always had a brittle shell, hard and fragile at the same time. Maybe Vern understood this too, which was why he was playing this cruel game. Seizing her. Releasing her. Hurting her when he felt like it, and making damned sure Honeyman knew what was happening. It was all part of his control-freak act, a way of saying *You two are mine, to do with what I want, when I want. Mine to reward when I feel like it. Mine to damage too. And there's not a thing you can do to stop me.*

She rolled her eyes then came over, threw her arms round him, kissed him on the cheek.

'Sorry, Dad. I'm taking this out on you. Not your fault. Let's... leave it.'

Is it really that easy? Can't be, he thought. She was putting on a brave face. Perhaps the best thing to do in the circumstances.

She pulled off the towel. He touched her wet hair for a moment and saw again the little kid she'd been, a happy one for a while. If she'd been crying, the tears were gone.

'I'm going to get you out of this. I'm not going to let that bastard ruin our lives.'

A smile, then she said, 'He doesn't need to, does he? We turned out to be pretty good at that ourselves.' She threw the towel on the tiles and added, 'I need to eat.'

Lauren cooked the way her mother used to: quick and practical, food as nourishment, that was all. Just looking at her put a meal together took him right back to their house in Prosper. Without asking he got up and started to scrape some parmesan through the grater, the way he used to back then.

Fifteen minutes later, close to two in the morning, the hours starting to run into one another, night bleeding into day, they sat in front of two plates of penne with a dark red sauce, a couple more glasses of wine. She ate quickly, greedily, and halfway through, mouth full, said, 'I think I maybe remember the guy from school now. Vern Miller.'

'What was he like?'

'Don't know. He was older. Must have been graduating when I turned up. Lot older. No one talked to him much. Cop's kid. You wouldn't.'

'And he blames me for what happened to his father?'

The shrug, then 'Maybe. Kind of get the impression he pretty much blames the whole world for everything that pisses him off. Which is a lot.'

'What do we do?'

She put a finger to her cheek.

'Oh, I don't know. Get out of here. Go to a fancy hotel somewhere. I could use a vacation. Everyone thinks you get one working on those stupid ships. Yeah. Sure.'

'I meant—'

'I know what you meant, Dad. There's nothing we can do. You need to find out what he wants to hear. The truth he's looking for. Vern's truth. Maybe yours too. Who knows?' She thought for a moment. 'What's the name of the woman in that old story? The one I mentioned. She's got to keep telling a tale and never quite get to the end, because if she does the guy's going to kill her.'

'Scheherazade.'

'How did it finish?'

'It went on for a thousand and one nights. In the end the king had fallen in love with her.'

She laughed, the kind of laugh that came from nervous relief. Red sauce splattered the table. Always a messy eater.

'Happily ever after. Right. It *was* a fairy tale.'

'Vern asked where I was the night his father got shot.'

'So where *were* you?'

'All those years ago? On one specific night? I don't remember. He says I was in Burnsville. A book event. There's a story in the paper. Guess he must be right.'

Lauren frowned.

'Hell of a coincidence. Don't you remember? You were in the same town when his old man got shot? The same night?'

'It was all crazy back then. Two towns a day sometimes. You think I read anything but the reviews?'

'It was Burnsville. Close to home. A guy you knew, someone who was involved in Mohawk Lake, got murdered.'

'It didn't register 'til later. Your mom never mentioned it. It was on the news when I got back to Prosper. I never saw Fred Miller after he left town, not once. Sent him a couple of emails when I was writing the book. He didn't get back to me. The publisher sent him an ARC.'

'A what?'

'An early copy. Before publication.'

'Why did they do that?'

He shrugged.

'They said they had to. Seemed dumb to me. Maybe the guy would have sued.'

She raised a finger.

'Only if you got something wrong. I remember reading somewhere: Truth is an absolute defense.'

Honeyman didn't respond to that.

Somewhere among his files on the computer there were stories about Miller's murder. He'd collected them the way he picked up other pieces of research, automatically, not knowing if they'd be any use at all. It seemed a semi-tragic side note to the story he'd already written. An old, failed cop reduced to night security work in a place he was a stranger, shot dead one night, half-drunk, after an altercation outside a grim downtown bar. The perpetrator never found.

'Dad. If Vern thinks his father got killed because he knew something about Mohawk Lake then—'

'But a year later... why?'

She looked more worried at that moment than he'd seen her since she stumbled through the door.

'Well, maybe because Fred Miller was getting close to the guy who really murdered them. I don't know. Vern doesn't either, does he? I told you. He's crazy. Something's burning away in his head. If it's vengeance he wants for his old man, that explains it. All the rage. Jesus.' She shook her head. 'You haven't seen him. I mean, I really thought he was going to kill you after we got caught taking that boat.'

'But he can't. Not yet. He thinks I've got something he wants.'

'Yeah,' she agreed. 'A name.' She pointed her fork at him. 'Even if we come up with one, save it, Dad. Save it 'til the very last moment. That way we get a chance.'

But is it a real chance? he wondered. *Is Vern Miller really a man of his word?*

'I'm keeping him amused. At least I think so. I just gave him what he asked for. I wrote why I went to Rodriguez's trailer. First time ever. I dropped the whole story about getting the evidence from some anonymous informer. Told the truth, like he asked. It could put me in jail if it ever got out there. I broke into the trailer. Took the pictures myself.'

She blinked and gazed at him.

'What?'

'Mom never said?'

'Of course not. You made all that up?'

'Not the facts. After you said Rodriguez and Mia had a fight, I went to try and talk to him. He wasn't around. I went in and found all the material in there. The books he kept...'

'Vern says those books were legit. Kind of thing any firefighter doing his job might keep.'

'There was a printout. It showed the cabin. And ways to set it on fire. The guy had compromising photos of Mia on his camera, for god's sake. I took shots of them. They kind of clinched it.'

'Really?'

Lauren just stared at him, and he felt cold. If she wouldn't believe his story, who would?

'There were gas cans outside.'

'A month after he set fire to two people?' She waved her glass at him, and she could have been Diane just then. 'All this stuff still hanging around? Seems dumb.'

'It was there.'

'You don't sound so confident, Dad. You sure you're telling Vern everything?'

That was a question he wasn't going to answer.

'What's Miller got out there?' Honeyman asked. 'What's he using to communicate?'

'I thought you knew. A laptop. A generator. Lots of gas. Some kind of geek gear I don't understand—'

'He sent me copies of those photos. They look like the originals. Fred Miller must have sneaked them out of the files.'

She ate a little more, drank some wine and kept looking at him.

'Why would Vern do that? Send you the actual photos?'

'I don't know.'

Lauren cleared her plate, pushed it one side and got to her feet.

'This guy doesn't do anything without a reason. I wanna see.'

THE PHOTOS WERE STILL on the desktop. Lauren flicked through them, sipping at what was left of her wine.

There was one that stood out. Different shape, poorer quality. Maybe it had been taken with an old phone.

'What's that, Dad?'

A blurry picture of a silver pendant on a chain, heart-shaped, the clasp closed. There were burn marks around the edges and a distinct dent. The thing looked cheap, handmade even.

'Vern sent me this chapter he'd written about what his old man did the day of the fire.'

'*Vern* wrote something? Can I read it?'

'Later. This is the pendant Fred Miller found at Mohawk Lake. The one I told you about.'

'And like I said... I'm a Honeyman. We really don't do jewelry.'

'Chief Miller never showed it to anyone as far as I can work out. He was pissed off with the way they took the investigation out of his hands.'

'Is this really important?'

'I don't know. There was a message inscribed.' Honeyman scanned through the files to find the reference. 'It said, "To Mia. Always and forever."'

'Cute,' Lauren said, but she didn't seem interested. She pulled up the other images. 'Wow. I saw the photos you ran in the paper, but all the bits were blurred out. Mia looks happy. Wonder who it was.'

'Did you hear rumors? At school?'

'About what?'

'About who she was involved with.'

Lauren ran a finger down the screen.

'Just what I told you. Feels weird, doesn't it? Looking at her like that. Thinking she was going to live forever.'

'How well did you know her?'

The look he got might have been from the teenage Lauren.

'I didn't. Why would I? She was a teacher. Sure, we liked her. She was still... old. Old acting cool. Not good.' Lauren wrinkled her nose. 'Kind of weird too, in a nice way but still weird. People always thought she might be screwing around. Didn't know how much. Using weed as well. You know when people try to make out they're super-happy when really they're sad?'

'Yeah.'

'It was like that. Sometimes she looked like she'd been crying. I guess that creep Rabbitt was hitting on her. Other guys too. When you get a reputation... it's like it's open season. Maybe... maybe it gets hard to say no. And all the time that shitty town's looking down its shitty nose at her. Like she doesn't belong there. Prosper was way too good for a tramp from California. Just like it was way too good for some guy from Mexico who liked to drink and get into fights. God, I'm glad I'm out of there.'

'Mom went to Mia's apartment once. She never told me why.'

'Ah.' Lauren winced. 'That was me. I think I maybe had an attitude in class. An unhelpful one. Mia wanted to have the parent talk. I kind of begged Mom to do it instead of you.'

'Why?'

That shrug again.

'I dunno. Girl stuff. Things you wouldn't like.'

She zoomed in on a couple of photos. Even in these originals it was impossible to see who else was there. Just pale skin behind Mia's naked form.

'She wasn't right in that place. Belonged in the city, not a stuffy little dump like Prosper. You couldn't be happy if you needed to cling to people like she did. Like she wasn't really alive if there wasn't someone around.'

Lauren selected all the photo files then right-clicked. A bunch of windows full of technical information came up on screen.

'What are you doing?'

'It's called the EXIF data. Exposure, speed, camera type, when they were taken. I handle the photo sales from the camera guys on the ship sometimes. Useful to work out what's going on when you can't match a print to an order.'

She sat back and stared at the screen.

'That's odd.'

'What?'

'Here.' Her finger tapped on the entry. 'What kind of camera did Jorge Rodriguez have on his desk?'

'Like I said, I knew I had a book coming, so I made notes for myself afterwards, every day back then. The photos were on his Panasonic. I just snapped what was on the screen.'

'No, Dad.'

'I saw it—'

'No. They were on the SD card *in* the Panasonic. But they weren't taken *using* the Panasonic. Here.'

She pointed at the model type. He couldn't believe it.

'If Rodriguez took the pictures with that camera, it would say so.'

'Maybe... maybe he changed it.'

'Why would he do that? And why would he keep something so incriminating in his damned trailer anyway? There was a murder investigation going on.'

Honeyman was struggling.

'Lauren. The Feds, the state police, they picked up that camera after Rodriguez got shot. They must have been through this. If they believed the photos came from somewhere else—'

'You think?' She tapped the screen. 'Come on. You ran your story. They went in heavy-handed as hell. A SWAT team and everything, killed a drunk guy who was waving nothing but a BB gun. They got shit enough already. For the fact they never found the killer themselves. You think they'd want to admit they shot the wrong man? It was Prosper. He was a foreigner. Case closed. Everyone can go back to believing they were living in their perfect little dream worlds again— Fred Miller and Bunny Rabbitt and a few others apart. But Prosper probably thought they deserved it. Who the hell's going to ask awkward questions then?'

She glanced at the red blink of the camera, and he got the message. This was as much for the man outside as him.

'I don't know...'

'Someone planted all this, Dad. Rodriguez was a sad drunk. Someone went in there, put the card in his camera. Printed out an incriminating map of Mohawk Lake... I mean, shit. The cabin was ashes by then. Why keep something like that around a month later? Was he really that dumb?'

Honeyman couldn't stop staring at the screen. The EXIF said the shots were taken with a Casio EX-S12.

'You just wrote you used a Casio.'

'I don't know what kind. Everyone on the paper had one. And we'd given a bunch away in a contest. Plenty of people with a Casio back then.'

She glanced at the screen again and muttered, 'Someone framed that guy. We've got to work out what happened. But not now. I've got to sleep. Can't keep my eyes open.'

With a grunt she got up, winked at the camera and mouthed 'thanks'. Then walked to the door, retrieved the heavy winter jacket and retreated beneath the blinking light so she was out of its line of sight. Lauren glanced at him and pulled something out of the pocket.

He wandered over to join her, praying they couldn't be seen.

'I got us an advantage,' she whispered. 'Picked it out of his things while he was pulling his pants back on and too happy to notice. Here...'

It was a handgun. A semi-automatic.

'He's got like an arsenal out there. With any luck he won't even notice.'

Lauren drew out the magazine and checked the shells. She seemed to know how to do that. Which was good. He didn't have a clue.

9

VENICE

Friday
Deadline: 1 day. 13 hours. 3 minutes.

Honeyman let Lauren sleep. As long as she wanted. He knew he couldn't, wiped out as he felt. There were too many memories buzzing around his head. From the start, the moment he hit "publish" on that story about the illicit, incriminating photos in a trailer outside town, his career, his life to an extent, had formed around a single purpose. Telling the story of Mohawk Lake and how a lonely, sad outsider named Jorge Rodriguez came to spread gas around the cabin there, incinerating the two people inside and setting the little world of Prosper all on fire. How nothing was the same after—the police chief fired amid accusations of incompetence; the high school racked with rumors of scandal around a principal whose feet turned out to be made of the lowest clay.

But most of all—and Honeyman made much of this in the book—how the presence of a young, free-spirited, bohemian woman from California tore the cozy mask of hypocrisy away from the picket-fence homes and church-going families around her. The story of *The Fire* was about the way one young woman's cruel, savage death—and that of the young kid with her—demonstrated the people of Prosper were no different, no more or less honorable or decent than all the big-city people they despised. There, more than anything, was the bigger tale he struggled to tell. About a picture-book America, a quiet place where nothing seemed to happen, which was a myth, as big a lie as the fake prosperity that was unravelling all around them that year of Lehman Brothers and Bear Stearns, of crises and crashes, small and local, vast and international.

At least that was the deeper story Thomas Honeyman hoped for, though his editor in New York had other ideas, and so did readers. They just wanted a lurid and sensational mystery, a thick, juicy impenetrable one.

It was easy to speculate when the facts were missing. The principal players were all dead. The widow and son had gone back to Arizona after Rodriguez died, determined to avoid all publicity. Honeyman had tried to track them down, but with no great enthusiasm when it became obvious it wasn't going to be easy. The book needed to be written, quickly before memory of the story died or some other hack got in first. Sometimes a mystery was better than a plain, everyday solution, doubt more seductive than blunt certainty. The idea that Prosper got torn apart for no reason except its own hypocrisy made the story more compelling in a way. Myth sold more than truth, or so his editor believed.

When they went through the astonishing worldwide sales figures just before *The Fire* came out in paperback, that gray, intellectual man in an office in Manhattan declared there was an underlying truth to the tale that struck a chord with readers at that time. What happened in Prosper offered proof life was never certain, nothing truly solid. All the money and apparent power in the world might not save you when the tsunami hit. That was as true for a hypocritical school principal in a small town in upstate New York as it was for some big Wall Street finance guy finding all his past misdemeanors coming home to roost.

But even the myth was a lie. Vern Miller had proved that now, and there was no turning back. Rodriguez had been a victim too, framed for something he didn't do. The real perpetrator left to go free, with only Fred Miller still on the trail, from a dead-end job in Burnsville, a place where his life would, within the space of a year, come to a bloody end.

Right then, in the hot and airless study in Maledetto, Honeyman would have given his right arm for a web connection, a phone, anything that could put him in touch with the outside world. He wasn't used to research without those kinds of tools anymore. Deprived of the ability to settle or disprove an idea in a couple of keystrokes, he felt lost. The low and rocky shores of the tiny island in the lagoon formed the borders of his world, a small, dark, sweaty confined one where the only knowledge he had was the information that resided on his laptop, and any files Vern Miller deigned to send him.

There'd been too much of the last for his liking. This was a kind of chase, but one that had been defined by a distinct paper trail laid down by a man out in the chapel ruins. It was time to go through all the years of files he owned already and see if anything of use lurked there.

The week before Honeyman quit the *News-Ledger* to write *The Fire,* he'd gone into the office one night and downloaded two years of the paper's print and web editions onto his laptop. He had no right, but no one was there to stop him. The data was still on his new laptop, all five gigs of it, a record of a place and time he remembered only selectively.

Everything was in that sprawling web of pages and photos and links, from lost dogs to marriages and deaths, the odd court case and, for the few months that Mohawk Lake was the only story in town, every last piece the paper had carried. Honeyman believed he knew each and every story; he'd written most of them, after all. But there was more to life in Prosper than Mohawk Lake, even when it seemed the tragedy had consumed the town and everyone in it.

Time to look at the details.

～

VERNON MILLER WAS a bright student who went from Lafayette High to college in Seattle. There he'd worked freelance for tech companies around the West Coast, an engineering job in networking. A geek. One so obscure he might never have been written about again.

Except he joined the National Guard Reserves, a decision that provided a story and a picture for the *News-Ledger* when he took part in an annual military readiness event at Camp Grayling, Michigan, just three months before Mia Buckingham and Scott Sorrell had their fatal assignation by Mohawk Lake. There Vern was, just twenty-two, manning some kind of artillery position, looking the part next to the long barrel of the weapon: tough, determined, macho. Son of local cop proves patriotic too. Free copy. Free photo. Just the kind of thing Jeff McAllister liked to fill the pages of his rag.

Just the kind of thing that made Honeyman think that, even with Lauren's stolen handgun, the two of them weren't much of a match for Vern Miller.

The photos of Mia in the shack bothered him too, especially their provenance. Between advertising, editorial and accounting, the *News-Ledger* employed eight people, two of them part-time. Jeff McAllister had been feeling unusually generous when the offer of a prize promotion came in, along with some hefty discounts if he wanted to spread some more around. Pretty much everyone in the office had gotten one. Cheaper than a pay raise, Honeyman guessed. Jeff himself... he had some fancy Nikon DSLR. A real newsman's camera, he said, not that McAllister was even close to being that. The cops knew he was one of Mia Buckingham's lovers. The stains on her sheets left no doubt there. But he had that alibi: a girlfriend in the country. The Feds had checked it out. If they believed Jeff then maybe...

Honeyman typed 'Casio' into the search field for the *News-Ledger* database and got six stories up on the screen. Four were plugs for the contest, one an uncritical review for the camera. The last a list of the winners.

'Jesus,' Honeyman whispered. 'Who'd have guessed?'

ALMOST ELEVEN A.M. by the time he'd finished, another bright and sunny day outside. Honeyman grabbed the walkie-talkie and hit the button. Took a while but eventually Miller came back.

So what's the deal with the Casio?

The guy could follow everything Honeyman typed on the screen. He had to have seen the search. Probably could trawl through the newspaper archive himself.

'You know. You must, Vern. Those pictures weren't from his Panasonic.'

Oh yeah. My dad picked up on that when I showed him. He was old and couldn't figure out computers. Used to ask my advice. He sent me those files. First thing you do with a picture is check the EXIF. Panasonic does not equal Casio. So I guess you're right. For what it's worth.

'If we're going to get to the bottom of this we need to work together.'

No, Mister Honey Bee. You need to give me what I want. Or else I burn you both.

'How do I know you'll keep the deal?'

Only one way to find out, Tommy. Do what I want. You think you've got a choice?

'You don't really care about Mohawk Lake, Vern, do you? This is about who shot your father.'

Wrong. It's about both. My dad got killed trying to put a name to whoever set that fire. Seems logical enough to me that they're one and the same guy. Don't you think?

'I don't know.'

Well. That is a shame. For you and your kid.

'Your old man interviewed Jackson Wynn. You sent me that. Why?'

For god's sake, are you just dumb or something? I got all this stuff, and I don't know what to make of it. I was in Seattle when you were tearing that town apart. You're here to make sense of these things. I can't. Pop sent me all kinds of junk before he died. He was kind of going crazy. Drinking again.

Said someone was following him. He thought maybe they'd broken into his apartment and taken some stuff. I don't know what's real and what's not. That's your job. You tell me.

'Why couldn't he give up?'

Seriously? Giving up was never his thing. I thought maybe you'd noticed. What made it worse, those bastards chased him out of a job, chased him out of town. He wanted to hit back. Maybe he would have too if someone hadn't shot him.

Honeyman called up the story he'd found. It was just two paragraphs, and Vern Miller couldn't have spotted the details or surely he'd have mentioned the fact. Two paragraphs naming the winners of the camera competition. A woman from out of town. A retiree from the mill.

And Jackson Wynn.

'Jackson won a Casio camera from us. Amazing we gave him the thing, frankly. He had a record. Your old man knew. Everyone did. He was a creep. He liked spying on people. Women in particular. Did you know that?'

Silence.

'Vern. Let me ask this again. Do you think you know who killed them?'

If I did, do you think I'd be here?

The laptop beeped. Something coming in.

Here's something else. A kind of confession.

'Excuse me?'

Never mind. I'm gonna send you these things, and you write them up. Just like you wrote your own story. Same style. Same voice.

'Why?'

Because I want to see what it looks like when you tell it. Maybe things can get... I don't know... clearer.

There was a sound behind Honeyman. A cough. Light, young, familiar.

'Dad?' Lauren was at the door, dressed, clutching two cups of coffee. 'You getting somewhere?'

'Maybe. I'm not sure.'

But she didn't seem to be listening. 'What's that noise?'

Shit! Shit! Shit!

The handset was squawking louder than it seemed possible, and Vern Miller sounded furious again.

Honeyman. You do everything I say. Now. Every last thing. You understand?

Then he heard it too. The rattle of a boat engine, and this time it was getting closer. Something from the world outside.

Do what I tell you. Don't make me mad. Or she'll pay first...

THE REAL ESTATE business in Venice was usually quiet, midsummer. This year even more so, Giorgio Morosini felt. When he started out in his small office in San Marco, most of the sales and rentals were local, to Venetians or other Italians wanting a home in the city, maybe a job in tourism or simply the pleasure of living somewhere they'd never see a motor vehicle. Over the years, everything had changed. Foreign money, some of it from places he never expected—China, Russia, the Middle East—had poured into the city, much of it buying up apartments that had once gone to locals for cheap rent. Instead, they got converted to short and lucrative stays for tourists. He hadn't sold a property to a Venetian in two years. He wasn't surprised. The prices were far beyond local salaries.

The foreign income was welcome, but it came with a cost. His own son, just out of university at Ca' Foscari, couldn't even find a room he could afford anywhere and had gone to live with his mother on the mainland. A loss Morosini felt from time to time, and his not infrequent affairs with visiting foreigners never quite made up for it.

Then there were the oddities. People with a sudden urge to splash a million euros or more on properties that sometimes they'd only seen on his website. Black money was washing through the place. Over the years Morosini had come to notice that every blip in the financial world—crisis or major shock—shook money out of foreign banks the way storms loosened tiles from the city's ancient rooftops.

There had been a time when that didn't matter. But not now. The authorities were wary of the floods of cash running through banks and real estate agencies and local businesses. So, by law, he had to fill in forms and say where the funds for property purchases came from. And, if he was doing his duty, alert the authorities to suspicious approaches. A part of him, the guilty Venetian native, didn't even mind.

The American who'd been in touch about Maledetto fell squarely into the category Morosini deemed 'suspicious'. It wasn't just that the man had been happy to get ferried all the way out to the far reaches of the lagoon, then demanded to be left there for most of the day and picked up, all for free. The email address he left was wrong. The phone number no longer worked. Morosini could find no trace of the name he left on the contact form—Jerome Franklin—or anything else to say he was based in Switzerland as he'd claimed.

Something stank, and more than anything it was the way the fellow had asked so many searching questions about Thomas Honeyman. A writer whose star had once briefly shone but long waned. All the same, Mister Franklin had wanted to know how often he visited, when he would next be around, what he did when he came here. Morosini had answered enthusiastically, gilding the lily as any good salesman would. Maybe some fake glitter could put a shine on a dump like Maledetto. If it worked... who cared?

It was only later, when the elusive Mister Franklin seemed to be no more than a phantom, that he'd had second thoughts about the whole affair and begun to worry that, perhaps, he was a party to more than a simple sightseer wanting to look around Maledetto for nothing. There was, he felt, something odd about the whole affair.

So, one week after taking the mythical American out into the distant marshes of the lagoon, he'd steered his shiny private launch to a hotel in Cannaregio and picked up one of his latest foreign friends —on this occasion Magda, a Polish divorcee, early forties, very slim and blonde and talkative. An attractive companion on the surface who loved her food, even if she complained with every course Morosini fed her that she was going to wind up fat.

'I will,' he declared as he turned his boat out onto the broad lagoon beyond the Fondamente Nove, 'show you a side of Venice few people ever see. Then introduce you to my friend, the world-famous author Thomas Honeyman. You've heard of him, I'm sure.'

She hadn't. Not that it mattered much at all. Morosini, a perceptive man, had been concerned about the American ever since that curious conversation the day he arrived. Whatever the quiet and reclusive writer thought, he would receive a visitor, like it or not.

'WHERE ARE WE?' Magda demanded as the skiff approached the island. 'I see no restaurants.'

'I won't let you starve, sweetheart,' Morosini told her from the stern. 'How about your ex-husband? Is the divorce arranged? Has he sent you the money for an apartment yet?'

'The divorce is through. The money isn't.' She sat in the prow of the boat, occasionally trying to stroke Bruno, Morosini's black Labrador, then retreating when he growled. 'Is that all you're after, Giorgio? Typical Venetian.'

'Not at all, darling. I was worried about you wasting so much on rent in that *pensione* of yours. You deserve better. A home of your own. In your own style. Dorsoduro. You have the look of Dorsoduro about you. Elegant. Refined.'

She half-turned to look ahead. Morosini was more concerned with the state of the water. It was shallow all around Honeyman's private island, with only a single channel safe enough to take them in. One mistake and he could wind up grounded in the muddy shallows, then have to climb out to free them. Which would not go down well with his guest.

'You're a sweet-talking bastard. I hate you and will continue to hate you until you find me lunch. Are you sure we're in the right place? It looks a dump. Do writers always live in dumps?'

Quite often, Morosini thought from experience. But she was right. When he looked up he saw the boathouse was a burned-out shell, blackened timbers protruding out of caked and sooty earth. Honeyman's small dinghy was nowhere to be seen. There was someone around, however. A young woman in cut-off jeans and a t-shirt bearing the name of one of the cruise lines which, as a true Venetian, Morosini loathed with a vengeance for the way they despoiled the city, scarcely delivering a cent of local income in return.

Whoever it was, she was waving at them and smiling.

Morosini edged the boat into the jetty and docked by the best section of planking he could find. The rest was blackened by smoke. The smell of fire lingered.

'I suggest you stay here with Bruno,' he told Magda with a smile. 'Please don't pat him. He's choosy.'

'Hɪ.'

American. Young. Thin and twitchy.

'I was looking for Thomas Honeyman—'

'My dad.'

'Ah. He has company for once. I'm pleased. He's usually so solitary.'

'Yeah. I'm Lauren. And you are?'

She was glancing round, arms folded tight in front of her chest.

'Giorgio Morosini.' He held out his hand and she shook it, damp palms, very quickly. 'Thomas engaged me to sell this place.' He glanced at the burned-out boathouse. 'It seems in worse condition than I thought.'

'Can of gas went up the other night.'

'How?'

She shrugged and said, 'Can I help?'

'I would like to talk to him. About business.'

'Gone out.' She gestured at the pier. 'No boat. See? He said he had to go to Burano to get some things. Maybe he'd eat out. I don't know when he'll be back.'

'Oh.' He pulled out his phone. 'So I can call him then? He should have a signal. Not like here.'

'Don't think he took his phone.' She tapped her head. 'He's in that kind of writing space right now. Hard to talk to him, frankly. Also...' There was the briefest of smiles. 'I think having me here gets on his nerves a bit. So he dashed off.'

From the boat Magda announced, 'I am hungry. No. Correction. Giorgio, I am *starving.*'

'Lauren. Is everything all right with your father?'

She frowned and said, 'Sure. He's just busy, that's all. Why wouldn't it be?'

'It's just... Thomas seemed distracted when I talked to him. When he arrived.'

'Ah.' She wound her arms free and tugged at her hair. *A pretty kid*, he thought. Maybe troubled too. 'We had kind of a family argument for a while. We're working on fixing it. Takes time. And space.'

'Oh. I hope you'll find that here.'

He knew all about the family, of course. He could take a hint too.

'It's fine. We're getting there. Slowly.'

Now he felt guilty for the intrusion.

'I'm pleased to hear that. Perhaps another time then.'

The young woman was thinking.

'If you come back Sunday he'll be done. Some company then would be nice.'

'Ah, yes! Saturday night he enjoys the fireworks. Then Sunday we celebrate his new book. *Redentore.* Thomas always uses that as a kind of marker, doesn't he?'

'Yeah.' She held out her hand and he shook it again. 'Lauren. Like I said... me and Dad have been kind of... estranged for a while. A lot of personal stuff to get through. But Sunday would be great.'

'Lunch,' Magda declared, and a low growl from the dog seemed to concur.

'Sunday,' Morosini agreed and waved a finger at the woman in the boat. 'There's a place on Mazzorbo Thomas told me about, Magda. We'll all go. You'll like my American author friend. And his daughter.

Well, then.' He looked at the burned-out boathouse and the scorched grass that made a blackened fringe around it. All that would have to be fixed before he'd bring any potential customer here again. '*Ciao, Lauren.*'

HONEYMAN STOOD AT A SECOND-FLOOR WINDOW, watching them leave from behind a curtain, praying that Lauren would be fine, Morosini and the woman with him too. The launch backed out slowly from the blackened remains of the pier, turned in the narrow channel, then headed out to the open lagoon. The zigzag route it took was marked by the mud banks of the shallows and the darker water that indicated the deeps. It looked as if they were headed for Burano. Or maybe Torcello, its stump of a cathedral campanile visible on the horizon like a lone rock finger pointing to a god in the sky.

Lauren stayed by the jetty, hands on her hips, Vern Miller's orders in her head, he guessed.

Get rid of them or else. Don't give them anything. A note. Any reason to get suspicious. Or I swear to God I'll shoot them now. Take them on the boat—man, woman, dog and all.

He'd sent her out there with one of the security cameras attached to her belt, hidden beneath the t-shirt. He could probably hear every word, so long as the Wi-Fi still worked.

A man who'd come prepared.

A man who watched from the ruined chapel, perhaps in the tower. With his sniper rifle at the ready.

Morosini's boat worked its way through the shallow channels around the island, then found the deep water the larger vessels used. Honeyman could hear the whine of the engine shift up a couple of tones, see the nose of the boat buck skyward under the throttle.

Then the door downstairs opened.

Lauren was in the study by the time he got there, depositing the camera from her belt on the desk.

'What did you say...?'

'Not now, Dad.'

She was shaking as she picked up the walkie-talkie.

'Don't start, Vern. They're gone.'

Yeah. But you told them to come back.

'On Sunday. If we don't have a boat... any way to get out of here. We need that, don't we?'

I didn't ask for it. Did I?

She clutched the handset to her chest to silence it.

'It's OK, Dad. Thinking ahead.'

'Christ, Lauren. Don't push him too hard.'

'I'm sick of getting spied on. Sick of lots of things.' She uncovered the walkie-talkie and hammered the button again. 'Vern. The guy has no idea anything's wrong here. You heard. How about we get something in return?'

A long moment, then the laptop beeped and three new files appeared on the desktop: two text documents, one audio.

Time to go back to work. Here's your raw material. My old man. What he did. Some of what he left me. You can work out what happened. Like I said, a confession. Not yours this time. Get writing, Mister Honey Bee. Time's short. Oh, and put the security camera back on the wall where you found it.

When Honeyman looked Lauren was crying, slowly, reluctantly, tears of fury and fear, he guessed. He wiped the damp away with a finger and kissed her wet cheek.

'Dammit, you turned out brave.'

'No. Mom was brave. And then she killed herself, which wasn't brave at all. I never did understand that. Did you?'

There was that awkward moment of intimacy again, unexpected, almost unwanted. The family was fractured before Diane's death, in a quiet, unacknowledged way. After, there'd just been silence between him and Lauren. Now, it was as if there was an armistice, an agreement to let hostilities lie because the price of allowing them to fester then come out into the open would be too great.

'Did Mom talk to you much, Lauren? After you left for college?'

'About what?'

'About us. About me. About how she felt. Anything, really.'

'No.' Her answer sounded flat and full of regret. 'She always kept things wrapped up inside. Just like you. Just like all of us.' She grimaced. 'Why was that? What made us that way?'

'I don't know.'

'That day she killed herself I was in class. You were out here. It didn't feel anything but ordinary. Normal. Us all being apart. I grew up thinking everyone was like that. Not true, is it?'

'If I had any idea she was feeling that way I would have been on the first plane out of here. I'd never have left her side.'

She was looking out of the window, through the branches of the fig tree, back toward the chapel.

'I know. I'd have run right back to Prosper too. But we didn't. We didn't even notice.'

'Not your fault, Lauren.'

'No. Or yours. She killed herself and never once let on she was anything but Mom. Crotchety. Miserable. Mom. I'll never get around to forgiving her for that. Dumb, stupid. Not like her. Not like the Mom I knew. Or thought I did.'

Leave it there, Honeyman thought.

'We're going to get out of this, Lauren. We're going to start again. I promise.'

She laughed at that, and it was so odd he asked, 'What's funny?'

'Sometimes promises aren't a great idea, Dad. Best to just get on with things and see what happens. You kept on dreaming, didn't you? Writing more books. Thinking you'd get richer and richer. Somehow making up to us for all the holes in our lives. None of it ever worked.'

'No. And I didn't get richer and richer either. Sorry...'

He sighed and for a moment she took his fingers in hers, squeezed.

'You don't need to apologize, Dad. You tried. It's just... there's no time for dreams anymore. These are the lives we have. All we've got.' She glanced at the camera on the wall. 'And maybe our lives don't amount to much but, Jesus, I'd kind of like to keep them.'

Lauren reached down, tapped the keyboard and opened the first Word document.

It was a transcript of another interview with Jackson Wynn. The second document was a lengthy screed seemingly typed out by Fred Miller himself, full of misspellings, crazy punctuation and strange, unfinished sentences. Maybe he'd been drunk. The last file was twenty-two minutes of mp3 audio.

The transcript and the audio file were dated July 13 and 14, the year of the fire. Miller's rambling note seemed to have been written in October 2009, presumably when he was living on his own and working nights in Burnsville.

Honeyman picked up the handset.

'Vern. What do you want exactly?'

What I said. Go through your files. Then tell the story, Tommy boy. Work your magic. Give my old man his due. Set it out like it should be told. The bad and the good. Then tell me what it means.

10

PROSPER, NEW YORK

July 23, 2008

Fred Miller found Jackson Wynn in the ranger station in Prudeaux Wood at 11:30 that morning, marched in, liked the way Jackson leapt in shock as he came through the door. He took a seat by the desk and ordered Wynn to sit opposite and do as he was told.

'Jesus, son. This dump's your office?'

'Didn't invite you here.'

Miller laughed and clicked on his voice recorder. Molly could type this up when he got back. She'd moan if she heard him slap the kid around—she always did when that happened. But then she could always skip that part, let Miller write in something new for the record and make damned sure any incriminating sections on the audio file got erased.

'Just the kind of pit I'd expect from the likes of you. Smells of shit. You don't stink so good either. Time to start talking, boy. You and me all cozy here and alone in your cabin. Tell me who you saw with the Buckingham woman when you went peeking into the shack.'

Jackson swore and grabbed a can of soda, popped it with fingers shaking so much the drink went everywhere.

'My, you are nervous, boy. Tell me everything good and straight and maybe I won't haul you into a cell and throw you in court for spying on women even though I warned you not to. Now—'

'Didn't spy on no one, and you can't prove I did.'

Miller settled back in his chair. This was going well.

'Can't I now?'

'If you could you'd be doing it. Get off my back, old man.'

'Soon as you tell me the truth.'

'Didn't do nothing. Told the real cops that already.'

'Don't push my button, son. The real cops?'

'The ones that count. From Albany. Seem like good guys.'

'Good guys don't make good cops. C'mon, Jackson. Just the two of us here.'

Jackson stared at nothing, chin on chest. Miller leapt to his feet and strode over to an ancient gray filing cabinet in the corner.

'Hey, look! They gave an ignoramus like you somewhere to keep your things. Like you're a real person. Wonder what kind of stuff you got here—'

The ranger started yelling, then came over flapping at him with his puny hands.

'Don't touch that. You got no right. Ow!'

He yowled as Miller slapped him with the back of his hand.

'Lay as much as a fingernail on me again and I'm going to regard that as assault on an officer performing his duty.'

'Fucking duty...'

There they were, in the bottom drawer, hidden under a pile of letters from headquarters and organizations planning visits.

'Oh my, oh my! What *is* this? Got your girlie mags, I see. All neatly tucked away and filed under correspondence. Who are you corresponding with, boy? Sure you can even write?'

Jackson was holding his cheek. It was only a little slap. Couldn't have hurt much.

'Yeah, I can write. What I read's my business.'

'Don't think the park people are paying you to jack off, door locked, thinking no one can see.'

'Leave me alone!'

'We are alone. No one else works here but you. No one's gonna disturb us. All nice and intimate, ain't it?'

'The real cops said to tell 'em if you started in on me again.'

'Did they? The real cops aren't here.'

'Everyone knows you're on the way out. Whole town's got your number now and—'

Miller pretty much lost it then, and by the time Jackson Wynn was on the floor shrieking and weeping and holding his bloody mouth he knew he was going to have to ask Molly to skip over this part of the tape altogether.

'See! See! That's what I mean. Get your freaking hands off me. You think you own this place. You don't. Touch me one more time, I swear I'll...'

The kid couldn't even carry through on a threat.

'You'll what? Start talking?'

'I said everything I got to say to you.'

Miller balled a fist. Thought about beating the kid some more. Something stopped him. Maybe it was the thought that people really were looking to steal his badge, and beating up a little creep like Jackson Wynn could give them the kind of excuse they craved.

'I could get you fired, Jackson. I could put you in jail. We could have all kinds of fun on the way there. Long time since I beat the truth out of a grubby little jerk like—'

'No, you can't. You can't do nothing anymore. They're taking all that away, you old fool, and no way you're getting any of it back.'

'All I want are some names.'

'Don't know no names.'

'Come on. Just one. To start with.'

'I don't know no names! If—'

To hell with it. He kicked Jackson hard in the shin as he crouched on the floor. Listened to him howling again, waited for the racket to die down, then said, 'You know who she was taking there. I think you watched. Didn't you? Snuck up to that one window when they were in there. Buck naked and screwing. Is that why you burned the place, Jackson? They see what you was up to?'

Jackson had scuttled into the corner, sat there, knees up, hands hugging them, blood leaking from his snotty nose.

'I didn't burn no one. You talk to the summer camp people. I was there all morning. They can tell you—'

'I think you're lying your skinny ass off 'cuz you're scared people are gonna see you for what you are. Creepy little pervert who sneaks around spying on people. Sticking your phone up ladies' skirts and taking pictures of them. Caught you doing that—'

'I stopped.'

'Don't believe you. Once a pervert, always a pervert. You think I should be asking the Feds to start spraying their jizz sprays all around this cabin? Your home? Mohawk Lake and see where you been jacking off—'

'Don't do that anymore. Now you get out of here. The state cops told me you got warned off messing 'round with their work. This is their job now. They don't like you sticking your nose in it.'

'This is my town—'

'*Was* your town.'

'Dammit, Jackson. I'm going to keep coming back until you talk, boy. Next time I find you here...'

He pocketed the voice recorder, ambled to the door, didn't say anything more, just grinned as he opened up and let the sweaty summer forest air sweep in to compete with the stench of sweat and blood and fear.

'You'll what?'

Miller grinned, blew him a kiss, said nothing at all.

Outside, he looked around the cabin clearing. There was a logging operation not far away. The trucks were making a pretty mess of the dirt road. No one near. When he came back he could do pretty much as he liked, and leave Jackson Wynn to stew in the meantime.

Best warn Molly about the tape, though. She'd have to do a little editing to take out the punches and the screams.

SEVEN IN THE morning three days later Chief Fred Miller sat in his office glaring at the computer and the latest story from the *News-Ledger*. Somehow Tom Honeyman had got hold of a forensic report on the DNA found in Mia Buckingham's apartment. It exposed the school principal, Gary Rabbitt, as one of her lovers. A meeting of the school board was being organized to discuss the man's future. Rabbitt had hightailed it out of town. His wife said she'd no idea where he'd gone.

The chief had seen this report himself. It came across his desk two days before, as part of the information-sharing agreement he had with the Staties. A deal that was now at an end after a furious phone call from Albany blaming Miller's office for the leak.

Not that they could prove it. They simply said no one on their end was giving the media anything except the skimpy material the information officers allowed. And anyway, if they *did* want to leak something they'd surely choose a better destination than a two-bit local paper on its knees. Which Miller thought was probably true. Those out-of-towners looked down on everyone in Prosper from the moment they arrived. There was also the interesting fact that the forensic report also named Jeff McAllister among the woman's partners, something the *News-Ledger* had never got around to mentioning.

It wasn't a busy police station. Only two people had seen the file when it came in: himself and his secretary, Molly Dunn.

So he waited until she turned up on the dot at eight as usual then called her into his office, turned the computer to her face, watched as she blushed and started to stutter out her denials.

'Jesus Christ, woman. You're as bad a liar as I ever saw.'

'Oh, Chief...'

She was getting redder and redder. Molly had worked in the station for eleven years and come to feel she was as much a part of its management as Miller himself, something the chief was inclined to ignore. She could be argumentative and overbearing, and of late had pushed that overstated opinion of her place in the workings of the Prosper police way too much. But she could type. Make coffee. Didn't nag him too much about his appearance and his behavior. Unlike the secretaries who'd gone before, she'd never done anything to piss him off greatly. She could bake a cake too, and brought one in from time to time, usually as an unspoken apology for one of her occasional outbursts. The one he got for his birthday, a cream cake he'd been finishing when the call came through about Mohawk Lake, was damned good. The last he was going to get as well.

'Don't give me the "Oh, Chief" crap. Why?'

She folded her arms and her eyes went glassy with tears, so much she had to take her heavy horn-rimmed spectacles off and rub at them.

'I am a decent woman in a town full of sinners.'

'Please...' Miller could feel himself getting mad. 'Couple of days ago you're giving me this shit about "Maybe I'm quitting, Chief, if you're going to give me tapes with you roughing up that creep Jackson a little." Today I find out you've been throwing confidential information into the lap of that nosy bastard Honeyman. I mean—'

'Who said I did?'

'Written all over your face.'

She didn't look so guilty anymore. Just mad.

'And what's written on your face, Fred Miller?'

'You tell me.'

'Yes. I will. Drink and jealousy. And fear. And hate. You're scared. You know this town's got your name on the shit list. Hell... Dirk and Frank and Pete don't even work for you anymore, not properly.'

That was true. His deputies had been assigned to the state team after the detectives from Albany decided they needed legmen and Miller's creaky and argumentative limbs ruled him out.

'Fuck it, Molly. Police matters aren't your business. You're here to answer the phone, type, make coffee and do what I ask.'

'See! There you go! All the foul language.'

'You just said "shit".'

'You made me!'

'How'd I do that?'

'By being you! Bad enough before, but you got worse and worse after this Mohawk Lake thing. You could do with taking a shower before you come into work as well. You stink like a farm beast sometimes...'

He pointed at the screen.

'Why?'

'I didn't say I did it.'

'Tell me that one more time and I'm gonna reach for the book and file charges.'

'What charges?'

'I'll find some. I'll make things up if I need to. I'm still the chief. I can do that.' He leaned forward, grinned the evil grin he'd developed for these occasions. 'You, of all people, understand me there, Molly Dunn. Don't you?'

'Not for much longer.'

He couldn't think of a thing to say for a moment. If his secretary was saying his time was running out, then it wouldn't be long before the rest of the town would be doing it too. Maybe they were there already.

It was a cruel thing to say but he couldn't stop himself.

'This is all about Frank, isn't it?'

'What?'

'Not my fault your husband died out on I-90. Stinking drunk with a Syracuse hooker in his cab.'

'Fuck you—'

'I thought you were bothered by the language, Molly.'

'Fuck you, Fred Miller. My Frank...' She was a short, squat woman, sweating now in the heat, glasses off, tears running down her cheeks. 'He'd have been fine if it wasn't for this place. This damned town. All sweet and perfect on the outside. Rotten as shit when you look in.'

'Molly—'

'A man like Gary Rabbitt. A school *principal*. Teaching one minute. Then hanging around with that whore he gave a job to. People like that have been poisoning this place for years and no one does a damned thing.'

'She wasn't a whore. Not that I know. Just a woman who liked company a lot.'

'A whore! All those men. Boys and god knows what else. Disgusting, filthy hussy. Gary Rabbitt would have got off scot-free if the likes of you let him. Don't want to upset things, do you? Not if it touches the people who run this town.'

Maybe that was true. Maybe a small-town police chief didn't have much choice.

'Principal Rabbitt didn't break the law as far as we know, Molly. Now you've cost him his job and his marriage too, from what I know of that tight-assed evangelical wife of his.'

'Like you care!'

He got a pen and reached for a sheet of paper then passed it over the desk.

'Can't say I do. About him. Or you. Here...' He clicked the pen. 'Write out your resignation now. Walk out that door. Don't come back. Try and see if you can get through a few days without talking to people. About this place. About what goes on. I don't want to hear you spreading more gossip, Molly. If I do I may tear up the letter you're going to write and look at putting you in court.'

He leaned forward, grinned again and winked at her.

'Now how would that look with all those lady friends of yours, huh? Molly Dunn. The paragon of virtue. The woman who sits in judgement on every last soul who walks these streets. Nothing but a common criminal standing up there in a pair of cuffs.'

Usually, Molly wore a fixed and somewhat forced smile. But that was so far gone he barely recognized her.

'You're a fool, Fred Miller,' she said as she scrawled on the paper.

'Everyone's laughing when you walk around this town. Beating up pathetic little creatures like Jackson Wynn. What kind of man does that?'

'A man who wants answers when no one's getting them. Like it or not, that's what I do.'

'Make the most of it. You'll be lucky if your fat butt's still behind that desk come fall.'

He grunted again, waved at the door as he watched her go. Then he thought about Jackson Wynn because, if he was honest with himself, he wanted to take out all his anger on someone and, seeing as Molly was a woman, it would have been wrong to expend it all on her.

The creep had more to tell. He felt sure. There was nothing else to do at the office, no one to make him coffee now. Molly would be on the phone to her friends already, spreading word she'd got fired, and soon, he guessed, she'd be proved right: probably before the leaves turned gold in Prudeaux Wood he'd be out of a job.

'Guess we need another visit,' Miller said and got his keys.

JACKSON WYNN DIDN'T SET fire to the cabin at Mohawk Lake. Miller knew that much was true. Pine Point Summer Camp gave him as solid an alibi as any man could get. The girls said he'd been hanging around the beach there for two hours that morning, watching them from his boat while they swam. After a while he didn't hide himself and came out to talk to a few of them, wondering if they'd like to go in the woods with him one day on a nature walk.

There were ten kids there, all fifteen and sixteen, a kind of gang, and not one Jackson Wynn should have been spying on if he had any sense. They knew what a creep he was. But they decided it was a game of sorts to lead him on, tease him, laugh at him, flaunt themselves as he watched goggle-eyed and dreaming.

Later that morning one of the counselors came down to check on the group swimming. He knew of Wynn from past years and had warned him off before. First, he got mad at the girls for not telling, and promised to yell at the junior staff for leaving them there on their own. Then he got madder still when Wynn began professing his innocence, flashing his work ID, saying it was his job to keep an eye on things. Especially young girls going out swimming.

As the argument escalated and Wynn planned his retreat, they saw smoke rising from across the lake. Sweating, worried, he'd put on his ranger hat and said he had to take his boat over there to look at it. That was his responsibility and no one argued as he pushed his motorboat out onto the green water. So there was firm evidence that placed him at Pine Point from just after nine that morning until after the fire started. Witness statements and some CCTV footage too. No way could he have had the time to burn Mia Buckingham and Scott Sorrell in the shack.

All of which Fred Miller knew as he drove back to Prudeaux Wood. Those reports had come across his desk as well. It was just that Miller also understood what lying looked like, and Jackson Wynn *was* lying, for sure.

THE CABIN WAS SMALL, meant to be manned by a single ranger, of late Jackson Wynn. It was a solitary spot, barely visible from the narrow forest road. All around was dense conifer, managed and worked by the local logging company. Miller rarely felt the need to wander out into that endless vista of tall pines and trees he couldn't begin to name. He knew local kids used to smoke weed there from time to time, hold parties, get up to all kinds of things. But that was outside Prosper, hidden away. What the town couldn't see, it didn't want to know about, and for the most part he was happy to go along with that.

There was a space in the trees where he could park out back. What he had in mind for Jackson wasn't going to be the kind of thing where you wanted a public record, though he'd keep his own phone recording just in case, and make some notes for himself after too. So best if no one saw he was there from the road. Also, Wynn would surely get the message when he saw the police truck tucking itself away in the trees.

The white-and-blue Ford slid onto a bed of pine needles behind the cabin. By the time Miller got to the door Jackson Wynn was out, half-running toward his own vehicle, scared as a squirrel that just heard a shot.

Miller got him by the truck door, grabbed a hold of his jacket, and slammed his face straight into the side window. Blood leaked down the glass. A little early for that, but all the same it felt good.

'All I came for was a little chat, Jackson,' he said with a cheery grunt. 'Rude to run away, boy. Outright impolite, if you ask me.'

He slammed his fist hard in the ranger's gut then dragged him back inside, threw him on the rough wood floor.

Miller scratched his nose with his forefinger. There was blood on there. Wynn's.

'Like I said before. Can't help but wonder what those clever crime scene people would find if they came poking around here.'

The ranger glared at him from the timber planks.

'You're gonna get into big trouble, old man. The State cops said to call if you came here again and—'

A hard kick to the chest killed that conversation. Miller picked him up off the floor and deposited him on a chair at the table next to the cabin's phone. Pulled the cord right out of the wall. No cell signal out here. No laptop.

'Well,' he said. 'Now we can be alone. Talk to me, kid. That's all I ask.'

Blood was pouring from Jackson Wynn's nose. His right eye was swollen and turning pink. Miller knew how to hurt people without marking them. It was a talent he'd developed over the years. This was not his best effort at all.

'Told you already, you old bastard—'

Another punch, hard into Wynn's flabby stomach, and that one just happened. Maybe he was still smarting at Molly's treachery. Or he just didn't care any longer. So many people telling him he was finished in Prosper. Even his own secretary. Leaking stuff to the paper. Straight off his desk. He ought to have done more than just fire her.

The ranger was dry-retching, weeping, scarlet-gray snot dripping from his nose and bruised, distorted lips.

'You look a sight, Jackson. A man in a uniform. What a mess.'

'I don't know—'

'Don't say that! Quit lying. Bad for you. All you got to do is spit out a name.'

Wynn went quiet and Miller thought, *He's going to talk.*

More calmly now, the chief went on, 'All I need to know is what you saw. I don't think you killed those two. I know you were too busy eyeing up those girls at Pine Point. They saw you. The counselors saw you. So you're safe. Which makes me wonder...' He took off his cap and scratched his head. 'Why in god's name are you being so secretive? You got to have something to hide. For the life of me all I can think of is you're scared shitless I'm gonna put you in a cell when I find out what it is. Take your job from you. Put you back in the hole this town dragged you out of back when they were stupid enough to give you another chance. Which I'm gonna do if you don't start talking. Either way you're screwed. Only chance you got, Jackson, is you come clean, come real clean, right now.'

He patted Wynn's hair, took a pack of tissues out of his pocket, handed it over, then took the chair opposite.

'Clean yourself up. Tell me what you know. Got bigger fish to fry than a little minnow like you. How hard can this be?'

Silence.

'You were watching her there?'

Wynn pulled out a tissue and started to wipe his nose, smearing the blood and snot everywhere.

'You *were* watching Mia Buckingham there. And maybe something else.' Miller put a finger to his cheek, thinking. 'Taking pictures again. That's what turns you on, ain't it? Taking pictures. Then bringing them back home.' He tapped the tissue pack. 'Putting Mister Kleenex's kids through college all night long while you whack off.

Caught you there before, Jackson. Should have put you away last time I found you up to your tricks and—'

'Fuck you, old man.'

Miller folded his arms.

'Now that is no way to talk, boy. You and me alone here. Jesus. I could do what I want. I could bury your miserable corpse out in those woods and no one would ever know.' He leaned down into the ranger's face and winked. 'Maybe I've done that before, huh? Killed people. Hidden them out here in your big green wilderness. Prosper's a quiet, tidy town, Jackson, and the wheels of justice do turn slow. Maybe I greased them a little once in a while. What do you think?'

Jackson's bottom lip quivered then he said, 'She took my camera.'

'What?'

'That teacher bitch. Came out all roaring mad, tits and bush and everything and didn't mind. Snatched my camera off of me. The one I won from the paper.'

'Who was she with? What was his name?'

Jackson Wynn looked as if his head was somewhere else.

'*My* camera. Best I ever had. Bitch.'

'Not going to keep on asking, son. I wanna know who he was. Tell me that and maybe I'll let you stay here. Stay a ranger. Just so long as you keep away from the women—'

'You ain't in no position to tell me anything. You're dead in this town. Just walking around like the old fool—'

Hell, Miller thought. *At least I tried.*

He was across the table, big fist raised, when Jackson lunged with the thing he'd held half-hidden below the table edge.

The chief yelped, and a spurt of blood flew through the air between them.

It was an army knife, one of its many blades upright.

'Don't come near me again, you bastard!' the ranger yelled and, quick as one of Prudeaux's lithe young bucks, he leapt for the door.

He had more than twenty years on Miller who was bleeding anyway, sucking at the slash across the ball of his palm from Wynn's knife, trying to work out what to do next.

'Run all you like, Jackson! I'm gonna find you. Get that name out of you. Then throw you in front of a judge.'

He lurched to the door.

Elbows working, legs flying out, Wynn was scooting down to the dock on the eastern edge of Mohawk Lake. Miller could see the Park Service's speedboat there, the fastest they owned, saved for chasing errant fishermen and hunters from time to time and showing off for the visitors.

A narrow blacktop road crossed in front of the pier, littered with logging debris, broken branches, leaves, and trails of fresh sawdust.

Miller wasn't going to be able to follow Jackson once he got to the boat. The ranger turned out not quite as stupid he seemed. Or so the chief thought until a truck came around the bend, way too fast, rolling sideways with its load: tall lumber, trunks stacked high and wide, horn blaring angrily.

The skinny ranger didn't stand a chance at all as the truck wiped him across the lane.

Miller watched from the shadows of the cabin, sucking on the wound across his palm. Not deep. Not long. Another time he'd maybe stop by the doctor and get it looked at. But not now. Nobody had seen him out in Prudeaux Wood. From what he'd witnessed of the end of Jackson Wynn—a broken corpse mangled under the giant wheels of the lumber truck, messed up in a way Miller didn't want to look at too closely—he wouldn't be telling anyone either.

So the little creep was taking photos of Mia Buckingham and her mystery lover. Got caught. Got his camera taken off him. Turned scared when Miller said he might wind up in court and ran away straight into the path of a lumber truck. *No great loss*, the chief thought. In principle anyway. Except he still didn't have a name for the other party or a clue where to start.

Miller went out the back door and took the police car down the narrow lane along the forest trail. No one used that. No one was going to know he'd been anywhere near the cabin. Not unless they came looking for tire tracks and evidence, and the only person who'd care enough about a sad loner like Jackson Wynn would be the chief of police of Prosper. Who'd write this off as an accident soon as he could.

The park service had just lost a ranger, that was all. On duty too. Maybe, he thought, they'd put up a plaque.

Eleven minutes later as he was driving into town his phone rang. There'd been an accident reported out at Prudeaux.

'On my way,' Miller said and turned around.

11

VENICE

Friday
Deadline: 1 day. 2 hours. 52 minutes.

Friday night, just after nine. Honeyman stared at the screen, scanning his words. Fred Miller's too. A life reduced to a few pages recounting a story that had stayed hidden for twelve years. So many revelations in those notes and the desperate confrontation recorded in the audio file. And the answer to something that had been bugging him for years too. The name of his one anonymous informer.

'Molly Dunn. Now *that* I never guessed.'

He grabbed the walkie-talkie.

'Vern. You knew it was Jackson Wynn who took those photos. You knew and you never said.'

No answer. It was dark by now. Night birds were hooting and cackling beyond the windows. Clouds scampered across a near-full moon, dappled light falling through the fig tree.

Of course Vern Miller never said. Understanding who took the pictures was only the smaller part of the puzzle. The real question was how they made their way into the camera he'd found in Jorge Rodriguez's trailer.

As always when the writing flowed, hours had vanished unnoticed. Honeyman had found himself lost inside the dead chief's shocking story and wondered how it had felt for the man himself. Miller went to pieces not long after, and that wasn't just because the town set the wheels in motion to kick him out. Something happened to him. Honeyman could see that at the time in the glazed, doomed look in his eyes. For all his bluster in Mia Buckingham's apartment, Fred Miller was, in his own eyes, a decent cop. Beating up suspects, tampering with evidence, throwing his weight around was part of the job for his generation, or so he thought. All the same, Honeyman felt the guy would certainly stop short of bending the law to frame an innocent man. Miller might not have regretted Jackson Wynn's death. The shakily written notes he left seemed to emphasize that. But the unexpected, unsought conclusion to that confrontation out in Prudeaux Wood surely acted as a catalyst. Confirmation that his tidy, ordered world was falling apart, and fast. Miller was a man who sought revelations in others but never himself. The stain of Jackson Wynn's blood was going to be hard to shake until that night in Burnsville, a year and a few months later, when it ceased to matter at all.

'Who's Molly Dunn?'

He hadn't realized Lauren was behind him. She took the seat by his side. What she'd been doing all this time… he had no idea.

'Miller's secretary. Prosper born and bred. Friendly on the outside and always staring at you with those judgmental eyes, asking: *Are you really good enough for around here?* A kind of uptight, churchy woman who looked down her nose at pretty much everyone. The kind—'

'I know the kind. I grew up there, Dad.'

'Looks like she was the one who leaked me the DNA results that got Principal Rabbitt fired. Sorry. I kind of got lost in all this. It's as if…'

As if the story was starting to come to life in a way it never had before. Not that he wanted to say that. Or welcomed the idea.

'No need to apologize, Dad. I saw you were busy, so I slept. For ages. Feel better now. So why would Molly Dunn do that?'

He tapped the arrow keys and handed her his chair.

'Read it for yourself. You always like to think people leak things out of a kind of sense of decency. That's a fairy tale reporters tell themselves to make them feel better. Mostly they're not whistle-blowers at all. The motive's something personal. A grudge. A way of getting back at someone. Sounds like Molly saw herself as some kind of moral guardian of the town. Watching all its dirty secrets get buried. Didn't like it. Didn't like Miller much either, or the way he was throwing his weight around. Mostly at the wrong people. Maybe she felt powerless and thought she was owed something. She sure as hell wanted Principal Rabbitt's scalp. Jeff McAllister's too, except I kept that quiet until the book came out.'

'Your old boss must really hate you.'

True, Honeyman thought. But there were worse things he had to live with.

'Big deal... I was gone from the *News-Ledger* by the time the book came out. And anyway I never left jobs on good terms. Didn't want to allow myself the chance to go back. That's me, I guess. Going back was always an admission of defeat. Of failure.'

'Except going back to Mohawk Lake now?'

'No. That just seemed to be a necessity. Maybe it was always coming.'

Lauren sat down and scrolled to the beginning of the chapter.

'Can I read it?'

'Not a pretty story.'

'Didn't expect it was.' She squinted at the screen. 'It's funny. My memories of all this are kind of bent. Mostly I saw it from Mom's point of view.'

'Because I was being an asshole writing all those stories. The book.'

'Quit being oversensitive. You weren't there most of the time. Also I was young. There were all those teenage hormones pushing and shoving inside me. Guess you know that.'

'You weren't so bad.'

'Not sure I believe you there.'

'Would I lie to you?'

She thought about that.

'If you thought you had to. Yes. You and Mom always wanted to protect me, even when I didn't need protecting. It's a parent thing. You weren't that unusual.'

Honeyman didn't say a thing.

'Dad.' Her voice was quiet, young again. 'I know this is all still real in a way for you. But not me. It's dead. Gone. In the past. Like Mom. A memory you're aware of but one you can't let keep you awake at nights. I don't think about her, because if I do, it makes me mad. Feels like she betrayed us, walking into Mohawk Lake. Choosing that day, the anniversary of when those two died. Leaving a stupid note no one understood. Why'd she do that?'

'I don't know. Did she... did she say anything to you?'

'No.'

'Nothing?'

Lauren tapped the screen, running her finger down the story there.

'Not a thing. I want to read this, Dad. You go take a break.'

HE LEFT her there and went to the kitchen, got a glass of San Pellegrino and sat at the dining table trying to think. His head no longer hurt. Vern hadn't beaten him as badly as he might have.

The notes from Vern's father were rambling, crazy in parts, so illiterate and furious, Fred Miller must have typed at least some of them drunk. They were full of such bitterness and only one regret. Not that he'd pushed Jackson Wynn into a violent end, then run away from the consequences. Just that the ranger died without ever saying who he saw with Mia Buckingham that day.

The chief wasn't the kind of man to give up on a task like that, even when they kicked him out of the police.

After a while Honeyman went back into the study and half-lay on the sofa, dozing while Lauren read, until he fell into a deep, dead slumber.

'Hey. Sleepyhead.'

It was dark outside and she was shaking him awake.

'What time is it?'

'Coming up to midnight.'

Less than twenty-four hours left before he was supposed to come up with a name.

'Has Vern said anything?'

'Nope. I tried getting him on the walkie-talkie but he never answered.' She looked at the desk. 'You can really write, can't you?'

'The one small talent I have.'

'You make it sound like you were there. Like you were watching these people. How do you do it?'

'You imagine yourself into it.'

'That's a creepy talent.'

'Yeah. The only one I've got.'

With Miller's notes and the audio, he'd fallen into the task very easily. It was the same with the first book. Take what facts you had then weave them into a convincing narrative. Turn someone else's story into yours.

Honeyman glanced at the wall camera, then at her.

'Want to take a break? Get something to eat?'

She was always quick.

'Sure.'

They went into the kitchen. He put his hand over the wine bottle when she went for it and poured water instead. Made sandwiches as if this was normal. Then he grabbed the radio.

'Hey. I know. Let's listen to the news. Remember, there's a world out there.'

There was a talk show on. Loud Italian voices, men and woman arguing about the fiery state of Italian politics, immigration and the EU, whether the heat and drought were because of climate change or just one of those things.

The bickering filled the airy kitchen, all the more when Honeyman turned up the volume.

They were close enough to hear one another.

Lauren leaned over.

'Maybe he can lip read. Maybe he's got some app on his computer that does it for him.'

She'd seen what Vern Miller's camp was like, close up. They went over it again. The big, military-style tent and the arsenal. The cans of gas, for the holed inflatable and the generator. Maybe for more than that too. A couple of sleeping bags. He'd let her use one, but only with plastic restraints around her wrists and ankles, the kind the cops had.

'Anything else?'

'He's got a phone. I saw him using it once. He was trying to hide it from me, but I'm pretty sure. Should have mentioned it before.'

'No cell phone signal out here, Lauren. Not for any of the networks. I'd know if there was.'

Mouth full just like when she was a kid, she said, 'Not that kind of phone. A satellite one. Big and bulky. We have them on the cruise ships in case there are emergencies when we're at sea and out of range.'

'You hear him talking to anyone?'

'No. But I've seen him using it near his laptop. They do data too.'

'You mean he's in touch with people?'

'I guess...'

'So he could call and get out of here any time he likes? It doesn't matter that he shot that dinghy from under us?'

She wrinkled her nose and said, 'Yeah. I never thought about that.' Lauren still seemed lost in the story. 'Why is Vern making you do this? Re-write the story for him. It's like...'

'Like what?'

'Like he wants to use it somehow. As if it's a kind of confession.'

'I've got nothing to confess.'

She looked straight at him.

'Do you think he believes you?'

Lauren grabbed the wine bottle and poured herself a glass. He couldn't stop her.

'I don't think he knows what to believe. How much did you read?'

'All that chapter. Some of what you wrote earlier. And I read your book. Had to. That was weird.'

'Just the first one? *The Fire*?'

Lauren grimaced.

'Just the first one. The others weren't my sort of thing.'

Honeyman closed his eyes and laughed. She was always honest. Too much so at times.

'Never mind. You're not the only one. Felt like I was writing for myself most of the time.'

'But you're good at this. When it's for real. Quick too. It reads that way, all slick and fast. There were a few typos in there. I corrected them. Hope you don't mind...'

'You're my editor now?'

She smiled.

'If you want me to be.'

'Your mom always mentioned the little mistakes first. Before anything else. She'd never help me correct them.'

'Well, that was Mom. No need to be offended. You were writing in a hurry.'

'Comes from being a reporter. When I was starting out, big stories close to deadline, you had to call it in, dictate it to the copy desk. Straight out of your head. No laptops, no cell phones. Back when I worked in Chicago...'

'And you gave that up for Prosper?'

'No. I gave that up for your mom. We met on an assignment I did there. A feature about the timber industry. We told you all this...'

'Sure you did. I was a kid. Did you think I was listening?'

He was the one who wasn't listening at that moment. Honeyman was lost in his memories.

'Diane was so much better at the fast stuff than me. She always had this quick, practical brain. Couldn't write well, not real writing. Always kind of clunky. But when it came to reporting...'

'You ever get things wrong?'

A pointed question.

'Not often.'

'But the book?'

'The book seemed right at the time.'

She waited, and then he said, 'Is there anything you want to tell me?'

'Not that I can think of.' A quick shrug. 'Anything you want to tell me?'

There was a squawk from the other room. The walkie-talkie. Honeyman was grateful for that.

'I think he wants me.'

'I think he can wait.'

She leaned in closer and whispered in his ear.

'Listen. I watched him when he's sending you the files. He's bent over his laptop in his tent like there's nothing else in the world. This guy's a maniac. Clever, but weird and obsessive.'

'Kind of got that message—'

'Yeah. Well, I stole us that gun. I can stay here now, make out like you're in the house and we're talking. But you're out of sight. You go shoot him. Shoot him in the head. Shoot him in the back. Or just in the leg, if you like. I don't care.'

He didn't say anything.

'Christ, Dad. Don't look at me that way. I'm not saying that because of what he did to me. I just think... maybe it's the best chance we have of getting out of here alive.'

'And if I screw up?'

'You won't.'

He'd thought of that already, thought of the photo of Miller in uniform, happy around weapons. Imagined the cost of failure. It wasn't just his life on his line.

'Or,' she added, 'you stay here and keep talking, keep typing, and I'll do it.'

'Not a good idea.' The walkie-talkie crackled again from the other room. 'The risk—'

'He's playing with us, Dad. Teasing. Tormenting. I keep telling you. The moment he's got what he wants, he's coming for us anyway. He wants to burn us just like someone burned those two at Mohawk Lake. He thinks he owes his old man. I can see it in his eyes.'

He took her arm, trying to find the right words. It was always easier to argue with Lauren than reason. That much, he knew, hadn't changed.

'That isn't going to happen.' Again the squawk. 'I've got to go talk to him. We've left it long enough.'

FOR ONCE VERN MILLER didn't sound too mad.

Hey, Tom. That chapter wasn't so bad.

'Thanks. I guess.'

You made my dad sound like my dad.

'I met him plenty of times, Vern. He said a lot in his notes. He always had his own voice, no one else's.'

That awkward pause, then the fury was back.

Don't give me that shit. Don't talk to me like we're friends or something. You didn't know him. I don't think any of us did. So what do you think?

About what? Miller seemed so sensitive, so quick to anger and close to the edge, Honeyman had to measure his reply.

'I think your old man must have been quite damaged. From what I recall he was a real law-and-order guy. Wanted to see justice done. Had a strong sense of right and wrong. Walking away from an injured man like that—'

He wasn't injured. Jackson Wynn was dead. Messed-up piece of meat under the wheels of that truck. Gone in a second. The paper covered the story, remember?

God, he'd done his homework.

'True. He didn't stand a chance. The point I was trying to make was...walking away wasn't your father's style. He searched trouble out if he could. Not that we had a lot in Prosper. Turning his back on Jackson Wynn that day must... It must have been like he was turning his back on the town as well. Had to hurt after all those years being king of the hill. He was on his own. No wife. No son.'

Cut the fake sympathy. You didn't give a fuck about my old man. None of you did. He was an old deadbeat you laughed at behind his back. You didn't give a shit about him getting fired. If it wasn't for you maybe he'd still be there.

'You know that's not true.'

You think? Don't try and put the blame on someone else. You own this, man. Not me.

Honeyman waited a moment for him to calm down, then said very carefully, 'I wasn't trying to blame anyone. Or sit in judgment.'

I had a life of my own. I wanted out of that stinking place.

'You weren't the only one, Vern.'

Right. I have to admit... you do have some insight, don't you? What do they call it? Emotional intelligence. Funny that when you came to write novels about people you'd invented, they turned out to be such shit.

'Your literary criticism is appreciated. I didn't realize you'd read any of my books.'

Outside the first one? Nope.

'Same as my daughter. Thanks for getting through one, anyway.'

Skimmed some of the reviews for the others. They mostly seemed like junk.

'So now what?'

You're still nowhere near giving me an answer, are you?

'Doing my best.'

Won't keep you alive. I want a name.

'I know.'

The laptop made a noise. Another incoming file. Audio. Big.

So you appreciate what's at stake here, Honey Bee, here's something else. A voicemail Dad left on my phone. The last thing I got. You don't need to write it. Not yet. Just want you to hear it. And think about it. We'll talk again tomorrow. Got things to do.

'Wait. If I—'

Sweet dreams.

The walkie-talkie crackled and fell silent. On the laptop the audio file opened of its own accord.

Then the voice of a dead man came out of the speakers.

Tom Honeyman had learned to read people early on. It was one of the tricks of the reporter's trade. Spotting when they were happy. Frightened. Nervous. Upset. Telling the truth. Hiding something. Or just plain lying through their teeth.

Listening to Fred Miller leave a long, incoherent and clearly semi-drunken voicemail for his son, he struggled to connect the sound of him to the man he once knew. As chief of police in Prosper, Miller had been taciturn, uncompromising, hard-working and, at least when he was in uniform, sober.

Now he was none of those things. Miller sounded lost and on the brink. So much so, Honeyman had to stop the audio from time to time to take a break from all the obvious pain and fury.

It began with a grunt. Then...

'*Vern. Christ, boy. Why are you never there when I want you? What the fuck do you get up to now? You lost that woman? You got a new one or something?*'

Music was playing in the background. Country and western. It sounded as if Miller was calling from a booth in a bar. The details of his shooting were on the laptop in an old newspaper story Honeyman had already looked at. The place was a dive called The Coot Shack, the wrong side of what passed for the tracks in Burnsville. Two blocks from where Miller was living in near-poverty. Maybe...

'*Not that it's my business. But why'd you go out there working on your own? Running 'round the country hunting work? Get a job. Settle down. That's what makes a man happy in the end. Yeah, and get a woman too.*'

He laughed, and the booze in him was obvious.

'*Why the hell am I talking to a frigging answering machine? Apologies, boy... voicemail. I know you computer guys like to call it that. Listen...*'

The music got louder. Miller swore, shuffled off somewhere more distant. Coughed, and sounded ill when he did that.

'I already said there was all these lies going around in Prosper about them two got burned down Mohawk Lake. Maybe you didn't believe a word of it, but I'm telling you now. It's real. I'm sending you some stuff of mine in the mail. Notes and other things I've been collecting.

'Those idiots from the Feds and the State cops thought they cut me right out of everything a year ago. Didn't know nothing. One of their guys was one of my guys once upon a time. Knew the meaning of gratitude. You don't need his name. Only get me and him in trouble. He was good enough to keep his old boss in the loop. So anyways...'

That long and rasping liquid cough again, and, as Miller struggled to speak, Honeyman thought, *Jesus, if a bullet in the night didn't take you, something else surely would have before long.*

'Anyways... I want you to keep these things. This shithole I'm living in ain't so secure and— Fuck off, boy! Grown-ups speaking—damned drunk kids coming 'round bugging you. This dump's just a room I got cheap for a while. Something better down the line when I get new work, and, anyways, someone's been rifling through my stuff and I don't want them seeing more. So I'm sending you a package in the mail. Files and documents and some things I put on a memory stick like you showed me. Hope I got that right. Yeah, I know, Vern, you said I could scan and email it but (a) I don't have the first clue how; and (b) who knows who might get their paws on it if I do things that way. At least the U.S. Mail's gonna be safe. God, I wish I could give this to you in person, but you can't get over here and I can't get over there right now, no problem, I know you can't. We'll meet up soon enough once I sort this thing out. And don't get mad at me when you find out where I've been. I got my reasons. So listen.'*

Footsteps then and the music got softer, finally vanishing altogether.

Honeyman could hear doors open, then the faint howl of wind and the murmur of distant traffic. Miller was outside. It sounded wet, and something told him it was cold.

'I been working on this Mohawk Lake thing off and on as much as I could. Damned store security boss wouldn't give me time off when I* *wanted. But I got back there enough to see people. Talk to them if I could, not that most would. Like I told you already, that stupid drunk Mexican got nothing to do with burning that pair like they was tinder. If he hadn't come out all boozed up and waving his toy gun he'd be in jail right now talking to a lawyer about all the compensation he was gonna get when finally they let him out and say... oh sorry, amigo, our mistake. Except those dumb Albany guys decided to play SWAT and now they daren't let on they killed the wrong guy all along. Damned outsiders. If they'd left all this to me, the bastard who lit that match... I'd have them nailed soon enough. But hey. We'll get there. I want you to have this stuff for safekeeping. Don't want to lose a thing. Too important. You keep it safe 'til I ask. No one else with a clue what went down for real back then.'*

There was a sound Honeyman couldn't quite place. Then he got it. A pack of cigarettes. The flick of a lighter. Miller sucking on something.

'Rainy here. But I guess you're used to rain out there in Seattle. Always seemed to be drizzling when I called.'

He laughed again, that sick and liquid sound.

'Longest message I ever left you, ain't it? Funny. Easier talking this way than face to face or when you pick up the phone. I used the job as an excuse to get out of the house. The hours. The work. It was an escape and your mom knew it. Maybe you did too. Truth is I was never good at all that family crap. Wasn't me. What the hell? Too late now.'

A vehicle pulled up. Tires in heavy rain.

'So I'm sending you these things. You keep them safe. Won't be long before I need them. Just got a couple of facts to... to close...'

A car door slammed. Back in the present, the real world, an owl hooted inches from the window, and the sound made Tom Honeyman almost jump out of his skin.

'To close this down...'

Honeyman could see it now. Knew what was coming. Understood the very moment Miller had left this message for his son.

'Hey! Move along, will you? I'm trying to have a private conversation. The bar's over there. Go get yourself a drink and outta my face.'

Miller was barking out the words in that threatening, furious way he had with drunks back home, just before he beat on them.

'Vern? You hear that? Some deadbeat stumbling 'round me in the pissing rain like they got nothing better to do. Burnsville's a shithole, son. Don't bother coming here.'

Then a bang.

Miller groaned.

Another bang.

This grunt was a cry, a scream of anger, pain and fear.

One last shot.

Gone, Honeyman thought. *Surely.*

Then there came a final sound, two mumbled words, barely audible, muffled by movement and whimpers of pain. Spat out with vehemence through clenched teeth and all the anger of a dying man.

Distorted, barely there at all, impossible to pin down.

'Oh...'

He said that for sure. Then a wheeze and a liquid choking sound.

And the second word...

Money?

Maybe.

Funny?

Not that it made sense, but maybe sense was the last thing you sought just then.

He rolled back the audio and listened again. Still unsure of what he was hearing.

There was another possibility.

He pressed play once more, then told himself he wasn't going to come back to it. No point. Every time it sounded more like a different word, the last thing Fred Miller ever said, coming at him from the grave.

Honey...

HONEYMAN PICKED up the walkie-talkie and stabbed the talk button.

'Vern. We need to talk about this. I mean... I can't... can't imagine...'

A voicemail of your father getting murdered. Vern couldn't have passed it on to the police. Maybe he felt that would have opened the floodgates to all the tricks his old man had been up to in Prosper, hiding evidence, being at least in part responsible for Jackson Wynn's death. If the cops had something like this, it would have come out. What a story.

Honeyman wanted to kick himself. The reporter in you never died.

He knew what he really should have been thinking too: *No wonder Vern Miller's so mad he can't wait to kill someone given the chance.*

'Vern! Will you please answer?'

The questions kept running through his head.

Maybe Miller didn't say 'honey' at all.

Maybe he just misheard, let his imagination run away with itself.

Or... this thought just came to him... maybe he was talking to a woman. Fred Miller was just the kind of guy who'd call them sweetheart or sugar or... honey.

'Vern! Are you there? We need to talk.'

If he was around, Vern Miller wasn't answering. It was after two in the morning. Tom Honeyman desperately wanted to sleep.

A gasp of wind rattled the wooden shutters on the window; after that the owl flapped its wings and let out a shriek. The unexpected sounds made him jump, made the silence within the house more obvious somehow.

He walked out into the kitchen and called Lauren's name.

Then went upstairs and did the same.

Lauren? Lauren?

They'd hidden the gun she'd stolen underneath the single bed in her room. He found the flashlight next to his bed and went in there.

The gun was gone. Like her.

If you won't do it I will, she'd said.

He should have known.

No point in hiding anymore. Honeyman went downstairs, walked

out of the front door and headed for the graves and the ruins silhou-
etted against the dim night sky.

MONEY. Funny.

Fred Miller's dying word was indistinct, but not so much in
Thomas's head. There it kept becoming clearer, the fire behind his
son's fury.

Honey.

The night was warm, the breeze strong and thick with the aromas
of the lagoon. Sweet-perfumed flowers, stagnant water from the
broken swimming pool, the hard tang of rotting vegetation and the
fishy brackish odor of water running into mud. Ahead the headstones
rose into the blue-black sky like broken teeth. The memory of the last
time he and Lauren ventured beyond the house kept coming back.
The pain. The warning: one more attempt at escape and you're dead.

And now Lauren was out there with a gun.

Soon Honeyman was out of the graveyard and half-running
across the shaky wooden bridge that led to the little island and the
remains of the old chapel. Somewhere by the shore he saw a brief
flash of light. No point in hiding now. He dashed through the gap in
the wall, past the stone angel, and found himself in what was once
the nave. Vern's tent was there, a large, military-style structure. Next
to it a generator whirred, a whiff of gas and fumes just noticeable.
The light came from inside the canvas. He went over, called Lauren's
name. Called Miller's too.

The beam flashed toward him. The canvas opened. He steeled
himself but Lauren walked out alone, wearing the heavy winter
jacket, shaking her head, flashlight in her left hand, the gun in her
right.

He tried to keep his temper, but all the same there must have
been heat in his voice.

'What the hell do you think you're doing? Running out like that?'

Lauren opened her mouth and stared at him.

'Dad. I came in to talk. Your head was in that laptop again, listening to something. You didn't even see me. I tried—'

'Where is Vern?'

'I don't know. I looked all over.'

She glanced down toward the line of shingle where they'd abandoned the deflated dinghy. It was empty now, just a silver ribbon of pebbles.

'The boat's gone. He must have fixed it. Just rubber, I suppose. You can patch it up.'

No wonder Miller wasn't worried about Morosini coming back on Sunday. He'd be away from Maledetto by then.

Lauren kicked her foot through some of the metal gear cases around the tent. 'He's got all kinds of toys. Do you think he maybe learned this kind of thing in the military?'

'I guess he learned a lot. Lauren. Give me the gun. We need to go back. This isn't a good idea.'

She laughed in the same kind of don't-be-stupid way Diane had.

'Dad. I've seen what he's like. He wants to kill us.'

'He's got... there's something in that audio file.'

'What?'

'I need you to hear it.'

He followed her to the side of the tent, where the generator was rumbling away.

Lauren kicked through the long grass.

'He had some cans of gas here. Nothing now. They're all gone. Maybe... he was running out. Is there somewhere he could go?'

The Lido, Honeyman thought. There was an all-night gas station for cars and boats near the vaporetto stop.

'Yeah.'

'How far?'

'Got to be thirty minutes or more in that boat. There and back. Lauren. We need to get out of here.'

She was staring at the tent.

'Doesn't make any difference. We broke the rules again. He's bound to know.'

'Give me the gun, Lauren. Please.'

Before he could say anything she was opening the canvas flap and crawling back inside.

IT WAS BIGGER than he expected, and everything was orderly in an obsessive, almost military kind of way. A low portable desk with a laptop, the screen off. Food and cooking utensils neatly packed to one side. A gas stove. Two sleeping bags rolled up to make room.

'I watched him type his password.' Lauren knelt in front of the computer. 'I think I can get in.'

The screen came alive. Code and code and code. Lots of windows for apps he didn't understand. Indecipherable text. Hacker stuff.

'Are we online?'

She shook her head and pointed at the taskbar.

'No. He must have his sat phone with him. That's the only way you can do it. All the same...'

She tugged her hair, thinking, then rifled through the bits and pieces on the low desk. There were four USB memory sticks next to the laptop. Lauren clicked them into a port one by one until she found a stick that was blank.

'I'm going to copy over his whole documents folder if I can—'

'What if he notices?'

'One out of four? I doubt that.'

'We need to go.'

'If you hear him coming, tell me. We've got time.'

'Please—'

'Dad.' Her voice rose. 'He's been trickling this stuff out to you all this time. Teasing us. Playing a game where only he knows what the cards are.' She tapped the keyboard and started copying files. 'If you won't let me shoot him, at least let me see his hand.'

'He'll know.'

'No, he won't. Pass me a bottle of that, will you?'

There was a six-pack of mineral water near the flap. He unhooked one from the plastic.

'See this stuff?' Lauren tapped a box at the back. Honeyman dimly recognized the logo: it was the same as the security cameras he had back home. 'This is the gear the bastard's using to spy on us. Well, let's see about that, Mister Miller.'

Somehow she worked out which app was monitoring the cameras and pulled it up. Eight views all around the house came alive, gray images on the screen, the whole place empty.

'Boom.'

She poured water all over the control box then, for good measure, unhooked the cables and dribbled some down the holes. The pictures vanished. Then she turned to the app, scrolled back to the point where the stored video captured the two of them just before they left the villa. With a quick tap of keys she deleted everything from that point on. Finally she rolled the control box on its side, poured out all the water and carefully dried it with a rag.

'As far as he's going to know this junk failed while he was gone.' Her fingers kept rattling away at the laptop, looking for something else, he guessed. 'Are you sure we can't just wait here and shoot him?'

'You're good at this.'

'I'd be good at shooting the bastard too.'

From outside they could just hear the distant rattle of an outboard engine.

'Not now. Not in the dark. Not...'

He couldn't go on. The engine was getting louder.

He held out his hand.

'Dammit. I was never very good at stopping you from doing anything, but right now... Give me the gun, Lauren. You're not doing this...' Looking at her angry face, it could have been one more argument twelve years before, in their front room in Prosper. 'Please...'

She swore then grabbed the weapon out of her jacket pocket and slammed it in his hand.

'Fine...'

The night seemed chillier, the approaching boat closer. They ran through the broken headstones, across the creaking wooden bridge, not looking back until they were home.

LOSING the spy cameras felt liberating. If that trick worked, they could talk freely now. They could walk around the villa, outside even, and Vern Miller would never know.

From the front porch it was obvious the motor they'd heard was him. They could see the dinghy approaching the island by the ruins, a tiny lamp on the bow as Miller piloted the craft into the shingle. Then it vanished, and soon after a flashlight beam broke the night sky as he walked to his base.

Maybe he'd made this trip before. Maybe there was an opening for them in that knowledge somehow. Not that Honeyman could see it. Lauren seemed to be the one attuned to the opportunities, as if she was thinking ahead all the time. But then she'd met Miller at close quarters. She knew the man a little, how he lived, what he had around him.

'He won't know, Dad. Quit worrying.'

'Who said I was?'

She punched him lightly in the ribs.

'I did. I can see it in your face. You always look like there's something bad waiting around the next corner. Even when there isn't. Mom used to say you took too much on yourself. Any problem, you'd put all the weight on your shoulders.'

'She never said that to me.'

That light little punch again.

'No. But then you guys never did talk that much. Anyway, she was the same. Always thinking she was seeing something... lying in wait, just watching.'

'She said that?'

'Yeah.' The brief moment of relief at escaping Vern Miller was gone. 'Her shooter in the shadows. That's what she called it, didn't she?'

The suicide note. Of course Lauren would have read it, not that the two of them were in any state to talk about it in the aftermath of Diane's death.

He opened the door. The camera lights were still blinking. Didn't matter. They were dead.

HE WENT STRAIGHT to the computer and the audio file Miller had sent him. The voicemail that began with his old man rambling drowsily in a bar. Then outside. Some kind of encounter. Shots.

She sat in front of it, listened, going pale as those final moments arrived.

'Jesus Christ. Imagine hearing that. Your own father...'

'I can't.'

'Nobody ever liked that guy.'

'What?'

'Everybody hated Chief Miller. I remember him picking on some kids at school just because he didn't like the way they looked or acted or something. They said he used to punch you around if he felt like it. Like we heard he did to Jackson Wynn. He was running everything, wasn't he? Who you gonna complain to? Anyway....'

'You met him?'

Lauren hesitated.

'Kind of.'

'When?'

'He came to the house and talked to Mom. When you were away. I think... I think he was out of the police by then. Maybe out of Prosper.'

Honeyman had never heard Diane mention Miller visiting the house.

'Why? Why did he come?'

She shrugged.

'I don't know. Soon as I saw that cop car in the driveway I turned straight around and rode away. Mom never mentioned it when I came back. From the look on her face I wasn't going to ask. I assumed it was about you. She never said? Really?'

'No...'

Lauren pulled up the earlier chapter he'd written, the first one Vern Miller had demanded. The story of the day Mohawk Lake happened, how the chief got called to it, soon sidelined, then met Honeyman himself in Maiden Lane.

'I mean... just read what you wrote. He was not a nice man. No wonder he got fired.'

He scrolled toward the conclusion of the audio and made it play.

'Vern? You hear that? Some deadbeat stumbling 'round me in the pissing rain like they got nothing better to do. Burnsville's a shithole, son. Don't bother coming here.'

Lauren covered her ears.

'Do we have to listen to that again?'

'Yes—'

'Burnsville *is* a shithole. Mom always said.'

That didn't sound right.

'I don't remember your mom going to Burnsville. What for?'

Lauren shook her head, yawned.

'God, I'm tired. Can we just sleep a while?'

'Why did she—?'

'I don't know! Maybe it was just the once. Shopping—'

'Burnsville's got no more stores than we had. If she wanted anything big, she went to—'

'Dad. Can we quit the interrogation, please? It's late. I'm exhausted. So are you. Getting so grouchy...'

Maybe she was right. He could barely think straight. Lauren either. She hadn't remarked on the final part of the audio. Fred Miller's dying words.

'I want you to hear this. Then tell me what you think he's saying.'

He found the place, hit play. She listened, intently he thought.

'Wow. I still can't get over Vern getting that on his phone.'

One more time, head close up to the laptop, she listened to Miller getting shot, then she pushed the chair back, yawned, stretched her skinny arms. The bruise on her lip was pretty much gone now.

'Well?'

'Well what?'

'Well, what did you hear?'

'A wheezy old guy getting killed. Mumbling stuff.'

'No...' He reached for the laptop and hit the keys. 'There's more to it than that. Listen...'

She did, then folded her arms.

'What do you think he says?'

'It's really rough. On Vern's phone. Can't hear it that well.'

'Try harder.'

Again he played it. Then one more time.

'I dunno...'

'Oh, come on. Money. Funny.' He hesitated then said it anyway. 'Maybe the start of a word. Honey...'

Lauren raised a finger.

'No, Dad. You can't take that one on your shoulders. You said you weren't there.'

'I said I was in town. I never saw him.'

'So he wasn't talking about you. Think about it.' She played the clip one more time. It was indistinct. No way of knowing what the dying Fred Miller was really trying to say. 'You left someone out.'

'No, I didn't—'

'You left someone out.' She said the word very slowly, like a teacher to a child. 'Bunny.'

He was tired, his head wasn't all there.

'What?'

'Gary Rabbitt. Bunny. The kids at school weren't the only ones who called him that. Here. The chapter Vern wrote for you. Based on his dad's notes, right?'

There it was on the screen in black and white.

'Hey, Bunny. Chief Miller here. Where does that pretty little thing of yours, Mia Buckingham, lay her head at night?'

'Like I said... wasn't just us who called him Bunny. But...' She got to her feet. 'I don't even know if 'Bunny' was what the old guy was saying. Could be just a dead man talking crap.'

The walkie-talkie buzzed. Vern Miller was back in business, maybe wondering what had happened while he was gone.

Damn well hope you've got something for me, Tommy boy. Time's running out for you and yours.

That was all. Nothing about his wrecked camera system or the fact that someone had been inside his tent.

Honeyman was about to answer when Lauren put her arm across to stop him.

'He can't see us anymore. Can't hear us. For all he knows we're sleeping. That's what we've got to do, Dad. Just for a little while. Neither of us is thinking straight right now.'

Tom Honeyman plugged in the USB stick they'd taken from Miller's tent and watched as the list of files began to fill the screen.

It was almost five in the morning. Saturday. The fireworks would burst over the lagoon in a little more than eighteen hours. The Night of the Redeemer.

'You go, Lauren. I've got a couple of things I want to look at.'

She sighed, kissed him quickly on the cheek, then vanished into the hall.

Gary Rabbitt.

The principal of Lafayette High.

Was it possible?

He opened the folder of files and searched on Rabbitt's name. The memory stick wasn't indexed. It seemed to take forever. He wished he had a printer. Things were easier to read on the page.

Just to get a break, he went and sat on the study sofa by the window, listening to the faint breeze outside, his head full of memories, doubts and worry.

Sleep took him anyway.

12

VENICE

D*eadline: 12 hours. 17 minutes.*

WHEN HONEYMAN AWOKE, his head was stuck back at a painful angle, and a bright morning had dawned beyond the glass.

There was a smell he couldn't put a name to at first, but it set an alarm ringing in his head and a churning in his stomach. Then it came: the iron tang of fresh-spilled blood.

'Lauren!'

He'd left her sleeping upstairs, been so out of it for hours anything could have happened.

Honeyman ran into the hall and found himself sliding, bare feet losing grip on the old brown tiles.

It was smeared there, a long trail, red and fresh. Across the floor from the open door, up to the stairs, where it ended on the first step. Not broad. Not heavy. Still real.

He stumbled up the steps, calling out her name, imagination alive with wild ideas. Vern Miller had been spitting out so many threats over the last few days. Such vivid promises of retribution. The night before they'd broken the rules again, and he was never as sure as she was there was no way Vern could work out what they'd done.

'Lauren...'

There, on her bed, spread out in bloody pieces across the crumpled sheets. A bird. A lagoon cormorant, he guessed, a gaping red tear in its chest, a bloody neck that looked as if the head had been torn straight off.

He gagged, picked the creature up by a broken wingtip, raced to the window and threw it out into the wild and straggling weeds of the back yard.

As he tried to focus, the walkie-talkie came alive. Vern Miller's crackly electronic laughter echoed up the steps.

Honeyman walked back to the study, and picked up the handset.

'What have you done to her?'

Nothing she didn't deserve. Shit, Tommy boy. You don't think things through well, do you?

'It was my idea. Don't hurt—'

Quit begging. You two are really dumb, you know. So you killed my cameras. I still got a window into your computer. I can see what you've been looking at. I know you been out there stealing my stuff while I've been gone. Stupid...

Honeyman cursed himself. Of course Miller would know they had the files from his laptop on the memory stick. He could see straight into everything Honeyman was doing, watch every keystroke as it happened. It was Lauren's idea to take the files. He should have seen the flaw in their thinking immediately. But they'd both been so exhausted.

'We're still trying to help you here, Vern.'

Don't fuck with me, Honeyman! All you're doing is trying to save your ugly hides.

'Same thing, isn't it? Where is she?'

With me, man. Where do you think? For the duration now, what's left of it. Maybe you don't ever get to see your little girl again, not 'til she's bones and ashes. It's nearly midday. The fireworks get lit less than twelve hours away. And there you are, still making out like you got nothing to offer. Can't trust the two of you together, can I?

'Give me more. Give me something to work with.'

She thinks my dad said "Bunny." Right at the end. Not "honey." Not something else. What about you?

'I honestly don't know. It's not very clear. What's your guess? He was your father.'

I'm here to ask the questions. Not answer them.

Not good enough. Honeyman sat down at the laptop, found the mp3 file, took a deep breath and played Fred Miller's last words again.

'Vern. I need to know.'

A moment, then Miller came back and didn't sound quite so mad.

One more mystery for you to solve, huh? You were in Burnsville that night, Tom. Didn't leave 'til the next morning. For a book event in Albany. I got your whereabouts down pat even if you haven't. I know every step you took.

'I didn't shoot your father. I didn't even meet him. So, please, give me a lead. I'm trying to help.'

You've been here since Tuesday, and you've given me shit.

Honeyman couldn't get Lauren out of his head. One wrong word and she was going to pay.

The laptop beeped. Incoming files.

One more try, Tom. I've been working on all this for eighteen months or more. Put together lots of material on all kinds of people. Almost as much as you. Gary Rabbitt. Your old boss McAllister. You and your family. Just sent you something. Take a look. Write me a chapter. Let me see it in your words. Bunny Rabbitt's story. All the evidence. Strong, weak, everything.

'If you had enough to nail him, why do you need me?'

See. You can be smart. When you want. Truth is I just don't know. Maybe I missed something. Maybe it isn't there. If that's the case...

He broke off, and in the background Honeyman heard Lauren yelp, a curse.

Point me somewhere else, and do it soon.

'The Burnsville cops must have looked into your father's murder. If they couldn't—'

Those sons of bitches could barely file a parking violation. I'm doing you one last favor. Use it.

Lauren was squawking again. Miller yelled at her to be quiet.

I picked out the files from the ones you stole. What I want you to look at. Start with Mia Buckingham. Or should I say... Mia Schoon. Go through them. Make a good enough case and we can call Mister Rabbitt and ask him. Just this once I'm going to let you peek beyond this little world of ours and see what's on the outside. All under my control, naturally. Make the most of it, Tom.

Lauren squealed once more.

'I need her here to help me. Let her go.'

There were shrieks and maybe punches too, and there was nothing Tom Honeyman could do to stop them.

He stared at the laptop. There was a whole folder devoted to the former principal of Lafayette High. Documents, audio, photos.

Ten minutes after he began to browse through them, the message box popped up.

A picture on it now, live again. Lauren tied to the statue of the crippled angel in the ruined courtyard.

You get reading, Tommy boy. Then you get writing. Only a few hours before the sky lights up. Screw with me again and I'll have just one Honeyman left to burn when it does.

13

SAN FRANCISCO

October 25, 2009

Four days before he died, Fred Miller left Burnsville, wondering if he'd ever go back. He got the cheapest ticket he could find—$250 on Frontier—and flew from Syracuse to San Francisco via Denver. When he reached San Francisco he checked into a rundown dump in the Tenderloin next to a dismal strip club, and slept okay in spite of the street noise and the traffic.

He'd been to the city a couple of times for vacations when he was married. Never liked the place, but Sue thought it was somehow cute. They'd always stayed with the other tourists at Fisherman's Wharf. That was a different kind of dump than the Tenderloin. The city seemed to him to have no clear idea of its personality. The sumptuous lived next to the sleazy, the raw and crude alongside the elegant. From the Tenderloin, Nob Hill wasn't far away, though it was a long steep incline up Leavenworth that would take him to the last address he had for Robert Schoon. If he couldn't find a bus or a cable car, he'd have to walk. No way he could waste money on a cab.

As strapped as he was, he felt there was no choice but to make this trip. Ever since he left Prosper the previous autumn, Mohawk Lake had been nagging at him, festering in his mind, a mix of anger and resentment. For sure the cops who'd stolen his job and the investigation had got it wrong. But a visit back to the town the previous week seemed to show he was alone in that opinion. Prosper had, in the vernacular of the young, 'moved on', or was trying to. Though that illusion wasn't going to last when Tom Honeyman's book came out a few weeks later.

The Fire: An American Tragedy. A pompous title for a pompous hack turned wannabe author. Honeyman's editor had had the brazen audacity to send him a pre-publication proof of this 'true crime' account of the murders. To Miller's astonishment, his name was up there in the credits for those Honeyman thanked for help during his research. He'd swallowed that down then scanned the first few pages with a sense of growing, aggrieved fury. Even at a casual glance it was clear the whole thing was an opportunistic pile of half-truths and bigger lies bolstered with speculation and some downright fantasy. Honeyman must have known as much himself. There was such a desperate sense of feigned certainty and fake philosophy in the tale he told. This came to a head when he rambled on and on about Jorge Rodriguez's so-called motives. Not that he came to any conclusion as to why an alcoholic firefighter would pour gas around a school cabin, lock the door and window, then set the place alight with a naked Mia and her schoolboy lover trapped inside.

The truth was Tom Honeyman didn't have a clue and went all the way around the block time and time again trying not to show it. Miller was certain by now: Rodriguez never had a motive because he never set the fire. Honeyman's book might have been headed for the bestseller lists—from what Miller read, it seemed that was a certainty, after what the publisher paid for it. But the fable it told was as full of holes as Jackson Wynn's story, right up to the moment that strange and solitary loner perished beneath the wheels of a lumber truck out in Prudeaux. The more Fred Miller thought about the book, the more he became convinced Honeyman knew it was a fake too.

Lies. Miller hated them. They offended him. Of course he'd lied himself about Jackson Wynn, overseen the investigation into his terrible 'accident', made sure no one ever guessed he'd been anywhere near. Got away with it as well. But that was a necessity. Even if the guilt it sowed in Fred Miller's head maybe kept lighting the spark that nagged him, whispering that the truth about Mohawk Lake was nothing like the crooked tale that crooked Tom Honeyman told to make his crooked fortune.

There were three bodies demanding a decent burial now: Mia Buckingham, the Sorrell kid and the wretched Jackson Wynn. And no one to lay them to rest but him.

Maybe when he was done he'd call Vern and go see him. Or try to find work in San Francisco, though in truth it wasn't his kind of town: too big, too easy-going, too willing to turn a blind eye to things that were right out there in the bright light of day and no one cared. There were other, better places in California, must be. It all depended on what he found. Fred Miller was making the last investigative journey of his career, with no authority, and nothing he could do even if he located what he was looking for: more on the woman who called herself Mia Buckingham and where she came from.

In his own head he thought there were maybe two outcomes to this strange adventure. Either he got a clue to what really happened at Mohawk Lake. Or he drew a blank and tried to work out what to do with what little money he had left.

Then he rang the doorbell of a guy named Robert Schoon.

IN THE ADVANCE copy Tom Honeyman's publisher had sent him, Miller had found barely a mention of Mia Buckingham's background. Lack of time, maybe. Honeyman thought he had his story and wasn't interested in anything that might contradict it. The woman came from a Nob Hill family, fancy, with money, and then something went wrong. Robert Schoon was a pilot with a regional airline flying out of SFO. Honeyman talked to the guy on the phone, listened to him weeping, persuaded him to send a photo of his FAA logbooks. They showed very clearly he was flying the weekend Mia died. Schoon provided the background Honeyman needed for the story. A sympathetic portrait of a woman fleeing a broken marriage and a husband who still loved her. And that, as far as Honeyman was concerned, was it.

Fred Miller did a little more. He went through the records. And nowhere could he find any marriage between Robert Schoon and a woman named Mia Buckingham. Or even a woman *of* that name. Then, finally, he came across what he was looking for. And that was the moment he knew he had to fly to San Francisco.

'Mister Schoon?'

He was a lean, good-looking man in his forties. White shirt and black tie, black trousers, flight uniform. All ready to go to SFO to pick up a plane.

'Can I help you?'

'I came about Mia.'

The guy blinked.

'I've got to be at the airport in two hours.'

'Don't take long to get there. I only need a few minutes. Can I come in?'

There was the usual 'and you are?' Miller pulled out his old chief's ID card from Prosper for a few seconds; when they tried to take that off him he claimed he'd lost it.

'I'm looking into Mia's death. Come all this way. It's just routine. A couple of questions and them I'm gone.'

'I told you. I'm going to work.'

'Well, you do that, sir. But in that case I'm going to have to ask the SFO police to pull you out of your cockpit so's I can ask you why you were pretending your sister was your wife. Which...' The guy was white in the face by now. 'Which may be a good story you can tell over the phone to some two-bit reporter on the make. But it won't wash with me. Not at all.'

'How did you—?'

'Because finding out what people don't want me know is what I do. Now do we have an embarrassing encounter at the airport? Or do I come in? I could use a coffee, by the way. A cookie too.' He smiled at the house. It wasn't big, but in a place like this it must have been worth millions. 'Bet a guy like you got good cookies too.'

SCHOON WAS DIVORCED. That, at least, was true. Ex-wife and two kids living out in Palo Alto. Plenty of money from his folks, from what Miller had seen. A man of substance flying planes because he loved to, not that he needed the work.

The cookies were good. The coffee too harshly European for his liking. San Francisco all over. They sat in the front room overlooking the street, and Miller wondered what it must be like to be comfortable, to have money like this. Robert Schoon probably had lots of women too. He had that look about him, and the place had the feel and smell of an active bachelor.

'So?' The guy had said barely a word after he let him in. 'Let's start with your sister. Ten years younger than you. You didn't even come to the funeral. Guess you weren't close. Not in that way.'

Schoon just glared at him.

'Robert... I'm not leaving until I hear.'

'Hear what?'

'Who she was. Why you went through this act.'

'And this is your business because?'

'Because I'm interested.'

'Why? That was a year ago. The guy who killed her is dead. Why do you want to poke at an old wound and see if you can reopen it?'

'Because it's still bleeding.'

'Meaning?'

'That dumb drunk Mexican didn't kill her. He was set up. Made to look like he did. Then the drunken idiot was dumb enough to wave a BB gun at a SWAT team and get himself shot. Whoever murdered your sister's still out there. I'm going to find him. Don't you want that?'

'The police in Albany told me it was closed. The FBI.'

'Dumbasses. Every last one of them. Look. You don't have to believe me. Just tell me a few things. Who Mia really was. That's all. Then I'm out of your hair.'

'For good?'

'Yeah. For good.'

The guy went to a fancy desk—walnut, antique, French or something—and retrieved a photo album. Then knelt next to Miller and flipped through the pages. Robert Schoon was young and fit. He could kneel easily. He could cry easily too, Fred Miller was disappointed to see.

TWO KIDS, two parents. A yacht. The house on Nob Hill. Vacations in fancy places. Italy. France. Cruise ships. Lots of cruise ships.

Mia was gorgeous even when she was little. A real Shirley Temple, round face and lots of blonde curls, always pretty in a designer skirt or shirt and jeans. Their mother died when she was eleven. By then they'd sent Mia off to a co-ed boarding school in Ojai, supposedly a track straight into an Ivy League college. The place was meant to straighten her out after more than a few unruly episodes at home. Didn't work. She was thrown out when she was fifteen after being found in bed with two boys and came home more out of control than ever. Home to a sick father and a brother ten years older, distant, who was looking to grow up.

Two years later their old man died. Robert was in Florida trying to build hours for his commercial license, flight schools and the weather being better there. Mia got left on her own in the house on Nob Hill for months on end. No job, but the allowance from her brother gave her money to spend, mostly on dope and booze and a rapidly changing army of friends and hangers-on who'd party so hard the neighbors began to put the cops on speed dial.

Five years that went on, her in the house, him away. There were wrangles about their father's will. He had cut Mia out of everything, saying all the money had to go to Robert, who'd surely look after his sister. It was just not a good idea to give several million dollars to her direct. Everyone knew she'd just piss it down the drain.

Mia fought for her share, naturally, because she never walked away from a battle. All the same, by the time she was twenty-eight the lawyers had seen to most of the money she had left. Drugs and drink had taken firm hold by then. Robert was back in the family home, not that she'd speak to him. She was living somewhere in the city, he didn't know where.

Schoon stopped the story and put the album away. Then he took the chair opposite and said the interview had to come to an end. He was flying to San Diego that afternoon and he was never going to be late for the job.

'A regular guy.' Miller felt bad asking these questions for once. 'Must have hurt. Having a sister like that.'

Robert Schoon pinched his fingers together.

'We were that close when we were kids. Big brother, little sis. I was going to protect her whenever I could.'

'You can't change people, Robert. They are what they are. In a way...' It surprised Miller he was saying this. 'In a way sometimes it would be wrong if you could.'

Schoon looked at his watch then tapped it.

But Miller wasn't going until he heard.

'All I want to know is why she wound up on the other side of the country, in a little town saying she was this divorcee named Buckingham. Every word a pack of lies.'

Schoon closed his eyes.

'There was this thing with the police. She'd been working...' His face screwed up with pain. 'She called it an escort agency. It was... prostitution. Maybe quite well-paid. I dunno. But that's what it was. She got caught in some scam on a guy. The cops were going to charge her, maybe. Just a minor thing, but nothing was ever minor with Mia. She was either up or down, and back then it was mostly down. The smallest problem could send her there.'

'And?'

'And she came to me finally and said she needed out of California. It was no big deal with the cops. They wouldn't chase her out of state or anything. She just wanted to be gone. A new name. A new story. A new beginning. Help her, and she'd never ask for anything from me ever again.'

Miller felt a little cold. He understood that need.

'Never going to be easy, that kind of thing, Robert.'

'There was some guy she'd met. A customer, I think. He'd been over here on business. A teacher or something. A teacher chasing hookers.'

'It happens.'

'I'm sure it does. She said she could get some papers giving her a fake degree. Some qualifications. Mia always liked art. She could draw. Could make things. Little sculptures. Pottery. Jewelry too. No qualifications, but if she could buy some she could find work in a school upstate in New York somewhere. Get a new name. Tell a story about her being someone else. A divorcee from California looking to pick up the pieces. But I had to pay for it. I had to confirm everything and make it possible. Me playing the former husband, but still on good terms, you understand.'

That didn't stack up, Miller thought.

'What? That wouldn't work.' Even the idiots back in the store security department knew enough to spot fake papers when it came to giving people a job. 'Couldn't have got past first base.'

'The... the customer she had was the guy who was going to give her the job. He was the one who'd go through the files. The one who'd decide. All I needed was to make sure the paperwork was there and write a letter saying all of it was true. She picked the name Buckingham herself. Like the palace. She always had fantasies about being royalty, about being somebody. Mia Buckingham, my former wife. A good woman. A reliable woman. We were still friends and would remain so. Then...'

Dammit, the guy was weeping full on. *No way you can fly a plane like that*, Miller thought.

'Then what?'

'Then she was gone. And I heard nothing. Until I got the call from the cops saying she'd been found dead. Murdered. They'd got the school papers that said I was her ex-husband. It was... I didn't know what to do. What do you do?'

'Telling cops the truth's one option.'

Schoon scowled at him, picked up a black leather pilot's bag by the chair and pulled out a couple of charts, looked at them, put them back.

'I said—' Miller began.

'I heard what you said. Telling cops the truth is what gets you into trouble. They weren't coming here. They knew pretty quickly I was working that weekend she died. So I just told them the same story I put in the letter I sent the school. You don't know what Mia put me through. Hell ten times, back ten times. God knows I wish she wasn't dead, but I spent years clearing up the shit she left. I wasn't going near whatever catastrophe she got herself into, in some place I didn't know a soul.'

Which was understandable, Miller thought, not that he said it.

'And that was it.' He picked up the case and got to his feet. 'That *is* it. She's dead. Gone. I did my best. It wasn't enough.'

Miller got the message and struggled out of the chair. Maybe it was the ten hours cramped on planes, but god he was feeling old.

'Sometimes nothing's going to be enough, Robert. Take it from a man who's seen it for years. When you're dealing with people with problems like that. Dope. Booze. Screwing around. Sometimes there's not a lot you can do.'

Robert Schoon looked like he was ready to punch him.

'Mia wasn't promiscuous.'

Miller laughed.

'If you said that to people back in Prosper they'd think they didn't hear you right.'

'She was looking for love. Some kind of connection to make her feel real. Wanted. Human. My sister tried to find that in all... all kinds of people. Didn't matter... it never worked.' There was a bitter expression on his face then, some hate in it. 'Never looked for it in me, not after Pop sent her off to that school in Ojai. Never asked. It was just money. Or getting her out of whatever shit she'd found herself in now. Never... affection. I wasn't there for that. Don't know why.'

Miller knew that money never guaranteed anyone happiness. Sometimes the misery bug just floated through the window and bit you in the ass while you slept.

'The customer... the john she hooked up with. His name was Rabbitt?'

'She never said.'

'Gary Rabbitt.'

'I just told you. She never said his name. Now will you get out of here? I need to go to work, and this conversation's getting me down.'

'I really need a—'

'He was the boss. He ran the place that was going to give her a job.'

'Principal Gary Rabbitt. Bunny.'

Robert Schoon blinked. A memory came back, and it was obvious it wasn't a pleasant one.

'Bunny. Yeah. I think I remember her saying that.'

'Thank you, sir.'

'You really think that Mexican didn't kill her?'

'I know it.'

'And you can find out who did?'

'I believe so.'

Schoon went and opened the door.

'So why's it just you here? Some old guy with an expired cop ID? Doesn't look as if he's got two dimes to rub together?'

Some questions weren't worth answering.

OUTSIDE IT WAS WARM, which surprised him. He always thought of San Francisco as a chilly city.

Principal Gary Rabbitt.

Who now was living in Dunston, Burnsville's neighboring town, alone supposedly. Getting by as a part-time teacher at a private school mostly for foreign students.

Miller checked his money. Just over five hundred dollars. Why he did that, he wasn't sure. It was the same as when he walked out of the dump in the Tenderloin.

Getting old, he told himself again. He ought to call Vern. Fly up to Seattle. Maybe see if there was a job there. A place people could use an old cop and not be too worried about checking out his past back home. What Robert Schoon said about his sister touched a nerve, in a way. He'd never grown apart from his son like Schoon and his sister did. But there was a distance now, and it wasn't simply measured in miles.

The trouble was he bore the blame. It was in his character never to let things go. If he went to Seattle he knew it would be a one-way trip. He'd stay and get some low-grade job there, then sit around getting older and grumpier, like that cop on the funny TV show he used to watch, except without the limp and the dog. He'd never get to the bottom of what happened in Mohawk Lake. At night that would come back to taunt him. Fred Miller wasn't one for self-deception. He knew himself, his flaws, his strengths. Without putting to bed the case that forced him out of the chief of police's seat in Prosper, he'd go to his grave unfinished.

There was a travel agent a block from the hostel in the Tenderloin. An overnight flight would get him back into Syracuse at ten the next morning. Three hundred bucks, which left him a couple hundred in cash and the last couple thousand he had in his checking account.

He sat on the plane and for some reason found himself remembering the old timer his mom used to use when she cooked eggs on the stove. A glass one, full of sand you turned upside down. When the pink grains had fallen from top to bottom they were done. Or supposed to be. Mom often forgot about them and the sand was way through before she ever came back.

Mohawk Lake was like that. Sand running through a timer.

Running out on his life too. He didn't know it, but very soon the last grain would trickle through the glass.

JUST AFTER ONE in the afternoon on October 29, 2009, Fred Miller parked outside a rundown cottage on Buckhart Lane in Dunston, New York, the address he'd gotten for Gary Rabbitt. Nothing like the fancy townhouse the guy had owned when he was principal of Lafayette High. This was one last throw of the dice, and if it didn't work Miller would just get drunk, wake up with a bear inside his head and let the bear decide what's next.

The long night traveling he'd spent rereading the proof Honeyman's publishers had sent him, getting madder and madder with every sentence. That gave him two enemies to hunt down now. Whoever really killed the teacher and the kid. Then the lying hack who took their sorry corpses and made himself rich out of their ashes.

He called the one number he had for Honeyman. The wife answered.

'Is he there? This is Fred Miller.'

A long pause then, 'You again?'

'Yeah, me again. Got more questions.'

'Tom's away working. I told you we didn't want to hear from you anymore.'

'Never heard that from him. Just you. I don't have his cell. I want it.'

'Why's that?' She always did sound awkward when he came poking around asking questions about Mohawk Lake. 'You're not a cop here anymore, Miller. You don't have the right to ask for anything.'

'Read that piece of shit he called a book.'

'Good for you.'

'Does he really think he can get away with a fairy story like that?'

'Tom's a good reporter. He worked his ass off on it.'

'I want to talk to him.'

'Why?'

'Because I do. Your man got it all wrong. Everything. Who killed those two. What Mia Buckingham was really like.' He laughed. 'Didn't even get her name right. A good reporter? Huh. He's just a lying snake-oil merchant panning for gold.'

Nothing on the other end.

'You going to give me his number or what?'

'No. You're a stupid old man out to make trouble for people who don't deserve it. You can go to hell.'

'Oh, lady, hell's not ready for me yet. I got plenty of others to send there first. Your husband, for one. I'm going to stalk that guy like I should have from the beginning. You two thinking you struck it rich with this pile of shit he wrote. God, he fouled up there. I got proof as well. I'm going to put it out there, and when that happens—'

'Tom's in Burnsville tonight. Book event. You live there, don't you?'

'How'd you know? You been checking me out the way I checked on you?'

'Go to the town bookstore. Eight p.m. Ask him yourself.'

Miller chuckled. Dumb idea.

'You think I'm gonna waste what I've got on a bunch of idiots turning out to see your lying husband in Burnsville? No. I'm biding my time, lady. I'm waiting till that lying fairy tale of his is out there all big and everywhere. Your man on the TV looking smug. Then... then I tell the papers what really went on.'

'You know that, do you?'

'Oh yeah. Not everything. But I'm getting there. And when I do, Tom Honeyman's gonna be back in the gutter where he belongs. I will destroy him. I will destroy his lies and everything and—'

There was a click. The line went dead.

He thought about calling back, then looked at the crappy peeling paint of Gary Rabbitt's front door and thought again. There was more immediate, more pleasant business to be done.

EIGHTEEN MONTHS before the fire at Mohawk Lake, Bunny Rabbitt had gone to San Francisco on school business and decided part of that business involved hiring an 'escort,' who turned out to be Mia Schoon. A drunk, doped-up, desperate young woman anxious to get out of town and start life anew. With her 'art'. Drawing, making stuff.

Miller still remembered the first impression she made when they met one time he gave a bunch of bored teenagers the standard school drugs talk. Some women just had a look, and she was one of them. Men stared, and it was hard not to join the line. There was a fragile, damaged loveliness about her, something that came from a hurt a guy surely felt needed healing. Maybe that was part of the act. Whatever, he could maybe understand why Rabbitt would have fallen hard for the pretty young hooker he'd hired under the guise of an escort service. Couldn't say no to her either when she pleaded with him to help her get out of San Francisco, take on a new name, and a new career. Mia Schoon didn't have a qualification to her name, but Principal Rabbitt knew all the rules. He could tell her what online degree to buy, which courses to make up, and promise that when the papers came across his desk he'd check off every box, interview her like he did every other new teacher at Lafayette, then smile and say, 'Welcome to school, Miss Buckingham. I'll see you six-thirty tonight, and don't wear your panties.'

Those visits would be regular, of course, so she could pay her dues. All those favors, all those debts couldn't remain outstanding. A school principal, a man with a severe, forbidding woman for a wife, had his needs as well. Someone like that would always have another side. It was just a question of whether it came out through some illicit sex on the side or a furious hellfire condemnation of everyone else who had a pretty little thing waiting for him to call and say his wife thought he was working late and oh, sweetie, will you remind me to take a shower before I go home.

He didn't know Rabbitt well. The man wasn't the kind of person who opened up to others easily. Especially when they came in a uniform. But it seemed pretty obvious from the conversations they'd had over the years he could be a selfish kind of guy, not the sort to share. Especially with a spotty sixteen-year-old kid like Scott Sorrell.

Miller rang the bell and kept his finger on the button. Gasping and cursing after he popped his eye to the spy hole, Rabbitt opened the door. Miller couldn't stop laughing. The man looked so different. His hair, always a buzz cut like he'd been in the military, was longer and clearly dyed a ludicrous shade of brown with ginger edging. He'd grown what he must have thought was some kind of trendy beard. A downturned mustache leading to a Vandyke shape around his chin. But Rabbitt wasn't a beard guy. He didn't have the whiskers or the real pigmentation. He just looked like one more sad, middle-aged bachelor trying to re-create the kind of youth he'd clearly never had.

'Hey, Bunny. Love the beatnik look. Is it working?'

'What do you want?'

'Love to see inside this little home you got. That's first.'

Rabbitt tried to close the door but Miller was there first, foot out to stop him. 'Don't be so rude, man. I been doing a lot of traveling on your behalf these last few days. Came all the way out to Dunston to see you.'

'I don't want you here, Miller. Beat it.'

He pushed his way in and took a look around. The place was clean. Spartan. Like Rabbitt had no money.

'Don't get it, Bunny. You, all dolled up like a failed gigolo. And this dump... could be a monk's cell or something. Times hard, huh?'

'Go away. Prosper and I are in the past.'

'So I heard. Kicked out of Lafayette High. And now you're boring another bunch of poor kids to death—'

'I'm gonna call the cops.'

Miller walked into the front room, found the cordless phone and picked it up. Rabbitt had followed him, squawking all the time.

'Do that, Bunny. Bring them here. We can all have a little talk.'

'About what?'

'Christ, man! Mia Buckingham. What else?' He grinned at the guy and winked. 'Or should I say... Mia Schoon.' Miller didn't smoke much, but it seemed a good time to light up, the place being so clean and pristine and obviously entirely unstained by the presence of tobacco. 'Want one?'

'I don't. I don't like it.'

'Mia's brother sends her regards, by the way. He's really grateful you took her off his hands.'

Rabbitt swore, blinked, then just stood there, mouth open, gaping and flapping like a goldfish out of its bowl.

'Truth be told... I don't like smoking either, Bunny. It's a bad habit. But we all got them. Me... it's tobacco and beer and whisky from time to time. You... going all the way to San Francisco at Lafayette High's expense and picking up hookers there, thinking no one's ever going to know. Then...' He laughed, slapped Rabbitt on the back. 'And then... this I can scarcely believe. A guy like you... You fall for her. You actually fall for her. Shit...'

It just came to him in a flash.

'It was you who bought her that necklace, wasn't it? *To Mia. Always and forever.*'

Miller still had the picture of it on his phone, along with the material the State cops had passed on. He called it up on the screen and showed it to Rabbitt.

'A bit sooty after she got burned.'

Rabbitt looked ready to throw up.

'I don't know anything about this. I don't know why you're here—'

'Please, Bunny. No lying. We're past that.'

Another chuckle, another slap of the back. And Rabbitt looked just like his name: a creature trapped in the headlights.

'Sit down.'

It wasn't a request. Miller was already pushing the guy into a chair, pulling up a stool, taking it, setting himself a foot away from that scared face with its puny beard and staring eyes.

'Here's what happened. You paid to bang Mia Schoon in San Francisco. Seems you two struck a chord. When she said she needed out of there, good old Principal Rabbitt couldn't wait to help. Got her brother to pretend to be her husband and give her some kind of back-story you could sell to the school. Failed marriage. New life. All that crap. Then you helped her fake all the credentials she needed to work as a teacher—'

'She was a good teacher.' Rabbitt's voice had gone down a touch in volume and tone. He wasn't angry. Maybe wasn't even scared. Just sorry. 'She had the gift. The students loved her.'

'She was a phony.'

Rabbitt glared at him then, and Miller thought: *Maybe there is a little backbone in this weed after all.*

'That town was full of phonies. Me pretending to be something else and all the while itching to be free. Lots of other people feeling the same way. Watching the world go to shit and wondering if we could get a little life in before there was no way out at all.' He nodded at Miller. 'You were as big a phony as the rest of us. Pretending you were some serious kind of cop. When all you did was cover up for the people who mattered. Take the little guys to court when it suited you. Beat up kids for being kids—'

'I did what I was asked, Mister Principal fucking his teachers!'

'Teacher. Just the one. She was beautiful. She was hurt. She needed saving.'

'Oh, Bunny, *Bunny*. You are a conscientious soul. You helped that girl, didn't you? Helped her in and out of bed. Helped her get a job she shouldn't have had. Man, you're Saint Bunny of Prosper. And no one even knows. Not yet.'

Rabbitt shut his eyes tight and swore again. He wasn't even good at that.

'I lost my job. I lost my marriage. I'm stuck here trying to make ends meet. In this rented dump. Having to pay alimony I can't afford—'

'Is there another room you got for sympathy? 'Cuz it don't seem to be working on me in this one.'

To Miller's amazement the guy went for him. More nail-scratching and palm-flapping than a punch. Couldn't have been in a real fight ever. All the same, the tiredness he felt from the journey and getting the run-around lit a fuse in Fred Miller's head right then. Next thing he knew he had Rabbitt on the floor in a headlock, squeezing his neck so tight the guy was fighting to breathe. The kind of move he used to make on young kids who pissed him off back when he was on the job.

Not a good idea. He let go, booted the idiot once in the shins, then picked him up yelping and threw him back into the chair.

'Gonna ignore you did that, Bunny.'

'You're nothing, you old fool. They kicked you out too. Prosper doesn't want to see either of us again.'

It was so hard not to punch his lights straight out at that moment.

'I called and told you she was dead. You never asked how, did you, Bunny? Never asked how.'

That seemed a lifetime ago. Maybe to both of them.

'Didn't like sharing, did you? Didn't like the fact she was banging all kinds of guys. That creep McAllister from the paper to pay the rent. Kids she picked up from school because she liked it. You bought her a cheap necklace and believed what it said there. Forever.'

'We had a bond. It was more than—'

Miller couldn't help but snicker.

'A *bond*? First time I heard it called that. Truth is you couldn't take her screwing around. 'Specially with your kids. So one day when she was in that cabin you went there and—'

'I didn't mind what she did. Believe it or not. I didn't care. She was too... alive for me to be offended. That was who she was. We didn't have that kind of *luminosity* in Prosper.'

'"Luminosity." What the fuck does that mean?'

'I doubt I could explain it, Miller. I doubt you could ever understand. I don't know why I'm telling you this, but our relationship—'

'Your *relationship*?'

'Our relationship had come to an end.'

'Marjorie find out?'

'No. Not 'til that damned paper named me.'

'Your little hooker dumped you.'

'I wasn't going to force her. I'm not that sort of man.'

Miller could scarcely believe his ears.

'No. You're the kind of guy who'd pay to get her to open her pretty legs. Lie to get her on your payroll. Remind her she was in your debt and still had to welcome you beneath the sheets. But you wouldn't *force* her. Not the kind of thing a principal does, huh?'

Rabbitt got up and pointed to the door.

'I want you out of here. Or I *will* call the cops. There's nothing you can say or do that will stop me. This is my home. You're a sad and lost old man, and you're putting a stain on this place that I don't appreciate.'

Miller thought about that. Rabbitt meant it.

'I still think you killed her—'

'Don't be so damned ridiculous! After the newspaper story came out I had Marjorie screaming the place down. The school demanding to know what was going on.'

'She dumped you and you got jealous she was balling the Sorrell kid. So you waited 'til they were in that cabin—that *school* cabin— and set the place on fire.'

'You're an idiot. It's a miracle the town didn't fire you years ago. Get out of here.'

Suddenly there were no questions left to ask. Nothing in his head to say. Except...

'Must have hurt when she told you to get lost. You being the big school guy. The one who saved her.'

There was a liquid sheen in Rabbitt's eyes then, and Miller wondered where that had come from.

'For what it's worth, I would have left Marjorie for her. I told her that. I wanted her to marry me. It would have cost me Lafayette High, and god knows I worked for that for years. All the same I'd have done it. I didn't care so much about... what she did. She taught me that didn't count. What was important was who you were with. What they meant to you. She meant a lot. Everything. I think I meant something to her too. It just wasn't enough.'

It wasn't Bunny Rabbitt who killed her. Fred Miller knew that now. He wouldn't be so keen on bringing in the cops if that was the case. This was another dead end, and all he could think of at that moment was at least he could maybe hurt this stuck-up creep one more time.

'You weren't enough, Bunny. There were others. So many of them. Those guys, those boys... they must have bugged you.'

'No.' He sounded certain of that. 'Not really. One or two, maybe. When she sounded really sweet on them.'

'Who?'

'She didn't say. I don't know. I don't...'

'A name. Give me a name.'

'We didn't talk about the others. Why would we? Why...?'

He was weeping, and that was something Fred Miller never could come to terms with.

'You don't connect to people,' Rabbitt mumbled. 'That's the truth. I didn't either, until she came along. That was the one gift she left me.'

'You don't look too connected now.'

'Just get out of here, will you? Get out and don't come back.'

Miller walked outside and thought: *Beer and whisky. Tomorrow's another day.*

14

VENICE

The walkie-talkie came alive.

That was the best chapter so far, Tommy boy. You're getting the hang of this. Caught my old man dead-on. All that anger and violence waiting to come out. See where I got it from now?

'I want to talk to my daughter. I want to know she's safe. That you haven't hurt her.'

A video window appeared on the computer screen. Live, it seemed, from the light. Lauren was sitting outside on the ground eating what looked like a granola bar. Not tied up or anything, though he could see the feet of the crippled angel at the back of the frame.

A voice from outside the picture barked, 'Say hello to your father.'

'Hello, Father.'

There was a familiar sulky resentment behind it.

'Hi, Lauren.'

The video vanished and they were back to the walkie-talkie, faceless, impersonal, controlled. Vern Miller's preferred mode of communication.

There's a couple of things I'd want to change in there, Tommy. Won't trouble you with them now. You don't have time for that, do you?

'Don't you dare hurt her.'

That's more your choice than mine.

'It isn't, Vern. We're all free to make our own decisions here. You could let her go. We could call it quits. I've given you what you asked for. Could be more, once we're out of here.'

Like what?

'Like me pursuing this story back home. Really trying to get to the bottom of it. I accept now that I got it wrong. It wasn't Jorge Rodriguez. Your father was on to something. Maybe that was what got him killed. We can take what we have, go back to Prosper and Burnsville, the cops there, see what they say.'

They'll yawn and say they don't do history.

'No.'

Do not contradict me! I'm telling you, Honey Bee. Those places don't like people digging up their dirty past. Hell, my old man would have sent you away with his boot up your ass. They read that crappy book of yours. They know Rodriguez lit that fire. They know they don't have a clue who killed my dad, and they couldn't give a shit. It's history.

That, Honeyman thought, *was probably true.*

'I'm trying...'

Not enough, is it, moron? Have you seen the time?

Honeyman hadn't. Time had lost its meaning over the past few days. When he was in Maledetto working on a manuscript it wasn't unusual for him to get as little as three hours sleep a night as he struggled to improve what was on the page. This was different. Short periods of intensive activity, some mental, some physical. His constant worry about Lauren. Night merging into day, moon to sun.

He checked. In his head it was still morning. He couldn't be more wrong.

Four thirty in the afternoon.

It seemed impossible. He must have slept somehow and scarcely noticed. One of those brief moments closing his eyes on the sofa had vanished into lost hours of wasted slumber.

You got seven hours left before the fireworks begin. Seven hours, and you still owe me that last chapter—who really burned down that cabin—or I kill you both. So focus. My old man spoke to Schoon. He flew home. Then he went to see Bunny Rabbitt. A few hours later he was dead. Same time as you were in Burnsville, Tom.

'So it seems.'

Did you see Rabbitt there?

An odd question, Honeyman thought.

'You mean did he turn up to my book event? No. I think I would have remembered. Gary Rabbitt would have made quite an impression. Given he was one of the people who got nailed by my story.'

Did you see anyone you knew? Your wife? Your kid?

'They never came to my events. Or maybe once. At the beginning, where it looks like getting a book out is some big kind of deal. After that, they'd be as bored hearing the same things as I am saying them.'

For Diane, *The Fire* had almost seemed an irrelevance. Something that interested her insofar as it meant they were no longer broke. Paid the bills and got her husband out of the house for weeks, months sometimes, on end. Beyond that... she never asked about it. As far as he knew she hadn't even read it, and he was never going to press that point.

'I didn't see anyone I knew in Burnsville. I was on a book tour. Thirty cities in twenty-five days or something. Your feet don't touch the ground. It's just planes and hotels and people asking you to sign their names and never telling you they spell them weird. Then when it's done, you don't remember much at all. Just a feeling of emptiness. Exhaustion. The book you just sold people as something fresh and new... it's old in your own imagination. Yesterday's news. The only thing that matters is the one to come, the one you ought to be working on, that's supposed to be in your head.'

And it never was, was it?

'Guess not.'

Until now. Look what else the Miller family's giving you.

Something was happening on the laptop. A new app being installed, by the looks of it.

'Vern. If you think Gary Rabbitt killed your father, why didn't you track him down?'

Think I didn't try?

'I didn't say that. You seem pretty good at finding people.'

You're easy. You got a website. Social media presence. You want people to know where you are, what you're doing. Not that so many are interested anymore. I thought about picking you up in Manhattan just for fun. Would have been so easy. Fly in, fly out. No tracks, no obvious motives.

'Why didn't you?'

No need. I thought you might be useful breathing for a while. Especially just the three of us out here.

'You couldn't find him, Vern. Could you?'

The app had finished installing. It looked familiar.

Not 'til now. Took a long while. Principal Rabbitt's a guy who knows how to hide. Here. I'm sending you some personal details.

A new document appeared on the desktop. At the top was what looked like a screenshot from a local website in Winter Haven, Florida. A photo of a man Honeyman could just about recognize as Rabbitt. Older, much older, any beard long gone, along with most of his hair. His face was thinner, almost gaunt. But he looked happy, which almost made him appear a different man altogether. A toddler was in his arms, bouncing on his knee. Behind him stood a dark-skinned young woman. The story was about a new couple taking over a long-established grocery store and deli, one that had been struggling for a while. A retired businessman from Trenton, New Jersey, by the name of Robert Ashford. A young wife from an Iraqi family somewhere out west. A kid with them. They hoped to revive the store and keep the place open for the locals.

A happy couple by the looks of it. Honeyman felt sick to his stomach at the thought of what was going to come next.

I got his address. His phone number. His new name. And the fact his new wife used to be his pupil back in Chicago when he called himself Jay

Waller. Pretty much all an ace reporter like you needs to know. I hope you're grateful.

'Thank you, Vern.'

Want to talk to him?

'You know I can't. No phone. No signal.'

Oh, but with my permission you can. Even better, you can talk to him face to face. Rabbitt, not that he calls himself that now, just put in one of those fancy new home screens in his living room. He can speak to his A/C and tell it what to do. Turn the lights on from bed. Check his bank balance. Ask for the news. And even better...

The app Vern had installed fired up. A video calling program bloggers used when they wanted to record live interviews during an online tour.

Even better, it can do this.

The light at the top of the screen next to the laptop camera began to wink. Which meant it was working.

A picture appeared in the window. A living room, a shiny marble fireplace, a fan whirling away in the ceiling.

Honeyman was struggling to imagine what he was going to say.

A face appeared, curious at first, then furious at what he saw.

'Fuck me, fuck me, *fuck me*...'

'Hi, Principal Rabbitt. Or should that be Ashford? Or Waller, maybe?'

'Jesus Christ. Is that you? Tom Honeyman?'

'Guess so.'

'How the.... How the hell did you find me?'

Rabbitt looked just like he did in the news story: older, with the worn air of a middle-aged family man. And, until the moment he stared into the camera, decidedly less stressed.

'I'm turning this shit off. Don't even think of calling back. You'll be blocked.'

An arm reached out in the picture. Skinny, tanned and, to Honeyman's surprise, there was a trendy tattoo of a chain around his wrist, what looked like a name inscribed above it.

'That wouldn't be a good idea, Gary. We need to talk.'

'Fuck you.'

'No. Listen to me. Won't take long. Winter Haven thinks you're some retired guy from Jersey. Not a disgraced principal. Or a busted teacher from a private school who, I'm guessing, vanished with one of his pupils. If you don't want your neighbors to find out, we need to talk.'

A woman came into the picture. Young, long dark hair, a round and foreign face, puzzled at that moment. There was a child in her arms, a little girl of maybe two in a pink skirt and top, giggling as she played with a plastic toy.

The woman stared at the screen and asked, 'Is something wrong?'

Rabbitt waved at her angrily with his right arm, and the look on his face, shame and fear and worry, made Honeyman feel as guilty as hell.

'You take Layla and go play out back. I got to deal with this.'

Vern Miller maximized the app so it filled the screen. The woman's anxiety was plain and all too real. The kid was holding out her arms and calling, 'Daddy, Daddy, Daddy.'

'Jay—?'

'For pity's sake, honey, don't call me that now. How many times do I have to tell you? Just get outside.'

The two of them left. The kid had started to cry as they moved out of the frame.

'The mother of your kid doesn't even know your real name, does she?'

'What is this?' Rabbitt snapped. 'What the hell do you want?'

The message box popped up in the right-hand corner above the app. Of course Vern Miller couldn't use the walkie-talkie. This was Tom Honeyman's job. All the same, he wanted his say.

The words came out one by one on the screen.

You do this good, Tom. I'll be watching. Every word.

W HAT M ILLER HAD SENT through was a report from a detective agency in Chicago dated two days before. Just a couple of pages, but that was enough to show the last thing the man who called himself Robert Ashford would want was his true identity laid bare in Winter Haven.

Rabbitt had lost his job at the private school in Dunston not long after Fred Miller got shot. Then he'd moved to Chicago and seemingly vanished, leaving his ex-wife back in Prosper broke, chasing alimony from a ghost. The agency had tracked him to a new school in Evanston where he called himself Waller, the maiden name of his mother. He'd lasted there just eighteen months before getting fired over rumors of an affair with a pupil. The school had kept that hushed up and away from the cops. But the young girl involved later vanished too. Then a couple calling themselves Robert and Sora Ashford appeared in Winter Haven with a child and just enough money to rent a store.

The business hovered in the red constantly. His young wife was working part-time as a receptionist in a dental practice to try to make ends meet. All the same, being Rabbitt—or Ashford, now—he tried to keep up appearances. The rented house with its faux-elegant furniture and techno toys was just the kind of thing he'd loved back when he was principal at Lafayette. It was all a façade. The credit reports told a different story. This was a couple slowly going broke, probably about to run again, hoping to leave their debts behind them.

'What do you *want?*' Rabbitt repeated.

Honeyman looked at this familiar face from the past, both the same and changed, and felt the faint shadow of nausea he used to get as a reporter out on a death knock or some other assignment that was about to cause someone pain.

'First I want to hear about Fred Miller.'

'What the hell for?'

'Because I do.'

'Got nothing to say…'

The hand was reaching out again, for the off switch.

'I ruined you once, Rabbitt. I can ruin you again.'

The arm went back.

'Why are you doing this? Why do I have to pay twice?'

'Listen—'

'No. You listen. I've got a wife—'

'She's not your wife. You're living under false names. You can't get married. She's the twenty-three-year-old daughter of an Iraqi diplomat who claimed asylum after the war. She was a pupil of yours in Evanston, and you're damned lucky the school chose to hush that up instead of calling in the cops.'

'I—'

'Listen to me. I got it all here. I know you ran away with her. I know her family spent eighteen months trying to track you down. And if they ever do, well...'

Here, Honeyman was ad-libbing, and it came so easily.

'I don't think it's hard to work out what that might mean. For you. For her. For the kid. At best you end up broke or in jail. At worst... who knows?'

The face that stared back at him from the laptop was the picture of fear and misery.

'Jesus Christ, Honeyman. What did I ever do to you? What did any of us in that town do? You came and ripped us all apart. You got rich on our misery—'

'Mohawk Lake—'

'Mohawk Lake was just the trigger. The weapon you picked. You were looking to bring us all down anyway. I talked to people afterwards. You're a wrecker. It's what you do, and you like it. Tearing people to pieces. Picking at everything 'til it falls apart in front of your eyes.'

Fine, Honeyman thought. *So be it.*

'Very good, Gary. Or Jay. Or Robert. Whatever. Does—Sora, her name is?—know about Mia Schoon? Does she know you were the kind of guy who'd raid the school expense account, go on some junket to San Francisco and pick up a hooker when you felt like it? Then, when you liked what she had, set her up with a job at Lafayette High so you could keep on sleeping with her? Hide her away like a secret little pet—'

'Enough of this shit. No one hid Mia...'

A hand went over something, the speaker probably. Rabbitt was staring around wildly. It was only when he was sure he was on his own that he spoke.

'That guy's gone. You hear me? Not coming back. Ever. I got a real family for the first time. If you take them from me I don't know what I'll do. What do you want? Money? You want money? After all you got—'

'I don't want money. I don't...'

The message box beeped.

Don't go soft now, Tommy. You're doing good. Keep him on the ropes.

'We... I want the truth. I got it wrong. Jorge Rodriguez didn't murder Mia and Scott Sorrell. Chief Miller told you that, when he tracked you down in Dunston.'

'Huh! Yeah. Miller. Made out like it was me. Crazy old bastard.'

'Was it?'

Rabbitt screwed his eyes tight.

'No. He knew that. I'd had the cops all over me when my name popped up on their list. They'd got CCTV of me and Marjorie shopping that morning. God, that's all she ever did. Shop. It wasn't me—'

'Miller got shot that night. After he talked to you.'

'I know.' He said it lightly, easily. 'Damned right I know. Burnsville cops worked out he'd been out to my place, and ran me through the wringer all over again. I was at the school that night. We had a production of *Romeo and Juliet*. Got an audience of fifty as an alibi. Doesn't get any better than that. Didn't stop the school getting spooked by the interest the cops were taking. Damned good job I had there, and all that shit from Mohawk Lake came and took it away. Thanks, Honeyman. Hope you're happy.'

'Not exactly...'

Rabbitt leaned forward, stared into the camera.

'Ever since that Saturday I've been running one way or another. I knew it was going to come out about Mia. Even without your stinking stories you put up on that rag for every last hypocrite in Prosper to see. In a way... I didn't mind. Sick of living a lie. Me and Marjorie had been running on empty for years. It was like everything else in Prosper. Just a pretense. A myth that we were happy. With Mia, just for a while, I was.'

'And now?'

'Now I'm content. I have a wife. She *is* my wife. Doesn't matter about a piece of paper. We've got a beautiful daughter together. I have... ties. A connection finally. Don't take that away. Please, I'm begging. You just cut this call and never come back. Leave us here. I have nothing for you. Nothing at all.'

The laptop sounded.

Keep going, Tom. He's trying to wriggle off the hook, and if he does that and leaves nothing behind...

'I need to find out who really murdered her and the boy. I have to. For my family's sake too. And I have to work out who killed Fred Miller. If there's anything you can tell me. Anything...'

'Why? You writing another book?'

'Kind of. Kind of like to... set the record straight.'

'You can't do that, Honeyman. Too many broken lives. Can't put them back together.'

'Maybe I can try. Fred Miller—'

'The paper said he got shot outside some bar in a part of town no sane person would walk that time of night. Madness.'

'Yeah. I know. He was broke. Lost.'

'He was an idiot. Anyway, how about you? I know you were in town that night. I saw all the notices in the press. You showing off at Barnes and Noble or somewhere.'

'I wasn't showing off. It was work.'

'Work. Yeah. You know, if I hadn't had that school play I might have come along and yelled at you from the audience. Told everyone what a pack of lies that was—'

'You hadn't read it. The publisher tried to send you a proof and couldn't find you.'

'I didn't need to read it! I saw all the crap you ran in the paper. You just decided what the story was, Tom, then dug up whatever shit you could find to support it.'

Another message on the laptop.

Boy, this guy has got your number.

Honeyman couldn't think of anything to say just then.

'Yeah. They pulled me in about Fred Miller. Just like they pulled me in over Mia. At least in Prosper they kept it quiet like I asked. They were decent guys. Not like you. Not like that vicious old bastard Miller. God, I've paid.'

He glanced toward the light of a window Honeyman couldn't see.

'They're my life. Punish me. Don't punish them.'

'Gary. Just give me something.'

'Like what? I don't want those two out there to pay. It's tough enough here already. I don't know if we can make it. Please, just leave us alone.'

'Who do you think shot Fred Miller?'

He was staring straight into the camera then. 'I don't know. Maybe you?'

'Why would I do that?'

Rabbitt shrugged and looked as if he'd enjoyed taking that one pop back. 'Why would *I*?'

'Because he came around that same day threatening you.'

'You think that stupid old bully frightened me? After what I'd been through? He busted in my place asking all kinds of weird questions. About Mia. Saying the cops had got it all wrong with Rodriguez and he was going to prove it.'

'He knew you sneaked her on staff.'

'So what? She was dead. I was fired. So what? I think... I think he actually thought if he could prove it was someone else, they might give him his job back. So he could return to Prosper a local hero. Delusional old fool. They couldn't wait to get his ass out of there. The guy was an embarrassment.'

Honeyman was going back through what he'd written.

'You told him you loved her.'

'What?'

'I have Miller's notes. He made lots of notes after he saw you. You said you loved her. You said you'd told her you'd leave Marjorie for her. You bought her that pendant they found.'

Again that glance at the window, the sudden swift shadow of shame stealing across his face.

'No I didn't. I never bought her a damned pendant. She used to make that stuff herself. She didn't need jewelry from anyone.'

Honeyman thought of the picture Vern Miller had sent him, the one he got from his old man. A silver heart, battered, stained with smoke and soot. Maybe it wasn't the kind of thing a man with pretensions like Gary Rabbitt would buy his lover. This was petering out with nothing to show.

'I need more than that. I need you to give me something, or I swear I'm packaging up everything I got and sending it to anyone I can find in Winter Haven. You know how news travels fast in small places. Especially when it's hot and bad.'

Rabbitt came closer to the camera and for a moment looked like the teacher he once was.

'And why would you want to do that, Tom?'

'Because I'm desperate. Hadn't you noticed? Who did she dump you for? Mia? Who was it who meant something?'

He shrugged.

'I don't know. Truly. Scott Sorrell? Nah. He was just a good-looking teenager with a bit of muscle on him. She liked that. Liked young. Kid thought he'd struck lucky. Nothing more than that.'

'Who?'

'I. Don't. *Know*. She never said. I never asked. We were over by then.'

'She must have—'

'One time. In school. She said something about someone getting heavy with her. Too close. Mia was like that. You kind of fell head over heels, and she never noticed what she was doing. It was all just... unreal. I don't think she ever connected with anybody. Or maybe she connected with everybody on the same level. Never noticed some of us wanted more, and you couldn't have that. It wasn't on offer. Though what you got... that made you feel so alive it didn't really matter. You thought you were the one. She could do that.'

There was a glassiness in his eyes then, the same kind of sheen Miller must have noticed hours before he died.

Honeyman persisted.

'Someone followed them to that cabin. Poured gas all over the place. Locked them in there. Burned them to a crisp.'

'Yeah. I know.'

'An innocent man got shot by the cops thinking it was him. Fred Miller died—'

'Is there a point to any of this? I keep telling you. I wasn't there. I wasn't responsible. At least no more responsible than anyone else in that damned town.'

'I don't want to hurt you—'

'Then don't. I'm begging.'

'This someone special...'

'I told you! She never said! The students, McAllister, she told me about them. She thought your old boss was a joke. And the kids... it was like she was doing them a favor. Bringing them into the big world. I told her she'd go to jail if Miller found out. Like she gave a shit.'

The screen sounded, another message.

Ask him about women, Tom.

I did, Vern. Didn't you notice? He's come clean about her.

Not him and women. Her.

Honeyman hesitated.

I'm telling you. You do it. I got your kid here. I want that question asked.

'Can I go now?' Rabbitt looked terrible.

'This other person... could it have been a woman?'

There was a flicker of anger in the guy's eyes, and Honeyman thought: *That's it. Caught.*

'Who told you that?'

'I'm asking.'

Again that shrug, a sign of defeat.

'Yeah. It could have been. Mia said she liked them just as much as she liked men. I told her to go careful in Prosper. It wasn't San Francisco. Being gay and getting found out was one sin some of the stuck-up prudes in that place were never going to forgive. I...' He glanced around, determined to make sure he was on his own. 'One time she asked me if I wanted to join in.'

'Who with?'

He shook his head.

'I don't know. The whole idea freaked me out. It wasn't for the sex. That wasn't what I wanted from her. Something... sordid like that. I wanted her. Just her. All to myself. Normal, like man and wife with kids and some comfort, some security. What a goddamn fool I was. But I didn't kill her. And I can prove it. Just like I can prove I never killed Fred Miller.'

The face came close to the camera.

'How about you, Mister Honeyman? You got guilt written all over your face that I think it must go deep right into your soul. If you got one. How about—?'

Honeyman abruptly closed the app.

The walkie-talkie came alive so loudly it made him jump.

No avoiding this, Tom. It's the million-dollar question. How about you?

IT WAS HOT, even for Venice in July. Five-thirty, humid, had to be close to a hundred degrees. Outside, across the lagoon, the preliminaries for the Feast of the Redeemer would have started. Honeyman had been there a couple of times, once with a teenage Lauren, who'd been mildly amused by the spectacle. Tens of thousands of visitors crowding the city, making the Piazza San Marco and the Rialto more impassable than ever.

Around four the celebrations would have started outside the grand basilica of Redentore on Giudecca, the symbol of salvation after terrible plague. First, children would row their twin-oared *pupparini* boats down the canal. Later there'd be a regatta of two-man gondolas along the same route, then the temporary pontoon bridge spanning the canal from Zattere to Giudecca would open to the teeming crowds.

On every canal and *rio* there'd be private boats cruising idly up and down, packed with people swigging *prosecco* and spritzers. Giorgio Morosini would be among them, he guessed, always with an attractive woman on board, perhaps wondering what time he might come out to Maledetto the following day. If indeed the Venetian did. Like all the locals, his timekeeping was erratic at best.

The Festa del Redentore was a night to feel alive, to celebrate the arrival of high summer and with it the lassitude that fell upon the city at that time of year. When he was there with Lauren they'd wandered to the Riva dei Sette Martiri waterfront by Giardini and watched the spectacular finale to the opening night, the gigantic fireworks show over Saint Mark's Basin, a riot of color and noise that tore into the sky near midnight. Diane was still at home and, thinking back, it seemed Lauren was almost glad her mother hadn't joined them in Italy. The two of them had been close that night, as close as it got. Maybe that was when he got the idea of using Redentore as a kind of milepost for his books. A target to be hit, not that it ever really was.

Except, perhaps, this year, in the strange way a dangerous and violent man named Vern Miller had engineered.

The walkie-talkie buzzed. He looked at it, walked into the kitchen, made himself a Negroni so powerful he almost winced when he took the first swig.

It was time to think. Honeyman sat down at the table, listening to the squawk from the adjoining room.

Back home he had something like thirty-five thousand dollars left in the bank. Here, there was a gun hidden away in the room Lauren had been using.

That was something. He went upstairs and dug it out from under the spare mattress.

He'd never used a weapon in his life. But it wasn't hard to work out how. Or that the magazine contained five shells. He guessed he could shoot a man too. If that was what it took.

When he was downstairs the walkie-talkie was still squawking.

Where've you been?

'I was hungry. I needed a drink.'

Jesus, timing's not your thing, is it? Looked at the clock?

Just turned six.

'Yeah.'

And still not finished, are you? One more chapter to go. The last one. The one that tells me who set that fire.

'And who killed your father. I got the message, Vern. Don't worry.'

Silence, then a video window came up on screen.

Lauren. Calm. Pale. Determined. Standing by the crippled angel. In the golden light of late afternoon she looked older.

'Dad?'

Her voice was a tone lower than usual. It looked as if she'd been crying.

'Your kid says she wants to talk to you. On her own.'

Lauren snapped, 'I'm not saying anything when you're around, Vern. Gimme a minute alone with my dad. You promised.'

Miller swore. The picture moved, and it was easy to see what was happening. He was passing the camera, the phone, whatever he was using, over to her.

A long wait. Footsteps falling away somewhere out of view.

'He's gone now.'

Honeyman couldn't work out what was happening.

'Where?'

'I think he's checking over the dinghy. He means it, Dad. We're out of time. I know I said you needed to hold things back, but not now. Either he gets what he wants or we're both dead.'

'I have money in the bank—'

'He doesn't want your money! You've got to tell him.'

She was staring straight at the lens, tears streaming down her cheeks.

'Tell him what?'

'For god's sake, do I have to say it? You've got to write it, Dad. The truth. No way out. No other...'

Lauren moved further into view so she was staring straight in his face.

'Dad. I know.'

'Know what?'

'Something happened with you and Mom. I *know*.'

She glanced around. He wondered if Miller was listening.

'What have you told him, Lauren?'

It all came out in a rush.

'I didn't *tell* him anything. I didn't have to. You're lying, Dad. I watched Mom going to pieces while you were gone. Old man Miller coming over to the house. Always asking questions. Pushing her. I thought she'd told you.'

He took out the gun and put it on the desk.

'You mean when he was a cop?'

'No. After he got fired. She said he wouldn't let go. He kept saying you got it wrong in all that stuff you wrote for the paper. He was going to put it right. Get back to Prosper.'

He knew that last part now. Didn't realize Miller had been visiting while he was away.

'Why did he want to talk to her?'

'She never said. She always made me go out when he was around. I thought... I assumed she'd told you.'

'He was just fishing, Lauren. That's all. The guy did that with everyone.'

Her eyes, bleak and a little damp, glared back at him.

'You wrote that stuff. About him coming back from San Francisco and leaning on her. That's not all.'

He felt cold. Felt the clock was ticking away too fast. Wondered how quickly he could write something, anything, that might keep Vern Miller dangling on the line.

'When you were doing the book event in Burnsville—'

'I didn't see Miller. That's the truth.'

'You mean you didn't see Mom either?'

Honeyman shook his head. This was crazy.

'Of course not...' He'd tried to remember, but the event was a blank. One more evening of talking bullshit, then signing books. 'She wasn't there.'

Lauren swung her head from side to side, checking they were still alone.

'She told me she was going. I... I said I'd like to come too. You and a book, that was cool. But she said I had to stay at home. Do school-work. She'd asked you, and you agreed.'

This was new. This was wrong.

'No, no. She never said anything about that. Never asked me. I'd have wanted you there.'

He couldn't take his eyes off her face. It wasn't just fear. There was something else there too.

'I thought you knew. I didn't dare say.'

'Say what?'

'She came back late. After midnight. I was in bed. Heard her crying and shrieking. When I came down she was a big mess in front of the fire. Drunk as hell. Like she was going crazy. She was, wasn't she? I mean... we both know that. What she was like after...'

But he didn't. He was either on tour or in Italy most of the time. Soon, Lauren was at college. Diane living on her own. He felt she'd preferred it that way. If he hung around the house too long she'd be asking him... *Are you going somewhere soon?*

She'd said that before he made that trip to Italy, just before she killed herself.

'Are you trying to tell me *she* shot Fred Miller? Mom?'

Again her eyes fixed on him.

'She was wasted. I wanted to call you. She said no.'

'Lauren—'

'There was a gun. She showed me...'

Lauren was weeping full on.

'What?'

'She said something needed doing. Something bad. If anyone asked, I was to say the two of us had been in the house all night.

Watching TV. I wasn't ever to say anything to anyone. To you. Anyone.'

He craved a drink. Didn't dare.

'We never had a gun—'

'I thought it was the two of you. I was scared.'

A memory. A phone call from the West Coast somewhere when he was on tour, a week after Miller died. He'd read about the murder online. When he mentioned it to Diane she blanked it out as if it was nothing.

'Lauren. This is all new to me.'

'Yeah, well, I've lived with it for years. I took the gun straight out that night and threw the damned thing in the river. You're not asking me, Dad.'

'I never knew how bad it was. If I had I'd never have left her on her own.'

'You're not asking me.'

'What?'

'Why she'd want Fred Miller dead. What she thought the two of you needed to hide.'

Dammit, he needed that drink. Honeyman walked away from the computer in a daze, went to the kitchen, poured himself a big one with shaking hands.

When he got back Lauren was still there, wide-open eyes staring down the lens.

'That was cowardly,' she threw at him. 'Walking off just when I asked. Never thought of you that way before, Dad.'

He thought maybe he mumbled 'sorry' but he wasn't sure.

'I've been choking this down for years. Not knowing. How much of it was her. How much of it you. Can't do it anymore.'

'I don't—'

'You've got to let it out now. Mohawk Lake wasn't like you said. I think maybe the two of you invented that story just so you could cover up what really happened. Can't do that anymore, Dad. You've got to write it. That's the only chance we've got. Write it. What really happened. I know you've been hiding something, Dad. I know some of this stuff you've fed him can't be true. You've got to put everything straight. Tell it like it really was. You've got to do this now, or he's going to kill us both.'

She pulled away from the camera and swore at something, someone.

'He's back.'

Vern Miller's face came up instead of hers. It was the first time Honeyman had truly seen him clearly. A man in his early thirties, stubble, dark eyes, fiery with anger.

'Hell, Honey Bee. I *am* a bad man. I did listen.' He had something in his hand, and it took a moment to work out what it was: a blow-torch. Miller pressed a button and a roaring jet of blue and yellow flame came out of the barrel. 'See. Like I said. I'm your muse. I'm your spark. Do what she said, or you and your kid here are lighting the sky tonight, just like the fireworks across the water.'

15

PROSPER, NEW YORK

August 8, 2008
(Revised)

'I heard guys talking...' Lauren sat there, mouth full of pasta, hair still wet from the shower. 'They said—'

'Oh, Christ. Again?' Her mother glared across the table. 'Just one time. One meal. One day where we don't talk about Mohawk Lake and that damned teacher, please.'

'Mom. It's all we got to talk about. Word is...'

Tom Honeyman did his best to intervene when it turned like this between them. Of late, it seemed to be happening a lot.

'Listen to your mom.'

'I *am* listening.'

Always a smart answer. Still, he persisted. It was expected.

'Is this really important? Right now?'

Lauren stared at Diane across the table.

'You tell me, Mom. What do you think? Want me to go on?'

'Fine...'

'I heard this morning that Mia was seen arguing with Billy

Rodriguez's dad the week before she was killed. Someone saw them out by the parking lot, and he was so mad it looked like he'd hit her.'

'Jesus...' Diane reached for her glass. It was wine again, not half cut with water like Tom had been asking. Lately, Diane always seemed miserable. He never could work out why. And it didn't feel right to ask. That was just the quick way to a fight. 'Jorge Rodriguez. What the hell's that guy got to do with anything?'

'Wait.' This was all new to Honeyman. 'Who's Jorge Rodriguez?'

'Dad. If you ever took any interest in school you'd know. Me and Billy are in the same year.'

'I didn't—'

'Everyone knows it wasn't just Bunny Rabbitt she was balling. Or Scott Sorrell. Everyone—'

'I don't think this is dinner table talk,' Honeyman said.

The two women glanced at one another and smiled. He got the message: Dad being pompous again.

'Some reporter you are, Tom. Maybe your daughter's come home with a story.'

'Huh?'

Lauren took over.

'Jorge Rodriguez. Guy works for the fire department. Or did. They say he had a fight there or something and got fired. Used to beat up on his wife. Billy too, sometimes.'

'He knew Mia Buckingham?'

'Yeah. I mean... who didn't? Everyone said she was real easy once school was out.'

'Everyone?' Honeyman asked. 'The woman's dead, Lauren. One of your classmates too.'

'I *know*. Me and Scott kind of dated a couple of times. Not that you'd notice. He was OK. So was Billy Rodriguez. Neither of them what you'd call *smart*.'

'Try and be respectful,' Honeyman said.

She put down her fork and stared at him, mouth open.

'Respectful? Wait a minute. You've been *personally* pissing off the whole town for weeks, lifting up the sheets and looking at what's stuck to the mattress underneath. Now you're taking a pop at me for *dissing people*?'

'It's my job—'

Diane grabbed the wine bottle and topped up her glass.

'You could always try listening to your daughter for once.'

'Why?'

'Because Mohawk Lake's going stale right now and you have no other story to keep your name up there. Bad news, Tom. No book deal coming your way soon if this goes on.'

'A book?' Lauren looked astonished. 'You think Dad could write *a book*?'

'Miracles happen, honey. We may need it. The *News-Ledger's* getting skinnier every week. No ads. The economy's shit. Your father could be out of work before long. Think about it. If he's got no job, then what do we do?'

'Then he'll find another one, won't you, Dad?'

Diane's laughter wasn't a pleasant sound.

'Kids. Fucking clueless.'

'Diane. Language.'

Lauren laughed.

'Yeah. Like I never heard *that* word before. We won't go broke, will we?'

'No—'

'We could.' Diane waved her glass at him. 'Don't lie to her, Tom. Get real. How many reporting jobs do you think there are anywhere right now? There's banks going under. People getting kicked out of offices all over—'

'Mom. This is Prosper. Dullsville. Things like that don't happen here.'

'Teachers getting burned alive while screwing one of their kids doesn't happen here either. Except when it does.'

Honeyman took his daughter's hand, and immediately she snatched it away.

'Don't worry. We'll manage. Maybe this story... maybe it's got legs.'

'Yeah. Legs.' His wife thought that funny too, and he wondered how much she'd had to drink, how long she'd been going at it before he came home from the office. 'Tanned and skinny ones like the lovely Mia's. So are you even trying to write this book?'

'I haven't... haven't started it yet.'

'Is it going to write itself?'

'No. I'm getting people interested. A publisher. It's a big story. Good story.'

She scowled. 'Isn't all this a little sordid for you?'

'Sordid sells.' Lauren said that with a nod. 'Sordid always sells.'

'But your father.' Diane was loving this, amused they were both teasing him. 'He's better than that. He sees himself as a *writer*. Isn't that right, Tom? Isn't a grubby little sex twosome turned bad just a touch... opportunistic?'

'Someone's going to do it. And maybe I can make it... more than that.'

'Hard to write a story without an ending. Looks to me like the cops are out of ideas. Miller's wandering all over town yelling at anyone he can find. The state cops and the Feds don't have a clue.'

From what he'd heard she was right. The case had ground to a halt. No forensic leads. Nothing in Mia Buckingham's complex private life. The two adult lovers they *could* name seemed to have unshakable alibis.

'These things take time.'

'No killer, no book, is there?'

'Maybe. Maybe not. I don't know. I'm working on it.'

Lauren got to her feet, a piece of pizza still in her fingers. 'I'm done with you two. Going to Rosie's. Me and her are doing schoolwork.'

'You mean listening to stupid music and pretending you can dance?' Diane sniped.

Lauren sashayed right there in front of them.

'Maybe, Mom. Who cares? Like you said, the world's going to shit anyway. If you two don't want to listen to what I have to say... not my fault.'

'Yeah, yeah.' Diane was shaking her head as if this was inevitable. 'Come on, then. Out with it.'

Lauren pouted like a little kid.

'You sure? I don't want to interrupt your conversation. You want me to do this, don't you?'

There was something odd in her voice then.

'Yes.' Diane turned serious for a moment. 'I do. Tell us, please. Tell both of us. Then go.'

'Thanks. What I was going to tell you is the day after someone saw Mister Rodriguez arguing with Mia, Billy got taken out of school by his mom. The two of them left for Syracuse. Never coming back. She and Mister Rodriguez are getting divorced. He drinks. He's mean, too. They think maybe he was banging Mia. Or Mia was banging Billy, and his old man found out and went wild. Or both. I don't know. But he had a fight with her. Then he got fired.'

'School gossip.' Diane stabbed a fork in the cold and clammy pasta. 'Why do we have to listen to this?'

'Because, Mom, nothing ever happened here before. And now it has. Billy's gone, isn't he? Mrs. Rodriguez too. Guess they didn't like living in that shitty trailer out in the woods. With a weirdo for a dad. They all got hated on 'cuz they were Mexican—'

'They came from Arizona.'

'Yeah, well, wherever they came from, I'm telling you. Him and Mia had a big fight. A week later the cabin gets burned down with her and Scott in it. Just saying.'

Then she was gone, and not long after, in the silence, they heard the gate open as she wheeled her bicycle out into the road.

DIANE KEPT DRINKING, not looking at him. Lost in something he couldn't quite imagine. Though watching her over the table gave him a sick feeling in his stomach. A realization how far they'd drifted apart over the years as he struggled to write, to find a way out of the *News-Ledger*.

'You knew this Rodriguez guy?' he asked.

He couldn't figure the expression in her eyes. Contempt? Guilt?

'Not exactly, Tom. I knew *of* him. If you went to school meetings a bit more maybe you'd learn things. If you could meet people without always wearing your damned reporter's hat.'

'I seem to recall we both did that once.'

'Yeah. And then I stayed home to bring up Lauren. And you just... vanished somewhere.'

'Right.'

She hesitated.

'It's true. What Lauren said. There was bad blood between Rodriguez and Mia. She told me herself. He'd been... rude.'

'Mia told you?'

'Correct.'

This was going somewhere he feared. Still, he couldn't stop himself.

'And you never told the cops?'

Diane closed her eyes and shook her head.

'No. When did you last talk to a teacher?'

'I don't—'

'They get shit from kids. They get shit from parents. If you were more of a father you'd be in there with me giving some of those lazy SOBs at Lafayette shit too. Starting with Gary Rabbitt. School's even worse than when I went there. Not that he matters anymore. You've seen to that. Who *did* send you that stuff?'

'The forensics report?'

'Yes.'

'I don't know. It just came through the mail.'

'Cue the hungry reporter. Roll some bait in front of Mister Honeyman, and you can guarantee he'll take it.'

'What does that mean?'

Diane got to her feet and began clearing the dirty plates. It was an automatic act. If he tried to help she always objected. Right now he could see she didn't want to look him in the face. Didn't want him to notice when she went back to the wine bottle, either.

'You should see what you can find out about Rodriguez. Go do that. Then we can have a talk.'

'About what?'

When she turned, glass in one hand, cloth in the other, she looked like the confident woman he'd first known. Someone he'd found a touch scary at first—and he'd liked that.

'About... lots. Now.' She nodded at the door. 'Off you go.'

Honeyman grabbed a beer and went upstairs, turned on the laptop. He could get into the *News-Ledger* database, lots of others too.

Plenty of places to look.

Though quite why, he still wasn't sure.

HE TALKED to the fire chief, Lou Barclay, established a few facts about Rodriguez, then sat at the desk, eyes on the screen, taking in nothing at all.

'Tom?' Her voice up the stairs was different too. Older. Deeper. 'You done up there or what?'

'Kind of.'

'Kind of. Are you coming down?'

She was in the front room, no booze this time. Arms crossed, waiting for him. 'So what do you think?'

'Don't know. Maybe I ought to go and try to talk to him.'

'That's tough-guy reporting. Not your kind of thing. You're the observant kind. Good with words.' She paused and smiled. 'Good with your imagination. Excellent, I'd say. You know confrontations aren't your style. You hate them with everyone. Me especially.'

Maybe, he thought, he barely knew this Diane at all.

'If it's my job I'll do it. If he's got something... If there's a story.'

'Sure sounds that way.' She lit a cigarette. Diane hardly ever smoked in the house. 'Are you going to ask him who was screwing Mia? Him or Billy?'

'I thought I might tell him there was a rumor going round town saying he got fired. Ask him if it was true and whether he wanted to talk about it. Then drop Mia into the conversation...'

She laughed.

'You can never come right out with something, can you?'

No. Certainly not then, given the hard and troubling look in her eyes.

'Let me save you the trouble. Mia didn't touch either of them. She wasn't entirely without taste. It was just an argument about Billy getting bad grades.'

The silence between them was long and painful, and he knew he had to break it, though he understood he'd hate the answer.

'You... asked Lauren to bring this Rodriguez guy up?'

Diane squinted at him. 'You're really quite quick sometimes.'

'Why?'

'Looking for a new story, aren't you?'

'What was she like?'

Diane shuffled up in the chair and decided she did need a drink after all. 'You?'

'I'll pass. I may have to drive.'

Back with a fresh tumbler of chardonnay, she said, 'Great figure. Hell of a looker. Why ask? You know that. You saw her at school. You printed that picture of her in bed with the Sorrell kid. I bet there wasn't a soul in town who wasn't jerking off to that when they had the chance. Something about pretty dead people. Especially ones you've known. Can't quite put my finger on it somehow, but... well.' She winked. 'I knew you wouldn't mind. You never have before. You've never even asked.'

There was a silent agreement that they didn't talk about what happened outside the house. And who with. That was her business. Not his. They had a daughter to look after, to try to bring up as well as they could. Problems enough with money and work. If a quiet affair kept her happy, he could live with it. So long as he didn't know any names and it never crossed the threshold of their home. Nor did he care to join in. Life was difficult enough without making it more complicated.

They'd talked a couple of times, after drink was taken, usually, about what might happen when Lauren was gone, settled somewhere. In the meantime... they'd try to make the best of it. The way the economy was going, there wasn't much choice. They were trapped with one another. Perhaps his urge to write, to start a new career as a writer, was part of a subconscious urge to escape the life they had together as much as the drudgery of being a lowly hack in Prosper. He wasn't sure and didn't want to think too hard about it.

'Did you like her?'

'More than that. Up it a notch. Quite a few actually.'

'Oh.'

'I don't... I don't think you'd call it love. More a kind of... losing your mind and being in thrall to every second. Not that I profess to be an expert when it comes to emotions. Who is? Not you. Not me. The two of us just fell into things. Me pregnant and knowing there was no way out.' She gestured at the room. 'We live this way because it helps us get by. Mia was different. You won't understand. You don't have a single wild gene in you. She was like color in a world that was black and white. A fancy, exotic flower in a bed of gray and boring weeds. Hard to ignore even though all the bees kept buzzing around, looking to edge you out of the way and sniff at her the way you did. Dying to get close, didn't matter what it cost.'

He kept quiet, not wanting to hear. She said it anyway.

'Pissed me off no end when she dumped me. Pissed me off even more when I found out she'd started balling kids from school. Not just Rabbitt and your idiot boss. I mean... she had a reason for those two. But kids. Children. It's insulting. Me a grown woman. Giving way to teenagers.'

A slug of wine went down, and she closed her eyes.

Honeyman said, 'I don't believe this. Any of it.'

'Like I give a— Thing is, by the time it got to that Saturday I'd had enough. I thought maybe I'd scare her.'

'You really want to tell me this?'

'Why not, Tom? Man and wife. Don't you deserve to know?'

'I don't believe for one moment—'

'Your choice. Want to run away upstairs and pretend to write that book you're never going to finish?'

'You wanted to scare her?'

'Yeah. Is that so hard to accept?'

A part of him said this was nonsense. He knew Diane, or thought he did. There'd been men in the past. Never women. Or maybe she just never mentioned them.

Another part said all the pieces might finally be starting to fall into place.

'If you're dousing a wood cabin with gas, you're not trying to scare someone. You're aiming to kill them.'

'Well...' She shrugged. 'Maybe. I was kind of mad. I mean... *mad* mad. That's what sitting here on your own all day long pretending you're a happy, everyday homemaker, doing the wash and the dishes, picking up your kid, dropping off your kid... that's what it does to you. To me anyway.' She screwed up her eyes as if trying to fix on a thought that was just out of reach. 'When Mia came along I felt alive. Hard to explain. It was like I could feel the breath in my lungs. Like everything we did was somehow more real. There was a kind of meaning to it. Nothing big. Just skin that felt like skin, warm, close... thrilling. There was a buzz to everything. She did that to you. Wasn't just the fact'—her eyes were wide open now and fixed on him—'the fact she could do more with one finger than you could manage with your whole body.'

'I didn't need to know that.'

'True. I've got a cruel streak, Tom. A crazy streak. And all these years I've tried to keep that hidden. Thing is... you try to tell yourself everything, this life we live, it's all safe and constant and maybe shitty but at least the ground's all firm beneath our feet. Nothing going to open up and swallow us. Except... you remember on September eleventh? Remember sitting here, looking at the little kid between the two of us, thinking everything we took for granted—maybe it was all just sand running through our fingers? What we had... what little we had... it could all get snatched away any minute? Seven years ago, that's all that was. Now we're back there. Every day some bank going down. Some company closing. Wall Street going crazy. We don't even know if the few pennies we've got are safe anymore. This house. You. Lauren. Nothing lasts. Nothing's permanent. Then... then you find some little bit of happiness pops out of nowhere in the here and now. You think anyone's going to say no? That it's *wrong*? I'll *wait*?'

She went over to the table and picked up her phone.

'I feel better already. Letting it all out. If you want to call Fred Miller, feel free. He keeps sniffing around. Came here a couple of times while you were out, not that he had anything on me. Maybe those other guys, the ones who want his job, they do. I don't know. But still... best be prepared.'

She held out the phone, and all he could think of was to ask, 'What do you want of me?'

'I want you to choose. Whose side you're on. Ours or theirs. Either do the noble thing and tell the truth. Or the two of us get our asses out of this and weave one big, big lie. Which do you think we're best at, Tom? What have we perfected all these years?'

'Two people have died. You... You...'

'Yeah. I killed them. I know. Hard to get stuff like that out of your head. Still... one day maybe.' She came close and pressed the phone on him. 'Truth? Or lie? You decide.'

When he still did nothing she went to the kitchen, pulled on a pair of rubber gloves, then retrieved a black-and-silver pocket camera from a drawer.

He shook his head.

'What's the camera got to do with anything? McAllister gave it to me for work.'

'Not this one. Mia grabbed it off some creep spying on us out in the woods. Trying to take photos through the window. Dirty little bastard. She gave it to me as a kind of present. A now-we're-done present, it turned out.'

Diane began flicking through the images, then hitting a button on the back.

'What are you doing?'

'Making damned sure there's none of me on here. Not like the guy who took them is going to be saying anything now.'

The gloves were a lurid yellow, the ones she used for the dishes. She extricated something from inside the camera then held it out in the rubber fingers. A memory card.

'Rodriguez has a place in that trailer park a mile out on Consett Lane. Silver one, set out on its own. Take a left when you drive in. You plant this thing and leave it there. The guy spends half his life in a bar anyway. There's a big camera on the desk. You pop this card in there, bring up these photos on the screen, take pictures of them. Then you run them on the web tomorrow, say someone sent them in the mail. The cops go to his place, push it all his way. We...' She grimaced. 'We try and survive.'

'I don't believe—'

'Stop saying that. This is now. This is real. Truth or lie. It's going to hurt either way, but one so much more than the other.' She winced and he saw the pain there. That was genuine enough. 'I don't want to go to jail. I'm not going to let that happen. I can't...'

She started crying, for real, not effect. He couldn't remember the last time.

'Thing is... I got to get this out of my head, Tom. Got to. Ever since, what with that bastard Miller hanging around, Lauren looking at me like she suspects something, I see... I see... God...'

He went and knelt by her, put an arm round her shoulders, couldn't think of a word to say.

'It's like there's something out there. Something waiting. Watching. Pointing right at me. Like it's real. Someone—a shooter in the shadows. Laughing, picking his moment, and then I'm dead. Could be tomorrow. Next month. Next year. I don't know.' Her face fell against his, damp cheeks, warm breath quick and hurt. 'I've got to shake this whole thing off, Tom. Close it down. Either call the cops or help me. Nothing in between.'

So close to her just then he felt he could see it too, that thing in the dark, could understand how it might stalk you. How, if you couldn't avoid its distant stare, you'd crave to share that burden with someone else.

'Whoever took these photos. The guy in the woods—'

'I said. You don't need to worry about him.'

He didn't dare ask what that meant.

'What if Rodriguez has an alibi?'

She didn't look him in the eye when she said, 'He hasn't. He's a drunk living on his own. No one knew where he was that morning before he showed up for work.'

'How—?'

'You don't need to know.'

'Dammit, Diane. He's innocent.'

Her voice rose. Angry, and usually she never needed the volume to make that clear.

'You know how long these cases take? Years. Miller won't be pulling him in and beating a confession out of him. He's not going to plead. Some lawyer will come along. A bunch of hearings. When it finally comes to trial maybe a good one can get him off. Who cares? We'll be gone from here by then. And you...' She leaned over and kissed his cheek, quick, eager, desperate. 'You're going to have your book. The mystery of Mohawk Lake. You can take this town apart just like you always wanted. I mean...' She leaned back and reached for the wine. 'You keep saying you want to save us. Here's your chance.'

Honeyman stared at the memory card.

'Your choice, Tom. You decide.'

'Lies always come back to bite you.'

She shrugged, and there was the faintest of smiles.

'Maybe. But not today. Not tomorrow. Lies can give us time, and a little time's all I need. If this crashes down when Lauren's older, then fine. But not now. Not the way she is.'

'How the hell could I get into his trailer?'

Her smile grew wider. He was lost and they both knew it.

Diane reached into her jeans pocket and pulled out a key.

'You use this. Rodriguez is in the Hawkeye every night 'til ten or eleven getting wasted. Trying to pick up anything that moves.'

'How—?'

'He's got a bunch of books about fires in there. Some of them weird. The cops will love all that. Supporting material. If they find the photos as well...'

Honeyman pointed at the key.

'Oh, for chrissake don't ask for details! I said. He hangs out in the Hawkeye looking for company. You've been out working most nights, haven't you? Never asked once where I was, what I did. I got this thing looking at me all the time, Tom. I need it gone. I want an escape route. For all of us. Can't do it on my own.' She blinked, and for a moment he thought she might break down completely. 'I'm sorry. I wish to god I'd never seen her.' Just for a second there was a wry look, amused almost. 'No. That's wrong. I won't lie to you. Not anymore. I wish it hadn't turned out this way. That's all.'

Sometimes there was a fork in the road and you didn't know which way to take. Left or right. Up or down. Didn't know what lay at the end of any of them. Just that something was pushing you forward, saying you had to decide. No way you can stay where you are. No chance you can go back to a time when everything seemed simpler, safer, predictable.

The strange thing was this moment felt almost tender, intimate, more full of meaning than any they'd enjoyed in years. It was as if they were a team again, the way they were almost two decades before, when they were reporters on the *News-Ledger*.

He squeezed her hand and said, 'Your plan sucks.'

She sighed, leaned back in the chair.

Quickly he added, 'I think we can do better. A lot better.'

Suddenly, her arms were around him, her tears on his skin. Her voice soft and hoarse in his ear. It was so unexpected he didn't know what to do.

'I'll never forget this. You be my rock. I'll be yours.'

He went upstairs, and sat down at the computer. In the newspaper's files there was a photo of the cabin from when it was first built. He made some notes and sketches about how a fire might be set around it, printed everything and stapled the pages together.

It was a warm night, dark, thick cloud, no stars, not much in the way of traffic either. All the same he wore a hood over his head when he stopped off to buy three jerry cans, one full of gas, from a station on the edge of town, and made sure to park the VW down the road and walk to the trailer, all the way there and back.

It was midnight by the time he arrived home, after putting the story to bed in the office and hitting the "publish" button to schedule the piece for the next morning.

Lauren was in her room—no music, no lights for once.

Diane was in bed. He came in, showered, joined her. She never said a word, just reached for him. Then they made love for the first time in months—real love, anxious, mindless, a physical act beyond thought and speech and maybe even memory.

When it was done, sweaty, still locked together, her damp, tear-stained cheeks against his, she whispered, 'You're done?'

'Yeah. Done.'

She kissed him and it all began again.

THE DAY JORGE RODRIGUEZ died in a hail of bullets, Tom Honeyman almost gave up. He'd never foreseen that happening after his story went online that morning. Though maybe Diane had. The cops told him later someone had called Rodriguez on his cell just before the SWAT team arrived. They didn't know who; the number was blocked. But Rodriguez had been whining in the Hawkeye about how he believed someone was out to cause him trouble. So the guy's fuse was lit already. That anonymous call was just the kind of thing Diane would have done. Honeyman suspected she had his number from the time she got the key, and maybe knew about the BB gun as well.

He never asked. Instead he dithered about going to the Feds—not Miller, never Miller—and telling them what had happened. But he didn't. There was their future to think about. And Lauren, sixteen, facing the prospect of both her parents in jail.

All the time Diane acted as if nothing had happened—never nagged him, never said a word except a muttered 'oh' when they turned on the TV and saw that live report, the same dread clip that greeted him when he turned up in Maledetto, triggered by Vern Miller on his hacked laptop.

As Mohawk Lake turned from news to recent history, life went on, though it had a strange, two-dimensional quality that meant Tom Honeyman felt as if he was walking through a dream. The book deal came and freed him from the newspaper. Lauren went to college, and by then he could afford the tuition. He absented himself from life in Prosper as much as he could. Even so, when he was home, from time to time, Diane would seize him at night, demand they make love, just as she did after he sneaked into Rodriguez's trailer and planted those incriminating pictures. It was as if somewhere in the old, lost ritual there was a kind of comfort, a meaning they might find together. Though usually she cried too, and the memory of her tears against his cheeks was one he could never erase.

They didn't speak of the cabin in the woods again. Of Mia Buckingham. Lafayette High. Or Fred Miller when he got shot.

Mostly they never talked at all.

Then one day—the fourth anniversary of the blaze in which Mia Buckingham and Scott Sorrell died—she walked naked into the gray-green waters of Mohawk Lake. Just a note left by her clothes.

There's a shooter in the shadows, and I can't bear this anymore.

Of course he told the cops he had no idea why she'd killed herself. No sense of what was on her mind, no clue what she meant in those final words.

Tried to tell himself too and almost believed it. Though in truth he knew exactly what she was talking about. The shooter in the shadows was the guilt, an ever-lurking creature that peered at her day and night while she suffered in silence, too proud or scared to say.

It was as if what had happened to them was an alternative statement of events, a tragedy choreographed to another narrative. The wrong one. It had to be, because Thomas Honeyman, author, had set down the correct version in his acclaimed nonfiction book *The Fire: An American Tragedy*.

Before going on to write a bunch of novels no one wanted at all.

16

VENICE

Saturday
Deadline: 8 minutes.

Honeyman was exhausted by the time he typed the final line, and had quite forgotten about Vern Miller, who must have been following every word a few hundred yards away on the island.

His mind was still in Prosper. Still trying to remember what their old life was like, and a time when he and Diane had been happy, as carefree as a broke, newly married young couple could be.

That had happened.

That had been real.

He put his head down on the desk, barely able to keep his eyes open. Sleep stole upon him unbidden, unwanted. Soon he found himself lost in a dream world that never existed, a place of possibilities, lives that could be changed, made happy, by taking that left turn instead of the right.

There was Diane in the hospital, tears in her eyes, a baby girl in her arms, Honeyman holding their hands, one sweaty and wrinkled, one tiny and newborn, surprise, fear, love binding the three of them together.

A toddler Lauren playing on the pebbles by Mohawk Lake, giggling as her father splashed her from the water.

Then the bitterness that followed with age and work and doubt, constant worry about money and career and a world that seemed to go to pieces from time to time, in crises made by others, though it was always the little people who paid the price.

It all ended suddenly as he half-fell from the desk, and only just managed to stop himself winding up on the hard tile floor.

It was dark. A sudden chill of fear ran through him.

Honeyman scrabbled at the keyboard to bring the screen alive.

No message.

He grabbed the walkie-talkie and held the button down in his left hand while trying to find something, anything that would get a response from outside.

It was almost eleven-thirty. The fireworks show across the lagoon was only minutes away.

Miller wasn't answering. Not by voice. Not on the laptop either.

A sudden explosion almost shook him out of his skin.

Too close to be the fireworks in Saint Mark's Basin. It had to be a display from across the water, Burano maybe or Mazzorbo. They got in on the fiery act too.

'Vern,' he yelled down the walkie-talkie. 'I gave you what wanted. Now let Lauren go. You hear me?'

Then he heard another sound, a low, deep rumble like a distant roll of thunder, and knew the show had begun for real.

Vern Miller's deadline was here.

Honeyman walked to the front of the house and gazed out of the long, arched Gothic windows as he did most years, usually with a Negroni in hand and a desperate attempt at some new fiction freshly finished on the desk. A manuscript waiting to go nowhere, not that he allowed himself to think that at the time. There was always hope when he wrote something new. Without that he had nothing. There was no chance of going back to journalism, no future work of any other kind at all.

Maybe this time was different, in a strange and dangerous way.

The night sky was the color of shot silk, dark, full of motion, wavering between blue and black and purple. Across the moonlit lagoon a burst of fire rose white and red, yellow and blue, rockets shooting to the heights, streams of cascading sparks trailing across the distant, spiky city horizon, exploding stars of flame above Saint Mark's Basin filling the space between the Doge's Palace and San Giorgio Maggiore with their brilliant incandescent light.

The noise—booms and cracks and a rattle like artillery—came after, as it always did at this distance.

Tom Honeyman tried the walkie-talkie one more time, then looked again at the laptop.

Both were silent.

Then he grabbed the gun, tucked it into the deepest pocket of his cargo pants and walked outside.

THE SKY WAS alive with fire. On his little island the rattle of explosions was sending birds scattering though the trees, mice, rats, lizards scurrying through the dry brush and scrub.

Miller's deadline had passed. Honeyman had provided what he'd asked for. A kind of truth. His own wife had set the fire by Mohawk Lake—locked her former lover and a teenager in there, poured gas all around them, lit the flames. Then, she persuaded him to place the blame on a troubled and innocent outsider. And finally, when she came to believe a solitary, disgruntled former cop was closing in on their lies, shot him dead one night in Burnsville.

A very different narrative from the story he'd outlined in his original book. One that, in part—he'd never guessed about Miller, because Diane had never said the old bastard was on her trail—he'd lived with in silence over the years.

One he still found hard to accept.

There seemed nothing left to hide. No need to play the game. If it weren't for Lauren's presence on Maledetto and the very real threat to her life, Honeyman might have coughed up the whole strange tale days earlier.

'Vern! Lauren!'

All that came back was the terrified chatter of unseen birds, the scampering sound of tiny creatures, the distant roll of thunder across the lagoon.

He called their names again and set off on the straggling path through the spiky undergrowth and wayward trees and palms. The lights of the northern coast from Punta Sabbioni to Lido di Jesolo fringed the horizon. A hail of explosive fire started to puncture the darker sky there too. Everywhere, it seemed, the world was burning as the Night of the Redeemer came to its inevitable midnight climax. In his head he could see the teeming crowds in Venice, the lines of people packing the pontoon bridge from Zattere to Giudecca. All the happy faces, astonished by the scale of the occasion, the noise, the color, the way night was exchanged for brilliant day.

Somewhere close by there was Lauren, terrified Lauren. A man too, damaged, dangerous, who'd trapped them on Maledetto seeking a narrative Tom Honeyman had fought long to hide, from himself as much as the world.

'Dammit, Vern! I gave you what you wanted.'

His sudden anger echoed through the crooked headstones of the cemetery. Nameless monuments to nameless dead. The bridge had lost one of its railings somehow. He took it in three strides over the stagnant ditch, the gun slapping hard against his leg as he stumbled furiously along.

'Lauren!'

Ahead, the silhouette of the crippled angel stood out against the bright horizon of the coast. The generator was no longer buzzing away. No lights anywhere in Miller's camp inside the nave. The moon was full and bright, but the tent was in the shadows of the ruins, its outline barely visible.

'For god's sake... Lauren!'

He was scared, and that was rare. Honeyman didn't usually feel enough regard for himself for fear. So it was more for his daughter, though still it felt the same. Cold, unnecessary, a sense of dread that sought a target, a reason, and found nothing there but a chilling, pointless void.

'Where are you? Where—?'

Gas.

The stench hit him like a noxious cloud, strong and chemical, so fierce it took his breath away. He might have been standing in a pool of it for all he knew. Then he felt the puff of warmth, heard the soft exhalation of explosive breath. There was a sudden blaze of light, a searing yellow smokiness beyond the walls, small at first but rising, upward, outward.

He swore, or at least he thought he did. By then, Tom Honeyman was running, racing past the ruined masonry of the chapel, past the crippled angel.

The noise and heat stopped him. Miller's military tent was ablaze, flames tearing through the disintegrating fabric, shooting six feet, ten, into the hot night air. Flecks of fabric and soot spiraled upward on the fire's smoky breath into a starry sky. The parched grass around was burning too, flames licking and racing everywhere.

In the midst of the inferno he could see something writhing on the ground—a figure, struggling, rolling side to side, trapped, screaming, shrieking, high-pitched and terrified. Trapped. Just like Mohawk Lake.

Arm out, trying to shield his eyes, he edged forward, desperate to force a way in, to reach the struggling figure on the floor. But the heat was so powerful, like a beast itself. He could barely get within six feet of the searing fire before the force of it beat him back. What was left of the tent would soon be gone. Inside the remaining frame he could see the figure, rolling in agony on the ground, flames licking all around, hungry to devour everything in their path. Though the movement was less marked. An end approached.

By the dead generator three jerry cans lay on their side, dripping flaming fluid onto the caked earth. All around the tent the dry grass was well-lit. Soon the blaze might spread to the whole of the tiny island on which the chapel sat. Maybe even the shallow ditch wouldn't stop it, and in minutes the rest of Maledetto might be ablaze.

There was a bucket by the cans. Empty. He raced to the pebble beach, scooped up what water what he could from the muddy shallows, ran back and threw it on the burning tent.

By now the figure inside was a miserable, pained shape crouched in the midst of the inferno, black as coal, immobile.

Dead.

The word just came and wouldn't leave.

Again he stumbled to the shore, again he filled the bucket. Staggered back, threw the pathetic contents onto the greedy flames, watched as they did nothing but hiss and fizz then burn all the more brightly.

What lay inside was unrecognizable, a still, sad, carbonized shape, a carapace of black matter lost to everything.

He fell to the ground, knees grating against hard earth, eyes filling with tears, from the smoke and heat, from a nameless grief rising like a cold, dead tide. The same bleak sorrow he'd felt that day in Burano when he'd called home and a stranger's emotionless voice had told him Diane was dead. That she'd killed herself. Then asked him what that note meant...

There's a shooter in the shadows, and I can't bear this anymore.

At the time he knew only half the story. Not now. What lay hidden in the dark, always waiting, was the heavy weight of conscience, three corpses ready to rise up in the imagination at any moment.

'Christ...'

He didn't know what to do. Didn't care about anything. Himself. Vern Miller. The world outside.

How long this lasted he had no idea. But the show across the lagoon had ended. The sky was returning to its usual velvet. The birds moving, squawking nervously through Maledetto's thickets of shrubs and trees.

A hand fell on his shoulder and he felt at that moment that

maybe the breath would vanish from his lungs, let him give up on everything, drift away and leave nothing but his own corpse here, as mute and useless as the shapeless black form inside the smoldering remains of Miller's tent.

'For god's sake, Dad. We've got to do something about this.'

'How...?'

Eyes stinging, Honeyman was on his feet, arms around her, fighting to convince himself this was real.

'Not now...' She pushed him off. The smell of gas around her was so strong it brought a sudden pain to the back of his throat. In her hands was a portable fire extinguisher, the kind they took on camping vacations in the woods. 'Got work to do.'

Lauren walked toward the tent, fired the thing, directed its noisy, spurting froth at the blaze.

She turned then, and the hard, commanding tone in her voice might have been her mother's.

'Stamp things out or something, will you? Or use the bucket. Jesus. We don't want this whole place going up in flames.'

IT SEEMED to take forever to get the fire under control, bucket after bucket of water, hour after hour, constant journeys to the shore and back. There were two more extinguishers she'd somehow retrieved from Miller's gear. After that, as the rest of the lagoon fell into silence and slumber, they ran around the small island stamping out the flames, only for the most persistent to return and threaten to cross the wooden bridge.

Beyond was the straggling forest of palms and scrub, a wasteland waiting like tinder. A few stray sparks made it and began to catch. Patiently, time and time again, they tracked them down, beat them out, every last burning stalk, and watched to make sure they stayed dead.

They didn't talk. No space for that. Lauren seemed too preoccupied. And Honeyman couldn't find the words. Or perhaps feared to.

When it was done they stood amid the stinking ashes and looked at what was left. The stone of the ruined chapel was charred and stained with smoke and soot. In the center, the frame of Miller's tent stood like a warped metal skeleton, a few blackened threads still hanging to it. There was a shape in the middle Honeyman didn't want to look at. A smell too, and it reminded him of the comment the late Jackson Wynn had made to the late Fred Miller.

Meat.

He was still staring at the ruins when Lauren took his arm, hugged him, and the sudden presence of her almost made him jump.

'We made it, Dad.'

'Thank god you're safe.' The words were a struggle. 'What... what the hell happened here?'

Honeyman knew from her face in the silver moonlight she wouldn't offer up a quick answer.

'What's happened is we're alive. Don't ask how. I want out of here. I want this stink off me. Guess...' She glanced at him, up and down. All the dirt and smoke of the blaze was on him, but he wasn't sure he wanted to lose it. Not until he understood why it was there. 'Guess you do too.'

'I—'

Another quick squeeze of his arm. 'Not... now.'

Already she was moving.

In silence they went back to the villa. She walked straight upstairs without even looking at him. He made two Negronis with shaking hands. Checked the laptop. No messages. He went to the status bar and, finally, turned off the Wi-Fi. Nothing stopped him. The walkie-talkie stayed dead.

And Vern Miller was a crouching corpse, a blackened shape in the ruins of the old chapel.

Tom Honeyman looked at the clock on the screen.

Four thirty in the morning. Silent outside. Even the birds seemed to have given up. On the horizon over the eastern coast he could just make out the rosy finger of the coming dawn.

IT WAS light by the time Lauren came down in a fresh shirt and cut-off jeans, her hair damp, hands working at it frantically with a towel.

Honeyman was slumped on a chair on the patio, staring at the bright, fresh morning, desperately wishing he could sleep, not knowing when that might happen. The photo album from upstairs was by his side, pages open, old pictures from Prosper there, memories of a different time, another life.

She came and sat next to him, threw the towel on the tiles, set Miller's satphone on the table, and said, 'Don't you want to clean up? We can call for a boat out of here whenever you like.'

'Soon.'

'You're still in the same clothes.'

'Yeah.'

Something weighed against his leg. The gun. He'd forgotten it. He put the weapon on the table.

'What happened?'

She frowned, that downturned mouth he'd first seen when she was two or three.

'I said. What happened is we're alive.'

He waited.

'What happened was I fooled him. He thought...' She blinked. 'You don't need to know the details. After he read what you wrote, Vern went outside. I could smell the gas. He was mad as hell. He knew you were going to come.' She touched his hand. 'You had to. And when you did, he was going to tie you up and put you in that tent. Burn you.'

'Why? I gave him what he wanted.'

She stared at him as if he wasn't following.

'You lied, Dad. In your book. You made up that story. In Vern's head that was what got his old man killed. By Mom. If you'd stayed out of it maybe Fred Miller would have found her. Arrested her. Be alive today. She's gone. Who else is he going to take it out on?'

Honeyman was lost for words.

'It was always going to be like that. I thought I told you. Weird thing was he said I was OK. I wasn't *responsible*. He'd let me go. And maybe me and him...'

'What?'

Lauren gulped at the drink.

'Vern Miller was one very strange guy. He really thought he could kill you and I'd still go off with him. What an idiot...' She winced at what she'd said. 'Sorry... dead idiot.'

Lauren took a comb out of her jeans pocket and began to run it through her long, damp locks.

'There was a hammer in the tent. When he came back I smacked him on the head. As hard as I could. For us.' She tapped his chest. 'God, what he put us through...'

More booze and she glanced at the gun on the table.

'Then I tied him up as best I could and came looking for you. Hadn't got more than a few yards and the whole thing went up. Never realized he'd put so much gas around the place. I think he was trying to get out and pushed over that stove he had. Or the electrical gear sparked something. Dunno. Don't much care.'

Honeyman didn't say anything, didn't do anything. Just sat there.

'What else I could do? I tried to get him out. You saw. I knew he had some extinguishers somewhere. I was looking for them when you turned up. God... I never expected the thing would go up like that.'

'I thought it was you in there...'

She nodded.

'I didn't know what else to do. Vern really wanted you dead.'

'Why? I gave him what he wanted.'

'Breakfast booze,' she cut in and chinked the empty glass in his lap. 'Boy, that tastes good. Not the kind of thing you talk about, is it? Mom killing Mia and Scott. You two covering it up. Shooting Chief Miller 'cuz he was threatening her.'

'I didn't know about Fred Miller.'

'No. Sorry. I thought maybe you did. Stop looking at me like that. I knew something was wrong. Broken. Didn't know what exactly, but how was I supposed to throw any of this into the conversation? You were always gone. Mom was silent and angry and always at the bottle. Me at college, then on a ship somewhere. Seemed easier... a lot easier... to just... stay out of things. Took my lead from you. Hope whatever ghosts were out there never came back to haunt us. Hey...'

She'd spotted the photo album on the floor. Her face lit up when she flipped through the pages.

'Where did you get all this?'

'One of the things I retrieved from Prosper. After Mom died. One of the few things.'

She picked out a photo from when she was seven or eight. They'd just moved to the house. Playing in the yard on a plastic bike, laughing for the camera, Diane kneeling, pushing her along.

'I loved that bike.'

Diane always said he shied away from confrontations. She was right. He hated them. Maybe if he'd faced things down before...

'I remember,' he said and took the album from her. 'Can I show you another one?'

It was near the back. A photo he'd noted that first night after reading Vern Miller's initial contribution to the story. One that had taunted him ever since.

'I kept wondering about that pendant. The one Fred Miller found. Inscribed to Mia. Didn't come from Rabbitt. All he said was... Mia used to make things.' He found the picture and put it in front of her. 'Then I thought. If you really liked someone perhaps you'd make something for both of you. One for Mia.' He pointed to the photo. 'One for you.'

It was the picture from school. Lauren half-smiling for a portrait. Around her neck a silver chain, a crude heart shape at the end.

When he glanced up from the page her face had the look of old, of Lauren angry as hell in the little house in Prosper, arguing about everything.

'You could have told me all this stuff, Lauren—about Mom, about Fred Miller—right at the beginning.'

'I said. I thought you knew. It's just a stupid pendant.'

He grabbed the satphone off the table before she could stop him.

'To hell with a boat. I'm going to call the cops.'

Lauren snatched the gun, held it up tight in her right hand, barrel not quite at him. Not quite.

'You've always got to ruin things, Dad. Don't you?'

He needed to get this straight. For him. For her. For Diane.

'Your mom shot Fred Miller. I believe that. But she never set that fire at Mohawk Lake. Deep down, I never thought she did. You need to care to kill someone like that. She never cared that much. Not for herself.'

'Stop this now.'

'Your mother only cared for one thing. You. That was all. You were so precious, maybe the only precious thing she had. She'd do anything, say anything to protect you.'

He could picture the two of them together back in Prosper. The Lauren and Diane Show. They were tight, a pair, a fortress against a cruel, uncaring world. He was always the outsider. Just there when they needed him.

'Tell me, Lauren. Please.'

'Tell you what? *What?*'

There was the heat, the hate, the fury. It was never far away even if she'd mostly managed to hide it here on Maledetto. He was aware, too, that he possessed the gift for giving it life. Looking at her, the guilt, the cunning in her eyes, something else became obvious. Something he should have realized before.

'That chapter that sounded like me. It wasn't Vern Miller. He supplied the evidence. You wrote it up. You were always good at that. Must have taken weeks.'

She laughed.

'Nah. I can be a hack as good as you. Couple of days when Vern said we were coming out here to meet you. Couple of hours skimming through that crappy book of yours to make me remember what you sound like.'

'Why?'

'Why what?'

He couldn't believe she was asking.

'Why did you go along with all this?'

'Because I had to! Vern's been nagging me for eighteen months, email, chat. Saying he's sure you told a pack of lies about Mohawk Lake and somehow something connects that to what happened with his old man. He was coming for you anyway, Dad. You think I should have let him do that alone?'

The gun flashed in front of his face and he realized he didn't care.

'No. I meant why did you kill them? Mia Buckingham. Scott...'

Her voice rang high and young and hurt again.

'Why do you think? They took something from me. Something I wanted. What else was there? You were never interested. Not in me. Not in Mom. All you ever did was go on about how you wanted something better. A job with a real newspaper like you deserved, not that useless rag in Prosper. Except that didn't work. And then it was your name on a book. Being with us... that was never enough.'

For a moment she pointed the gun straight in his face and he knew then: she could use it. Vern Miller didn't die by accident.

'I couldn't breathe in that place. No friends who counted. No life. Mom drowning in a lake of fucking chardonnay.'

'I tried—'

'You didn't. You didn't care. No one did. Just Mom. Then...' She stopped. Choked up for a moment. 'A teacher. And she's old. Doesn't make sense. Except it did. Mia listened to me. It wasn't just... that. There was something real there. Real. For me. Me! First time ever. Someone who... connected.'

He remembered Diane's words that night. The confession that wasn't hers at all. The affair with Mia, the discovery of her unfaithfulness, the pain. It was all Lauren's. All the sentiments and the feeling. Probably the words as well.

'I'm sorry—'

'Sorry doesn't work. I thought me and Mia meant something. The day she stole the camera off that creep stalking us in the cabin, it was like... we were a couple. A pair. Jackson Wynn... she ripped him a new one, said she'd run him out of Prosper if he told a soul. Gave me the camera. Said I could keep it.'

'Did you tell her? Mom? About Mohawk Lake?'

He got a savage stare for that, one that said... *you idiot.*

'God, you really don't get it. I didn't need to tell her. She found Jackson's camera in my room. I think she went looking, after the fire. Mom knew me. She understood something was wrong.'

'You begged her to set this whole thing up? To tell me it was her?'

That juvenile scowl creased her face in a look of mock pain.

'No! It was Mom's idea. Not mine. I was past thinking, almost past caring by then. Waiting for the cops to call. Mom's idea. I was never that quick. And let's face it...' The scowl became an accusing stare. 'You couldn't come up with a scheme like that, could you?'

'I went and framed an innocent man. Got him killed.'

'For Mom. Not me. Then you were gone. Maybe if you'd stuck around, she wouldn't have walked into the lake.'

The gun touched his shoulder. He didn't flinch.

'Mia was like... I was the love of her life. For a month or two. Next thing I know she's banging Scott Sorrell and god knows who else, like I'm some insect on the ground who just doesn't count. As if we never ever happened.'

'And for that you killed her?'

Lauren shrugged, closed her eyes for a moment. Maybe he could have snatched the weapon, but he didn't even try.

'I just wanted to... do something.'

'You locked the door. The window.'

'Yeah. I was mad at her. Not everyone's like you, thinking things through 'til they hurt. Real people just go crazy for a while and then it's done. Oh, shit. I don't know... I wish it hadn't happened. But it did.'

She was crying. Her face shiny with tears. Real or not, he had no idea, and maybe it was the same for her.

'When I locked them in and spread the gas I thought I'd yell and let them know. Thought I'd peek through the window like Jackson Wynn and holler, "I saw you, I know, I will tell, Mia Buckingham, I will scream it all over Prosper 'til they run you out of town, calling you out for the whore you are." Then when they got scared I'd let them out.'

She stopped.

'What happened?'

'When I looked they were just there, together. All done. Happy. Wrapped around each other. Mia looking at Scott the way she used to look at me. Like she could love anyone if she wanted. It didn't matter. We were all just the same. I didn't want to be the same. I wanted to be special. To someone. Anyone...'

'You were special to us.'

Then she laughed, but not for long.

'You were my parents. That was owed. Mia... I thought I'd earned.'

Somewhere, far away, an engine whined. A small boat out fishing for clams, Honeyman guessed. It got louder then diminished. Vanishing into the depths of the lagoon.

'Dad.' Lauren's left hand came out and touched his chest. 'Listen to me. You helped Mom out. You put your neck on the line for her. Help *me* now. That's all I'm asking. The two of us. We can do this.'

What was right? What was wrong? Honeyman couldn't work it out. Nothing was ever black or white.

'Say something, will you? Mom wasn't going to go to jail. Me neither. I won't. I won't let you do that. We can get through this. Together. Vern is just one dead guy. He doesn't matter. All we've got to do is lay low for a while. Stay out of things 'til we know nothing's coming back at us from here. Please. I'm begging. We keep our heads down. God knows I've been doing that all these years. No reason you can't... No reason...'

She was sobbing so freely it took him back to when she was little and how much that hurt him when it happened. How hard he'd tried to put things straight, for her, for Diane. And failed.

Honeyman said, 'Two men dead, don't you mean?'

No answer.

'The gardener, Lauren. The deaf-and-dumb guy with the beard.'

The tears stopped. She glanced at him sideways and it was as if there was someone different there. As if two Laurens lived inside her, competing with each other for attention, for control.

'Oh, *him*.' She made air quotes with her fingers. '"Gianni". Vern paid off the gardener and wrote out that note. He said you had to be scared right away, the moment you showed up. He wanted you to understand this was serious.'

Honeyman pointed back to the ruins. A couple of wisps of smoke were still rising from the previous night's blaze.

'I saw...'

'You saw Vern. With some crappy fake beard, making out like he's deaf and dumb and working here.' She pointed at him with a finger like a gun and said, 'Bang, bang. It was me with the rifle. Shooting at the air. Vern falls down, pretends he got hit. You run back to the house. Scene set.'

'Dammit, Lauren.'

'I had no choice!'

'You could have shot Vern.'

She shrugged.

'Maybe. Told him he should have thrown around some blood. Stupid. That's why he came back with that dead bird, to scare you some more. It was all him. Not me.'

'Never you.'

'No. Never, ever me.'

'Vern *is* dead. I need to call the police.'

'Hear me out, Dad, will you?'

Lauren sat down on the ground, arms clasping her knees, a teen again except for the handgun nestled in her fingers.

'You can't bring in the cops. Think about it. Do that and they'll start asking all kinds of questions. Digging up everything. You. Mom. Mohawk Lake. You'll be inviting them into our lives. That's what *he* wanted. You writing it all out yourself. Then he kills you, you're dead, and it looks like suicide. With a confession.'

She squinted at the bright horizon.

'I could have said no. I could have stayed on the ship and let him come here all on his own. You'd have been dead days ago. Would be nice if you sounded grateful.'

Honeyman swatted away a busy mosquito. He realized this was like that moment back in Prosper when he knew a corner had been turned. He was never coming back to this place.

'Lauren. We need to do something right for once.'

'Yeah! We do. Listen. We bury him in the graveyard. Who's going to find out? Vern was a loner. A weirdo. Didn't work full-time for anyone. No girlfriend. No relatives. I don't want to get thrown in a cell and told I murdered that evil bastard—'

'I thought you didn't.'

She smirked.

'Yeah. And Jorge Rodriguez didn't kill Scott and Mia. Neither did Mom. But you just wrote that too. We invent the lives we've got. Either that or people invent them for us. Besides, this is Italy. We don't know how things work. What the lawyers are like. You call the cops and there's no guarantee we get out of this at all. For once can we stick together? Can we? We do what's needed here. Then we make ourselves scarce for a while. Piece of cake. Gimme the phone, please.'

She raised the gun.

'Gimme the phone.'

Honeyman handed it over, then got to his feet.

'I didn't ask for any of this, Dad. I was just playing along. Trying to keep him happy. Doing the same for you. What choice was there? Really? I wasn't going to let Vern kill you. I just needed to find a way out. We're going to bury him, get out of here. We can start again. Who's to know different?'

'*We'll* know, Lauren, won't we?'

She winked at him.

'Exactly. And we're family. We keep our secrets...' She tapped her chest, her heart. 'In here.'

Honeyman leaned forward and kissed his daughter on her warm, damp cheek. She recoiled just a little at his touch. It was turning into a beautiful morning. The kind he loved on the lagoon, bright, peaceful, solitary. A day that spoke of redemption, of the release the city sought, in prayer and fire, in song and jubilation. The sun was rising over the forest of crooked graves and the ruins of the chapel, where a few fat flakes of soot were floating on the gentle morning breeze.

Tom Honeyman ignored the gun, didn't look at her as he walked away, along the winding path, through the dry weeds and the sharp thistles, toward the lines of crooked headstones, the snag-toothed tower of the chapel.

Ahead, past the smoke-stained silhouette of the crippled angel, lay the shining expanse of water. In the distance the familiar city horizon of spires and towers rose from the summer blue.

Maledetto.

He didn't believe in curses.

He didn't believe in ghosts.

The living were more to be feared, the visible more threatening than the unseen. Except for that creature Diane called the shooter in the shadows, an invisible specter of guilt and conscience that stalked her all the way into the chilly waters of Mohawk Lake. Then followed him. Lauren too, perhaps, though of that he wasn't so sure.

Honeyman kept going, didn't look back. One way or another he was leaving this place. Abandoning an island of fractured dreams and a story he'd never come to finish. All gone for good.

17

VENICE

Sunday

Giorgio Morosini was in the stern, steering his little boat out from the island of Mazzorbo, south toward Murano and the city. The restaurant with its tables by the water was fast disappearing behind. Lauren sat in the bow, Magda on the bench in the middle, a little drunk and garrulous after a Campari spritzer and a bottle of wine.

She swept her arm over the side into the brackish water and declared, 'That was a wonderful lunch, Giorgio. How do you find these places?'

Bruno the black Labrador had decided to crouch close enough for Lauren to stroke him from time to time. Whenever Magda tried, he growled.

'How? You should ask our new friend, Lauren. It was her father who introduced me to Ai Cacciatori. I never knew the place existed. A Venetian too. Shame on me.'

'I loved those duck dumplings,' Lauren said, holding tight as the launch rocked against the wake of a passing vaporetto crammed with tourists headed for Torcello.

'Gnocchi,' Morosini corrected her. 'Your father adores them too. I was hoping he'd be here.'

Lauren had rehearsed the story well that morning, before the Venetian turned up with his launch around eleven. The previous day, her father had told her he had to leave on a sudden business trip. He departed in his dinghy that afternoon. She was to wait for Morosini on Sunday.

Not that the real estate agent was to come ashore under any circumstances. Her bag was packed, the precious laptop with its documents safe inside, when he arrived to pick her up. Using Vern Miller's satphone and her father's travel account, she'd booked herself two weeks in a hotel near the Accademia Bridge. It was an arty establishment beloved of authors, both famous and unknown, as well as painters familiar with the nearby Guggenheim.

'It was all very sudden. Him going away. Unexpected. Sorry.'

She made sure she sounded upset when she said that.

'Where's he gone?'

'I don't know. Dad was... evasive. Not himself really.'

'Maledetto.' The Venetian shook his head as if the word alone was sufficient. 'That place can get to people.'

'Writers,' Magda declared. 'You can never trust them. I had a boyfriend from Krakow who was an author once. Not... not a *published* author, to be precise. Or perhaps a poet. Maybe just a journalist. I don't remember. Very untrustworthy.'

Morosini scowled at her.

'Well, my very good friend Thomas is extremely trustworthy. A decent, hard-working gentleman. As I said, every year he comes here to finish his next book. In time for Redentore. I am sorry I missed him.'

Lauren tapped her bag.

'He did finish it. Yesterday. During the day. First draft, of course. It needs some revision, some expansion in places. He asked me to edit it for him. From the hotel. Then send the manuscript to his agent.'

Morosini appeared impressed. 'You work in publishing too?'

'Writing... storytelling... it runs in the family.'

He leaned back against the stern, set the throttle and began to steer with the tiller between his knees.

'Excellent news. I fear he will have to get some work done on that place. You must tell him. The fire seemed much worse than I thought. Larger. This dry weather. Everything is like tinder. At least the villa is untouched. But the old chapel, the graveyard...'

'*I* could never live near a graveyard," Magda declared. "More wine, please.'

He handed Magda the bottle. Lauren had the impression the garrulous Polish woman was not to Morosini's taste.

'Even if a buyer were to appear, and there's none on the horizon, it would not be wise to take them all the way there in its present state. A lick of paint. Some tidying up would make a great difference... Your father was willing to buy a ruin on the basis of hopes and dreams. Most people want to pay their money and have all that delivered to them, ready-made.'

'Great advice. He said you were always free with that, Giorgio.' She smiled at him very pleasantly, and he seemed to like that. 'Dad said to tell you. He's grateful for all the work you've put in over the years, and it's not your fault it didn't sell. Or rent. Now he wants the island taken off the market. He's going to keep it. Or rather...' It was easy to improvise. 'We've been out of touch for a little while. He wants me to have it. A gift. Soon there'll be money to bring it back to how it should be.'

'How it never was,' he grumbled. 'A ruin is all Maledetto's been as long as I've known it. A leper colony and a cemetery for plague victims, among other things...'

'Lepers!' Magda's voice went up a few tones in horror. '*Lepers!*'

'Long dead. There's nothing anyone need fear there anymore. Also, we should refer to it by its proper name in any case. Santa Maria dell'Umiltà. Magda, I will drop you off at your hotel before taking Lauren to hers. There are some chores I must tackle this afternoon. I trust you enjoyed your lunch, dear.'

'Very good, Giorgio.' Magda looked bored, sleepy and quite drunk. 'I shall not be buying property in Venice, however. It's too damp a place, for one thing.'

He cast her a vicious glance.

'The point of this city is that it rises from the water. The lagoon is part of who we are. A dream that comes and goes like the ocean, never set or fixed or certain.'

'I love it here,' Lauren cut in, beaming at the friendly dog beside her. 'I always have. In a little while I'll be back to think about what work we can do.'

Morosini looked cheered by that idea and upped the engine a notch to drown out the litany of complaints from his unwanted companion.

'If you need advice on workmen, I have contacts,' he added when Lauren fell silent, almost shouting above the noise and spray. 'Reliable men. That place could be lovely one day soon. It would help if you learned a little Italian, of course.'

'*Sì. Certo.*'

'Ah. I'm impressed.'

'I've worked here now and again. You pick things up.'

'I'm sure you do, young lady. I'm sure you do. Will you come to live among us?'

'Perhaps. I always like it when writers say they divide their time. New York and Venice. That suits me fine.'

'An author! Like father, like daughter!'

Lauren raised her glass.

'Exactly...' she agreed.

HALF AN HOUR later Morosini dropped off Magda at a *pensione* in Cannaregio. The two of them barely exchanged words let alone a kiss. Then he pointed the launch down the Grand Canal and they travelled along the busy waterway at a leisurely pace, among vaporetti and water taxis, commercial boats, dinghies full of raucous parties sipping wine and picking at food. It was the Sunday of Redentore, one of the highlights of the year. All the while Morosini gave Lauren an insider's view of the palaces, museums and churches they passed along the way, scowling at the tourists flocking around the Rialto Bridge, telling her there was another Venice away from the places outsiders congregated like flies. A real city to be found, one he'd be glad to show her if she wanted.

He was a good-looking man—fit, tanned, an interesting talker with a quick and attractive smile. For once she couldn't work out if this was flirting or not. Perhaps Giorgio Morosini, puzzled by her father's absence, didn't know himself.

After a leisurely cruise they passed beneath the elegant wooden curve of the Accademia Bridge, moored near the vaporetto stop, and Morosini pointed the way to the Agli Alboretti hotel.

'A charming place with its fair share of history. Though take some of the stories you hear about Peggy Guggenheim with a large pinch of salt. Venetians are fabulists at heart, all of us. It's a medical condition brought about by living in this strange world of ours.' He climbed onto the jetty and tied up the launch. 'Do tell reception Giorgio Morosini sent you and insists you are given the finest suite in the house. Here...' He handed over a card. 'Call me any time. The island is off the market as of now, but I will always be here to help. And if you wish...' She wondered if he was embarrassed. 'If you would like company sometime—'

The dog woke up and wagged his tail as Morosini helped her clamber off the boat onto the busy landing.

'Bruno loves a walk along the waterfront. Or anywhere, really, should you—'

'Thanks, Giorgio. I'm going to be really busy working on my dad's manuscript.'

He seemed so very Italian, she was expecting a quick, polite embrace, perhaps a kiss. But instead he held out his hand. And she took it.

'Is your father's new book a mystery?'

'Most books are.'

'I believe he's a man who's no stranger to that sort of thing. Perhaps it runs in the family.'

'We're very boring, really. Don't worry on our account.'

Morosini returned to the boat and blipped the throttle.

'Of course,' he shouted over the racket of the outboard. '*Ciao*, Signora Honeyman.'

'*Ciao*.'

She didn't correct him. Honeyman it would be from now on. There was a track record to that name, even if it was marginal of late.

Morosini could be kept occupied with requests for building advice and contractors. Perhaps even a walk with his dog and dinner sometime. He was the only man alive who'd seen her father on Maledetto that week, and there was a curious, perhaps suspicious, side to his nature. One she'd deal with in due course if necessary.

The hotel receptionist said he'd never heard of Giorgio, not even when she showed him the card. Fabulists, all. But the room they gave her was quiet and spacious enough, a suite with a balcony overlooking a neat and pretty garden of palms and flower beds. Maledetto might look like that one day, she thought. The fragrance of the flowers would be enough to hide the smoke and ash and memories that lurked in the small cemetery on the islet with the chapel.

'You're on vacation, *signora*?' the porter asked as he placed her luggage on the bed.

'Not at all.' Lauren patted the bag. 'I'm a writer. I'm here to finish a book. I hope the Wi-Fi's good.'

'*Sì*. But this is Venice. You're here for two whole weeks. There's much to see, I promise you.' He waved at the sunny afternoon beyond the window. 'Don't spend all your time indoors at a desk.'

Still, mostly, she did. Day and night, going through the material her father had written, excising some parts, adding others. Back in Prosper she'd shown him her schoolwork from time to time, and he'd always said she could be a writer if she wanted. He was right. The words came easily. She felt she'd pretty much mastered his style, writing that opening chapter for Vern Miller: plain, straightforward, more a storyteller than a journalist. This was the way he must have approached the completion of a book on Maledetto in that run-up to the fireworks on the Night of the Redeemer. Set a deadline, tell yourself you were going to meet it. Nothing mattered but the words, the structure, the story. Not food, not drink, not the hour. There was only the work. The few times she left the room were mostly to get out of the way of the cleaner. There was much to be done.

The bare bones of the book were pretty much complete, sketchily written but easily expanded. After that it was mostly a question of adding in revised material from the first version of *The Fire*. Background on Prosper and the people who lived there. All carefully attuned to fit the new narrative and the sequel's selling point: naming the killer of Mia Buckingham and Scott Sorrell as her mother, Diane Honeyman. Revealing that she'd shot Fred Miller dead when the former chief began closing in on her.

Vern never got a mention, naturally. She wasn't lying when she told her father he was a loner no one would miss.

And as for Tom Honeyman... that was a key part of the proposition.

Her father was missing, vanished after inviting her to Venice, confessing what he'd done, then leaving her with the evidence and a final request to make it public.

In the end it all seemed to fit. A convincing narrative, a new one that took the original story somewhere else, with shocking detail and, ultimately, a public, pained confession. All told by a daughter who was a victim too, living in ignorance from the fallout of Mohawk Lake.

On the ninth day she realized suddenly it was done. Not finished. A real editor would be needed for that. But there was nothing left to add to the material she had, no way she could think of to improve it. The conclusion seemed to come out of nowhere, so quickly it left her thinking there had to be something she'd missed.

But no. Another day of reading convinced her that to tinker further would only make things worse. The time had come to go to the next stage. Contacting her father's agent in New York. One last piece of fiction to set down in a simple email and an attachment.

. . .

Hɪ, Suzanne—

My name is Lauren Honeyman. You represent my dad. I know you were expecting something from him. He told me here in Venice.

I don't really know how to write this. To be honest, I don't really know what to do. Dad's gone, no clue where. He told me lots of things about Mohawk Lake, things I never guessed at. Terrible things that explain a lot of what broke up our family in the first place. He wrote down some of it. Then he told me more, and begged me to finish what he couldn't. A new book that was the truth, not the big fat lie he sold us all before.

It's kind of done now, so I'm enclosing what Dad suggested. He called it a 'partial'? The start of the story and some of the things he wanted out there. There's more if you want it. Pretty much the whole book, I think. But I'm new to all this and Dad's just gone and I...

Sorry. Can't deal with that in an email.

He said this is mine now. I get to choose what to do with it. My book. My deal, if you think it's worth one. I want his name on the cover, though. I owe him that. I owe him lots. I wish I could have stopped him from leaving. I wish to god I knew where the hell he is.

Damn. I'm rambling now.

Please read it and tell me what to do. Even if it's just to get lost. I promised I'd do this for him, and that's a promise I've kept. You say what happens next. I'll send you my number. You can call or WhatsApp me if you like. Maybe a message would be better. The time's different here, and I'm not sure I can talk that easily on the phone right now.

Yours,

Lauren Honeyman

Iᴛ ᴡᴀs three in the afternoon in Venice. Nine in the morning in New York.

She hit "send."

Then, for the first time in days, she went for a walk.

T<small>HE WEATHER WAS BALMY</small>, perfect, the lagoon sweet with the smell of the sea, the neighborhood quiet once she escaped the crowds around the Accademia.

Wandering aimlessly, she found herself on the Zattere, a broad stretch of waterfront by the side of the Giudecca canal.

When she reached the vaporetto stop she could see a cruise ship, huge, white and blue, six or seven stories tall, making its steady way out to the Adriatic behind a tug, the handrails on the roof crammed with tourists gawping at the view. She'd made this slow and cumbersome exit across the lagoon several times herself while working for the Apollo line. The ship was from a different company, but the experience looked much the same.

It got the usual response from the locals too. They were gathering in boats by the vaporetto stop, raising banners that read *No Grandi Navi*—no to the huge cruise ships—that were causing environmental havoc in the city.

Lauren hung around, watched a couple of guys getting ready to take their dinghy out to yell at the liner as it departed.

One smile and she was on board, laughing as they made their way into the gray channel, a small and angry flotilla, many Davids surrounding a hideous Goliath and its cargo.

The protest was over in twenty minutes. One of the guys on the boat, a student at the university in Dorsoduro, invited her for a drink with his friends.

She chose a light Hugo spritzer in a bar opposite a yard repairing sleek black gondolas.

Then her phone buzzed. A message.

This is Suzanne Barclay. First things first. Are you safe? Do you need help?

Hi, Suzanne, Lauren replied. *I'm confused and I don't know what to do really. But Dad loved me... loves me. He left me money and a place to stay and this thing he said I had to send you. I want to come home but...*

She left it there.

Where's Tom?

Wait. Don't answer right away. She smiled at the student, got another drink, then tapped out a reply.

I don't know. I wish I did. He just left. He wasn't in a good way. I couldn't stop him.

Have you told the cops?

He told me not to. I was to give you this stuff and see what you thought.

There was a long pause at the other end. Then...

Yeah. I read it. You say it's all finished?

He asked me to work on it. Gave me some tips. It was almost there. But yeah... I think so.

You need to report Tom missing.

I know. I should have already, but he made me promise.

Talk to the police. Then let me have everything you've got. If the rest is as good as this, I'm putting up the barricades for an auction.

Really?

Yeah. Really. You have no idea where Tom's gone? Is he well?

A pause. Lauren thought for a moment of using an emoji. Weeping. But that wouldn't have felt right.

No. I don't think he's well at all. God, I should have told the cops sooner, shouldn't I?

She had the entire book on her phone. It only took a few seconds to put it into an email.

You should have the file any moment.

The guy was still there when she hung up.

'Good news?' His name was Toni.

'What makes you say that?'

'You look happy.'

'I lost my dad.'

His face fell, and he looked so ashamed she almost laughed.

'But hey.' Lauren took his arm. 'He goes off on his own sometimes. I'm still here.'

They went to the Lido, an all-night party on the beach. She came to the next morning in a chaotic bachelor house, snuck out with a thick head before he could wake up.

There was an urgent message on her phone from New York. Suzanne Barclay wanted her to take the first plane home, all expenses paid. Business class.

The room in the Agli Alboretti had a couple of days left to run. She was enjoying Venice now she had money for once.

All the same, it was time to leave.

18

NEW YORK

The day after she got back the summons came.

Suzanne Barclay's office was on the forty-third floor of an office building on Broadway. There was a panoramic window behind her with a gorgeous view out to the Hudson. Tom Honeyman's agent was much as Lauren expected: elegant, serious, beautifully dressed, the kind of woman who turned up by accident on the cruise ships from time to time, and looked around the place thinking *I've got two more weeks of* this?

Next to Suzanne was someone who might have been her sister. Same age, mid-forties, maybe fifties, with some work. Same perfect hair and too-smooth features. Neither was the kind of woman Lauren would have hung around normally, and she guessed all three of them knew that. But this was work. A printout of the manuscript sat on the shiny walnut desk, the title on the cover page the same as she'd typed out in the Agli Alboretti: *The Fire Revisited: A True Story by Thomas and Lauren Honeyman.*

The second woman introduced herself as Gillian Sharp, senior executive vice president for one of the big New York publishers—not that the title meant something, Suzanne said later, since executive vice presidents were a dime a dozen in the book business. Though it seemed Gillian Sharp *was* one of the few who counted.

She'd read the material Lauren had sent from Venice and was willing to make a pre-emptive offer for the whole thing at an attractive price. There were just... questions to be answered.

Lauren had dressed down, the cheapest, oldest clothes she had: frayed jeans, frayed shirt. Done a little with her hair but no make-up. This was a kind of a job interview, maybe the most important she'd ever have.

After the preliminaries—how much they loved the book, how it needed the right treatment when it came to publication, the way it told an important story, a true, human one concerning the impossibility of escaping the ever-stalking shadow of guilt—Suzanne asked straight out, 'Where's your father? We really need to know.'

'If we don't,' Gillian added with a frown, 'I'm not sure this is possible. The contract. The book—'

'Jesus Christ!' Lauren's voice was high, close to a shriek. Tears came and glistened in her eyes. 'You think this is about a goddamn book?'

'Your father's been my client ever since Mohawk Lake.' Suzanne sounded almost defensive. 'I'd like to think we're close after all that time—'

'You're his agent. Not his friend. You've been telling him for years everything he's written since was shit. You have any idea how much that hurt him?'

Suzanne blinked and cast a quick glance to her side. 'Hard to sell, honey. It's not necessarily the same thing. The market's really difficult these days.'

'My dad's been living with all this... darkness ever since that first damned book came out. Eating away at him. Trying to find something else to bury it—'

'Lauren.' It was the publisher. 'You can't bury something like that. Knowing he was party to what your mom did. That's the point, isn't it? That's the story he wants us all to tell.'

'You think I don't know that?'

She sounded like a hurt teenager and didn't mind they clearly noticed.

'Of course you do.' Suzanne again. 'The thing is there are... legal issues here. To do with copyright and ownership. Your father wrote this—'

'Not all of it. It wasn't finished. He gave it to me. Asked me to do it. Edit what I could from what he'd told me.'

'All the same—'

'Oh, for chrissake, he's dead somewhere! Do I have to spell it out?' Lauren was crying now, tears rolling down her cheek, as real and watery as the blurry river beyond the window. 'He gave me all this, then went off in his boat. I don't know where. It wasn't to the airport. I tried to stop him. I was begging. He took the boat into the marshes. I went looking. Paid one of the local fishermen. They said you could vanish for good there if you wanted.'

Their eyes never left her.

'He said not to tell anyone. Not to call the cops. Just take what he gave me, finish it the way he asked. Send it to you. See what you thought. The book. That island he bought. His place there. He said he'd... he'd fouled up everything. It was all mine now. And then he left. Then...'

Stop, she thought. *Enough.*

'Wow.' It was the publisher, Gillian, again. 'If we just clean her up a little and work on the language, she's going to be a killer on TV.'

'Yeah.' Suzanne Barclay nodded. 'You're sure he's gone, Lauren?'

'What do you want... a body?'

'I didn't—'

'He was my dad. I loved him. I knew things had been weird between us for years, just couldn't work out why.' Lauren leaned forward and jabbed her finger on the pages on the desk. 'This is why. Dad is.... He was a good guy. My mom was a good mom. They were ordinary people. Decent. Something just... just worked its way into our lives. He wanted everyone to know that. He didn't...' More tears came, like a sudden flood. 'I don't think he wanted to be around to see it. It wore him down. Just like it did Mom. Maybe one day something, someone turns up—'

'You need to report him as missing,' Gillian cut in.

'Done that. Told the cops in Venice just before I left. They're kind of looking. Needle in a big wet haystack. *Foreign* needle. You think they care?'

They looked taken aback by that outburst.

'Obviously we're hoping he turns up...' It was Suzanne now, and it occurred to Lauren that this had all been mapped out in advance. The deal too, probably. All that was needed was the choreography of its closing. 'But for all our sakes—you, me, Gillian, our companies— we need you to sign a legal waiver saying that this work is now your copyright alone. If anyone appears out of nowhere at any time to challenge it, the legal consequences are your problem. Standard procedure, to be honest. Specially need it here.'

A pause.

'I'll sign whatever you like. But I want Dad's name on the cover. Before mine. Bigger.'

'Bigger's not a good idea, honey. Not if your father's gone.' Suzanne seemed sure of that. 'Missing authors don't do promotion. And this isn't the music business. Dead authors don't sell. If you wrote some of this—'

'Lots—'

'Lauren,' the publisher said. 'It's going to be your name up there. This is your story more than his.'

'You think?'

'We do,' Suzanne agreed. 'Two parents with a terrible secret, and their poor kid never knows what's eating at them, what's tearing the family apart, 'til the very end. Damned right.'

'Also...' Gillian tapped the manuscript. 'The title. *The Fire Revisited: A True Story.* It sucks. No point in looking back. Hell, half the people who'll buy this won't even remember the first book.'

'We're going to call it *Shooter in the Shadows.*' The way the agent said it, it was clear there was no arguing. 'An ordinary family. Ordinary mom and dad. One wrong step and then there's always something lurking, something waiting, coming out to kill you when you thought you could bury it.'

'Right...' Lauren murmured.

'Your name on the cover. Your book. Your job to promote the hell out of it when the time comes. But...' Suzanne shrugged. 'If you're not fine with that...'

Silence. This was the moment Lauren had been waiting for. The offer was coming.

The two women looked at one another. Suzanne said, 'If you're willing to sign that waiver, we have a deal.'

'I thought you said something about an auction.'

The publisher wriggled on her seat, glowered at the agent, and said, 'We've talked this through. I'm prepared to offer what we call a pre-empt. You take the book off the table. We'll pay $2 million, all languages and audio worldwide. No point in an auction. You'll never get a better offer. This is going to be the biggest nonfiction title we push next spring. I'll put everything we have behind it. It's a hit. Guaranteed. With the money I'm going to spend, it's got to be.'

'Bigger than *The Fire?*'

'Oh yeah.' Gillian seemed very sure of that. 'So what do you think?'

Lauren let that question hang in the air for a while, then said with a shrug, 'Kind of funny, talking about lots of money. I'm dead broke at the moment. The cruise company fired me over losing all this time looking for my father. How long... I mean... I don't like to ask. If I sign something...'

Suzanne Barclay got out of her chair, came over and put an arm around her as if she was her mom or something—which was strange, not that she mentioned it.

'You don't have to worry about that, honey. You're Tom's girl, a trustworthy kid. I won't even wait for your name on the contract. If you say you're happy with this, just tell me what you need. I'll forward something on the advance. From me personally. You've been through hell. We need to make that right. It's what your father would have wanted.'

Lauren found she was crying again, and for the life of her she didn't know whether it was gratitude, relief or just plain amusement.

THAT EVENING SUZANNE BARCLAY emailed and said she'd gotten Gillian to up the offer to $2.4 million. The manuscript was being sent to four TV streaming services overnight and could get maybe another million or more there. Fifty thousand dollars was going into Lauren's checking account the following day as a personal remittance from Suzanne against the advance coming from the publisher.

Lauren wrote a quick and grateful message in return and said yes, she'd take it.

Ten in the evening in Manhattan. Her father's laptop was sitting on the desk in his study, sand and dust from Maledetto still between the keys. Lauren pulled up the messaging app on her phone and hit her own name. The old one, just an initial, the way she'd set it up: L. Taylor.

It took a moment, then a face came up.

'Hi, Dad,' she said.

19

LAMMA ISLAND, HONG KONG

T om Honeyman was having a late breakfast in a small café next to the fish stalls in Sok Kwu Wan, one of the ports on Lamma Island, Lauren's old phone propped up in front of him just in case she called. That, a handful of clothes and a dwindling bundle of cash were pretty much all he had.

It was her idea for him to lie low until they agreed it was safe to show their faces. Maybe Vern Miller had told someone he'd gone to Venice. Or Giorgio Morosini was going to come back that Sunday and poke around. Best thing to do: get out of there for a while. She could go back to the cruise ships and vanish on the sea. One was due in Venice in a couple of days, and they'd give her a job.

Stay out of sight. Don't talk. Live off what money they had. Then, when they were sure events on Maledetto were never coming back to bite them, they could emerge and live their lives again. Together. Apart. He had no idea, and he guessed she didn't either. But in the strange confusion after the Night of the Redeemer, he was content to hide. To know she was safe.

The two of them buried the incinerated remains of Vern Miller in the dry and sooty soil of the Maledetto cemetery. Then he left Lauren to deal with Morosini the following day and piloted the patched-up dinghy slowly, carefully, on a circuitous route back to Venice before dumping it in a side canal near the rail station.

A train ride across the country to Naples. Two days was all it took, hanging around the bars of the shady district called Spaccanapoli, to get word out he needed a passport. Five thousand euros from a guy with no name. Good for pretty much everywhere but North America, where they'd surely ask too many questions. A train back to Rome, a cheap one-way ticket from Fiumicino Airport to Hong Kong via Bangkok.

All those years of reading thrillers had given him something back after all. The knowledge of where to look for counterfeit passports in Italy. How to bury yourself on a remote lump of rock in the South China Sea where no one was much minded to ask awkward questions. Lamma was almost a larger Maledetto in a way, a respite from the teeming crowds of the city. The food was cheap and good and different. There was a bar too, Annie's, named after the lugubrious Australian woman who ran it. A louche, bohemian place, the kind of hangout people with interesting histories frequented knowing no one would ask who they were. A good enough place to stay out of sight until he knew it was safe for Tom Honeyman, author, to emerge again.

'Wow, Dad. You're growing a beard.'

'Start of one. Best I can manage. Meet the new me.'

He held up the passport. Canadian, in the name of Laurence Taylor, which matched the 'L. Taylor' of Lauren's credit card and the ID on the phone.

'The temporary me. Pretending to be a hoodlum on the run is fine for a while. But not forever. I thought you'd never call. I was getting worried.'

'Oh, you know. Things to do.'

'Hope the cruise ship you picked up worked out.'

No answer.

'I'd like to get back into the world, Lauren. Soon as it's safe.'

'I'm sure,' she said.

The cafe had the smell of Lamma about it: fish, fresh, dried, old, stale. Gasoline and sewers. Fried food, strange spices. And behind everything the faintest note of sweetness, the fragrance of incense and joss sticks from so many windows. In a month or two, when Lauren got money to him, maybe he'd move on. The Philippines. Malaysia. He'd always liked old stories from writers like Somerset Maugham, tales about a lost colonial world of danger and uncertainty. There was something beguiling about the idea he could lose himself for a month or two, the way people did a century or so ago. Then re-emerge, maybe with a new and better story to tell. He had a couple of ideas in his head he'd put in front of Suzanne Barclay before long.

Lauren looked good on the phone as he rested it against the ketchup bottle on the table. Different. Confident and older somehow. All the same he couldn't take his eyes off the background behind her. It seemed familiar.

'You *are* on a ship, aren't you?'

She winced and did that little shrug and grimace he recognized.

'Not exactly.'

He watched as she moved the laptop around. It was his apartment in Manhattan. The few paintings he owned. The TV. The wide windows out onto the street. Just looking at it made him pine for the place, for normality, for home. He'd left his keys, his credit cards, everything in Maledetto. It had seemed safer that way. Of course she could have used them.

All around him cackling porters were lugging crates of strange tropical fish, crabs and gigantic shrimp, placing them out on the stalls for all to see. The noise was constant, the smell not so great. Honeyman felt tired and stupid.

'Where are you?' Lauren asked. 'It looks... really something.'

'I'm where you said. In the Far East. Quickly getting broke. Why are you in New York?'

'Business,' she said with a wrinkle of her nose.

'Lauren—'

'Thing is... that book the two of us wrote.'

'The two of us?'

'Yeah. The two of us.'

'You said you'd delete all that.'

Her eyes lit up with amusement.

'C'mon, Dad. Best thing you've worked on in years. Way too good to waste.' A long pause and then she added, 'Suzanne thought so too.'

'Suzanne?'

'Barclay.'

'What the hell has she got to do with it?'

'She's my agent now. Got me a hell of a deal. Two point four million and rising.'

Before he could say a word she rattled off some details and numbers. More than he'd ever got. But then this new story played upon the earlier book, leapt up on its shoulders, flew along propelled by Lauren's story as an added, modern twist. A fresh perspective told by the unwitting daughter of a couple who'd covered up three murders, blamed someone else, got rich for a while then fell to pieces when the lurking specter of guilt finally came to claim them.

'I said thank you in the credits. Least I could do. They think you're dead. Best it stays that way for both of us. You can't come home. Ever. God knows you'd never get out of jail. Best if you just—'

'*This* is what you wanted? This was why you played along with Vern?'

She leaned forward into the camera.

'No, Dad. Vern played along with me. You still don't get it, do you? Life's about opportunities. Taking them when you can. Like you did at Mohawk Lake. You taught me there. Dammit, dancing on a cruise ship's no career. I thought you might appreciate that. Writing, though...'

She squinted then pretended to type in front of him, her tongue stuck out of her mouth at an angle like a puzzled kid.

'Writing's cool.'

The sea off Lamma wasn't the still and muddy gray of New York or the placid flat lagoon around Maledetto. The constant waves moved to a living, swelling rhythm, stained a sheen of turquoise that gleamed like a precious stone. Head south from the island and there was nothing but ocean and the endless deep for a thousand miles or more until you hit Brunei. Plenty of places a man could lose himself forever.

'They don't like Vern's title.'

'Really.'

'Wrong for today's market. They say they're going to call it *Shooter in the Shadows*. That'll sell better. Kind of makes it a more human story. Everyone's going to assume you're dead. So, in a way, this is really about me.'

'I could walk into the American embassy here. Give myself up. Bring this little show of yours down around your ears.'

She laughed right at him.

'*Our* ears, Dad. Our ears.'

'Yeah.'

'Well, you could. But face it. Think of all the lies you've told. All there in your own words. Got them right here in front of me. Who the hell's going to believe you now? Who are they going to trust? You?' Her smile was wide and confident. 'Or poor, damaged me?'

Tom Honeyman struggled to find the words. The story of Mohawk Lake apart, he never could.

'We won't talk again. But try to have a good life, Dad. Wherever... whoever you are.'

Then she smiled and ended the call.

ABOUT THE AUTHOR

David Hewson is the author of more than thirty books and audio dramas. *Shooter in the Shadows* was his fifth audio original after his adaptation of *Romeo and Juliet*, narrated by Richard Armitage which won the Audie for best original digital production in 2018.

A former journalist with the London *Times* and *Sunday Times* he lives in Kent.

You can sign up for notification of promotions and forthcoming titles at www.davidhewson.com

twitter.com/david_hewson

instagram.com/david.hewson

Printed in Great Britain
by Amazon

62837371R00182